THE GRAND GAME
BOOK 5: WOLF IN THE VOID

THE GRAND GAME
BOOK 5: WOLF IN THE VOID

TOM ELLIOT

COPYRIGHT

THE GRAND GAME

A House established.
A Wolf on the run.
And with his foes multiplying,
Can Michael accomplish all that he must?

Michael has taken the Game by the throat. No longer content to lurk in the shadows, he has started down a path that will inevitably bring him into conflict with the Powers.

But the Powers are no easy foes. Nor are they Michael's only adversaries.
Other enemies stir. Some confront him openly, while others watch patiently from the sidelines. A lone wolf no more, and with many of his own pieces in play, Michael may find himself more exposed than he believes.

The stakes are high. And the schemes of the players convoluted.
Evading entanglement will not be simple. Avoiding the ire of the Powers will be even harder. And escaping the attention of beings beyond his ken may well be impossible. Can Michael strike a delicate balance between obscurity and strength? Or will his dreams for House Wolf end in ashes?

Follow Michael on his epic journey and find out!

PRAISE FOR THE GRAND GAME

"Interesting portal litrpg. Well-paced and the start of a new series. Curious to see where it goes..." —**Tao Wong on goodreads.com.**

"... Great action, great storyline and I honestly binge read it, start to end..." —**Alex Kozlowski on goodreads.com.**

"Smart MC. Great Tension. Full of Action." —**CookieCrumble on RoyalRoad.com.**

"Everything I look for in a LitRPG." —**CosmereCradleChris on RoyalRoad.com.**

"Oh I liked this very much!" —**The Enlightened Beard on amazon.com.**

"One of the best in this category this year." —**kindle customer on amazon.com.**

Author's Note

Dear Readers,

Thank you for reading the Grand Game. This is a self-published book. Even though care has been given to the review and editing of this novel, some mistakes may have slipped through. If you spot any grammatical errors or typos, please get in touch with me via email.

This book also contains game-like elements. They are generally unintrusive and integrated into the story, but beware, they exist. Otherwise, I hope you enjoy Michael's story.

Happy reading!
Tom (**TomLitRPG.com**)
Support me on PATREON[1]

---

[1] https://www.patreon.com/grandgame

CONTENTS

MICHAEL'S EVOLUTION

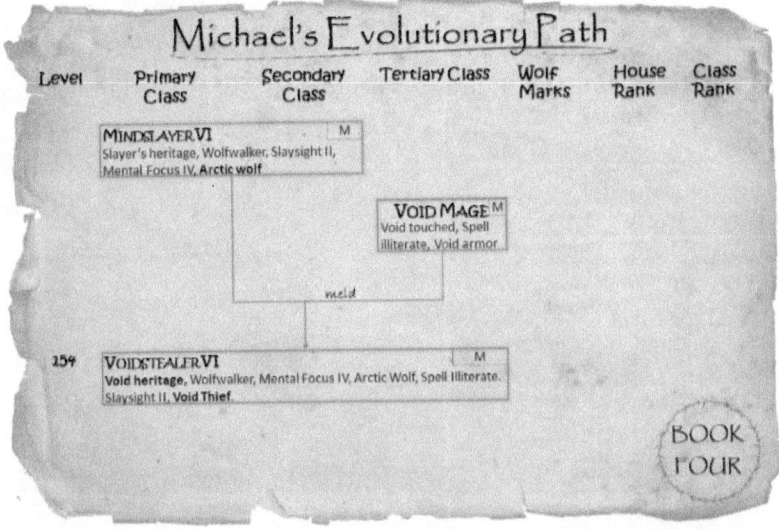

Michael's Evolutionary Path

Level	Primary Class	Secondary Class	Tertiary Class	Wolf Marks	House Rank	Class Rank
	MINDSLAYER VI M Slayer's heritage, Wolfwalker, Slaysight II, Mental Focus IV, **Arctic wolf**		**VOID MAGE** M Void touched, Spell illiterate, Void armor			
		meld				
154	**VOIDSTEALER VI** M **Void heritage**, Wolfwalker, Mental Focus IV, Arctic Wolf, Spell Illiterate. Slaysight II, **Void Thief.**					

BOOK FOUR

As always, Michael continues to grow during his adventures in the Forever Kingdom. The chart above only illustrates his latest achievements (as accomplished over the course of the last book). If you wish to view Michael's earlier evolutionary charts, please visit my site at the link below.

tomlitrpg.com/michael

THE SYSTEM OF THE GRAND GAME

The universe of the Grand Game continues to expand with every book in the series, and at this point, it no longer makes sense to include all the maps, charts, and diagrams in each new book.

If you wish to learn more about the world of the Forever Kingdom or understand the system of the Grand Game better, please visit my site at one of the links below.

tomlitrpg.com/game-lore
tomlitrpg.com/world-lore
tomlitrpg.com/glossary

MICHAEL AT THE END OF BOOK 4

Player Profile: Michael (Details)

Level: 154. Rank: 15. Current Health: 32%.
Stamina: 7%. Mana: 0%. Psi: 13%.
Species: Human. Lives Remaining: 2.
True Marks (hidden): Pack Alpha.
False Marks (fabricated): Lesser Shadow, Lesser Light, Lesser Dark.

Active Buffs

Damage reduction: Life: 0%. Death: 5%. Air: 40%. Earth: 40%. Fire: 40%. Water: 40%. Shadow: 5%. Light: 5%. Dark: 5%. Nether: 20%. Physical: 54%*.

Additional resistance (excluding inherent resistance provided attributes): Life: 0%. Death: 2.5%. Air: 20%. Earth: 20%. Fire: 20%. Water: 20%. Shadow: 2.5%. Light: 2.5%. Dark: 2.5%. Nether: 10%. Physical: 0%.

Immunities: Entanglement: tier 2 spells*. Mind spells: tier 2 spells*.
denotes buffs affected by items.

Attributes

Available: 0 points.
Strength: 21 (13)*. Constitution: 27 (19)*. Dexterity: 79 (55)*. Perception: 35 (31)*. Mind: 75 (71)*. Magic: 31 (21)*. Faith: 0.
denotes attributes affected by items.

Classes

Available: 2 points.
Primary-Secondary-Tertiary tri-blend: voidstalker (fabricated). voidstealer VI (hidden).

Traits

void heritage (hidden): +2 Dexterity, +2 Strength, +4 Mind, +4 Perception, +6 Magic.
beast tongue: can speak to beastkin.
Marked: can see spirit signatures.
wolfwalker (hidden): improved senses in all conditions.
anointed scion (hidden): bound to House Wolf.
inscrutable mind: +8 Mind.
secret blood (hidden): conceals bloodline.
mental focus IV: increases effectiveness of Mind skills by 40%.
budding explorer: all key points in newly discovered sectors logged.
arctic wolf (hidden): +5 Constitution, +2 Mind, +3 Strength.
spell illiterate: cannot cast mana-based spells.
potion resistance II: potency of potions reduced by 2 ranks.

Skills

Available skill slots: 0.

dodging (current: 125. max: 550. Dexterity, basic).
sneaking (current: 127. max: 550. Dexterity, basic).
shortswords (current: 139. max: 550. Dexterity, basic).
two weapon fighting (current: 121. max: 550. Dexterity, advanced).
light armor (current: 126. max: 190. Constitution, basic).
thieving (current: 102. max: 550. Dexterity, basic).
chi (current: 124. max: 710. Mind, advanced).
meditation (current: 143. max: 710. Mind, basic).
telekinesis (current: 127. max: 710. Mind, advanced).
telepathy (current: 116. max: 710. Mind, advanced).
insight (current: 147. max: 310. Perception, basic).
deception (current: 111. max: 310. Perception, master).
channeling (current: 101. max: 210. Magic, basic).
elemental absorption (current: 81. max: 210. Magic, master).
null force (current: 15. max: 210. Magic, master).
null life (current: 4. max: 210. Magic, master).
null death (current: 11. max: 210. Magic, master).
nether absorption (current: 48. max: 210. Magic, master).

Abilities

<u>Constitution ability slots used:</u> **10 / 19.**
load controller (10 Constitution, expert, light armor).

<u>Dexterity ability slots used:</u> **41 / 55.**
crippling blow (Dexterity, basic, shortswords).
minor piercing strike (5 Dexterity, advanced, shortswords).
improved backstab (10 Dexterity, expert, sneaking).
improved trap disarm (5 Dexterity, advanced, thieving).
superior lockpicking (5 Dexterity, advanced, thieving).
superior set trap (10 Dexterity, expert, thieving).
whirlwind (5 Dexterity, advanced, two weapon fighting).

<u>Mind ability slots used:</u> **57 / 71.**
superior mass charm (10 Mind, expert, telepathy).
stunning slap (Mind, basic, chi).
windborne (10 Mind, expert, telekinesis).
heightened reflexes (10 Mind, expert, chi).
twin astral blades (5 Mind, advanced, telepathy).
long shadow blink (10 Mind, expert, telekinesis).
quick mend (10 Mind, expert, chi).
simple mind shield (Mind, basic, meditation).

<u>Perception ability slots used:</u> **31 / 31.**
improved analyze (5 Perception, advanced, insight).
improved trap detect (5 Perception, advanced, thieving).

conceal small weapon (Perception, basic, deception).
superior facial disguise (10 Perception, expert, deception).
superior ventro (5 Perception, advanced, deception).
lesser imitate (5 Perception, advanced, deception).

Other abilities:
improved slaysight (hidden) (Class, advanced, telepathy).
basic void thief (hidden) (Class, basic, any void skill and telepathy).

Known Key Points
Dungeon Sector 14,913 (candidate's dungeon) exit portal and safe zone.
Kingdom Sector 12,560 (wolves' valley) nether portal and safe zone.
Kingdom Sector 1 (Nexus) safe zone.
Dungeon Sector 101 (scorching dunes) exit portal and safe zone.
Dungeon Sectors 102, 103, and 104 (haunted catacombs) exit portals and safe zones.
Dungeon Sector 105, 106, 107, 108, and 109 (guardian tower) exit portals.
Kingdom Sector 18,240 nether portal 1 (guardian tower), and nether portal 2 (Draven's Reach).

Equipped

Weapons
stygian shortsword, +3.
ebonheart (+30% damage).

Armor & Clothes
ranger's kit (+40% damage reduction, +4 ranks stealth).
bomber's belt (5 x acid bombs, 5 x smoke bombs, 5 x ice bombs, and 5 x fire bombs).
belt of the chameleon (11 x rank 4 nether protection crystals, 11 x rank 4 disease protection crystals, 10 scent concealment crystals, 5 x mental concealment crystals, 4 x rank 6 disease protection crystals, 2 x rank 5 poison protection crystals, 2 x rank 4 strength enhancement crystals, 1 x rank 4 dexterity enhancement crystals, and 3 x rank 4 magic enhancement crystals).
wayfarer's boots (legendary item, +8 Dexterity, move soundlessly).
wayfarer's gloves (legendary item, +8 Dexterity, hands immune to hazardous substances).
magister's cloak (legendary item, +4 Magic, +8% physical damage reduction).

Rings & Accessories
adept's ring (+6 Magic).
goliath's ring (+8 Strength).
acrobat's ring (+8 Dexterity).
sharpshooter's band (+4 Perception).
hale stone (+8 Constitution).
savant's ring (+4 Mind).

troll's talisman bracelet (+6% damage reduction).
gift of the unbound ring (immunity to tier 1 and 2 entanglement spells).
band of stillness ring (immunity to tier 1 and 2 Mind spells).
aetherstone bracelet (2 / 5 stored locations, 0 stones charged).
simple potion bracelet (3 / 3 full heal potions).
veteran's trapper's wristband (198 / 200 trap-making crystals).

Other
backpack, small bag of holding (50 slots), large bag of holding (200 slots), hunter's alchemy stone.

Backpack Contents
Money: 73 golds, 5 silvers, and 3 coppers.
20 x field rations.
2 x flasks of water.
2 x iron daggers.
1 x bedroll.
bounty letter authorization.
1 x coil of rope.
tavern bill of ownership.
Tartan token.
2 x full mana potions.
3 major mana potions.
2 x minor mana potions.
Vivane token.
Kesh Emporium access card.
cat claws.
spectacles of ward seeing (detect tier 4 wards).
BHG ID (junior member, 1 / 10 active jobs).
simple map of Nexus.
1 x rank 6 cure disease potions.
commune rod.
superior analyze, greater trap detect, ability tomes.
enchanted leather armor set (+20% damage reduction, -35% Dexterity and Magic).
10 x acid bombs, 14 x smoke bombs, 10 x ice bombs, and 10 x fire bombs.
slotted-potion belt (2 x rank 4 cure poison, 1 moderate heal, 2 full heal, 2 full mana potion, 3 major mana potions).
faithful (+40% damage).

Miscellaneous Loot
None.

Alchemy Stone Contents
None.

Bank Contents
Money: 1,655 gold, 0 silvers, and 0 coppers.

2 x full healing potions.
2 x full mana potions.

<u>Tavern Money</u>: 9,850 gold, 0 silvers, and 0 coppers.

<u>Open Tasks</u>

Find the Last Wolf Envoy (hidden) (find Ceruvax).
Heist in the Dark (steal chalice from the Power, Paya).
Silent Brethren (find out what has happened to the guardians).
A Perverted Trial (stop the Triumvirate abuse of the Combat Trial).
Brokering Peace (establish peace in sector 12,560 within 4 months).
Brotherhood Obligations (report to the brotherhood after 4 months).

If you wish to view Michael's earlier player profiles, please visit my site at the link below.

<u>tomlitrpg.com/michael</u>

CHAPTER 305: DRAVEN'S REACH

Transfer through portal commencing...
Leaving sector 18,240. Entering the Endless Dungeon.
...
...

Journeying through a portal was instantaneous.

One stepped into the depths of a shimmering gateway in one sector, raced through the ley line connection, and emerged in another sector barely a split second later. The passage was seamless and without interruption—always.

Or almost always.

Only once before had my transition through a portal been disrupted—when I'd attempted to return to the guardian tower from sector 18,240 with a stygian creature on my heels. But even then, despite my pursuer trying to break through the gateway, my passage had resumed of its own accord.

That did not happen this time.

Transfer halted!

Dungeon sector 73,102 is corrupted. The area around the exit of the one-way portal may be unstable or occupied.

Assessing dungeon viability...

I stared at the Game message in shock. *A corrupted dungeon?* What the hell was that? I'd never heard of such a thing before. But just as concerning was the description of the portal as 'one-way.'

Given the horde of nether creatures at my back, I'd known leaving Draven's Reach the same way I entered would be difficult, if not impossible. But having the option to retreat would've been nice.

Now, I didn't even have that.

And why do I have the time to ponder all this? Portal travel was instantaneous. Why was I stuck in a ley line and left at loose ends?

A moment—at least I thought it was only one—ticked by. I was disconnected from my senses and could neither see nor hear—only think. An eternity could have passed, for all I knew. *What now?* I wondered, dearly hoping the portal was not broken.

Right on cue, another Game message unfurled in my mind.

Assessment completed. Analysis inconclusive.

The corruption in sector 73,102 is too severe to evaluate the dungeon's parameters accurately. The sector's overall threat level and creature population cannot be guaranteed.

Do you still wish to enter Draven's Reach?

The question was superfluous. Of course I did.

Given what awaited me back in the nether-infested sector, I had no choice. But the Game seemed reluctant to send me on my way. Why, I had no idea. Regardless, my decision was made.

Impatiently, I willed my desire to the Adjudicator, and after another long, indeterminate pause, more text scrolled through my mind.

Resuming transfer...

About bloody ti—

Before I could complete the thought, I was jettisoned through the ley line, out of the gateway, and into a lightless room.

Ground formed beneath feet unready for it.

Catching myself before I could fall, I swept my gaze across my surroundings. The room's design was familiar, similar to other dungeons I'd visited. It was an entrance chamber. The walls were cold, gray rock, and the floor was more of the same. None of that mattered though, so much as that the area appeared free of threat.

It's safe.

The observation was the signal my exhausted body had been waiting for, and before I could consciously will it, my sagging legs gave way under me, dropping me to my knees.

Another Game message flashed for attention.

You have entered sector 73,102 of the Endless Dungeon.

This sector is part of a closed region named Draven's Reach. It consists of 1 unclaimable sector and 3 one-way portals: the primary entrance, the exit, and the secret entrance.

There is no restriction on the number of players who may be in Draven's Reach at any one time. The dungeon is repopulated on a continuous basis and has an exceptionally slow respawn rate.

Recommended player levels: 200 to 249.

Recommended party size: 4.

Players currently inside the dungeon: 0 (excluding you).

Sector bosses remaining: 1 of 1.

I barked out a laugh, the sound bleak and absent of joy. Draven's Reach was a tier five dungeon. *Really?*

I'd barely reached tier four myself, and a dungeon of this caliber was a challenge I was most emphatically not equipped for. *Great job, Michael*, I groused. *You couldn't have chosen a worse escape route if you'd tried.*

But further remonstrations would have to wait. A new and not particularly pleasant sensation was coursing through my body. Beginning in my stomach, it exploded outward. There was a vileness in me, and I urgently wanted—no, *needed*—it out.

Slapping my palms to the ground, I hung my head and vomited, ejecting what seemed like a river of pale-yellow spittle and bile. *Yuck, that's horrible,* I thought, crawling away from the mess.

My body was not done yet, though. My chest was also on fire. Rolling onto my side, I coughed, forcibly trying to oust the filth polluting my lungs.

"*Prime, are you alright?*"

Caught up in my misery, I'd almost forgotten about Ghost. Craning my neck in the direction of the spirit wolf's mindglow, I managed a vague half-nod, glad she had made it safely through the gateway too. But before I could inquire after her own experience, I coughed again—this time involuntarily—and ejected another stream of yellow gunk.

An entire chain of coughs followed, and for the next few seconds I lost track of Ghost and my surroundings. Finally, my heaving subsided, and I rolled onto my back. "Ah," I murmured, "much better."

My body remained weak and my chest and stomach felt delicate, but I no longer had an irresistible urge to cough or vomit. Hopefully, that meant I'd expelled the last dredges of the stygian overlord's noxious fumes.

"Prime?" Ghost asked again, concern threaded through her voice.

Wiping my mouth with the back of my hand, I sat up shakily. "I'm alright. I just need a few minutes to recover." I required a lot more time than that, but a few minutes were all I could spare right now.

"What happened?" she asked.

Raising my head, and glad for the distraction, I fixed my attention on where I knew the spirit wolf was. "You don't know?"

"I saw the overlord's blob land and those ugly spikes drive into your boots. Did they do this to you?"

Dully, I stared down at my feet. A handful of ebony shards were still embedded in my wayfarer's boots. How could I have forgotten them? They hurt horribly.

No wonder my legs gave out earlier.

Reaching forward, I yanked out the shards, wincing at the little shivers of agony that followed each extraction.

When I was done, I flopped back against the ground, exhaling noisily. "It was the nether that did this to me, Ghost. Not the spikes. The overlord's spell created a concentrated cloud of blight."

"Couldn't you have run around it?"

"Of course not! A cloud that big, how would I have—"

I broke off, belatedly remembering Ghost couldn't see free-floating nether. I exhaled and continued more calmly, "No, I couldn't. The blob covered an area a few hundred yards in diameter."

"Oh."

My thoughts were still fuzzy, I realized, and I was missing things I shouldn't have been. I couldn't afford that—not in a tier five dungeon. I need to heal. But before I turned my attention inward, I had to ensure that a certain inquisitive companion of mine didn't go exploring.

I turned back to Ghost. "Promise me you won't wander off. I'm in no position to rescue you if you get in trouble."

A riot of emotions, shame chief amongst them, wafted off the spirit wolf. "I won't run away again," Ghost said, her tone muted. "Promise."

"Thank you," I said, deciding not to belabor the point further. "This chamber should be secure, but don't leave it. I'm going to see to my wounds. If you spot any danger, tell me immediately."

Ghost perked up, contriteness, shame, and guilt all vanishing beneath a new emotion—excitement. *"Yes, Prime!"* she replied, her mindvoice practically quivering with eagerness. *"Nothing will get by me!"*

I sighed. Ghost's response was a little too enthusiastic for my liking, leaving me to wonder if I should've phrased my request differently. But I hadn't been lying earlier; all my energy pools were swimming in the red and needed urgent attention.

Besides, it was not a bad thing for the spirit wolf to learn more responsibility. If the two of us were going to get out of the dungeon alive, Ghost would need to play her part.

And I would have to trust her to do it.

Leaving the spirit wolf to her 'guard duty,' I closed my eyes and called up my status.

You are no longer afflicted by noxious fumes. Your health, psi, stamina, and mana have stopped degenerating.

Current Status

Health: 32%. Stamina: 7%. Psi: 13%. Mana: 0%.
Void armor: inoperative, damage reduction, and resistance buffs deactivated.
Stolen spells in your mana pool: 1, necrotic spike with a remaining duration of 4 hours.

Alright, I thought, *let's get to it.* Unwrapping a travel ration, I bit off a chunk and chewed mechanically.

✳   ✳   ✳

You have replenished 30% of your stamina with 3 x field rations. Your stamina is at 37%.

You have healed yourself of all injuries. Your health is at 100%.

You have restored 100% of your psi.

You have replenished 100% of your mana. Void armor charges remaining: 100%.

Long minutes later, I was done. Opening my eyes, I surveyed myself. I was fighting fit once more.

Or as close to, I amended, eyeing my stamina.

Unfortunately, the field rations I had consumed had only restored a small portion of my stamina, and from experience I knew eating more would do no good. Without a stamina restoration skill—or potion—only sleep would completely renew me.

Resting, though, would have to wait until after I'd scouted the area. Then there was also the necrotic spike spell I'd stolen. It was a tier six spell, and I couldn't afford to waste it by sleeping away the next few hours.

I was a tier four player, alone and equipped with only tier three spells, in a tier five dungeon. If Ghost and I were to survive, we would need to utilize every advantage at our disposal.

Rising to my feet, I scanned my surroundings again. The second, longer study revealed that my initial impressions had been incorrect. The walls and floor, while smooth, were formed from uncut stone. Moss and lichen grew in clumps in the corners, and water dripped down from the rocks above. What I'd mistaken for a chamber was more properly a cavern.

I frowned. Did that signify anything? Was the dungeon older than others I'd been to? Or just more primitive? I turned to Ghost. The spirit wolf had positioned herself next to the cavern's only exit, and from the feel of her mindglow, I could tell that all her senses were trained on the tunnel beyond. *"Anything out there?"* I asked.

"The tunnel is empty," she replied curtly. *"No intrusions to report."*

My lips twitched upward at her response. Ghost had the makings of a warrior already. Perhaps all she'd needed the whole time was to feel useful. *"Well done,"* I murmured and strode forward to join her at the cavern mouth. Peering out, I saw that just as Ghost had reported, the tunnel was empty.

Dropping into a crouch, I gestured for her to follow in my wake. *"Come on, then. Let's find out what this dungeon is about. The sooner we get through, the sooner we can rejoin the pack."*

And perhaps, along the way, we'd discover just why the Game had labeled the place 'corrupted.'

Chapter 306: Lying in Wait

Before leaving the cavern, I wrapped myself in shadows but didn't cast my buffs yet. On this, my first venture into the tunnel, I only intended on scouting.

Time was of the essence in more ways than one. Safyre and the pack were waiting for me back in the arctic tundra, as were Loken's agent and Saya in the valley, not to mention the fact that I wouldn't retain memory of the stolen spell much longer.

Still, rushing would be foolish.

Until I understood the dungeon's true challenge, Ghost and I would take things slow. I also couldn't forget this was a tier five dungeon. After all the stories I'd heard about elite players and creatures, I was a little anxious about fighting foes above level two hundred. Would I be up to the challenge of facing them?

Only time would tell.

Setting aside my musings, I focused on my surroundings. Like the cavern, the tunnel appeared to be a natural formation. But where the entrance chamber had been spacious, the tunnel was... cramped. There was no way I'd be able to navigate it upright, and swinging a sword in its depths wouldn't be a good idea either.

That was not all, however.

Formed of irregular boulders, the tunnel floor was replete with tiny crevices and cracks, each eagerly awaiting a misplaced foot. Making matters worse, lichen grew everywhere, fed by the tiny rivulets of water trickling between the rocks. There was no light source either, which didn't bother me but would hamper most players.

The burbling water made it hard to pick out aberrant sounds and the lichen's strong fragrance masked other scents. My night sight also failed to reassure. Up ahead, the corridor turned sharply, rendering the rest of the tunnel invisible.

The overall effect was... unsettling and made me reluctant to advance. Not budging from the cave mouth, I tallied up the results of my observations. Treacherous footing? *Check.* Dulled senses? *Check.* Tight confines? *Double check.*

I didn't need to be an expert scout to figure out what all that meant: ambush. It was a strong possibility...

I snorted. It was a near-certainty, more like. Something—or many somethings—were waiting ahead to jump me. The question was what should I do about it? Ordinarily, I would have trusted my abilities to see me through.

But this is a tier five dungeon. This time my abilities may not suffice.

I swept aside the doubting inner voice. Regardless of the danger, I had no choice. The tunnel was the only way forward, and I would have to risk its confines. But caution was not unwarranted. Opening my mindsight, I swept the area.

No mindglows popped into view. Other than for me, Ghost, and the rampant lichen, the tunnel was barren of life. Not reassured, I cast trap detect.

You have failed to spot any traps.

I sighed as it, too, came up empty. I'd not expected either ability to uncover anything. Still, it had been necessary to try. There was only one other precaution I could take. I turned to my companion. *"What do you think, Ghost? Is it safe?"*

I sensed her confusion and immediately realized I'd asked the wrong question. As a spirit entity, Ghost had little concept of physical dangers. *"Does anything about the ground ahead strike you as odd?"* I amended.

Ghost took her time answering, her attention flitting from me to the tunnel and back. *"No...?"*

I bit my lip, realizing I would have to be content with her answer. And really, there was no reason to doubt her. Dire wolves were strong natural telepaths, and the spirit wolf's mindsight was more finely attuned than mine.

Over and above that, Ghost had been a disembodied entity for years which had honed her mindsight even further. By now, I expected her telepathic abilities rivaled that of the pack elders. Ghost *would* spot things I had missed, and if she said the patch of space ahead was clear, it was likely true.

But what about the rest of the tunnel?

"It's clear. I'm sure of it," Ghost added in the face of my continued silence.

I nodded absently. *"There is something else I need you to do."*

"Yes?" she prompted when I didn't immediately go on.

I hesitated, considering my next words carefully. It had not escaped my notice that Ghost would make an ideal scout. Most corporeal creatures would be oblivious to her presence.

Unfortunately, most did not equate to all.

There was always the chance that there was something in the dungeon that could see—and attack—her, and if that happened it would spell disaster. Ghost had no defenses to speak of, and it would only take one hit to snuff out her lifeforce.

But then, I thought wryly, *a single strike from a tier five creature would likely do for me too.*

The stark truth was that I couldn't shield Ghost from the dungeon's perils. To get out, we would both have to shoulder more risks than I was comfortable with. *"It's dangerous,"* I cautioned.

Unsurprisingly, my warning did not daunt her. *"I'm ready,"* she huffed.

I wasn't so sure, but I set aside my doubts. *"I want you to scout the rest of the tunnel beyond the bend. If you find something or sense anything odd, return here and report."*

"Got it," she replied and slipped by me, impatient to begin.

"Ghost," I called. She halted. *"This is important: if you detect anything amiss—anything at all—you head back at once. Clear?"*

"Understood." She fell silent for a moment, thinking. *"What if I don't find anything? What if the tunnel is empty?"*

It was a pertinent question and reassured me somewhat. Ghost was thinking ahead and beyond my basic instructions. *"Then you scout the passage's entire length. Give it... ten minutes. If by that time, you don't reach its end, return to me. But under no circumstances are you to leave the tunnel."*

"Yes, Prime." The spirit wolf bounded forward, then paused again. *"Can I begin?"*

I waved her on. *"Go ahead, and be careful please."*

* * *

Ghost zipped into the tunnel, and I gripped my blades, ready for anything, but nothing reacted to her passage and a moment later, I relaxed.

There was no guarantee that Ghost would uncover any lurking creatures—especially if they were hidden and their minds shielded—but I fancied her chances better than I did my own.

Tracking the spirit wolf with my mindsight, I watched her make her way around the bend ahead without pausing. Five yards beyond that she kept going, accelerating. I wanted to urge her to caution again but refrained. I'd said all that needed to be said, and Ghost knew her own capabilities better than I did. I had to trust her.

A little later, Ghost disappeared.

I'd expected it, of course. She'd hit the limit of my mindsight's range—twenty yards—but that didn't stop my own concern from redoubling. If anything happened to the spirit wolf now, I wouldn't know until too little.

All I could do was wait.

My mouth twisting sourly at the thought, I sat down cross-legged. A minute passed. Then another.

What was taking so long?

Unable to help myself, I cast my buffs and strained my senses. If I heard anything, the slightest hint that Ghost was in trouble, I would set off.

Another minute went by.

That's nearly four minutes gone. Why hadn't Ghost returned yet? Was it time to go after her?

No.

Schooling myself to patience, I clenched my hands together, and to distract myself, contemplated my slaysight ability. It was what dictated the range of mindsight. Was it time for an upgrade?

Definitely.

The urge to do so immediately was strong, but I could no more afford to act rashly than Ghost could. Gathering my thoughts, I considered the matter carefully.

Slaysight was one of my only two Class abilities—the other was void thief—and the last time I'd upgraded it was before I'd entered the guardian tower. It was past due for an upgrade.

But...

But, I conceded, I had only two Class points remaining. I'd used the other four advancing my mental focus trait to tier four. In as short supply as Class points were—I gained one every twenty levels—I couldn't spend them carelessly.

So, was investing in slaysight further the right approach?

I thought so.

Not only would upgrading slaysight improve my mindsight range—and consequently increase the distance over which I could communicate with Ghost—it would also add another mental manipulation to the ability. The first tier of slaysight had given me mind-blind, the second, terrify. What would the third bring? Something equally good, I was sure.

There were other considerations too. While my other Class ability, void thief, had potential, it was still something of an unknown, whereas slaysight had already proven itself.

The telepathic-based Class ability had been especially useful against higher-tiered foes—like the savants in the guardian tower—and I expected that would hold true in Draven's Reach as well. Given my rank seventy-one Mind attribute, high telepathy skill, *and* the forty percent boost provided by mental focus, of all my abilities, slaysight had the best chance of succeeding against a tier five foe.

For all those reasons and more, it made sense to advance the ability. Reassured that my choice was not a rash one, I closed my eyes and called up the class upgrade interface.

You may advance your Class to rank 7 at this time. Class points available: 2. Do you wish to proceed?

I signaled my intent to do so and selected slaysight for advancement.

Commencing Class upgrade...

...

Upgrade complete. Class points remaining: 1.

Congratulations, Michael, your voidstealer Class has advanced to rank 7!

You have upgraded your slaysight ability to <u>superior slaysight</u>. The third tier of the slaysight adds another mental manipulation to your arsenal: <u>sleep</u>. Additionally, the range, number of targets, and duration of the spell have increased.

With superior slaysight, you may detect any mind within 50 yards and <u>sleep</u>, <u>terrify</u> or <u>mentally blind</u> any 4 targets for 20 seconds. This is a Class ability and does not occupy any ability slots.

"Perfect," I murmured as I felt the bubble of awareness around me expand to fifty yards. My mindsight range had expanded to the same limit as long shadow blink, thereby doubling the distance I could teleport when using Ghost as my target.

In fact, the ability's new range made coordinating with the spirit wolf easier in nearly every aspect, leaving me wishing I could upgrade slaysight again. Unfortunately, to do that, I would have to first raise my telepathy skill to tier four. *I will make that a priority,* I decided.

A moment later, I had more cause for celebration as a familiar mindglow entered the range of my awareness. A relieved smile slipped on my face. Ghost was finally on her way back, and from the taste of her mind, she was unharmed.

Rising to my haunches, I prepared to meet her. It was time to find out what secrets the tunnel held.

CHAPTER 307: MEETING AN ELITE

Ghost drew to a stop before me. *"The tunnel is empty,"* she reported.

I frowned. *"Empty?"*

"Yes, Prime. I traveled its entire length. After about fifty yards, it straightens out and continues that way before coming to an end two hundred yards later."

"I see," I murmured, still puzzling over the fact that Ghost hadn't found anything. *"And did you see what lies beyond?"*

"No," she replied. *"After I spotted the exit, I swung back like you told me."* She paused. *"Should I have explored farther?"*

I shook my head. *"You did the right thing,"* I assured her. *"Two hundred and fifty yards,"* I said, musing over the length of the tunnel. *"Is that why you took so long?"*

She did not reply immediately.

"Ghost?" I prompted.

"On my way out, I thought I sensed something, but when I checked again, it was gone."

My interest sharpened. *"What was it?"*

Ghost hesitated. *"I'm not sure. It wasn't another mind. Those are easy to spot. It was..."* She fell silent, struggling to articulate her thoughts. Patiently, I waited.

"...less," she finished finally.

"Less?" I repeated.

"Not a whole mind," Ghost clarified. *"Like... a part of one maybe?"*

"Huh." I rubbed my chin, wondering what she'd detected.

It was possible that Ghost had sensed a stray thought from an imperfectly shielded mind. Or worse yet, that she'd caught the tail-end of a communication between two hidden entities. I probed further. *"On the way back, did you feel it again?"*

"No. I waited to see if anything would reveal itself, but nothing did." She regarded me somberly. *"You think it was something?"*

I nodded. *"I do."* Dropping into a crouch, I checked my blades. *"Come on, let's go find what."* And how many of them there are.

✳   ✳   ✳

You are hidden.

I followed on Ghost's heels as she led me into the tunnel, making sure to keep at least twenty yards between us and to stop every few yards to run my gaze over the surroundings. As Ghost had reported, the bends and twists in the tunnel ended after fifty yards.

I sighed in relief as I entered the new tunnel section. Finally, my line of sight was unimpeded by rock. Squatting on my haunches, I examined the passage ahead.

The second tunnel section remained as constricted as the first but was arrow straight. At the end of it was a narrow slit. *The exit.* Beyond the opening, the darkness was less complete, leading me to hope it led to the surface.

"*It was here,*" Ghost said, drawing my attention to her. She had come to a stop thirty yards ahead of me.

I swept my eyes over the area she indicated, but nothing seemed out of place. The spot in question was indistinguishable from the rest of the tunnel, and if it did hide one or more tier five creatures, they had to be pretty small given the cramped quarters. "*You're sure?*"

"*Yes,*" Ghost replied confidently.

"*Alright. Advance another twenty yards, then hold your position.*"

I sensed her puzzlement. "*Why?*" she asked.

"*You'll see.*"

Doing as I instructed, Ghost moved farther down the corridor until she reached the very edge of my awareness. "*That's perfect,*" I said and picked up a loose pebble. "*Now, don't move.*" Winding back my arm, I flung the stone.

The pebble struck a side wall about three yards from the spot Ghost had marked and clattered softly as it bounced off the rocky surface.

The reaction was instantaneous.

A handful of nearby—but otherwise unremarkable—rocks transformed from dull stone to glistening scales, revealing a coiled serpentine form. Its movements a half-seen blur, the reptile reared up and spat a viscous blob of green.

A hostile entity is no longer hidden!

The venom streaked through the air and struck the errant stone. The pebble sizzled, and a moment later, dissipated into nothingness.

Alrighty then, I thought, shrinking back in horrid fascination. I suspected that whatever the serpent's spittle contained, it would as easily dissolve *me* as it had the stone.

"*Prime,*" Ghost began excitedly, "*did you see—?*"

"*Shh,*" I interrupted. "*I did. Don't move.*" Drawing in psi, I readied a casting but didn't release it. Instead, I waited.

The serpent had not coiled back down again. Standing tall, it scanned the tunnel—looking for whatever had disturbed the stone, I thought. While it did, I observed it in turn.

The creature was small, less than a yard in length from its diamond-shaped head to its spiked tail. I wasn't deceived, though. It had to be a tier five foe. I was sure of it. What I was *not* certain of was how many of its kind were hiding in the tunnel.

Even though the serpent had revealed itself, its scales rippled continuously, attempting to mimic its surroundings, but now that it was in motion the illusion was imperfect, and I was able to pick out its shape. Still, the creature's camouflage was excellent and, if not for Ghost, would've defeated my own senses.

Tricking the serpent into revealing itself had been a risk—as was sitting still and waiting to see if my stealth would suffice against it. If the serpent *did* find me, I would flee—I'd positioned Ghost for just that eventuality—and not look back.

The serpent's head rotated in my direction, and I tensed in anticipation.

A hostile entity has failed to detect you! You are hidden.

I exhaled in sharp relief. The creature's vacant white eyes had passed over me without pause. Tier five critter or not, its gaze couldn't pierce the thirty yards of inky darkness separating us.

Now to find out exactly what I'm facing. Marshaling my will, I reached out and analyzed my foe.

The target is a swarm viper of indeterminant level.

I grimaced at the Game's response. 'Indeterminant level' meant the viper was above level two hundred—my improved analyze only worked on creatures below that—and confirmed my suspicions that it was not to be taken lightly.

What was a swarm viper though? And where was the rest of the 'swarm'? One viper did not a swarm make. But I couldn't risk throwing more stones in search of them, not with one serpent already on the lookout for danger. And, I reminded myself, Ghost *had* only sensed the one anomaly.

Maybe there is only the one? The thought made me smile—somehow, I doubted I would be so fortunate.

The viper, meanwhile, had coiled back on itself and stilled, and even though I knew where it was, I could no longer pick out its form. I pursed my lips, considering my next move. The serpent appeared to lack any real physical defenses. Its scales were pliable and unlikely to resist the bite of my blades.

A single backstab should kill it.

But appearances could be deceiving, and I was leery of entering close quarters with the thing until I understood its capabilities better.

Better to kill it from afar and take every precaution possible.

Formulating a plan, I spent a few minutes going over it with Ghost. Then, I got to work.

It was time to put my stolen spell to use.

＊　　＊　　＊

Drawing mana, I cast my first magic spell.

Although 'cast' was perhaps a misnomer. I did not so much as create the spell weaves—lacking the skill to do so myself—as let them take shape under the direction of my mana. But regardless of how the spell was enacted, it functioned perfectly, and in short order, a shard of stygian black hovered before me.

You have cast necrotic spike. Duration: 5 minutes.

Intently, I studied the thin sliver of darkness. Lacking any physical components, the spike was invisible and would remain that way until activated—which suited my purposes admirably. Directing the shard with my mind, I placed it less than a foot from the concealed viper.

A necrotic spike ward has been successfully configured.

When a hostile entity enters the ward's activation range, it will be triggered, dealing 5% nether damage to the target.

Mana remaining: 80%.

I winced upon seeing the last Game message.

The necrotic spike spell was a tier six ability, and its mana requirements were as high as I'd feared. At best, I would only be able to place five spikes, and then only by draining my mana pool *and* void armor completely.

It was far from ideal.

But there wasn't anything I could do to rectify the situation either. So, gritting my teeth, I accepted the mana cost and placed three more spikes in close proximity to the first. It was only with the last shard that I held off.

Each spike would last five minutes. That was not enough time to fully restore my mana pool through channeling, but if I bespelled the viper into sleep, I could retreat, regain my mana, sneak back, and lay another five spikes.

Four iterations of that and my foe would be dead.

It was a tedious, but solid plan—assuming that I *could* in fact sleep the serpent. A big assumption, and one that I was not at all confident about.

Which was why I needed a backup plan.

Rubbing my thumb across the blue rune on my trapper's wristband, I activated the item.

You have passed a thieving skill check!

You have removed 2 trap-making crystals from your trapper's wristband. Remaining trap-making crystals: 196 of 200.

I was conscious that my store of trap-making elements was finite, and with no hope of buying more while in the dungeon, I had to use them sparingly. With that thought in mind, I set just the one trap instead of doing what I really wanted—which was to seed the tunnel with enough traps to kill the viper many times over. I would use the trap to buy me enough time to escape, and nothing more.

Placing the trap at my feet, I aimed it in the direction of the viper.

You have connected a lightning trap element to a remote-control trigger.

A tier 3 trap has been successfully configured!

My work done, I sat back. I was ready at last. Closing my eyes, I began my final casting.

It was time to kick things off.

CHAPTER 308: THE SWARM OF ONE

You have cast necrotic spike.

The final spike materialized beneath the serpent and, just like I intended, triggered immediately.

Necrotic spike activated! A swarm viper has sustained nether damage.

The serpent flashed into sight once more, this time with a shard of darkness piercing its slender body. I smiled tightly. *So far so good.* Hands on my blades, I waited patiently. The next move was my foe's.

Quicker than I expected the serpent calmed, and I guessed its initial frenzied motion had been spurred by surprise rather than pain. Now though, the predator was back in control. Rearing up, it searched the darkness impassively.

A hostile entity has failed to detect you!

My smile broadened. My stealth was holding. The viper allowed me scant time for further celebration, though. Dropping back down, it slithered across the rocky floor. Whether by happenstance or not, it headed in my direction.

Necrotic spike activated!
Necrotic spike activated!
Necrotic spike activated!
Necrotic spike activated!

Four more ebony needles materialized from the ground to skewer the serpent anew. Its forked tongue flickering out, the viper hissed in pain at each new piercing, but that was the sum total of its reaction. Despite the shards decorating its torso, the creature did not abort its advance.

A hostile entity has failed to detect you!

My eyes narrowed. The viper had already covered a quarter of the distance to me and showed no sign of slowing. I couldn't afford to delay further. Releasing the casting I held ready, I drove my will into its mind.

You have cast slaysight.
A swarm viper has passed a mental resistance check! You have failed to induce your target to sleep.

My smile turned grim. The failure was not unexpected, but disappointing, nonetheless. Spinning psi, I tried again.

You have failed to induce your target to sleep.

God damnit! I swore. The distance between me and my foe had reduced to ten yards and soon my stealth would fail. There was no time for a third attempt, I realized. Wrapping my fingers around the remote in my pocket, I pressed down on it.

You have activated a trap.

A jagged bar of lightning burst into existence in front of me and shot down the tunnel to strike the onrushing serpent dead center.

A lightning bolt has grazed a swarm viper.
Your target has passed a magical resistance check! You have failed to stun a swarm viper.

Damn, damn, and damn. One failure, I'd anticipated. Two, I'd planned for. But three... that left me with no other choice but to flee. *Time to go.* Drawing in psi, I focused on the waiting form of Ghost.

A hostile entity has detected you! You are no longer hidden.

The shadows cloaking me dissipated, baring me to the viper's sight. My alarm growing, I kept casting. *Almost there. Just a—*
The serpent flowed upwards, and its head darted forward. Knowing the horror it was about to unleash, I threw myself against the closest wall.

You have evaded a swarm viper's venom spit. Your spellcasting has been interrupted!

Green spittle blistered the air, passing scant inches from my face. I'd dodged the lethal projectile, but in the process, I also lost control of my teleport spell. Worse yet, the viper hadn't paused to study the results of its attack. Rushing forward, it closed the remaining distance between us.

I drew my blades and tried to set my stance, but there was barely room to maneuver. Fighting blade-to-fang was the last thing I wanted to do, but my foe was leaving me no choice.

Two yards away from me, the viper went airborne. It snaked through the air, jaws open and fangs ready to bury themselves in my exposed face.

Reflexively, I slashed down with ebonheart.

But even as I did, I knew the blow to be useless. No matter how physically vulnerable the viper appeared, it was sure to have some hidden defense mechanism.

The blow landed.

And to my surprise, cut through—slicing away scales and flesh without hindrance.

A swarm viper has been dealt a fatal blow!

I gaped in disbelief as the two halves of the viper's bisected body landed on the ground with soft thuds.

I'd done it. I'd killed a tier five monster.

And it had been ridiculously easy too.

The laughter bubbling inside me escaped, and I chuckled involuntarily. To think that after all the planning and preparation, it had taken only a single strike of ebonheart to—

"Prime? Are you alright?"

"More than alright, Ghost," I murmured. Sheathing my blades, I stepped gingerly over the twitching corpse. *"Our foe is dead,"* I said, then, with immense satisfaction, added, *"I killed it."*

Ghost's mind tasted confused. *"Are you sure?"*

"I am." Her confusion was understandable. I was also more than a little puzzled by the encounter myself. It had been easy, true—I glanced over my shoulder at the corpse—but there was no mistaking the evidence. The viper was dead.

Still, something about the skirmish didn't feel right. It *had* been too easy, after all. I hesitated, then asked, *"You have some reason to believe otherwise?"*

Ghost shifted uncertainly. *"Uhm, it's only... the thing's mind, it hasn't vanished. I can still feel it."*

My eyes narrowed. What Ghost sensed was impossible. A mind did not survive its body's death. But I didn't doubt her. So, what was going on? Turning around, I crouched down to examine the viper's corpse anew.

My blade had caught the serpent mid-torso, severing it neatly in two. Each half was about two feet in length and continued to twitch. Blood and other fluids leaked out of the exposed ends, creating a rapidly expanding pool. I edged backwards, not wanting to let the stuff soak into my boots. There was no telling what toxins it contained. *Wait...*

Mid-motion, I paused. My subconscious was screaming at me. Something I'd observed about the remains was off. Squeezing my eyes shut, I replayed what I'd seen in my mind's eye.

A heartbeat later, my eyes snapped open.

I had it. I knew what was wrong.

In life, the viper had only been a yard long, if that. *So, why is each of its severed halves two feet in length?* My gaze jerked downward, seeking confirmation.

Each piece was not two feet in length. Not anymore. They were two and a half feet now. The damn things were growing!

Unease gathering in the pit of my stomach, I retreated warily. Whatever was happening to the corpse, it did not bode well.

A swarm viper's deathwish ability has been triggered!

✳   ✳   ✳

In the wake of the Game's message, any temptation I felt about hanging around vanished. Spinning psi, I hastened my flight and retreated into the shadows.

You have teleported 48 yards to Ghost. You are hidden.

"Oh my," the spirit wolf exclaimed excitedly when I emerged from the aether beside her. *"Do you see that? Its mind is changing!"*

I nodded grimly. *"I think it's reviving itself."*

As maddeningly vague as the Game message was, I was sure now that whatever was happening to the swarm viper, it was not in fact dead. In hindsight, I realized that should have been obvious to me earlier.

The Game had not awarded me any experience after the encounter, nor had the Adjudicator pronounced the swarm viper dead. Both were important tells that I'd missed. Thankfully, the lesson had not been as costly as it could have.

"What do we do now?" Ghost asked.

"We wait," I answered, my own gaze fixed on the far end of the tunnel where the two halves of the serpent's body were still twitching—and growing. *"And watch."*

As far back as I was, there was little chance of the reviving serpent spotting me, and before I resumed our skirmish, I needed to better understand what was going on.

It did not take long for the spell wreathing the swarm viper's corpse to finish, and when it was done, I saw that I'd guessed wrong.

The viper had not revived itself.

It had done something altogether different—and infinitely worse.

Deathwish spell completed. A swarm viper has cloned itself.

Aghast, I stared at the two very-much-alive vipers slithering languidly through the blood pooling around their progenitor. *Two*, I thought. *I have two foes now in place of one.*

Both creatures appeared identical to their predecessor. But were they? Surely that couldn't be so. They had to be magical constructs with a timed lifespan. Otherwise... otherwise, I was in a lot more trouble than I'd originally imagined.

Ignoring the impulse to cut and run, I reached out with my will and analyzed the distant creatures.

The target is a level 191 swarm viper.
The target is a level 191 swarm viper.
Swarm vipers are amongst the most intriguing monsters in the Forever Kingdom. While they possess a host of other menacing traits and abilities, it is for their unique deathwish ability that the serpents are feared.

A deathwish ability is triggered in the instant between a creature being dealt fatal damage and the spirit fleeing the body. The swarm vipers' variant of this ability is a cloning spell, which creates two marginally weaker copies of the host.

Extraordinarily, the copies are not transient beings, but fully-fledged individuals. In a very real and frightening sense, swarm vipers can be said to give birth when they die.

It is this bizarre—but nonetheless efficient—method of procreation that makes swarm vipers such fascinating creatures.

"It has split its mind," Ghost marveled. *"There are two of them now!"*

I nodded numbly. Ghost's observations tallied with the Game's message. It was a safe bet, too, that both of the newly created swarm vipers also had the clone deathwish ability. If I killed them, they would only multiply again.

I sighed, finally understanding the true meaning behind my foe's name. The viper wasn't part of a swarm. It *was* the swarm.

A swarm of one.

CHAPTER 309: THE BETTER PART OF VALOR

It was not all bad news, of course.

There were some definite benefits to facing two weaker creatures instead of one higher level foe, especially since the 'new' vipers weren't elite-ranked monsters anymore. That not-insignificant fact was what had allowed me to analyze the clones.

It was also why my telepathic abilities were more likely to succeed the second time around too. And after the next iteration of clones, it would be *even* easier. In fact, I thought, grinning in sudden realization, from here on things could only get easier.

I can still win this.

The insight reignited my enthusiasm, and I nearly resumed the battle there and then, but I reined in the impulse in time. There was something else I had to attend to first—namely, restoring my mana.

Both the clones appeared content to remain where they were, but just in case, I retreated another fifty yards up the tunnel. The exit, and I was certain now that it was indeed an exit—light, albeit of the weak and dull kind, was streaming through—was only a short hop away. Nothing had ventured through yet, and I didn't think anything would, but it wouldn't do to leave it unguarded.

"Keep watch on that," I instructed Ghost, gesturing to the exit, then sat down and closed my eyes.

✳ ✳ ✳

You have replenished 100% of your mana. Void armor charge remaining: 100%.

Your channeling has increased to level 104.

A little later, I opened my eyes to find Ghost standing patient sentry by my side. Rising silently to my haunches, I peered down the tunnel. The two swarm vipers were still where I'd last seen them.

"Are you going to try killing them?" Ghost asked.

I glanced at her. *"I am."*

"Won't more just appear?"

I shrugged. *"It matters little. Each successive group will be lower-leveled and easier to kill."* I paused. *"It will likely be time-consuming, though."*

"What do you need me to do?" she asked.

I looked back over my shoulder. *"Return to the exit and keep watch. Make sure nothing interrupts us."*

"On my way!" she responded, energetic as ever, despite the trivial nature of the task I'd assigned her.

I smiled fondly. As frustrating as Ghost could be at times, her unrelenting good cheer never failed to surprise me. It made her a pleasant companion and I was glad to have her around.

"*Try to stay within fifty yards of me at all times,*" I said, adding a final word of caution. "*If I need to flee, I will teleport to your location.*"

"*Of course, Prime,*" she replied.

Leaving Ghost to her task, I turned back to the swarm vipers. Their minds were as opaque to me as their predecessor's had been, but neither had concealed itself yet. *Hmm...* Was that because they had lost the ability to do so, no longer being elite creatures?

I didn't know and it didn't really matter. Drawing psi, I began casting.

There were multiple tactics I could employ against the swarm vipers, but the simplest—and most effective—was to let them do most of the work for me.

Sending tendrils of psi forward, I assaulted the minds of both serpents simultaneously.

You have cast mass charm.
A level 191 swarm viper has failed a mental resistance check!
A level 191 swarm viper has passed a mental resistance check!
You have charmed 1 of 2 targets for 20 seconds.

I exhaled in relief as I wrenched control of one of the clone's minds. I'd not been entirely sure my charm spell would work and had been afraid that whatever ability the vipers were using to shield themselves from my mindsight would also make them immune to mental manipulations.

But it hadn't. And now the rest of the encounter would be easy. *Right, time to get them fighting,* I thought and reached across the mental link binding my new minion to my will.

A hostile entity has detected your spell! A level 191 swarm viper is now hostile to your minion!

I faltered, momentarily distracted by the surprising Game message. The unaffected viper had detected my influence over its companion. Something like this had never happened before!

The second swarm viper did not hesitate. While I was floundering, and before I could finish issuing my attack orders, it struck. Uncoiling rapidly, it darted forward and clamped its jaws around my minion.

It didn't stop there, though.

Powered by the momentum of its lunge, the serpent coiled the rest of its body about its victim, trapping it in steel bands of flesh. My minion attempted to respond in kind, but the second swarm viper had executed its first strike too well, and it was unable to sink its jaws into the other.

A swarm viper has critically injured your minion.
Your minion has failed to hit a swarm viper.

My mouth twisted sourly as I watched the two writhing serpents. It seemed all but certain that my minion would lose the battle, and I wondered if I should intervene. But after a moment's consideration, I decided not to.

After all, it didn't matter which viper came out on top.

The loser would still clone itself into two weaker variants. Stilling my hands, I waited for the battle to resolve itself.

*   *   *

Inevitably, the aggressor won.

Your minion has been dealt a fatal blow.

About time, I thought grumpily.

Even with a death-grip on my minion, victory had not come easily—or quickly—for the second serpent. Sliding free from the corpse, the battered victor reared up to its full height and stared down triumphantly at its defeated foe.

I, too, watched the 'dead' viper intently. My next move would depend very much on what happened. The corpse trembled minutely, then more vigorously and, a heartbeat later, burst apart.

Deathwish spell completed. A swarm viper has cloned itself.

As expected, two new vipers emerged from the fresh spatter of blood and gore. It was the moment I'd been waiting for, and without delay, I interrogated the newcomers with analyze.

The target is a level 181 swarm viper.
The target is a level 181 swarm viper.

I pursed my lips. *So.* Each time the swarm vipers replicated, they lost ten levels. I could work with that. Drawing in psi, I began a second casting.

Again, the second swarm viper surprised me.

Not giving me a chance to finish my casting, the bloody survivor of the first battle struck again. Its jaws opening impossibly wide, the serpent flung itself at one of the new clones.

And swallowed it whole.

What the hell?

My mouth dropped open, revulsion battling shock, as I watched the frantically struggling younger clone slide down the mouth of its fellow. There had been no reason for the older clone to attack. I hadn't even cast my charm spell yet!

So what had prompted the assault? *And what sort of attack was that anyway?*

Obligingly, the Game answered.

A level 191 swarm viper has consumed a level 181 swarm viper and has advanced to level 196.

Consume is a rare and somewhat macabre ability that allows some creatures to ingest their weaker fellows. In the process, the attacker becomes stronger, absorbing a fraction of its victim's power. Note, consumption does not trigger an entity's deathwish ability.

My eyes widened. *Now, that's... dastardly.*

The older swarm viper was not done yet, though. Pinning its gaze on the second clone—which was frantically slithering away—the engorged serpent darted forward and clamped its jaws down on the fleeing clone's tail.

Then, it sucked it in, too.

A level 196 swarm viper has consumed a level 181 swarm viper and has advanced to level 201.

Well... damn.

I stared disbelievingly at the newly empowered swarm viper. It might have been my imagination, but to my mind, the thing looked smug and self-satisfied.

More depressing, I was right back where I started: facing off with an elite creature again.

✳   ✳   ✳

The older clone—which I was quickly coming to hate—had yet another surprise for me. Less than a minute after digesting its 'meals,' the sated serpent coiled around itself and faded from sight.

A hostile entity is hidden!

God damnit! I cursed, suspecting what had happened. An elite once more, the swarm viper had regained its camouflage ability. *I can still kill it,* I thought mulishly.

Yet, despite my confidence, I made no move to attack anew.

Like I'd told Ghost, slaying the swarm viper would take time and, in the face of the clones' new consumption ability, my estimate of how long that would be had gone up. Drastically.

I'd spent an hour fighting the viper—and had nothing to show for it. I could resume my battle with the creature and likely waste another few hours slaying it or...

Or I could find another way to employ that time and put my stolen knowledge to use. After all, the entire reason I'd ventured out of the entrance chamber without resting in the first place was the necrotic spike spell—and given the swarm viper's nature, the spell would be wasted against it. Any one of my blades would serve me better against the clones.

Slaying the swarm viper was not a priority, I reminded myself. Maximizing the benefit I derived from my stolen spell was. I glanced at the waiting exit behind me. At the very least, the area beyond warranted a look-see.

And I can always come back and kill the swarm viper later. Turning around, I headed for the exit. As I made my way towards Ghost, I felt the muscles in my legs strain harder. The ground beneath me was rising, I realized. Steeply, too.

"We're leaving?" Ghost asked when I drew level with her.

I nodded. *"We'll return later. But for now, it's time we did a bit of exploring."* I jutted my chin towards the tunnel opening ahead. Over the last few feet, the walls and sides of the underground passage had compressed sharply, leaving the exit no more than a tiny slit in the ground. *"What's out there?"*

"Nothing," she replied dismissively. *"Just rocks and more rocks."*

"Hmm," I mused, not sure if I was more disappointed or relieved to hear that.

Squeezing through the narrow opening, I went to see for myself.

※　※　※

The first thing I noticed was the purple sky.

It was enough of a surprise that I instinctively dropped into a crouch and cloaked myself in shadows. Only then did I turn my attention to the surroundings again.

I was in a deep basin formed of stony ground and rimmed with rocky cliffs. My first thought was that I was in a mountain range. But no, there were no tall peaks darkening the horizon. Instead, the cliffs' tops had been sheared off, and their heights were hidden from sight.

I'm in a chasm, I thought. *A cauldron-shaped chasm.*

Sheer walls curved around nearly the entirety of the basin, except for a small gap in one section. And in that direction the chasm extended onwards, zigzagging like a jagged scar across the face of the world.

Above the towering gray cliffs—each a few hundred feet tall at least—the sky shone violet. There was no sun in evidence. Nor stars for that matter. But the sky was not uniformly purple. Here and there, the horizon was marred by patches of pale white.

Clouds perhaps? I wondered.

But there was something off about the 'clouds'—I couldn't quite put my finger on what, though—and it made me hesitant to label them such. Frowning, I tore my gaze away from the gray haze—the mystery could wait for later—and turned my attention to the rest of the sky.

In other spots, the sky's violet tinge thickened, deepening to a metallic hue. The familiar sheen reminded me of the scorching dune dungeon where I'd seen something similar.

Was the violet band stretching across the horizon the sector's protective barrier? The one that shielded the dungeon from the dark miasma of the Nethersphere? *Most likely,* I decided and dismissed it from further consideration. Dropping my gaze, I studied the stony, pockmarked ground ahead.

That's when the *second* intriguing thing caught my eye.

It was a moving mountain.

Two moving mountains rather, each vaguely man-shaped and with arms and legs.

But they weren't really mountains, I realized. They were monsters, and the dungeon's next challenge.

"The sky looks funny," Ghost remarked suddenly. "I... like it. Can we climb the rocks and take a closer look?"

I glanced sideways at the spirit wolf, then back again at the mountain-sized humanoids. The cauldron's floor extended a few hundred yards in diameter, and the pair were far off and of no immediate threat. "I thought you said there was nothing out here?"

"There isn't," she replied. "Now can we go see the sky? Please?"

I pursed my lips. Ghost wouldn't lie to me, but the two rock creatures were clearly visible. Despite being over two hundred yards away, their size made them easy to spot. "What about those two?"

"Oh, them," Ghost replied with barely a hitch. "What about them?" She paused, then added helpfully as if I might have missed the fact, "They're just rocks, Prime. Weirdly shaped and large, but just rocks."

"They're moving, Ghost," I retorted in exasperation.

"So what? Rocks move."

"Rocks roll," I growled. "They don't walk. Living creatures do that!"

"Huh?" Ghost exclaimed, finally sensing some of my irritation. "But they have no mind!"

I blinked. "They don't?"

"No. They don't," Ghost replied emphatically.

I scratched my chin, considering this. The rock creatures were too far away to appear in my own mindsight, but I didn't disbelieve Ghost. What then did that make the two entities? Constructs? Probably.

Narrowing my gaze, I examined them anew.

Both creatures were as tall as the cliffs bordering the cauldron and while they were humanoid in shape, nothing about them screamed human. For one, they were formed from solid rock, for another, their faces were devoid of features, and their hands and feet lacked digits, ending in flattened stumps instead.

The two weren't identical either. The creature on the left was missing an arm, while the one on the right had a chunk missing from one of its legs. I frowned. It almost looked like the two had been injured. But what could injure such behemoths?

"Are they really alive, Prime?" Ghost asked, sounding miserable.

I glanced back at the spirit wolf. She had been trying so hard to be useful, and now, she thought she'd failed me. And she hadn't, not really.

"They might not be," I admitted, ashamed of my earlier anger. "They could be constructs." Realizing she probably didn't know what that was, I added, "A construct is a made-thing, something created and given false-life. While they have no mind, they are still dangerous."

"There are creatures with no mind?" Ghost asked, seemingly startled by the notion.

I nodded. "There are."

"B-but... but how do I spot them then?" she moaned.

"You can't unless you see them behaving strangely, in a way natural things won't." I hesitated before adding gently, "Then you should tell me."

"I'm sorry, Prime," she said dejectedly.

"*The fault was mine,*" I reassured her. I realized that if I was going to continue employing Ghost as my scout, I would have to expand her education. There were things other than constructs she needed to know about, and I resolved to teach her at the soonest opportunity.

"*Come on,*" I said. "*Let's go take a closer look at these things.*"

CHAPTER 310: MOVING MOUNTAINS

Before moving away from the tunnel, I cast my buffs, more out of an excess of caution than anything else. I'd yet to decide whether to engage the rock giants.

You have cast heightened reflexes, increasing your Dexterity by +8 ranks for 20 minutes.

You have cast load controller, granting you a 10-minute encumbrance aura that slows any armor-wearing foe within 2 yards by 20%.

You have trigger-cast quick mend. When your overall health falls below 30%, it will instantly heal you for 20%.

After further consideration, I also swapped out my secondary blade—the stygian shortsword—and replaced it with faithful.

You have equipped the sword, <u>faithful blade</u>, gaining the recall ability and increasing the damage you deal with your offhand by +40%.

Ready as I could be, I tiptoed across the bowl-shaped cauldron. While I did, I scanned the surroundings, searching for anything else Ghost might have missed, but spotted nothing alarming.

The cauldron itself held most of my attention. The cliffs bordering it were too sheer for an ordinary human to scale. I, on the other hand, could likely manage the feat with windslide. It was not, though, the most obvious route out; that was the narrow canyon whose entrance lay beyond the two rock creatures.

Where it led was anyone's guess, but that was not my chief consideration right now. My gaze slid back to the rock giants and for lack of anything better, dubbed them One-Arm and Limp.

The pair strode along a ravine that meandered from one end of the cauldron to the other, dividing it in two near-equal halves, and looking for all the world as if they were patrolling it. I frowned.

Now why would they do that?

The constructs walked alone and in opposite directions, their footfalls heavy and ponderous as they marched along the ravine from the center of the cauldron to its rim, then back again.

Limp—the one with the missing chunk of leg—had a definite hitch in his stride and moved slower than One-Arm, forcing him to wait in the middle of the cauldron while Limp finished his own half of the patrol. But even One-Arm was no speedster, and I judged I was many times faster than both.

Unfortunately, speed seemed the only advantage I had over the pair.

Limp and One-Arm were larger than me, undoubtedly stronger, and if appearances could be believed, their skin and innards were rock-hard too. Worse yet, if the pair lacked minds of their own, they were also immune to all forms of mental manipulation. That made them impervious to *both* my blades and telepathy. A sorry state of affairs that would have me gladly avoiding the behemoths entirely.

If not for my stolen spell.

It gave me an edge that, provided I stayed out of range of the giants' ham-fisted hands, *should* win me the encounter. My lips twisted sourly. A lot depended on that 'should.'

Two hostile entities have failed to detect you! You are hidden.

Drawing to a halt, I crouched down. I was now just under fifty yards from my targets, and near enough to the ravine to peer within. While some parts of it remained shadowed from sight, I could see enough of its depths to determine the ravine was as barren as the rest of my surroundings. Deciding there was no need to approach any closer, I unfurled my mindsight.

Not unexpectedly, no mindglows appeared.

"You were right, Ghost," I said. *"These two lack minds of their own."*

"They are constructs then?" she asked.

"There's only one way to be sure," I murmured. Reaching out with my will, I analyzed Limp, the closer of my two foes.

The target is a stone golem of indeterminant level.
Your analyze attempt has been detected! You are no longer hidden.

Limp's featureless face creaked in my direction.

Uh-oh. Being discovered so quickly was unexpected and threw my hopes for a carefully choreographed encounter into disarray. Rising swiftly to my feet, I backed away. It was time to revise my plans.

The first order of business was securing an escape route, and unfortunately the tunnel would not do. *"Ghost,"* I ordered, *"search the—"*

I broke off. The ground under Limp was bubbling.

My gaze flickered downward. The previously solid-seeming ground beneath the stone golem was turning to mush. It was a safe bet that whatever was happening, it didn't mean anything good for me. Edging back faster, I wrapped myself in shadows.

Or tried to.

You have failed to conceal yourself. A hostile entity has detected you!

"The other one is turning to face you as well," Ghost reported.

My eyes darted to the second golem. The ground beneath One-Arm was churning restlessly too.

What are they doing?

A moment later, the stone beneath Limp liquefied entirely, flowed up the golem's legs, along his outstretched arms, and into his upturned palms.

Where it then coalesced into a giant boulder.

That explains the pockmarks, I thought, watching Limp sink into the newly formed crater beneath him. The golem was unfazed by his new position, though, and slowly drew back his arms—and the boulder still stuck to his hands. Anticipating what was coming, I threw myself backward.

Not a moment too soon.

Limp's arms extended again, propelling the enormous boulder in my direction. The projectile hurtled through the air with a speed that defied reason—it was three times my size and had to weigh a few tons at least.

But I was faster still, and on the move already. Tucking in my limbs, I held them tight as the rock screamed mere inches past me.

You have evaded a stone golem's attack.

Having missed me, the stone projectile kept going, only coming to a halt when it met the encircling cliff and shattered into a thousand tiny pieces.

Bounding back to my feet, I winced at the sound of the impact, finding it all too easy to imagine what the boulder would have done to me.

"Incoming!" Ghost shouted.

My head whipped around to see One-Arm lobbing his own missile. Without hesitation, I dived again and took cover as the second boulder whistled by.

You have evaded a stone golem's attack.

Right, no more time to waste. Not bothering to look back over my shoulder, I set off running, arcing away from the angry golems. While I did, I summoned psi, and willed two slim shapes of vibrant violet energy in my palms.

You have cast twin astral blades.

The instant the psi daggers materialized, I spun about and flung them at Limp. But I didn't wait to observe the outcome. Whirling around again, I resumed my flight.

Your astral blade has failed to harm your target.
Your astral blade has failed to harm your target.
Stone golems are immune to all forms of mental assaults!

My lips thinned at the Game messages. Just as I'd anticipated, Limp proved immune to psi damage. Although I had expected no less, I'd still needed to verify my suspicions.

"They're forming more boulders," Ghost reported.

"Thanks," I grunted. *"Let me know when they release."* In preparation, I drew more psi and cast windborne.

"Take cover!" Ghost yelled.

I could hear the massive stones hurtling through the air myself and laid down the ramp of air I held in readiness. Gliding along the windslide, I watched the projectiles sail harmlessly past me.

You have evaded a stone golem's attack.
You have evaded a stone golem's attack.

Somersaulting off the windslide, I hit the ground running and yanked free a brace of stoppered bottles from my belt. It was time for another test. Winding back my right arm, I threw all three objects at Limp.

You have ignited an ice bomb, creating a freezing cloud.
You have ignited an acid bomb, creating an acid pool.
You have ignited a fire bomb, creating a fiery explosion.
You have failed to harm your target. A stone golem is immune to cold, acid, and fire damage.

I wasn't sure what I was expecting, but total immunity to all my bombs was not it.

Damnation! What does it take to hurt these things?

I still had a few other tricks up my sleeve. I could try a lightning trap or a straight-up assault with my blades, but after the resounding failure of my bombs, I was skeptical of either approach working.

Enough quibbling, I decided. It was time to try the only real weapon left to me: the necrotic spikes.

Another pair of boulders sailed my way, but I'd opened the distance between me and the golems to about a hundred yards and barely had to break stride to dodge out of their path.

"Are you going back into the tunnel?" Ghost asked.

Taking stock of my surroundings, I realized that I was indeed heading in its direction, but that was more by sheer chance than conscious choice. *"No,"* I panted between breaths. *"The tunnel isn't safe. I can't risk being trapped in there between the viper and the golems."*

"Oh. Right. I'll find you somewhere else to hide, then."

I almost called Ghost back, but then realized I would need a place to recuperate—and soon. *"Alright, go on,"* I replied while neatly sidestepping the next pair of incoming boulders.

After the projectiles passed by, I ground to a stop and turned around. I was far enough from Limp and One-Arm that their missiles were no longer a significant threat. And neither golem, I noticed, was closing the distance to me with any great speed. *Here will do.* Tapping into my pool of magic, I let it form the weaves of my only mana-based spell.

A necrotic spike ward has been successfully configured.
Mana remaining: 80%.

The ward spell materialized beneath the ponderously advancing Limp and, a heartbeat later, triggered as his foot crushed down on it.

Necrotic spike activated! A stone golem has sustained nether damage.

I grinned and the tight knot of dread in the pit of my stomach unraveled. I'd been half-convinced that even the stolen tier six spell would fail.

But it hadn't, and my relief knew no bounds.

Now we're in business, I thought. Setting off on a run, I began a second casting.

✳   ✳   ✳

A stone golem has sustained nether damage.
A stone golem has sustained nether damage.
A stone golem has sustained nether damage.
A stone golem has sustained nether damage.
Mana remaining: 0%.

A little later, I'd set and triggered four more necrotic spikes, all while kiting the golems and dodging their sporadic boulder-fire. Despite its premature start, the battle was turning out to be easier than I expected.

The wide-open nature of the cauldron left me plenty of room to maneuver, and even after enduring repeated hits of nether damage, Limp did not change tactics. Despite the golems' toughness, I realized they were no more than unthinking constructs.

A weakness I'd intended on ruthlessly exploiting.

"Find anything yet?" I called out. The first stage of my assault was complete. I'd focused all my attacks on Limp, and by my reckoning, I'd eaten through a quarter of his health already. Three more waves of spikes and he'd be dead.

First, though, I needed a hidey-hole to recover.

Ghost did not respond to my hail which likely meant she hadn't heard me. Unfortunately, I had no idea where she was; she'd long since dropped out of range of my mindsight.

I grimaced, realizing I had erred by not asking the spirit wolf to report back regularly. *A communication protocol, that's what we need,* I thought. In situations like this, neither Ghost nor I could afford to be left wondering if the other was alright. Somehow, we still needed to stay in contact. I sighed. It was another problem for later. For now, I just had to find her.

Where is she?

Lifting my head, I scanned the cauldron's perimeter. Ghost had gone looking for shelter, and the only likely spots for that were the base of the cliffs or the ravine. There was nowhere else to hide from Limp and One-Arm. Unintelligent though the golems were, there was nothing wrong with their senses, and despite multiple attempts, I'd failed to hide from either.

I needed somewhere out of direct line of sight if I was going to lose them. Cutting left, I headed towards the closest edge of the cauldron and away from both golems.

I hadn't taken more than a dozen steps, though, when Ghost raced into view. *"Found it!"* she sang.

"Welcome back," I said, hiding my relief at her return. *"What did you find?"*

"A cave," she replied proudly. *"It's in the ravine and is small, dry, and empty."*

I smiled. Ghost had done well. Swerving north, I angled back to the golems and the ravine at their backs. *"Lead the way."*

*   *   *

You have teleported 50 yards to Ghost.

I didn't climb down into the ravine—that would only have let the golems know where I was heading—and instead shadow blinked directly into the cave using Ghost as a teleport beacon when I drew close enough.

Two hostile entities have failed to detect you! You are hidden.

I smiled at the Game message. I was safe at last, if only temporarily. *"Keep an eye on our friends,"* I instructed Ghost before closing my eyes and seeing to my recovery.

You have replenished 4% of your mana. Your mana is now at 4%.
You have replenished 4% of your mana. Your mana is now at 8%.
...
You have replenished 100% of your mana.

Thirty minutes later, I was ready to venture forth again. My short rest period had gone undisturbed. Rising to my feet, I crept to the cave entrance. Mindsight reported Ghost to be directly above me, likely standing on the edge of the ravine, but of the golems, there was no sign.

"Where are they?" I whispered.

"They've resumed their patrols," she answered. *"The one-armed one is near the cliffs and turning around, and the other is near the center but heading away from your position."*

"Perfect," I replied, and stepped through the aether to emerge by Ghost's side.

You are no longer hidden!

Immediately, both golems swung around to face me. But I was already running—and casting.

A stone golem has sustained nether damage.
A stone golem has sustained nether damage.

I hit Limp twice before he managed to form a boulder. Dodging the incoming missile, I cast again and laid down two more necrotic spikes.

A stone golem has sustained nether damage.
A stone golem has sustained nether damage.

"Ghost," I panted, while weaving mana for my last spell. *"Return to the cave. I'll be there in—"*

I broke off as the ground trembled violently.

Spreading my arms, I retained my balance and risked a glance over my shoulder. It sounded like one of the golem's missiles had misfired and hit something—the ground, most likely. The sight that greeted me was altogether different, though.

Limp was no more.

Where he'd stood was a pile of shattered rocks and stones. My brows drew down in confusion. Was he dead?

But he couldn't be.

I'd hit the golem with nine necrotic spikes so far. That equated to only forty-five percent damage. *He can't be dead, not unless—*

A Game message interrupted me.

You have killed a level 224 stone golem.

Of their own accord, my feet stopped moving, and I stumbled to a halt. This time there could be no doubt. I'd done it. I'd killed an elite!

More Game messages scrolled through my mind.

You have reached level 158!
Your dodging has increased to level 130 and reached rank 13.
Congratulations, Michael! You have accomplished the feat: Master Dungeoneer! Requirement: slay an elite creature in any dungeon. You have been awarded an additional life! Total lives remaining: 3.

I whistled softly in appreciation.

Killing Limp had netted me four levels, not to mention earned me the unlooked-for boon of another life. True, I'd only managed the feat because of the stolen necrotic spell. But even knowing that did nothing to dampen my mood.

I've killed an elite, I thought, still marveling at the fact.

If I could repeat the feat, it was entirely possible I would emerge from Draven's Reach as an elite myself—even accounting for the diminishing returns as the level gap between me and the dungeon's denizens decreased.

I grinned. *Now, there's a happy thought.*

"*Look out!*" Ghost warned.

My head jerked up and spotted the boulder taking shape in One-Arm's hand. In the aftermath of Limp's death, I'd nearly forgotten about my second foe. Throwing myself into motion again, I prepared another casting.

It was time to gain another bunch of levels.

CHAPTER 311: THE DUNGEONEER'S REWARDS

You have killed a level 226 stone golem.
You have reached level 161 and rank 16!
For achieving rank 16, you have been awarded 1 additional attribute point and 1 Class point.

It took me another two hours and sixteen necrotic spikes to kill the second golem which, while a substantial number of nether shards, was still short of the twenty I'd estimated I would need.

There was only one conclusion I could draw from that: both One-Arm and Limp had been injured before I'd encountered them.

How and why, I didn't know, but I was glad it had happened, nonetheless. It had taken me almost three full hours to kill both elites, and I wasn't sure I would've managed the feat if they had been uninjured.

But that was all behind me now.

You have replenished 100% of your mana.

I opened my eyes. After killing One-Arm, I'd retreated to the ravine cave to recover. This time around, Ghost had declined to accompany me and had instead gone sniffing around the cauldron; the cave bored her, or so she claimed.

Another Game message flashed for attention.

4 hours have passed. You have lost knowledge of the stolen spell, necrotic spike.

I sighed. The stygian overlord's spell had served me well, but now it was gone, and it was time to ponder my next move. The first order of business was spending my sudden profusion of points.

I had gained eight attribute points from the encounter with the golems, and one Class point too. Before deciding how to invest them, I turned my attention inwards and reviewed the status of my ability slots.

Unused Ability Slots

Strength: 13 of 13.
Constitution: 9 of 19.
Dexterity: 14 of 55.
Perception: 0 of 31.
Mind: 14 of 71.
Magic: 21 of 21.
Faith: 0.

My first instinct was to dump the new attribute points in Dexterity or Mind, but I couldn't ignore how poorly my tier two analyze was faring in the dungeon. It was simply not up to the task of inspecting elite-ranked creatures. Just as importantly, I already *had* a tier three analyze ability tome in my backpack. Unfortunately, though, I lacked the necessary Perception slots to use it.

But information was power.

Knowing my foes' level and something of their nature before I engaged them could make all the difference to the outcome of an encounter. *A functional analyze is worth the cost,* I decided.

Withdrawing the tome in question from my backpack, I made the necessary investment in Perception and learned what the tome had to teach.

Your Perception has increased to rank 36. Other modifiers: +4 from items.

You have upgraded your analyze ability to <u>superior analyze</u>, enabling you to inspect entities of rank 30 and below. The tier 3 analyze variant is more likely to provide you with additional information on a target. Additionally, it makes you aware of any effects and buffs that are active on the target. You have 0 of 36 Perception ability slots remaining.

Perfect, I thought.

I still had three attribute points remaining and, after further consideration, decided to invest them in Mind. Right now, boosting the performance of my telepathic abilities was more important than increasing my speed or the size of my mana pool.

Your Mind has increased to rank 74. Other modifiers: +4 from items.

My attributes seen to, I turned my attention to my two Class points. One, I was holding in reserve to upgrade slaysight again—which I would do when my telepathy skill advanced to tier four.

But the other...

Was now the right time to spend the second Class point? Truly, I could see little reason to hold back.

But how best to use it? I *could* improve one of my existing Class traits, acquire a *new* Class benefit, *or* upgrade void thief.

I bit my lip, uncertain which way to go. There was no way to know beforehand how void thief's tier two variant would improve the ability, nor for that matter what new Class benefits the Adjudicator would offer. But there was no reason to choose upfront either. The best way to make the decision would be on the spot—during the Class upgrade process itself.

Then let's do that. Closing my eyes, I willed my intention to the Game.

Assessing player's suitability for a Class upgrade...
Class points available: 2.
Player rank: 16.
Upgrade requirements met.
You may advance your Class to rank 8 by improving an existing Class benefit or by selecting a new one. Do you wish to proceed?

If I did proceed, there would be no going back. I would have to complete the Class upgrade; the Game would force me to do so. Taking a deep breath, I conveyed my response to the Adjudicator.

Commencing Class upgrade...

2 new Class benefits are available, and 5 of 6 existing benefits are upgradeable.

New benefit: <u>deft thief</u>. This trait increases the number of spells you may steal from a foe with void thief.

New benefit: <u>prepared mind</u>. This ability allows you to precast a single ability, releasing it instantly when needed with no additional casting time required.

Existing benefits that may be upgraded: void heritage, wolfwalker, mental focus IV, arctic wolf, and void thief.

Existing benefits not available for upgrade: slaysight. This ability requires a telepathy skill of rank 15 to advance.

Choose your rank 8 Class benefit now.

I sighed. This time around, the Adjudicator had seen fit to only provide me with a choice of two new Class benefits, and one wasn't exactly 'new' either. I'd already come across prepared mind the first time I'd upgraded my Class, and I immediately dismissed it from consideration again.

The other benefit, deft thief, sounded nice... but I wasn't convinced that being able to steal *more* spells would be helpful in my present circumstances. What I really needed was to be able to retain the stolen knowledge for *longer*, thereby increasing the benefits I derived from it.

No, I decided, *deft thief is a trait best left for another time.* That left my existing Class abilities and traits to consider.

It was easy to predict how void heritage and arctic wolf would advance—both provided bonus attributes—and I was sure the next tier would also increase the boost they provided. The only question was by how much. Likewise, I already knew from my previous Class upgrade what mental focus would do.

I frowned. Wolfwalker I was less sure about. The trait was a result of my Wolf Mark though, and I thought it likely it would evolve further on its own as my Mark deepened.

That left me with only one real option—upgrading void thief.

I'd suspected all along that my choice would boil down to this, and really, even though I was being forced to make the decision somewhat blindly, improving void thief was far from a bad option. Forgoing further deliberation, I willed the Adjudicator to advance the ability.

Upgrade complete. Class points remaining: 1.

Congratulations, Michael, your voidstealer Class has advanced to rank 8!

You have upgraded your void thief ability to <u>improved void thief</u>. The second tier of this ability makes it easier for you to filch knowledge from your foes by reducing the damage your void armor needs to sustain to trigger a theft from 50% to 40%.

The range of hostile spells that can be stolen has also expanded to include channeled spells. Additionally, the memory capacity of your void armor has improved, allowing you to remember your stolen knowledge for 8 hours instead of 4.

Improved void thief also provides you with a second method, called siphon, of disrupting your foes' attacks. After you perform a successful spell theft, a conduit is forged between you and your foe, enabling you to siphon a portion of their mana whenever they cast any further spells at you. Note like its first tier counterpart, siphon is a passive ability and dependent on a successful void theft to function.

"Wow," I exclaimed.

The benefits provided by void thief's tier two variant were significant—especially if siphon allowed me to replenish my mana in battle. It left me wanting to upgrade void thief again, but sadly, none of my void skills had reached tier three yet.

Ah, well, maybe—

"Prime, I've found something odd."

Opening my eyes, I looked about. Ghost had returned. *"Hostiles?"* I asked, hands dropping to my blades.

"I don't think so," she replied, sounding puzzled. *"It's a box. One moment it wasn't there, the next it appeared—almost on top of me!"* she added, sounding a bit indignant at the last.

My eyes widened. *"A loot chest,"* I breathed. *"Was it metal?"*

Ghost pondered the question. *"It was made from gold."* She paused. *"What's a loot chest?"*

I grinned. *"Our reward for defeating the golems."* I knew my answer had failed to enlighten her, but eager to see what the chest contained, I rose to my feet. *"Come. I'll explain on the way."*

✳ ✳ ✳

The loot chest was near the center of the cauldron besides the pile of rocks that One-Arm had transformed into upon death. As I drew closer, I saw that Ghost had not been mistaken.

The box was indeed gold.

Rubbing my hands in anticipation, I flipped open the lid and peered inside. There were only three items—fewer than I'd hoped. Still, I wasted no time inspecting each in turn.

The target is the rank 4 shield: mirror shield. This item bears the enchantment: reflect. Reflect is a passive ability that causes all tier 4 and lower spells blocked by the shield to be reflected back to the caster. This item requires a minimum Strength of 16 to wield.

The target is a piece of enchanted mosaic. It is one part of the Emblem of the Reach, an artifact of unknown rank. You are unable to discern its properties.

The target is the rank 5 ring: mage's surprise. This item increases your Magic by +10 and bears the tier 5 enchantment, spellhold, which allows you to store a single mana-based spell of tier 5 or lower. The spell will be held indefinitely within the ring and, when required, can be cast instantly and without drawing from your mana pool. This item requires a minimum Magic of 20 to use.

I sat back with a frown. The container's contents were disappointing, especially in comparison to my previous haul from a gold loot chest.

"Something wrong?" Ghost asked.

I shook my head. *"No. It's just that I was hoping for..."* I paused as Ghost's question forced me to consider the question: what *had* I'd been expecting?

Better loot, for one.

I sighed, realizing that unconsciously I'd been hoping to find something game-changing, like I had the last time with the master Class stone. *"... more,"* I finished.

Ghost didn't say anything further, and I picked up the ring, mage's surprise. It was the only item of immediate benefit but, even so, it was not what I considered a *great* item.

It would suit a mage or cleric perfectly. Me? Less so. Still, the ring's additional attribute buff was not to be sniffed at and in the right situation, having a tier five spell in reserve would come in handy. Quelling my disappointment, I removed my old magic boosting ring—attribute buffs did not stack—and replaced it with the new one.

You have unequipped the <u>adept's ring</u>, losing 4 Magic.

You have equipped the ring, a <u>mage's surprise</u>, gaining +10 Magic and the ability, spellhold.

That done, I inspected the shield. Like the ring, it was a nice item, just not for me. I couldn't use a shield, but I knew someone who could. *I'll save it for Terence*, I decided, and stuffed it into my bag of holding.

That left the jagged piece of stone tile to examine. The Game had called it an enchanted mosaic and 'part of the Emblem of the Reach.' That was certainly a reference to the dungeon's own name.

What does it do, though?

Picking up the tile, I turned it over in my hands but sensed nothing even faintly magical about the stone. For the most part, the mosaic looked plain and ordinary, a flattened piece of polished rock with etched lines on one side.

I traced my finger along one seemingly random swirl of lines. I had no idea what etchings were meant to portray but suspected deciphering their meaning would require the remaining Emblem pieces, and considering where I'd found the first one, the others were probably also hidden in loot chests.

Which meant killing more elites.

I sighed again. I'd only pitted myself against the golems because I'd seen a way to win—which would not necessarily be true of other encounters. Against certain elites, I would stand no chance.

While I'd killed the two rock creatures easily enough in the end, I had only managed the feat because of the necrotic spikes. Without them... the dungeon's other elites would not be so easy to take down.

I snorted. An understatement.

I focused on the mosaic piece again, studying it thoughtfully. Frankly, without its companion parts, the artifact was little more than junk. But I was not about to attempt slaying *every* elite in the dungeon simply in the hope of completing it.

That would be foolish.

Resigning myself to the mystery of the artifact remaining unsolved, I rose to my feet. It was time to move on. Dropping the mosaic into my bag of holding, I took my bearings. To the north lay the cauldron's exit and the rest of the dungeon. To the south was the tunnel and the swarm viper.

"*Which way?*" Ghost asked, echoing my own thoughts.

I pursed my lips. Like the golems, the swarm viper was an elite I thought I could defeat. And the opportunity it afforded for leveling could not be ignored. "*Back to the tunnel,*" I replied.

I glanced at the ravine. "*But first, I think it's time I rest up.*"

CHAPTER 312: LESSONS IN SPELLCRAFT

This time around, I forwent blinking into the cave Ghost had found for me and took the long way down into the ravine. Reaching the bottom, I looked left and right.

The long-ago waterway that had formed the dried-out riverbed had wormed through the underlying rock, exposing an untold number of cracks and crevices, all of which could be sheltering enemies. After only a brief hesitation, I set off west.

I could sense Ghost's confusion. *"The cave is the other way,"* she said.

I nodded. *"I know, but I want to scout the ravine for myself."* I glanced at her. *"It's not that I don't trust you, but it always pays to make doubly sure."*

"Oh ok."

The ravine's cave, as safe as it had proved so far, was not my first choice of refuge. I was uncomfortable with how exposed it was—its entrance was a gaping maw, clearly visible from the northern side of the cauldron. Anything could enter while I was asleep.

It was part of the reason I was so keen to clear out the tunnel. Given the underground passage's tight confines and concealed entryway, I didn't imagine many of the dungeon's denizens would find it, much less willingly enter—assuming they could fit through, which I doubted most would. All in all, I thought the tunnel would make for an ideal base for my dungeon run.

And something told me that it was going to be a long one.

In the meantime, I would have to make do with the ravine. But if I was going to sleep in the cave Ghost had found, I wanted to be damn sure the ravine was secure—just in case.

"Can I ask you something, Prime?" Ghost asked.

"Go ahead," I told her, not breaking stride. *"We can talk while we walk."*

"Those spells you threw against the golems, what were they?"

"You're referring to the bombs?" I asked absently, my head swiveling left and right as I swept the ravine's depths. So far, I hadn't encountered anything of concern. *"As I understand it, they're alchemical enchantments designed to explode on impact."*

"Not those... the spell you cast before."

I frowned. *"Before? I didn't cast anything—"* I broke off. *"Oh, you mean the psi daggers. The spell is called astral blades."*

"That's the one," Ghost agreed. *"Can you teach it to me?"*

I stopped walking. *"Teach you!"* I exclaimed.

Mistaking the cause of my amazement, Ghost's mind flushed with embarrassment. *"I'm sorry, Prime, I shouldn't have presumed. Please, forget—"*

I waved her to silence. *"No, it's not that. Of course, I'll teach you whatever you want."* The notion of Ghost learning my telepathic abilities had never occurred to me before, and for a moment, I was dumbstruck, simply wondering why. The spirit wolf clearly didn't lack for ability and was obviously more skilled than me in some aspects of telepathy—like mindsight.

But how would I go about teaching her? And were Game-gifted spells even something that could be taught?

"Do you think you could learn the spell?" I asked cautiously.

"I saw some of the weaves while you were casting," she offered. *"But the spell went by too quickly, and I failed to catch all of it."*

"You saw the weaves?" I asked, startled anew.

"Yes," she replied simply.

I pinched the bridge of my nose, thinking hard. *"What about the other spells I cast earlier, like the one I used on the swarm viper—mass charm? Did you see its weaves too?"*

"Some of it," Ghost admitted. Her voice turned brittle. *"I don't think I can cast that one, though. Sulan tried teaching me a similar spell, but I failed to grasp it."* Shame colored her mind. *"I'm not very good."* she finished forlornly.

I blinked, trying to unpack all that. I'd always known the dire wolves were strong telepaths, but I'd never sat down and compared spells with any of the elders—nor, come to think of it, had I ever seen the pack in battle. Now, I wondered what spells they might wield and whether we could teach each other.

"What did Sulan say when you failed?" I asked slowly.

"She said spells grounded in the real are beyond me because I lack a body," Ghost whispered. *"Which is why—"*

"—you asked about the astral blade spell," I finished, finally understanding why she'd brought up the matter only now.

Today was the first time I'd used the astral blade spell while near Ghost, and unlike my other telepathic abilities, the spell was purely psi-based. It had *no* physical components whatsoever. I rubbed my chin. Perhaps Ghost *could* learn it. She had no problems using mindsight after all, another pure psi-based casting. It was worth a shot at least.

"I'll teach you," I pronounced at last.

"You will?" Ghost asked, sounding shocked.

Smiling, I nodded. *"I'll show you the weaves while we walk."* Drawing psi, I formed the spell. *"Now, watch carefully..."*

* * *

For the next hour, I taught Ghost while we strode up and down the ravine. It was both harder and easier than I expected.

The spirit wolf could see the psi weaves I formed easily enough—an ability, which according to Ghost, all dire wolves had—but she struggled to memorize and duplicate the spell's intricate design in her own mind, and all it took was a single misplaced thread for the entire casting to fizzle.

I, of course, didn't have the same problem. Courtesy of the Game, the spell's pattern was etched indelibly in my consciousness. I could cast it by rote, without thinking about individual steps or the correct turn and twist each psi thread needed to take to complete the pattern. Teaching Ghost made me realize how complex spells were, and I despaired of ever learning any casting without the Game's help.

Ghost, though, was managing just fine.

Bit by bit, the spirit wolf committed the spell's design to memory and replicated more of its pattern during her casting attempts. Her spells still fizzled, but I was not discouraged. In only a few more days, I suspected, she would master the entirety of the spell.

An hour later, we finished exploring the ravine and slipped back into the now-familiar cave. I'd found two other likely spots where I could shelter assuming I had to abandon the cave, though neither were as good.

"Show me the astral blade spell again," Ghost demanded the moment I settled down on the floor. *"I'll get it this time; I know I will."*

"No," I replied firmly, knowing if Ghost had her way, her spellcrafting lessons wouldn't stop until she'd mastered the casting. *"I've taught you enough of that for one day. Perfect what you've learned so far before we move on."*

"Alright," Ghost groused, and I sensed a spell weave take shape before me.

Ghost has failed to cast astral blade.

"Save your practice for later," I said mildly. *"For now, listen carefully. There is something else you must learn."*

"Something else?" she asked, puzzled.

I nodded. *"It's time I taught you more of the Game..."*

✳ ✳ ✳

The night—I called it that for convenience, but what time it was, I couldn't say for certain; the sky remained unchanging purple throughout—passed in pleasant conversation. At first, Ghost had been reluctant to learn, but once I got started, she became intrigued by the intricacies of the Game and urged me onwards.

The spirit wolf was endlessly curious. It was in part why she'd latched onto me so quickly. She was also, I sensed, lonely, and once she realized I truly meant to answer her questions fully and honestly, she peppered me with an endless litany of them.

Eventually, though, when I could stifle my yawns no more, I called it quits and, after promising to resume our lessons tomorrow, turned in for the night. Ghost, not needing as much sleep as I did, volunteered to keep watch, and impressed by her performance in the dungeon so far, I let her.

✳ ✳ ✳

You have slept 6 hours. Stamina, mana, and psi reserves have been fully restored.

I awoke hours later, with my energy pools replenished but body and muscles still aching and sore.

"*Morning, Prime!*" Ghost greeted.

"*Morning,*" I replied with notably less cheer as I sat up gingerly. "*Anything to report?*"

"*The swarm viper remains in the tunnel, and nothing entered the cauldron.*"

Mid-yawn, I broke off. "*You went back to the tunnel?*"

The spirit wolf had the grace to feel ashamed. "*Only for a little while,*" she confessed.

I frowned but remained silent.

"*I thought you would want to know where it was,*" she added, her voice growing smaller.

"*I see.*" Saying nothing further, I contemplated admonishing her for her infraction—she'd abandoned her post, if only temporarily—but decided against it. Ghost already knew she'd erred.

"*From your words,*" I said at last, "*I take it you found the serpent.*"

Ghost pulsed relief. She'd been *expecting* a scolding, I realized. "*I did,*" she said. "*It's still hiding.*"

I unwrapped a travel ration while I considered this. "*Was the creature easier to locate this time?*"

"*No,*" she huffed. "*I had to comb through the tunnels four times before I caught even a glimpse of its thoughts.*" She paused. "*Its dreams are not pleasant.*"

"*Hmm.*" I bit through the ration. "*Did it move at all from the spot where it was... born, I guess, you would say?*"

"*It hasn't,*" Ghost replied.

"*Interesting,*" I said, chewing thoughtfully.

"*We're going back today?*" Ghost asked, unable to stifle her curiosity any longer.

"*We are.*"

"*You have a plan?*"

I nodded slowly. "*I think so. The tunnel is a far from ideal battleground to face the viper. The first step will be luring it out.*"

"*And then?*"

"*Then I kill it,*" I said grimly. "*And keep killing it until every last clone is dead.*"

After giving the matter some thought last night, I'd come to the conclusion that the true threat was *not* the viper's cloning trait but its consumption ability. It had taken only a little math to figure out that if an older clone managed to consume the horde of low-level vipers my killing spree created, I could very quickly be facing a single viper of even *higher* level than the original one I'd encountered.

And that was something I had to prevent at all costs.

However, maintaining control in the tunnel's tight confines would be nearly impossible, especially once the number of viper clones reached double digits—which they surely would. In the cauldron, on the other hand, I would be able to separate the swarm and keep individual serpents isolated until they could be slain.

That was the theory, anyway.

Rising to my feet, I dusted my armor free of crumbs and slipped out of the cave. It was time for round two with the swarm viper.

And this time, I intended on winning.

CHAPTER 313: ROUND TWO

DAY TWO IN DRAVEN'S REACH

It took me longer than I expected to find the tunnel entrance.

From the outside, the narrow slit leading into the swarm viper's den looked no different from the hundreds of other crevices riddling the cauldron floor, and in the end, I had to resort to asking Ghost for help to find it.

It got me thinking, too.

I'd entered Draven's Reach through a secret entrance that led directly into the viper's den, and if not for that happy fact, I was certain I would never have found the tunnel. The viper's den was akin to the slime's lair in Erebus' dungeon, I realized.

It's a hidden leg of the dungeon. A secret challenge.

Idly, I wondered if any other dungeon party had ever encountered the swarm viper. I shrugged away the errant thought. It certainly made the forthcoming challenge more interesting, but otherwise mattered little.

Dropping to all fours, I wriggled into the tunnel's narrow opening and reentered the underground passage, welcoming the familiar darkness for all that it sheltered a dangerous foe.

You are hidden.

A predator on the hunt, I crept forward, mind focused and senses extended. As dangerous as the serpent was, it was just a beast, and like all beasts, it could be tricked and trapped, making *me* the deadlier predator.

Or so I told myself.

Closing in to within fifty yards of my target, I drew to a halt and silently unsheathed ebonheart. Hefting the black blade in my right hand, I extracted an empty leather bag from my backpack. I was as prepared as I could be.

I glanced behind me at Ghost waiting near the exit. *"Ready?"*

"Ready," she confirmed.

I turned back to where I knew my foe to be hiding. Exhaling softly, I set down ebonheart and, picking up a small pebble, flung it at the concealed creature.

A level 201 swarm viper is no longer hidden!

The elite emerged from the darkness, and just as it had done the first time, uncoiled with startling quickness to strike down the bouncing stone with a blob of green venom.

I didn't wait to see what the serpent would do next. Retrieving my shortsword, I stepped through the aether.

You have teleported into a swarm viper's shadow.
Your target has detected you! You are no longer hidden.

Sensing my presence at its back, the viper swiveled around. But it was too late. Ebonheart was already arcing downwards, and in one fell swoop, the black blade put an end to my foe.

A swarm viper has been dealt a fatal blow!

There was no time to waste.

Dropping my sword—the soulbound blade would return to me of its own accord—I grabbed the viper's two bloody halves and shoved them into the waiting bag.

The corpse had already begun twitching, but if my first experience with the creature was anything to go by, I knew I had a couple of seconds still. Clutching my left hand tightly around the bag's opening, I dashed for the tunnel exit, spinning psi while I fled.

You have cast windborne.

It was impossible to stand upright in the tunnel, so I materialized the ramp of air as low to the ground as feasible and flung myself flat down on my stomach to zip along its length. It was perhaps not the most comfortable way to navigate the tunnel, but it was the fastest.

The corpse' twitching increased in pitch.

I had no idea if the ordinary leather bag could contain the viper's clones once they spawned—I doubted it—but the bag made transporting the creature easier and would perhaps buy me a few precious seconds.

I reached the end of the windslide and, with my chin tucked into my neck, heaved my body over my head, letting momentum roll me a few yards onwards. Seconds later, I was back on my feet—still crouched—and with the bag secure in my left hand. Not stopping, I crab-walked forward at the fastest pace I could manage.

The bag shuddered.

I was almost out of time. Keeping my gaze fixed on the tunnel exit, I spun psi again.

A swarm viper's deathwish ability has been triggered!

The bag tugged violently sideways, nearly pulling me off my feet as something—two somethings—came alive within it. Grounding my teeth in frustration, I clutched at it tighter.

Damnit! I'm going to have to—

I broke off as I crossed an invisible line, bringing Ghost—waiting outside the exit—into range of my awareness. Without hesitation I completed the spell I'd been holding ready and blinked to her.

You have teleported 50 yards to Ghost.
Deathwish spell completed. A swarm viper has cloned itself.

A tear appeared in the bag and a thrashing tail thrust through. Winding back my arm, I flung the bag and its deadly cargo as far afield as I could. Not delaying to observe the outcome, I whirled about and fled in the opposite direction.

✳   ✳   ✳

Leaving Ghost to watch the escaping clones, I raced across the cauldron as fast as my feet could carry me. Only once I was certain the intervening distance was sufficient to conceal me, did I wrench to a halt and wrap myself in shadows.

Two hostile entities have failed to detect you! You are hidden.

I turned around. It was time to see if my ploy had worked. Rising to my feet, I peered back the way I'd come. I spotted the torn leather bag immediately, and beside it, two serpentine forms snaking along in lazy circles. I sighed in relief. The clones had not slipped back to the tunnel as I feared they might.

"It worked!" Ghost exclaimed, approaching me. *"They're not going back."*

Smiling, I nodded. *"It's time for phase two."* Luring the swarm viper out of its den was only the first part of my grand plan, of course. The other bits, while less dangerous, were just as tricky and their success was by no means assured either.

Glancing down, I saw ebonheart had returned to its sheath. I didn't draw the black sword, though. If the next part went according to plan, I wouldn't need it. Dropping into a crouch, I retraced my steps back to the serpents while Ghost kept patient stride beside me. My targets seemed indifferent to their surroundings and hadn't yet moved far.

Two hostile entities have failed to detect you! You are hidden.

Twenty yards from the creatures, I stopped again. I was close enough. Drawing psi, I spun the weaves of a familiar spell.

You have cast slaysight.
A level 191 swarm viper has failed a mental resistance check!
A level 191 swarm viper has failed a mental resistance check!
You have induced 2 of 2 targets to sleep for 20 seconds.

Not taking the time to celebrate my success, I dashed out of the shadows and towards the two sleeping serpents. Without being told to, Ghost peeled off to her own position. She had a part to play, too.

In only a few seconds, I covered the intervening distance and stopped with brutal suddenness a foot away from my targets. After taking a moment to calm my breathing, I kneeled beside one of the unconscious clones.

For what I intended next, speed would not serve.

Reaching out with empty hands, I let them hover above my chosen target and glanced to the right.

"I'm in place," Ghost whispered.

I nodded in response, not daring to use mindspeech this close to the vipers, no matter that they slept. Spinning psi, I readied my next spell, then slid my hands beneath the serpent with glacial slowness.

The creature did not stir.

So far so good. Breath held in anticipation, I closed fingers about the viper's torso and lifted.

53

The serpent rose easily to dangle bonelessly in my outstretched hands.

I exhaled in silent relief. Until this moment, I hadn't been sure if the viper's induced sleep would hold through my actions or if they would be constituted as hostile. But my plan had worked, and now phase two was well under way.

"*Coming to you,*" I murmured, and shadow blinked.

You have teleported to Ghost.

I stepped out of the aether and into the bowels of one of the cauldron's many craters. The spot Ghost and I had chosen was about fifty yards from the other clone and, more crucially, out of its line of sight.

Moving as carefully as when I'd picked up the serpent, I set it down and took a step back, studying it for a beat. In slumber, the viper looked helpless. Harmless. But nothing could be further from the truth. Drawing ebonheart, I raised the black blade up high and brought it flashing down.

One surgical strike was all it took.

A swarm viper has been dealt a fatal blow!

Turning my back on the slain clone, I exited the crater using windborne.

"*That went well,*" Ghost commented as I made my way back to the other still-sleeping clone.

I nodded. "*Now we only need to do it a few dozen more times.*"

✳   ✳   ✳

Deathwish spell completed. A level 191 swarm viper has cloned itself into 2 level 181 swarm vipers.

Deathwish spell completed. A level 191 swarm viper has cloned itself into 2 level 181 swarm vipers.

If phase one of my plan had been to lure the swarm viper out of its den, then phase two was separating the clones after each kill. I couldn't do that indefinitely of course; there simply weren't enough craters and other hidey-holes in the cauldron for that.

But that wasn't my intention. My primary goal was to force the clones down to a manageable creature-level while still keeping them isolated.

Twenty-eight kills and about a hundred slaysight castings later, I accomplished what I set out to do. "*How many does that make now?*" I asked, sinking wearily down to the cauldron floor.

"*Thirty-two clones, each safely tucked in its own crater,*" Ghost answered promptly.

"*And none have attempted to leave their new homes?*" I asked.

"*They're content to remain where they are,*" Ghost confirmed.

I had charged the spirit wolf with the task of monitoring the serpents—a task she was more suited to than I—not that it seemed necessary. Each 'newborn' clone stayed where it was, seemingly happy to let its prey happen on it by chance.

In fact, the only time I'd seen the vipers motivated enough to move was when they spotted a hostile or ran across one of their younger clones. And so far, I'd been careful to not let either of those things happen.

"*Do we move on to the next phase?*" Ghost asked.

"*In a minute,*" I replied, closing my eyes. "*Let me restore my psi first.*"

CHAPTER 314: A MILLION AND ONE THINGS TO SLAY

A little later, I was at the rim of one of the craters, looking down.

This crater, like the others in the cauldron, had been formed by the stone golems tossing around their boulders. But there was something else special about it, too. Before luring the swarm viper out of its den, I'd spent nearly half the day preparing this particular bowl-shaped hole for my plan.

Using ebonheart—or misusing it, rather—I had dug a narrow shaft into the crater's center. But even with the aid of the indestructible soulbound weapon, hacking through the rocky ground had been near impossible. In the end, I had only managed the feat by repurposing an existing seam in the earth, enlarging and smoothening the mostly vertical crevice until I deemed it suitable.

But I was getting ahead of myself. I wasn't yet ready to employ the shaft; that would have to wait for phase four. Letting my gaze drift away from the shaft, I fixed my eyes on the crater's sole occupant.

The target is a level 151 swarm viper.

The serpent sat coiled and unmoving. It looked no different from the original swarm viper, but from what I'd observed of this generation of clones, I knew them to be slower than their older kin.

Are they less deadly too, I wonder? Picking up a pebble, I flung it at the resting snake.

The viper reacted as expected. Uncoiling, it spat venom at the stone. This time, though, the acidic spittle was not potent enough to dissolve the pebble, nor was the snake's aim as accurate.

I smiled grimly. *This may just work, after all.* Drawing ebonheart and faithful, I cast my buffs.

Your Dexterity has increased by +8 ranks for 20 minutes.
You have gained an encumbrance aura for 10 minutes.
You have trigger-cast quick mend.

Releasing the shadows cloaking me, I jumped into the crater. The drop was a short one and I landed lightly. My gaze flew to my foe. It had already spotted me, and predictably, was snaking aggressively forward.

Raising my blades, I waited.

I outclassed my foe and was both quicker and better armored. Slaying the creature would be easy. It was what came next that worried me more.

The viper's mouth yawned open and green vitriol spilled out.

With only a slight twist of my torso, I avoided the acid shot. Resetting my stance, I waited for the next attack, but no more projectiles were forthcoming; the serpent was already in melee range.

Coiling back on itself, the viper sprang upwards.

Slashing downward with ebonheart, I cut short the attack.

A level 151 swarm viper has been dealt a fatal blow!

The serpent's lifeless body, cleaved in two, thudded back to the ground. I took a step back, eyes peeled on the remains. It wouldn't be long now.

Deathwish spell completed. A swarm viper has cloned itself.

This time around, the clones only took a couple of seconds to spawn. But I wasn't taken by surprise. I'd noticed something similar with the four earlier generations. At each successive cloning, the vipers' deathwish ability triggered faster, spawning the next generation quicker.

It served my new foes naught, though.

I was already in striking range and moving. Before the newcomers could react to my presence, faithful ripped through the torso of the first while ebonheart chopped off the head of the other.

Both blows were fatal.

A level 141 swarm viper's deathwish ability has been triggered!
A level 141 swarm viper's deathwish ability has been triggered!

The bodies thrashed, moving more violently than they had a chance to do in life. Flicking my blades free of blood, I retreated a dozen steps, knowing I would need space to maneuver. Things were about to get interesting.

Less than two seconds later, four newborn clones writhed free of their sires' corpses. Catching sight of me, they rushed forward together. I watched them come. The one on the right was leading slightly. It would attack first. I raised ebonheart in readiness.

The serpent sprang. Ebonheart chopped downwards.

A blur of motion appeared on my left. Faithful flashed out.

Two more shapes hurtled through the air.

I stepped to the left and let them sail past, then whirled around with both my shortswords extended in outstretched arms.

Four level 131 swarm vipers have been dealt fatal blows!

The chunks of the lifeless clones rained down, hitting the ground nearly simultaneously. But eight more would soon appear. *Time to separate the herd.* Sheathing my blades, I dashed past the gory remains and toward the other end of the crater.

Deathwish spells completed. Four swarm vipers have cloned themselves.

I didn't bother looking around, knowing an attack was imminent. In preparation, I drew psi.

"Duck!" Ghost yelled from where she kept watch on the crater's rim.

Obediently, I threw myself into a roll and a handful of projectiles hissed past. Not all the attacks missed, though. A few still found their mark.

Three swarm vipers' venom spit attacks have injured you!
Your health has decreased to 91%.

I gritted my teeth, ignoring the sensation of the vipers' venom eating away at my skin. My void armor had done nothing to weaken the attacks;

they were acidic in nature and not magical. But as excruciating as the pain was, the venom's damage was minimal, far less than I'd anticipated. More to the point, my spellcasting hadn't been interrupted.

Springing back to my feet, I spun around and released the spell I held ready.

You have cast mass charm.
A level 121 swarm viper has failed a mental resistance check!
A level 121 swarm viper has failed a mental resistance check!
...

...
You have charmed 8 of 8 targets for 20 seconds.

In a single heartbeat, *all* my pursuers froze, and stillness descended upon the crater.

The battle had ground to a halt.

I laughed. I couldn't help it. My spell's overwhelming success had caught me flatfooted. I'd been preparing to jump back into the fray and slay the uncharmed vipers before they could consume my minions, then pick off the rest one by one. Instead, I'd unexpectedly bought myself some breathing room.

Don't waste it. Get moving!

My amusement faded. The battle was far from over, and the outcome still hung in the balance. Subdued though my foes were, the next batch wouldn't be. And they would number twice as many.

My gaze flickered across the crater, assessing my next move. By forcing the serpents to chase after me, I'd hoped they would spread out, leaving me room to maneuver between them.

But now, I had a chance to separate the clones more completely.

Reaching into the minds of four of my new minions, I ordered them to the far end of the crater. Docilely, the vipers did as commanded. I watched them go for a moment, judging how far they would get before my charms spell lapsed.

Far enough, I decided.

Turning back around, I drew my blades and strode towards the remaining four clones.

"*Prime?*" a puzzled Ghost queried. I was off script.

"*Not to worry,*" I murmured as I spun psi. "*Just a slight change in plans.*"

Reaching the bespelled vipers, I tightened my hands around my blades and planned my strikes. The clock ticked down and the distance between the two sets of clones expanded. Still, I waited. *Just a little longer...*

The charm spell neared end-of-life.

Now.

Bursting into motion, I struck, chopping and stabbing.

Four of your minions have been dealt fatal blows!

I spun to a stop, and lifted my gaze from the dead clones' shredded remains to search out the other viper-pack. They were still in range. Stepping through the aether, I blinked to the closest.

You have teleported 38 yards.

I flowed out of the charmed viper's shadow, blades flashing. Striking blow after blow in quick succession, I decapitated the remaining clones.

Four of your minions have been dealt fatal blows!
Deathwish spells completed. Four swarm vipers have cloned themselves into 8 level 111 swarm vipers.

Ignoring the newly blood-christened ground, I whirled around. The first slain viper-pack had already spawned into the next batch of clones, and the corpses behind me would follow suit shortly.

It was time to go.

Orienting myself on Ghost, I fled the crater, finally ready to launch the last phase of my plan.

✳   ✳   ✳

A few seconds later, I was on the rim of the crater once more, looking down. This time, though, it housed sixteen clones. Granted, each was four ranks lower than the previous rank fifteen one, but that didn't mean much. The serpents' numbers more than made up for what they lacked in levels.

The vipers below weren't idle either. Hissing angrily, they frantically searched the crater for me, but wrapped in shadow as I was, I was out of their line of sight.

"Do you think it will work?" Ghost asked.

She meant phase four of my plan, I knew. *"It has to,"* I replied simply.

There was no way I could kill every iteration of the swarm vipers by blade alone, of course.

By my calculation, if each successive generation of clones retained their deathwish ability, I would need to slay over a million of the creatures in total.

A clear impossibility.

But only if I attempted to slay them *individually.*

Killing the clones en-masse would change the outlook completely. Doing so would require more than an ordinary area-damage spell, though. If I firebombed the clones in the crater, there was no guarantee some would not live through the blast. If that happened, the survivors would simply consume the younger generation and advance in level, leaving me in a possibly worse position than when I'd started!

No, what was called for was a *sustained* area-damage spell.

A killing field that would persist for dozens of seconds, if not longer, and destroy each successive generation of clones before they had a chance to consume their fellows. Unfortunately, none of my consumables— bombs or traps—fit that bill.

That's where the shaft came in.

It was my answer to dealing with the remaining clones. The shaft was my way of creating a firestorm in a teacup, one that would hopefully burn hot and long enough to incinerate the next twelve clone generations as soon as they spawned.

Right, time to find out if all of this has been worth it.

Drawing psi, I reached out to the closest bunch of clones below and forced my will upon them.

You have charmed 6 of 6 targets for 20 seconds.

I waited a beat, but the other clones did not react to my charmed minions. It seemed the rank eleven swarm vipers did not possess whatever ability their rank nineteen sibling had used to detect the presence of my compulsion spell in our first encounter.

Satisfied that no attacks would be forthcoming, I ordered my six minions into the shaft. Obediently, they slithered in.

Six down, ten to go.

* * *

In short order, all sixteen vipers were in the shaft.

Accompanied by Ghost, I entered the crater and strode towards the trapped clones. For now, the shaft was just an ordinary hole, albeit one deep enough to hold the vipers captive and hide me from view. Drawing to a stop at the shaft's edge, I peered in.

Instantly, lines of green colored the air.

I yanked back my head, but none of the venomous spit made it out of the shaft. "Tsk, tsk," I murmured. "They aren't happy, are they?" Cloaking myself in shadow, I peeked into the hole again.

Multiple hostile entities have failed to detect you! You are hidden.

A thin film of green liquid coated the bottom of the shaft. Writhing furiously, the vipers swam unconcerned—and unharmed—through the mess.

Hmm, I mused, eyeing the pooling acid. *That can be useful.* Picking up a handful of pebbles, I dropped them in the shaft.

Predictably, more acid arced upwards as the clones attempted to obliterate the stones. I chuckled quietly. "Perfect."

"What are you doing?" Ghost asked curiously.

"Creating fuel for the fire," I answered laconically.

The acid the serpents spat was surely combustible, and once I kicked off things, the green pool would serve to keep the flames going until the fire raged hot enough to feed off the creatures' own bodies. Picking up another fistful of stones, I threw them into the shaft as well—prompting another angry volley of sprayed acid.

Then I did it again. And again.

Finally satisfied with my efforts, I withdrew one of the remote triggers tucked in my pocket for safekeeping.

I hadn't just dug a shaft earlier; I had also primed its depths with thirty-two firebomb traps, each connected to its own remote trigger. Thirty-two bombs sounded like a lot, but I didn't plan on using them all in one go.

Best case, one trap on its own would be enough to deal with *this* batch of clones—I hadn't forgotten the other thirty-one waiting in the nearby craters.

Worst case? The fire would die out after one bomb, and I would be forced to detonate a second trap, then a third and a fourth, or however many were necessary.

Actually, that wasn't the worst that could happen. The real doomsday scenario was if the bombs failed entirely, and the viper clones multiplied so quickly that they spilled out of the pit. This outcome didn't bear thinking about though, and if it happened, I had only one recourse: running.

So what will it be? I wondered. There was only one way to find out.

I turned to Ghost. *"Ready?"*

"Ready," she confirmed.

"Remember, if you sense any of the minds in the shaft growing, tell me instantly." That would mean one of the clones had begun consuming its fellows, in which case I would have no choice but to detonate more bombs.

"I will," she assured me.

"Then here goes," I muttered and pressed down on the trigger I held.

CHAPTER 315: THE GIFT OF SIGHT

You have activated a trap!
16 level 111 swarm vipers' deathwish abilities have been triggered.
32 level 101 swarm vipers' deathwish abilities have been triggered.
64 level 91 swarm vipers...
...

...

32,768 level 1 swarm vipers have died!

The shaft's performance exceeded all expectations.

Fueled by the swarm vipers themselves, the fire burned hot for nearly a full minute and was bright enough to turn the rock lining the shaft slick like glass.

"It worked," I murmured in awe.

"It did," Ghost agreed, seemingly not as impressed by the spectacular success of my plan as I was. *"Will you do the same with the next clone?"*

I glanced in the direction of the nearest crater, reminded of the other waiting rank fifteen clones, and pondered Ghost's words.

I could, of course, have attempted employing the shaft earlier in my plan—and not bothered with forcing the vipers down to rank eleven first—but I had wanted to give my fire trap the best chance of scoring instant kills, and I'd been worried the higher-ranked clones would have survived long enough to consume their younger kin.

"Yes," I said at last. *"The plan has proven itself. Best to stick with what works."*

Slaying the swarm viper took the entire day.

Thirty-two times, I lured a clone into my chosen crater. Thirty-two times, I killed it down to its rank eleven iterations. And thirty -two times, I enticed the pack into the shaft and detonated a fire trap.

I made sure, too, to train my telepathy skill in the process. At every opportunity, I charmed, slept, or blinded the clones even when it was unnecessary to do so. And when it was all said and done, the Game message I'd been waiting on all day arrived.

You have killed a level 201 swarm viper.

It was done. Finally.

Sinking down wearily onto the ground, I closed my eyes and waited. Sure enough, more Game alerts flooded my mind.

You have reached level 164!
Your thieving has reached rank 11.

Your sneaking, light armor, telepathy, and telekinesis have reached rank 13.

Your shortswords has reached rank 14.

Your meditation has reached rank 15, allowing you to learn tier 4 abilities.

Remaining trap-making crystals: 132 of 200.

A small smile stole onto my face. The rewards for the day's work were as great as I expected.

Not only had I gained three player levels, I'd advanced one of my skills — meditation — to tier four, an achievement in and of itself. While the skill was amongst my least useful when it came to related abilities, getting it to tier four was still a significant milestone in my player development.

The encounter's biggest winner, though, was my telepathy. It had advanced a whole two ranks, not surprising given how extensively I'd employed the skill during the day.

Unfortunately, achieving victory had not been without cost either. I'd exhausted a third of my trap-making crystals, and there would be no replenishing them until I escaped the dungeon.

"*Well done, Prime,*" Ghost said softly.

"*Thank you,*" I replied. "*I couldn't have done it without you.*" About to go on, I paused as another Game alert flashed for attention. Curiously, I opened it.

Congratulations, Michael! You have accomplished the feat: <u>The Bigger They Are!</u> Requirement: kill a tier 5 creature on your own while of lower tier yourself. As only the 132nd rank 16 solo player to defeat an elite creature, you have been awarded the trait: <u>Spirit Talker</u>. This rare trait is normally reserved for rank 4 aetherists and allows you to converse with any spirit capable of speech.

Note, the traits you earn from feats are based on the circumstances and manner of your achievement.

I stared nonplussed at the Adjudicator's message.

Spirit talker. It was a strange reward to receive. Sure, given the manner in which I'd gone about the deed, the trait made sense; Ghost had been an integral part of my success. But I *already* had a means of communicating with her. Why give me a trait to do what I could already accomplish?

"*What is it?*" Ghost asked.

"*Oh nothing,*" I said, glancing absently in her direction. "*Just an odd trait—*"

I broke off, my mouth dropping open in shock.

I *saw* Ghost.

Not just as a glowing awareness in my mindsight. No, I saw her in her full ghostly glory.

"*Trouble?*" Ghost asked, believing something to be amiss.

Shaking my head wordlessly, I let my gaze flit about her form. Ghost looked exactly as you would expect a spirit to look. Her visage was pale, colorless, and ethereal, and I could see through her to the walls of the crater beyond.

But for all that, Ghost's shape was still distinct and unmistakably wolflike. In size, she rivaled Sulan and the other dire wolf elders. Her coat was thick and luxurious, and her eyes deep and curious. Idly, I wondered what color they had been in life.

"*I can see you,*" I said at last.

Ghost was sitting on her haunches. "*See me?*" she asked, tilting her head to the side.

"*Yes. I can see your spirit form.*"

Ghost's jaw dropped open, exposing sharp canines. "*You can? How?*"

"*The Adjudicator,*" I explained, realizing what a tremendous gift the Game had granted me.

"*Then, can you see me do this?*" Ghost asked, spinning about in a jubilant circle.

"*I can,*" I replied, laughing at her antics.

Ghost froze.

My humor faded. "*What's wrong?*"

Ghost shook her head—an odd mannerism for a wolf, but then she was no ordinary wolf. "*I... heard you.*"

I frowned, not following, then realized what she meant. "You *heard* my laugh?" I asked aloud.

Ghost barked in assent.

It was my turn to blink. "Alright," I said, bemused anew. "So, we can both see and hear each other in the 'real' now." I rubbed my chin thoughtfully. "That neatly solves our communication problem."

And it did.

No longer was I bound to the fifty-yard reach of my mindsight to see or talk to Ghost. That elevated my new trait from an oddity to a prized boon.

"*Thank you, Adjudicator,*" I murmured and rose to my feet.

✳   ✳   ✳

The time had come to sleep again, and this time, I had no compunctions about where to do that. Reaching the tunnel entrance, I slipped inside.

"Once we get to the entry chamber, we'll spend an hour on your lessons before calling it quits for the day," I said to Ghost.

She bobbed her head in silent assent, enjoying our new form of communication.

I grinned back, just as pleased by the sight of the spirit wolf padding by my side. She was large enough that parts of her body passed through the tunnel's sidewalls though that did not seem to bother her in the least.

My gaze drifted down the passage. It would be a stretch to say my fortunes had turned around since entering the dungeon, but things were certainly looking up, and I was eager to see what the following days would bring. How many more elites would I have to kill before—

I stumbled to a halt.

My gaze had caught on an unusual shape up ahead. It seemed the tunnel had another surprise in store for me. In the exact same spot, where I'd first encountered the swarm viper was a... loot chest.

Not wooden.

Not bronze.

Not silver.

Not even gold.

Something altogether different—a type only spoken about in hushed whispers. A platinum chest.

"Wow," I murmured.

Ghost followed my gaze. *"More... loot?"*

I nodded emphatically and dashed forward. Drawing to a halt before the closed box, I flipped open the lid. There was a single item inside.

An ability tome.

Whatever knowledge the book contained, I knew it had to be spectacular—the platinum chest practically guaranteed it—I only hoped it was something *I* could use. Hands trembling, I reached within and picked up the tome.

You have acquired the fade ability tome. Governing attribute: Dexterity. Tier: expert. Requirement: rank 10 sneaking skill.

The fade ability is one of the most elusive in the Game. Only discoverable in the most dangerous of dungeons, it is sought after by assassins the world over. Few, though, are fortunate enough to find it. At lower tiers, the ability progressively blurs the wielder from sight. But it is not until the elite tier— when it grants true invisibility—that the fade ability's true potential is unlocked.

"*True* invisibility?" I repeated, wondering what the Adjudicator meant by that. My mind flashed back to the potion I'd used in Nexus to evade, however briefly, the guards atop the safe zone walls. That potion's effects had been powerful enough, yet the description of the fade spell implied it would do *more*.

I opened the book.

Sure, I already had an overabundance of dexterity-based abilities, but the prospect of having my own invisibility spell was too enticing to pass up.

You have gained the expert ability: fade. This ability blends your physical form into the surroundings, irrespective of the prevailing light conditions and whether or not you are in combat. At this tier, the ability makes you 25% harder to see for 1 minute.

This ability's activation time is very fast, consumes stamina, and can be upgraded. You have 4 of 55 Dexterity ability slots remaining.

"My, my," I exclaimed softly as understanding of the ability filled me. Fade complimented my skill set perfectly. It did not provide any direct benefits like additional armor or increased strength. Instead, it made me harder to see—which, in turn, made me harder to hit.

Even better, fade would continue to function *while* I was fighting, something that no other stealth or illusion ability I knew of would do.

True invisibility, indeed, I thought, smiling broadly.

Still grinning, I left the empty loot chest behind and headed into the entrance chamber, my thoughts full of plans for the future.

CHAPTER 316: THE VIEW FROM ABOVE

DAY THREE IN DRAVEN'S REACH

You have slept 6 hours. Stamina, mana, and psi reserves have been fully restored.

Your Dexterity has increased to rank 58. Other modifiers: +24 from items.

You have etched an aetherstone with the aether coordinates of nether portal 1 in Kingdom sector 18,240. Currently stored aether locations: 3. Charged and unetched gems: 2.

I awoke early the next morning, the dawn of my third day in Draven's Reach. Before lying down to rest, I had spent my available attribute points and tutored Ghost further in spellcraft and the ways of the Game. I'd also charged the aetherstone bracelet.

Unfortunately, the aetherstones were of no use in the dungeon. But as soon as I escaped its confines, I intended to use the bracelet to rejoin the wolves and the others. By now, they were all surely wondering what had happened to me.

I glanced up at the encircling walls of the cauldron. Ghost and I were at the ravine once more, ready to begin our day's adventures. It was time to move on from the starting area—although I don't suppose it could be called that.

I had entered Draven's Reach through a hidden portal and could be anywhere in the dungeon, including near its exit. "That's the next step, I guess," I murmured.

Ghost glanced at me. *"What is?"*

"Figuring out how this dungeon is laid out," I replied. From the welcome message, I knew Draven's Reach had only one sector and one boss. The dungeon boss mattered little to me, though, except that he was likely near the exit portal, and finding that was all-important.

"How will we do that?" Ghost asked.

I pointed to the cliffs. "By scaling those."

* * *

You have equipped a set of cat claws.

The cauldron's walls were smooth, near-vertical, and almost devoid of cracks and other handy outcroppings, but with my cat claws and Ghost's help, scaling their heights was almost too easy.

Devoid of a body, the spirit wolf did not need to climb.

She simply floated upward to a likely perch, and I teleported to her. Using my cat claws, I clung to the cliff and waited for her to reposition. Then we repeated the maneuver.

A few short hops later, I was atop the cauldron walls. Packing away my climbing gear, I took in the view.

I stood on a mountain plateau, one that seemingly stretched for miles and encompassed the entirety of the dungeon. The plateau was riddled with seams—jagged canyons, chasms, and rock valleys—and although I couldn't see into their depths, I realized they were not unlike the cauldron I had just exited and likely housed more dungeon denizens.

I turned about in a slow circle. The plateau itself was cold, barren, and uninhabited. Or so it appeared at first glance. To the south and west—less than a hundred yards from the cauldron's edge—the plateau terminated abruptly as the violet sky curved downwards to enfold it.

I was right about that, I thought, following the arch of the sky. The violet horizon I had spotted from below was part of the sector's protective barrier. The dome enclosed the entire plateau and was so large that its northern and eastern ends were shrouded from sight. But distance was not the only thing obscuring the view.

To the northeast, in what I judged to be the dungeon's center, hung a monstrous bank of pale fog.

It was so large that it extended from the top of the violet dome and disappeared beneath the plateau, eclipsing an area of over a square mile. There were other fog banks as well, but they were much smaller, with the next largest covering an area of only a few dozen yards. The gray haze I had spotted earlier streamed between the central fog bank and the smaller ones, as if it was feeding them.

Whatever the fog banks and gray haze were, I didn't have a good feeling about them.

"What could they be?" I mused, wondering if I should draw closer to inspect one. The nearest fog bank was a long way off though, and I would have to traverse a good distance to reach it.

"What could what be?" Ghost asked.

"The fog," I replied, thinking it self-evident.

"Fog?" Ghost swung around to study the sweeping vista. *"Oh, you mean the plumes of smoke in the north."*

I frowned. "It isn't just in the north, and I wouldn't call it smoke. It's more—"

My eyes narrowed. There *was* a column of smoke to the north. It was mostly obscured by the intervening fog banks, which was why I hadn't noticed it earlier.

"Well spotted, Ghost," I murmured, crouching down to take a closer look at the spiraling column. It appeared to originate from one of the dungeon's northern gorges.

The gorge was large enough that I could see into its depths despite the many miles separating us. At its center, there was a cluster of bright dots, although they appeared blurry at this distance. Squinting, I strained my eyes, and one of the dots swam into focus.

My eyes widened. "Those are campfires!"

Ghost looked at me uncomprehendingly. *"Is that significant?"*

I nodded. "Fires equals civilization. And civilization means people."

Ghost paused to consider this. *"Allies?"*

"They may become that," I allowed, "but it's equally possible they will prove hostile."

I contemplated my next move. Draven's Reach was obviously a large dungeon. The winding chasms and canyons made for a veritable maze and clearly spanned many dozen miles. Worse yet, there was no obvious indication as to the location of the exit portal. I could spend weeks, if not months, searching for it.

Or I can ask someone.

My gaze drifted back to the gorge. Someone there was bound to know something. "The gorge bears investigation," I pronounced at last. "Let's go."

✳   ✳   ✳

I was tempted to use the plateau as a highway and cut straight across to the gorge, but I was also curious about the dungeon and the other denizens that populated its depths.

So, rather than taking the direct path, I decided to follow the chasms and canyons that threaded through the plateau. That way, I could learn something of Draven's Reach's inhabitants, while also staying safely out of their grasp.

Walking along the clifftops encircling the cauldron, I made my way to the canyon leading away from it and peered down. The canyon was narrow, only about a dozen yards wide, and expanded eastwards as it zigzagged through the mountain. From what I could see, it was devoid of life. Unfazed by the drop, I strolled along the edge of the cliff, following the canyon.

Ten minutes later, I spotted something of interest.

Dropping into a crouch, I stared into the canyon. It had slowly begun to curve northwards, and so far, I hadn't come across any branches or, for that matter, hostiles.

Until now.

Less than a hundred yards ahead was a slumped shape. The thing was unmoving, and from this distance appeared formless, but given the vivid blue hue of its covering, it was certainly no rock.

"Do you see it?" I whispered.

"The blue body?" Ghost replied.

I nodded. "It's either sleeping, knocked unconscious, or... dead." My brows furrowed. "Can you sense its mind?"

"It doesn't have any," Ghost asserted. *"It's dead."* She paused. *"Unless it's another construct...?"*

"Unlikely. This one isn't moving." I reached out with my will. In this, an elite dungeon, I was more wary than was my wont to use analyze, but given that Ghost's observations tallied with my own, I deemed it safe enough to inspect the seemingly-lifeless hump.

The target is a level 214 dead frost ent.

I rubbed my chin thoughtfully. *A dead elite.* What had killed it, though?

Running my gaze across the surroundings, I searched for an answer but spotted nothing that could be responsible for the creature's demise. I hesitated, pondering my next move.

Draven's Reach was beginning to perturb me.

I'd not forgotten that the Adjudicator had labeled the dungeon 'corrupt.' Then, too, there were the unusual fog banks and the fact that Limp and One-Arm had been injured *before* I encountered them. Finally, there was the dead ent that I had most certainly not killed.

If I didn't know better, I would have said there were other players about, but the dungeon welcome message had been clear: I was the only player in Draven's Reach.

Of course, another party could have slipped in *after* I'd entered, but it was highly improbable that both Ghost and I wouldn't have sensed their presence if they'd come close enough to injure the stone golems. Whatever the case, the mystery was growing, and I was no longer sure I could ignore it.

"We go down," I said finally.

✳ ✳ ✳

Reaching the bottom of the canyon took only a little longer than scaling the cliff had. Touching down lightly, I tiptoed towards the body with Ghost by my side.

Now that I was at eye level with the corpse, its true size became apparent. The frost ent was nearly as large as the stone golems and covered in pale blue skin. But while the golems had been fleshless, the ent was a creature of blood and bone.

Drawing to a halt at the foot of the creature, I walked a slow circle around it. The corpse lay face down, so I could tell nothing of its features, but the ent had two arms and two legs and was clearly humanoid. It was naked, too, except for the tattered loincloth wrapped around its waist and the primitive club clenched in its right hand.

What drew my interest, though, were the corpse's wounds.

Cuts and slashes marred nearly every square foot of ent's body. An entire chunk of flesh had been bitten off its arm, and deep furrows scored its back. In places, the creature's skin had been seared off completely, burned or dissolved.

The ent had been assaulted. If I had to guess, I'd say there had been multiple attackers involved, and they'd used both tooth and claw. But *who* were they? This did not seem like the work of players.

It can only be other dungeon denizens.

Why was there no sign of them, though?

The rocky ground was too hard to capture footprints, but that did not explain the absence of other physical evidence. Except for the ent's own remains, there were no blood spatters, tufts of fur, or score marks in the rocks—nothing that I could ascribe to the ent's attackers. Surely an elite of the ent's stature had not gone down without landing a few blows of its own?

This makes no sense, I thought, bowing my head in silent contemplation.

"*There's more over here,*" Ghost said, sounding disconcerted.

I looked up to find the spirit wolf had wandered farther down the canyon and was studying something beyond my line of sight. "Another corpse?" I asked sharply.

There was a long pause before she answered. "*Yes.*"

Abandoning the dead ent, I hurried towards Ghost, but drew up short before I reached her.

Beyond the next bend in the canyon were three more corpses.

More dead frost ents. They, too, had been killed savagely, and once more, the attackers seemed to have left no evidence of their passing.

Damn. What is going on in this dungeon?

CHAPTER 317: THE REEK OF CORRUPTION

I examined the three corpses as carefully as I had the first, but my investigations revealed nothing new. Whatever had slain the ents had done so without taking any apparent losses of their own.

"We should return to the clifftops," Ghost said suddenly.

Glancing at her, I noticed the worry shadowing her eyes. I didn't think I was imagining it, and I was sure it was not for her own sake that she was concerned.

I shook my head. "I don't think we can."

"Why not?"

"Because," I said slowly, articulating my thoughts as they formed, "the mystery here has grown too great to ignore anymore. If there are things in this dungeon powerful enough to slay elites without leaving any evidence of their passing, sooner or later, we are going to run across them. And when that happens, I want to be armed with as much information as possible."

Ghost shifted uncomfortably. *"What do we do?"*

"We follow the canyon and see where it leads."

"And if we run across these... things?"

"We kill them." I sighed. "Or, if they are too great to face, we flee to the plateau."

*   *   *

Hours later, Ghost and I were still in the canyon. We had passed several smaller side tunnels and cul-de-sacs but had decided not to deviate from the main canyon.

We'd run across more dead elites, too.

All had been killed in a similar manner as the ents, and all were gigantic creatures of one sort or another. Colossal elites, I began to suspect, was the central theme of Draven's Reach.

Ghost had placed herself in the lead, and I had not demurred. It made sense, and I'd grown used to her passing unseen by others. And truly, my initial concerns with her had abated somewhat.

Some of the corpses we'd run across had smelled truly awful, their remains half-rotted and decaying. It was clear they had been killed long ago, which meant that whatever was killing the dungeon's elites had been at it for some time.

The realization eased my fears.

It would have been far worse if the things haunting the dungeon could cut through more than a dozen elites in a scant few days. All the evidence pointed to the invaders waging a sustained campaign—if they were in fact invaders and not part of the dungeon's own denizens. Still, some of the killings had obviously been recent enough that the blood had not congealed yet, and I didn't lower my guard.

Which was why when Ghost came racing back, I was primed to react.

"*What's wrong?*" I asked, drawing my blades in a flash.

"*Hostiles ahead!*" she exclaimed, the words spilling out of her in a rush. "*Come quickly!*"

My hands tightened around my swords. If it were ordinary hostiles, Ghost would not be as worked up as she was. "*Did they see you?*" I asked, wondering at the cause of her haste.

"*No.*" She shook her head. "*They're fighting each other!*" Not waiting for my response, she turned around and hurried back the way she'd come. "*Follow me!*"

I opened my mouth to call her back, then closed it with a snap. I would find out all the quicker what was going on if I did as she bade.

Sheathing my blades, I crept after the spirit wolf.

✳   ✳   ✳

It did not take long for the sounds of the battle raging ahead to carry to me. The combatants remained out of sight, though, blocked from view by a twist in the canyon. Ghost had already turned the corner and disappeared again.

Despite being eager to uncover the mystery of the dead elites, I didn't rush and took the time to cast my buffs.

You have cast heightened reflexes, load controller, and trigger-cast quick mend.

You have cast fade, blurring your form and making you 25% harder to see for 1 minute.

Ready for anything, I braced my back against the canyon side wall and inched forward. Reaching the bend, I peeked around the corner.

A remarkable sight greeted me.

Feet spread and arms akimbo, a frost ent stood in the center of the canyon. He was enveloped in a bubble of spelled ice that was as wide as he was tall. The cold sphere was so large that it cut through the surrounding cliffs, rimming them with frost and icicles.

The cliffs, though, were not the only things to suffer the touch of the ent's magic. The horde of creatures assaulting the elite were likewise afflicted. But while the lifeless rocks were able to shrug off the subzero temperatures, not so the ent's foes. The ice field turned many into frozen blocks and those it didn't, it chilled, leaving them slow and clumsy—easy targets for the ent's massive club.

That's a powerful spell, I thought.

The ent's enemies had numbers on their side, though. For every foe that the elite bashed to death inside the freezing sphere, ten more waited outside to take its place—which was why more than a dozen of the creatures had already managed to crawl past the ent's defenses and latch onto his naked torso.

Despite his impressive size and magic, the ent was doomed, I realized. Letting my gaze drift away from the elite, I focused on his attackers.

Ordinarily, I would've described the creatures as large—each was at least twenty feet in length—but in comparison to the ent, they looked tiny. In many respects, the attackers resembled armored caterpillars. Each had hundreds of clawed feet, and segmented bodies that rippled as they moved.

But unlike ordinary caterpillars, the attackers' bodies lacked the comforting solidity of physical beings, and instead were formed from billowing clouds of black mist. Mist that stank of filth and horror. Mist that emitted a palpable aura of evil. And mist whose origin I, of course, recognized.

Stygians. The ent's attackers were stygians.

"Bloody hell," I muttered, staring at their wavering forms.

It all made sense now—why the Adjudicator had labeled Draven's Reach 'corrupt,' why Ghost had not seen the fog, and why the dungeon's elites were dying.

And truly, I was not entirely surprised. Ever since spotting the gray haze in the violet sky, I'd suspected something like this, yet had steadfastly refused to consider the possibility.

Stygians in a dungeon were an impossibility, after all.

The Game itself shielded the Endless Dungeon from invasion. Nothing, not even the Powers, could breach a dungeon sector's protective barrier—or so I'd been led to believe. My breath escaped in a rush. That was not quite true. I knew better. I'd been *told* better.

Kolath, one of the very guardians tasked with upholding the barriers around the dungeons, had warned me that something was amiss. He'd even tasked me with finding his silent brethren, fearing the worst.

I glanced up at the violet sky and the gray haze scarring it. *Nether. Call it nether. You know that's what it is.* I sighed. It seemed clear enough that the guardians had failed their mission, at least when it came to Draven's Reach.

The dungeon's protective barrier had been breached. The stygians were inside the dungeon. And the insidious nether was spreading, blighting all it touched.

Which was bad for me on multiple levels.

If the nether infestation had spread far enough, then the sector's safe zone could be compromised, leaving me with nowhere to resurrect if I died.

I swallowed unhappily. As bad as that was, what worried me more was what effect the nether would have on the dungeon's gateways.

Would the exit portal still work?

I had no idea. But if it didn't... then Ghost and I could be stuck here forever. Drawing back from the corner, I slumped down dejectedly.

It was time to rethink the future.

*   *   *

I sat on the ground, head bowed. Behind me, the battle raged unabated. It concerned me little, though. I got the sense that the skirmish had been going on for hours and would likely continue for many more before coming to its inevitable end. Eyes closed, I pondered what the nether's presence in this sector meant for me.

After my initial bout of panic—had it been that? If not, it had been awfully close—passed, I realized things were not as bleak as they first appeared.

For one, the dungeon could not be in imminent danger of falling. Moonshadow had told me it could take months, if not years, for a sector to succumb to the nether. Granted, he had been talking about kingdom sectors, but I was sure the same principle applied to Draven's Reach.

And if I needed more evidence, sector 18,240—the blighted sector from which I'd come—was still unclaimed by the nether and conditions there were visibly worse.

In fact, given what I'd observed of the fog banks, I suspected the nether had only just begun to gain a toehold on this sector. Other than for the central region of Draven's Reach, most of the dungeon appeared untouched by the gray haze.

I have time, I concluded. *Lots of it. Years, probably.* My shoulders straightened and my unhappiness dissipated. There was no need to panic, rush, or take undue risks.

Something else occurred to me.

As strange as it sounded, the nether's invasion was not without benefits. In fact, the stygians had already helped me, albeit unknowingly. Without them injuring the stone golems—and it had to have been the stygians—I would have not killed the two elites.

It opened the way for some interesting... possibilities. *Hmm.* Rubbing my chin, I considered my next move.

"Aren't you going to watch the fight?" Ghost asked.

I looked up to find the spirit wolf sitting before me. "I'm thinking, Ghost." I glanced at her thoughtfully. "Do you recognize the ent's attackers?"

"Of course. They're those nether creatures."

I nodded.

Ghost wrinkled her nose. *"Do you think they followed us through the portal?"*

"Unlikely," I replied. "Besides, the ones here look nothing like the ones we fought back in the kingdom sector. They must be from a different nest. I'm sure they got here before we did."

Ghost didn't question my reasoning. *"Then you don't think they're a danger?"*

"Oh, they're still that," I murmured. "What I'm trying to figure out is what to do about it."

"I don't understand."

I jerked my thumb in the direction of the skirmish. "I mean what do I do about that? Do I help the elite? Or the stygians? Do I try killing both? Or do I ignore the battle altogether? Which is the right choice here?"

Ghost yawned. *"You think too much, Prime."*

I rolled my eyes. "Lots of help you are."

The spirit wolf sat beside me and scratched vigorously at one ear with a hind leg. I eyed her askance. Did she really need to do that? She had no physical form after all. *"Neither the stygians nor the elites are Pack,"* Ghost said finally, ignoring my look. *"And both are your enemies. You should kill them however you can."*

It was not an entirely unreasonable conclusion. It was one I'd reached myself, and ordinarily, I would have no scruples about pitting the stygians and elites against each other.

But.

But the stygians were no normal foes. The void was the anathema of life. If left unchecked, the nether would destroy not just the elites, but eventually those I'd pledged to protect, too.

Which left me in an unhappy predicament.

How far did I go in my fight against the nether or, for that matter, the dungeon's denizens? Did I try to protect the elites—or sacrifice them to the void? Should I attempt to stop the nether claiming the sector? Or should I ignore the future—and somewhat nebulous—threat the stygians represented and take the easiest path before me?

And I had no doubt what that path would be.

It would be simple, almost laughably so, to use the nether to slay the elites. Merely touching the stuff was fatal to non-players. All I had to was lure the dungeon's denizens into the fog banks and let the free-floating nether do the work for me.

Granted, I would gain no experience in the process, but killing the elites in this manner would be as 'risk-free' as it got. Then, I could walk out to the dungeon, without looking back, and without caring that I'd furthered the void's cause.

Easy enough.

If I was willing to betray my promise to Kolath—and the Primes of old.

I had only Kolath's word for it, but according to the guardian, the ancients were the void's sworn enemies. "It's not that simple," I said at last.

"Why not?" Ghost challenged.

"I can't allow the nether to claim the sector, not if there is a chance to stop it."

"Then don't let it." Ghost met my gaze. *"But you should still kill the elites."*

I stared at her blankly for a moment, then laughed helplessly. "Back to that, are we?"

Ghost seemed to shrug. *"You said it yourself: you need to get stronger."*

I frowned, but Ghost was right, and I didn't owe the elites of Draven's Reach anything. They were not Pack. By the same token, the stygian menace could not be allowed to spread unchecked. That *would* threaten my Pack. Perhaps not today, tomorrow, or even years from now, but someday, the void would spread to the sectors my allies sheltered in.

Rising to my feet, I came to a decision.

The dungeon's denizens were my enemies. But the stygians were more so. I would not use the nether against the elites, as tempting as the prospect was. I would stay true to the task Kolath had given me. I would protect the sector from corruption, but only the sector itself; the elites were fair game.

Meanwhile, there was a skirmish raging ahead, and while I was not in a position to defeat either of the battling parties, I could still manipulate the outcome to my own ends.

Recasting my buffs, I slipped around the corner.

Chapter 318: Iced, Chilled, and Frozen

Multiple hostile entities have failed to detect you! You are hidden.

The battle had not progressed much in the short time I'd been away. Dropping into a crouch, I studied the combatants.

The target is a level 217 frost ent. He is severely injured.
The target is a level 170 stygian crawler. It is currently frozen.
The target is a level 173 stygian crawler. It is currently chilled.
The target is a level 168 stygian crawler. It is near death.
Stygian crawlers are amongst the least armored of the nether's creatures. That does not mean they are not dangerous. Rarely found alone, crawlers prefer to swarm their victims, and like most other stygians, they have a highly developed sense of hearing which they use both to navigate the void's opaque mists and locate their prey.

I pursed my lips. The elite was more injured than I'd expected given that his torso was largely absent of the wounds I'd seen on the corpses I'd examined earlier.

So, how are the stygians killing him? I wondered.

My gaze roved over the crawlers clinging to the ent. Presently, they numbered a dozen. Some hung onto his naked legs, while others perched on his back. One and all, they dug their feet into their foe's skin, leaving deep puncture marks as they slowly crawled up his back.

Periodically the ent wrenched free some of the crawlers. Those on his legs were easy to reach, but those on his back were impossible for him to get to. Which was why the creatures were trying to nestle between his shoulder blades, I realized.

I padded forward a few steps.

Multiple hostile entities have failed to detect you!

Ghost made to follow, but I waved her back. *"Stay there,"* I ordered. Once more, the spirit wolf would act as my backdoor. If anything went wrong, I would use her to teleport out of harm's way.

Wrapped in shadow, I snuck closer to the battle. I was about a hundred yards from the ent—he was facing the other way—but despite my proximity, the elite's freezing sphere shrouded the crawlers, making details hard to pick out, and I needed to get closer to see what those on the ent's back were doing.

The rest of the crawler horde were gathered on the other side of the elite and while some did attempt to circle around their target, they succumbed to the effects of the elite's spell before they could. As soon as that happened, the chilled crawlers—those that could still move—readjusted their course and made directly for the ent.

Forty yards away from the elite and just outside the rim of his cold bubble, I drew to a halt. Squinting, I focused on the crawlers on the ent's back and slowly, more details emerged.

The crawlers' jaws were latched fast onto the elite and blood—by the gobfuls—coursed down their throats.

They're leeches, I thought, shivering in disgust. *Not caterpillars.*

The crawlers were sucking the ent dry. That's why he was weakening, despite his lack of wounds. It didn't explain the cause of the injuries I'd seen on the corpses, though.

But right now, that was of little consequence. The time had come for me to act. Drawing back a few steps, I summoned psi. Focusing on a single target only, I released my will.

You have charmed a level 172 stygian crawler for 20 seconds.

I smiled thinly as one of the creatures clinging to the ent's back fell under my spell. I waited for a heartbeat but neither the elite nor the other stygians reacted to my interference. My spell had gone unnoticed.

Excellent.

"*Release,*" I ordered, tugging on the leash I'd formed around the stygian's mind. Obediently, the crawler unlocked its jaw and retracted its feet from the ent's flesh. Bereft of any anchors, the creature fell.

You have taken hostile action against your minion and have lost control over it.

Ignoring the Game message, I watched the crawler to see what it would do next. Chilled and confused, the creature stayed where it was.

Unfortunately for the crawler, its new location did not happen to be a safe place. Not missing the sudden appearance of the stygian at his feet, the frost ent planted his left foot backwards and squished the hapless creature beneath his heel.

A stygian crawler has died.

My gaze flitted to the other crawlers, watching to see what they made of their fellow's demise, but none appeared suspicious. My smile broadened. My stealthy assault was off to a good start.

Focusing on another crawler on the ent's back, I reached out to it with my will. It fell under my spell as easily as the first and, without remorse, I forced my second minion to release its hold, then watched impassively while the elite killed it, too.

Two down.

Dropping down into a cross-legged stance, I made myself comfortable. It was going to be a long few hours.

✳   ✳   ✳

The day passed slowly.

Lurking in the shadows, I bespelled the crawlers that clung to the ent and sent them to their death. I picked my targets carefully, not charming too many or so often that the combatants would suspect outside influence.

Nor did I charm every stygian on the elite's back.

I could have done that, of course, but saving the elite was not my intent. Drawing out the battle and increasing the stygians' losses was. I still needed the ent to die, but in the process, I wanted as many of the crawlers to perish as possible.

And while my chosen approach lacked the excitement of a direct assault, my charm offensive and the time spent skulking in the shadows paid off.

Your sneaking has increased to level 141 and reached rank 14.
Your telepathy has increased to level 139.

It was good training—essential, even.

Before I escaped the dungeon, I was determined to advance as many of my skills as possible to tier four—if not higher. The training was only an added bonus, though. My primary objective was something else entirely. To make sure the opportunity did not pass me by unnoticed, I rechecked the elite's health every so often, and eventually, the message I'd been waiting for arrived.

The target is a level 217 frost ent. He is near death.

Releasing the weaves of the latest charm spell I'd been readying, I rose to my feet and advanced towards the ent until his bubble of ice loomed large in front of me.

Before I could reconsider, I plunged forward.

You have entered a cold sphere!
Multiple hostile entities have failed to detect you!

It was as if I'd re-entered the tundra. This time, though, I was not dressed for it. Between one moment and the next, freezing cold assailed me.

You have passed a magical resistance check! A level 217 frost ent has failed to freeze you!

I smiled tightly. It was nice that I'd managed to shrug off the ent's spell, however briefly, but I didn't expect my resistance to last. Wrapping my arms tightly about myself, I crept onward.

You have passed a magical resistance check!

The temperature plummeted further—although I was not sure how that was possible—coating my armor in tiny shards of ice. It seemed that even resisting the sphere's magic did not negate the very real cold it generated.

Only a little farther. Clenching my teeth to keep them from chattering, I took another step.

You have passed a magical resistance check!

Ignoring the aching cold, I looked around.

I was now almost fully encased in the ice bubble, and as I'd hoped, neither the ent nor the stygians had spotted me yet. *One more step should do it.* Bracing myself, I began to move forward.

"What are you doing?" Ghost asked in alarm.

Pausing, I glanced behind me to see the spirit wolf edging anxiously around the corner. *"Get back, Ghost,"* I replied gently. *"I need you to stay out of sight."*

She retreated, but that didn't stop her from interrogating me further. *"Why are you going so close? Are you going to kill the ent?"*

"I'm not going to slay the elite," I assured her. *"Nor am I going to fight the stygians."* Yet.

My words mollified the spirit wolf somewhat. *"What are you doing, then?"*

"Stealing the ent's spell," I replied, and before she could respond, stepped forward again.

You have failed a magical resistance check!

You have partially resisted the freezing effects of a cold sphere! You are <u>chilled.</u> **While chilled, you will sustain ongoing freezing damage and your movement speed will be reduced by 50%.**

Duration: infinite. The debuff will remain in effect as long as the source spell is being channeled.

I grimaced. This time, the pain was more than superficial; this time the tentacles of ice dug deep into my body, inflicting real damage.

You have sustained ice damage. Your void armor has reduced the elemental damage incurred by 40%.

Void armor charge remaining: 90%. Your health has decreased to 94%.

I rocked back and forth on my heels, trying to generate some heat. It was useless, of course. There was nothing for it, but to bear through.

You have sustained ice damage.
You have sustained ice damage.
You have sustained ice damage.
Void armor charge remaining: 78%. Your health has decreased to 76%.

The seconds ticked by and the damage to my void armor and health multiplied. I did my best to ignore it and keep my gaze fixed on the combatants. They were the real danger. I was taking a risk placing myself this close to the battle, but the reward would be worth it—or so I hoped.

You have sustained ice damage.
...
...
Void armor charge remaining: 66%. Your health has decreased to 58%.

My limbs shivered violently, threatening to spasm. I hugged myself tighter, trying to force myself to stillness. In front of me, the ent swayed and fell to one knee, setting the ground trembling.

It would not be long now—for him or me.

Drawing in psi, I prepared a casting.

"Are you alright?" Ghost asked, sensing my agony.

"I am," I rasped curtly, lacking the energy or focus for a longer response. *"Be ready."*

You have sustained ice damage.

Void armor charge remaining: 60%. Your health has decreased to 46%.

Void thief triggered! You have acquired the channeled spell, <u>cold sphere (stolen)</u>, from a frost ent and will retain memory of it for the next 8 hours.

Cold sphere (stolen) is a tier 5 spell that encases the caster in a bubble of ice with radius equal to your height. When hostiles enter the field of effect, they may be <u>frozen</u> or <u>chilled</u>. Both debuffs inflict elemental ice damage. The cold sphere will remain manifested for as long as the caster channels the spell.

Void siphon activated!

A conduit has been forged between you and a frost ent, allowing you to steal mana from your foe whenever he casts a spell at you.

I sagged wearily. It was done. I had stolen the ent's spell. I didn't have a use for it yet, but I didn't doubt it would come in handy.

Time to get out of here.

Releasing the psi I held ready, I shadow blinked to Ghost.

Chapter 319: Seeds of Corruption

Your elemental absorption has increased to level 85.
A frost ent has died.
You have reached level 165!

Less than a minute after I fled the field the elite died. Of course, no loot chest appeared. I'd not killed the frost ent myself, after all.

But somewhat to my surprise, I earned a level from the battle. After a moment's thought, though, I realized it was a result of the crawlers I'd charmed during the encounter. This time around, I invested the new attribute in Magic. With a channeling spell in my arsenal, the additional mana would not go unspent.

Your Magic has increased to rank 22. Other modifiers: +14 from items.

Safely tucked behind the sharp bend in the canyon, and with Ghost by my side, I watched the stygians closely to see what they would do next.

First, they ate their dead.

Or perhaps inhaled was a better term for it. In this sector, outside of the Nethersphere, the stygians' bodies didn't possess any real mass, and after the crawlers were done, the bodies of their slain fellows vanished entirely.

"That explains why we saw no evidence of the attackers earlier," I murmured.

"*But what caused the wounds on the corpses?*" Ghost asked, studying the crawlers as raptly as me.

"I suspect we're about to find out," I replied, pointing to the handful of stygians crawling over the ent's body.

Some of the crawlers were burrowing deep into the corpse's innards, others were tugging free long stretches of skin and muscle. It was a revolting sight, and having no desire to watch the nether creatures feast, I almost turned away in disgust.

But then, I realized I was wrong.

The stygians weren't eating. They were harvesting the ent's remains.

After stripping free manageable chunks of meat from the corpse, the crawlers held them aloft in their legs—upturned to point skyward—and carted them away. I frowned. It was the strangest behavior by far that I'd seen from the stygians yet.

What are they up to?

Puzzled, I watched the fully ladened crawlers—each with every third set of legs loaded with meat—gather at the far end of the dead colossal. *What use do the stygians have for the ent's remains?* I wondered. They couldn't possibly be feeding something with it, could they?

"*There aren't many crawlers left,*" Ghost interjected. "*Will you attack now?*"

I broke free from my musings and tallied the nether creatures' numbers. There were perhaps three dozen left. A lot, but still within my means to kill—especially armed with the ent's spell.

Still, I shook my head. "We wait for them to leave, then we follow."

My gaze found the meat haulers again. The crawlers were not on a simple hunt-and-destroy mission. They were gathering supplies for... something, and if I had to guess, that 'something' was waiting for them back at their base.

And I wanted to know where that was.

Ghost eyed me doubtfully. *"You want to follow them? Is that wise? What if they join up with others and end up being too many to kill?"*

"That's possible," I admitted. "Probable even. But I'm hoping the crawlers will lead us back to their nest. Finding it is more important than killing a few dozen of them."

In all likelihood, the stygian's nest was in the central fog bank, but that covered an area of a square mile. Too large to search easily, and besides, I could be wrong about what the crawlers planned on doing with their grisly burdens or where they were going with it.

I studied the stygians anew. They were still gathering, and I judged I had a few more minutes before they were ready to depart. "Will you keep watch?" I asked. "I need to attend to something before we set off."

"I will let you know once they start moving," Ghost promised and settled down beside me.

Nodding in thanks, I turned my focus inwards and called on my mana. I had a new spell, and it needed safekeeping.

Adhering to my will, my magic formed the weaves of the cold sphere spell. A silent passenger to the casting, I waited patiently while my mana worked. The spell finished in a flash, weaves charged and ready. Taking hold of them, I projected the casting, not outward and around me in a bubble of cold, but inwards and into the ring on my finger.

Spellhold enchantment activated.

You have successfully stored the <u>cold sphere</u> spell in the ring, mage's surprise. This spell may now be trigger-cast when required.

Note, cold sphere is a channeled spell and therefore, after it is initially triggered, the casting will draw from your mana pool in order to remain active.

I smiled. I hadn't been entirely sure my new ring would be able to capture stolen spells, and I was glad it had worked. Now, even after I lost knowledge of the cold sphere spell, I'd be able to cast it again—for one more instance, anyway.

I glanced up. The stygians were not done yet. Realizing I still had more time, I closed my eyes and set about restoring my defenses.

✳   ✳   ✳

You have healed yourself of all injuries. Your health is at 100%.
You have restored 100% of your psi.
You have replenished 73% of your mana. Void armor charges remaining: 73%.

"Prime, they're moving."

Nudged alert by Ghost's warning, I opened my eyes. The stygians had turned around and were headed back up the canyon.

I rose into a crouch. "Go," I ordered. "Don't let them out of your sight. I'll follow in a second."

There was little chance the stygians would spot the spirit wolf, and it was best I maintained a healthy distance between me and the crawlers in case of any untoward surprises. Ghost raced forward and when I judged her far enough away, I set off after her.

The stygians left no physical trail to follow, and if not for the fact that Ghost and I kept them in our sights, we would have lost them altogether. When they came to a split in the canyon, the crawlers unhesitatingly chose the left fork, and a little later turned left again down a narrow chasm. An hour later, they had navigated a dozen twists and turns, all without slowing down.

Trailing silently in the nether creatures' wake, my brows furrowed thoughtfully. The stygians knew the dungeon well—much better than I expected. I, on the other hand, was thoroughly lost and would have been worried if I didn't know I could reorient myself using the plateau above.

"They've stopped," Ghost reported.

I glanced up in surprise. Up ahead, I could see Ghost, but not the stygians themselves. We had traveled an appreciable distance, but I was sure we were nowhere near the central fog bank. So why had the crawlers stopped?

"You're sure?"

"Yes." Ghost paused. *"There are other stygians here. This might be the nest you were looking for."*

I frowned. A narrow chasm was the last place I expected the stygians to nest. *"The others, are they crawlers too?"*

Palpable silence, then, *"No."*

I began moving forward again. *"I'll be there shortly."*

✻   ✻   ✻

Reaching Ghost's side, I found myself staring into a fog bank. Not the large central one, but one of its smaller kin. Although from this vantage, 'small' was not the word I'd choose to describe it.

The fog bank stretched from one wall of the chasm to the other. Nor was its presence confined to ground level. A towering spire, the nether stretched upwards to wrap the chasm's full height with billowing clouds of gray, completely obscuring what lay beyond.

I glared at the free-floating nether. From up above, on the plateau, the small fog banks had appeared to measure only a few dozen yards in diameter, but down here, in the chasm's depths, there was no telling how widely it had expanded.

Or what monsters it hid.

"Describe what you see, Ghost," I said grimly.

She looked at me perplexed. *"The stygians are in clear view."*

"They're in a cloud of nether," I explained.

"Oh, I see." The spirit wolf's ears pricked up attentively. *"Are we inside the cloud right now?"*

"Not yet, but the path ahead is brimming with the stuff," I replied glumly and went on to describe what I'd seen from the plateau.

"So that is what you meant by fog," she said.

I nodded. *"But enough of the nether. Tell me what you see."*

Ghost's gaze swung forward again. *"The crawlers have met up with six other stygians."*

I frowned. Only six? This couldn't be the stygian's base, then. Not the main one, anyway. *"Describe them."*

"They're not big," she said. *"Smaller than the crawlers and with six barbed legs and two stick-thin pincers for arms."*

I didn't recognize the stygians Ghost described, nor could I try analyzing them just yet. We were more than fifty yards away from the fog bank and the creatures were out of range of my mindsight. *"What are the six doing?"*

"They're standing in a circle." Ghost hesitated. *"Guarding something, maybe? Whatever it is, I can't quite—"* She broke off. *"Oow, I see it now. It's small, shiny, and so dark. Blacker than your sword,"* she finished, sounding fascinated.

"A seed," I hissed. *"A damnable stygian seed."* I'd seen one only once—that time I'd entered a rift with Simone's party—but it had left an impression, and I had no trouble recognizing that it was what Ghost described.

"What's a stygian seed?" a confused Ghost asked.

I waved aside her question. *"I'll explain later."* What was a seed doing here? Were the stygians trying to create a rift?

Or had they formed one already?

I wasn't sure. I didn't know enough about the seeds to guess at this one's purpose. Nor, I reminded myself, did I know how the stygians were entering Draven's Reach. I'd assumed they had breached the sector's barrier and were streaming in directly from the surrounding nether. But what if they were using rifts to fuel their invasion instead?

It was certainly a possibility.

Still, regardless of why this seed was here, I knew it had to be destroyed. First though, I needed more information. *"What are the stygians doing with the ent's remains?"*

Ghost wrinkled her nose. *"They're packing the dead flesh around the seed."*

Urgh. My own lips curled in disgust. Were the stygians trying to hide the seed—or feed it? Did the seeds *even* need feeding?

It was something else I didn't know.

I sighed, realizing my knowledge of the stygians was sorely lacking. I would have to rectify that when I could, but for now, my ignorance was merely one more factor I had to take into account for the upcoming battle.

I inched forward carefully. Before I kicked things off, I needed to know the levels of the seed's guards.

"The crawlers are leaving," Ghost said abruptly.

Mid-motion, I froze. *"Are they coming back this way?"*

"No, they're heading deeper into the chasm."

I relaxed. *"Perfect,"* I said, then settled down to wait.

Five minutes later, the crawlers disappeared entirely from Ghost's field of view. That left only the six seed guards for me to deal with.

Returning my shortsword, faithful, to my backpack, I equipped my stygian blade. The nether creatures were immune to physical damage, and even ebonheart would not hurt them.

Next, I considered the enchantment crystals on my belt. After a moment of silent debate, I decided to forgo using any of them. Given what I'd surmised already of the nether's presence in the sector, I suspected the toxicity of the fog bank ahead was low, making this an ideal opportunity to train my nether absorption skill.

Lastly, I recast my buffs and stalked forward.

Six hostile entities have failed to detect you! You are hidden.

At the Game's message, I halted. I was still more than fifty yards from the edge of the fog bank. *"Have the six stygians changed position?"*

"No," Ghost replied. *"Only two are facing you. The other four are looking in other directions."*

"Tell me if that changes," I murmured. Resuming my advance, I padded forward until my mindsight was triggered.

Two bright mindglows had crossed the edge of my awareness. I paused to consider them for a moment, but seeing as they remained still and unmoving, I crept forward another few steps.

Four more minds entered into range.

Drawing to a halt, I considered the stygians ahead. Mindsight reported all six creatures to be stationary, and like Ghost had said, they were deployed in a circle, four guarding the east and west approaches along the chasm while the other two watched cliff walls. Reaching out with my mind, I analyzed the closest one.

The target is a level 182 stygian weaver.

"A weaver," I mused. It was another type of stygian I didn't recognize. Sending out more strands of my will, I inspected the other nearby hostiles.

They too were weavers and rank eighteen creatures.

Six rank eighteen foes. I rubbed my chin thoughtfully. Defeating the seed's guards was certainly doable, but the outcome was by no means assured. I turned my gaze upon the fog bank.

I was about twenty yards from its edge. Assuming the seed was in its center, that meant the nether cloud measured about forty yards from end to end. Not as large as I'd feared, which was good news at least.

I crept forward again. There was one more thing to verify before I initiated combat, and that was ascertaining the toxicity of the nether.

Reaching the fog bank, I slipped past its outer edge. Heavy banks of smog that I'd known to expect roiled all around me, transforming everything beyond a few yards into a wall of gray. I wasn't about to complain, though. While the free-floating nether reduced visibility, it concealed me, too.

Six hostile entities have failed to detect you!

Warning: You have entered the nether! The nether toxicity at your current location is at tier 2. You are unprotected. Your health, psi, stamina, and mana are degenerating at a rate of 15% per minute.

You have failed a magical resistance check!

Your void armor has reduced the nether damage incurred by 20%.

Tier two. The fog bank itself posed little threat. In fact, if not for how the free-floating nether impaired my line of sight, it would have minimal bearing on the outcome of the battle.

Smiling, I retreated out of the fog. It was time to plan my assault.

CHAPTER 320: THE WEAVE WEAVES AS THE WEAVE WILLS

Only a few moments later, I was ready to commence.

Ghost had been briefed on the plan and waited a few dozen yards behind in case I needed to make a quick getaway. I was once again outside the fog bank, a touch under fifty yards from my targets.

Drawing psi, I flung a net of bewitching at the six weavers.

Strands of my will surged forward and invaded the minds of the stygians. One by one, they fell under my spell. Sadly, though, some resisted.

You have charmed 3 of 6 targets for 20 seconds.

My casting was less effective than I'd liked, but the fact that it had succeeded at all meant the outcome of the encounter was assured. Seeing no reason to prolong things, I ordered the bespelled creatures into motion. *"Attack!"*

As one, the trio fell upon their surprised fellows, and if the wild bobbing of their mindglows were anything to go by, a frantic life and death struggle had ensued.

"It worked?" Ghost asked. She was far enough away that the stygians were no longer in her sight range.

"It did," I replied. *"It won't be long now."*

Rocking back on my heels, I made myself comfortable while I waited for the battle's inevitable conclusion.

Game alerts scrolled through my mind.

Your minion has injured a level 184 stygian weaver.
A level 184 stygian weaver has critically injured your minion.
Your minion has cast necrotic pulse, healing 6 targets.
A level 184 stygian weaver has cast necrotic pulse, healing 6 targets.

I blinked in surprise. None of the weavers were taking damage. Or rather they were, but they were *also* healing themselves.

"Ghost," I said slowly. *"I need you back here."*

The spirit wolf trotted to my side. *"What's wrong?"*

I pointed to the fog bank that remained opaque to my eyes. *"Tell me what's going on."*

"The stygians are fighting each other—just like you planned," she said.

"But how are they fighting?" I pressed.

Ghost appeared bemused by the question, but answered, nevertheless. *"The weavers are using their pincers to fling spells at each other. The projectiles they're summoning are bright yellow and eat away at whatever they touch."* She paused. *"Is that what you wanted to know?"*

I frowned. *"Just magic projectiles? That's all the weavers are using? You don't see any other spells in play?"*

Ghost's gaze slid back to the fog. *"They aren't—wait, I see something else."* Her ears pricked forward. *"A disc-shaped green glow is forming beneath each stygian's torso. They weren't there before."*

"The green discs, describe them."

"They're brightening by the second. I'm not sure, but I think they're growing too." Ghost stiffened. *"One of the discs just exploded."* She paused. *"The blast passed over all the weavers, but it didn't hurt any of the creatures. Instead, it—"*

"—healed them," I finished for her. *"It's a mass restoration spell."* To figure out just how problematic the stygians' healing was going to be, I reached out and inspected one of the distant mindglows.

The target is a level 181 stygian weaver. It is uninjured.

Analyze confirmed my suspicions. The cumulative effect of the weavers' necrotic healing pulses surpassed whatever damage their projectiles were inflicting. I sighed.

It didn't look as if things were going to run as smoothly as I hoped.

✳   ✳   ✳

You have lost control over 3 stygian weavers.

When my former minions regained control of their minds, the skirmish ground to a screeching halt. Unlike the other stygians I'd bespelled before, the weavers seemed smart enough to realize they'd been fooled into fighting one another.

"They sound unhappy," I commented to Ghost as I listened to the angry clicks and hisses that emerged from the fog bank.

The spirit wolf wagged her tail in agreement. *"They are."*

"Angry enough to charge out of the fog?" I asked hopefully.

"I'm sorry, Prime. But the creatures are not budging from the seed."

I sighed. It was too much to hope that the weavers would abandon their charge, but I had to ask. Drawing in psi, I began a second casting.

"Are you going to charm them again?" Ghost asked.

I nodded. *"I don't intend on forcing the weavers to fight each other, though. This time, I'm going to lure them out. One by one."* Isolated and alone, the weavers would be easier to kill.

My spell completed and I focused my attention on the fog bank again, searching for my first victim.

But there was none to be had. My mindsight was empty.

"Ghost," I said in a half-strangled voice, *"please tell me the weavers have fled."*

A moment of deliberate silence. *"They haven't."*

I lowered my head into my hands. It would have been better if the stygians had gone, because the alternative was worse: somehow, the weavers had shielded their minds.

"I can't see their mindglows anymore," Ghost added helpfully.

I nodded bleakly. *"Me neither."*

In one fell swoop, my options had narrowed considerably. Mental manipulation was now out of the question. If I wished to pursue the encounter, I either had to take the fight to the creatures—sword to claw—or employ my consumables. But my remaining bombs and traps were too precious to waste unnecessarily.

Looks like I'm doing this the hard way, I thought, unsheathing my stygian blade.

Ghost stiffened to attention.

"Stay here," I ordered before she could ask what I was about, *"and keep an eye out for the crawlers' return."*

Padding forward, I entered the fog bank.

✳   ✳   ✳

You have been afflicted by the nether.
Your health, psi, stamina, and mana are degenerating at a rate of 12% per minute (damage reduced by void armor).

I crept through the pale mists with deliberate care, ignoring the corrosive touch of the nether and the constant drain on my energy pools. If I rushed the encounter, the weavers would kill me long before the fog bank did.

Six hostile entities have failed to detect you!

My targets were close.

I couldn't see the weavers yet, but their plaintive clicks and angry hisses made them easy to track. From the sounds of it, the creatures were stationary again, and I could only assume they'd resumed their guard positions. My senses trained for the least hint of movement, I advanced cautiously.

Six hostile entities have failed to detect you!

One step. Two. Ten. Then, finally the intervening nether thinned enough to give me my first glimpse of my foes.

Six hostile entities have failed to detect you!

I stilled, studying the two creatures that had emerged into view. The pair were the forward sentries and guarded the closer end of the chasm.

The weavers' bodies were thin, elongated, and antlike. Their rear-ends were fat and rounded, and their heads tiny and oval shaped. They were small too, less than half my own size. In stark contrast to other stygians I'd encountered, the weavers were physically unthreatening.

But only if you ignore the stench of the void that clings to them, I thought wryly.

What the weavers lacked in physical presence, though, they made up for with magic. Sickly green light pulsed beneath their abdomens, yellow ichor that glowed eerily coated their legs and pincers, and brown threads of magic laced their bodies like a second skin.

They're pure casters, I guessed.

Narrowing my gaze, I searched the pair for any sign that either bore a mage's shield, but spotted none. That both reassured and worried me. I doubted the weavers had left themselves physically vulnerable, and if they lacked the obvious—if effective—protections of a magic shield, they had to have other hidden defenses.

Defenses I would only learn about *after* I attacked.

It did not deter me, though. My buffs were already cast, and I had only my final preparations to perform. *No sense in delaying any longer.* Raising my stygian sword, I empowered it with stamina.

You have cast fade, blurring your form and making you 25% harder to see for 1 minute.

You have cast piercing strike, doubling the damage dealt on the next attack.

You have cast whirlwind, increasing your attack speed by 100% for 3 seconds.

I was ready. Focusing on the closer of the two visible sentries, I blinked to him.

You have teleported into the shadow of a stygian weaver.
Six hostile entities have failed to detect you!

My stealth held, but I knew I had only seconds before I was spotted. Stepping *through* the weaver's body—outside the Nethersphere, the stygians lacked actual physical form—I struck down with my blade.

My body had passed harmlessly through the weaver. My sword did not do likewise.

The smokey stygian blade—forged from the nether itself—found flesh where my body had not and caved in the weaver's skull.

You have backstabbed your target for 5x more damage!
You have killed a stygian weaver with a fatal blow.

That was not the end of it, though.

The threads of brown magic lining the now-dead body surged upwards to form a mirror-copy of my sword, and before I could recover from my astonishment, it ran me through.

A stygian weaver's vengeful armor has injured you, reflecting a portion of the damage you dealt!
Your void armor has reduced the necrotic damage incurred by 20%. Your health has decreased to 70%.

I flinched, mouth forming a silent O. It was apparent now what form the weavers' defenses had taken. Anticipating the worst, I glanced down at where the bespelled blade had pierced my left thigh.

There was no blood.

The reflected attack had not been physical in nature and instead of inflicting a gaping wound, had left withered muscle and bone in its wake. That did not mean it didn't hurt. It did—mightily. Wincing, I lifted my left leg, flexing it in an attempt to lessen the pain.

The outside of my boot brushed a stone and set it rolling.

Five hostile entities have detected you! You are no longer hidden.

Damnit, Michael! I cursed, angry at my carelessness.

My misstep had cost me my stealth, and this was about the worst possible time to flounder. Gritting my teeth against the pain, I tightened my grip around the hilt of my sword and whipped my head left and right.

I didn't need to see my foes to know what they were about. The angry surge in the volume of their clicks made that evident: the weavers were converging on my position. One foe, though, was clearly visible.

On my right, two raised pincers—each bursting with yellow ichor—were pointed squarely at me. *It's about to fire.* Out of options, I played my trump card. Dipping my mind into the ring I wore on my right hand, I activated the casting it held ready.

You have trigger-cast cold sphere.
A stygian weaver has failed a magical resistance check! 1 of 1 targets have been chilled.

It was too bad the other four of the weavers were still out of range of the freezing bubble. But right now, they didn't matter as much as the dead sentry's companion. Realizing its predicament, the weaver turned around and attempted to flee.

But it was far too slow.

With my weight braced on my right leg, I spun around and brought my shortsword whistling downward in an overhead chop. Stygian blade met chilled flesh and hacked through effortlessly.

You have killed a stygian weaver with a fatal blow.
A stygian weaver's vengeful armor has injured you!
Void armor charge remaining: 57%.
Your health has decreased to 50%.

Once more, a spelled blade manifested in the wake of my assault and buried itself in my torso. This time, anticipating the attack, I rode the pain better, accepting it as the price to pay for the kill.

Unbidden, more messages from the Adjudicator scrolled through my mind.

Void thief triggered!
You have learned the direct-targeted spell, vengeful armor (stolen), from a stygian weaver.
Warning: you have reached the limit of your stolen spells. Do you wish to replace the tier 5 cold sphere spell with tier 4 vengeful armor spell? If you refuse, knowledge of the new spell will be lost.

Angrily, I banished the Game alerts. *Bloody hell! Not now. I'm still in a—*

A blight thorn has injured you!
A blight thorn has injured you!
...
Void thief triggered!

The four magic missiles struck me near-simultaneously. *Ta-ta-ta-ta!*

They ricocheted off my chest in sharp order, my cold sphere, unfortunately, doing nothing to slow them.

I flew backwards, mind nearly white with pain. Each of the thorns stung as much as the vengeful armor attacks had, and I could feel my mind shutting down from the sensory overload. Grimly, I held on to consciousness.

If I fainted, I was dead. It was that simple.

To make my already dire situation worse, a plethora of new Game alerts flashed open for attention. I dismissed them without a second thought. Only one imperative drove me now: survival.

I landed hard after traveling airborne for nearly a dozen feet, and my back hit the rock ground with an audible thud. The air escaped my lungs in a rush. My chest was on fire, as were my leg and stomach.

Still, I set aside my body's agony and wove psi.

Over the sounds of my own heavy breathing, I heard four sets of insect-like feet scuttling closer. I ignored them as I had my own injuries and kept casting. Flight was my only hope.

You have cast windborne.

The moment my spell completed, I manifested the casting and rolled onto the ramp of air. Four projectiles shrieked through the air on a collision course with me, but before they could reach me, the windslide bore me away.

You have evaded 4 blight thorns.

Face pressed against the ramp of air, I heaved in relief. I was free and clear.

Now, it was time to regroup.

CHAPTER 321: UNBRIDLED CURIOSITY

The windslide carried me ten yards, far enough for the mists to shield me from the gazes of the furious weavers.

Four hostile entities have failed to detect you! You are hidden.

I smiled wanly. Ironically, the very nether that was responsible for my current peril was now sheltering me from its minions. Stretched flat across the ground, I raised my head slowly and listened to their angry calls.

The weavers were not drawing closer.

I lowered my head carefully, more relieved than I cared to admit. The stygians had elected not to pursue me, choosing instead to guard the seed. It made things easier and meant I could finally acknowledge my body's sorry state.

Void armor depleted. Your health has decreased to 30%.

The blight thorns had wreaked havoc on me, shredding my void armor *and* forcing quick mend to trigger. It was a wonder I'd escaped at all. Nor was I safe yet. In my reduced state, the constant drain from the free-floating nether hit hard. I urgently needed to heal, but first I had to escape the fog bank.

Opening my mindsight, I searched for Ghost and found her quickly. By the looks of it, the spirit wolf was anxiously pacing the edges of the fog bank. Drawing in psi, I blinked to her.

You have teleported 25 yards to Ghost.

Ghost spun to face me the moment I appeared at her side. *"Are you alright?"*

"I will be after I tend to my injuries," I rasped. *"Keep—"*

"—watch," Ghost finished. *"I know. I'm on it. See to your wounds."*

I smiled through the pain. My companion was growing more confident by the day, and I no longer questioned her competence. Forgoing further comment, I closed my eyes and gathered psi.

✳   ✳   ✳

You have fully restored your health, mana, and psi.

You failed to acquire the spells: blight thorn (stolen) and vengeful armor (stolen).

Your nether absorption skill has increased to level 61 and reached rank 6.

Your channeling has reached rank 11.

Your chi has reached rank 13.

Your dodging has reached rank 14.

Your insight has reached rank 15, allowing you to learn tier 4 abilities.

A little later, I opened my eyes. My health, mana and psi pools were fully restored, and the pertinent Game alerts attended to.

In some respects, the encounter's outcome was discouraging. I'd gained no levels, taken more damage than I expected, and had lost the opportunity to learn two potentially useful spells.

My new fade buff had had no perceptible influence on the skirmish either. The weavers had targeted me easily enough throughout. Perhaps, though, I was being too harsh. It was still too early to judge the ability's performance, after all.

Enough naysaying.

Despite everything, I *had* killed two of the weavers, I reminded myself. That made my opening foray a success. I had learned much of value, too, and was certain to do better the second time around as well.

I rolled back to my feet. It was time for round two.

✳   ✳   ✳

I re-entered the fog bank wrapped in shadows and cloaked by the nether. The weavers remained agitated. Crouched and hiding only a few yards away from the seed, I watched the four stygians pace around their charge in an unhappy circle.

The weavers were also keeping their buffs active, and every few seconds, the green light beneath their torsos would flare. Clearly, the creatures were going to great lengths to not be caught flat-footed again.

Their precautions would aid them little, though.

Drawing my stygian blade, I gripped it with both hands and held it aloft. Then I waited.

Four necrotic pulses flared outwards—healing spells needlessly cast on creatures already at full health—and in the next instant, the light beneath the weavers' torsos dimmed. *Now*, I thought. Choosing a target at random, I shadow blinked.

You have teleported 3 yards.

I emerged from the aether less than two feet from my chosen victim, blade already in motion and seeking blood.

You have killed a stygian weaver with a fatal blow.
A stygian weaver's vengeful armor has injured you!

The shortsword struck cleanly, cleaving through the joint connecting the weaver's head and its torso. The corpse crumpled beneath me, and I whipped about.

Three hostile entities have detected you! You are no longer hidden.

The other stygians reacted instantly—and predictably. Swinging around to face me, they released a flurry of projectiles in my direction. I'd learned my lesson though and did not stay to face the onslaught. Rolling out the path of the incoming projectiles, I spun psi.

You have evaded 3 blight thorns.

I leapt back to my feet, a casting ready. Laying down a windslide, I hopped on and vanished into the mists.

✳ ✳ ✳

My second assault had been surgical. Neat. Clean.

Other than for the unavoidable damage I sustained from the dead weaver's vengeful armor spell, I'd walked away from the encounter untouched.

Now, I prowled the fog bank again.

Despite my twin successes, the weavers had still not altered tactics and remained stubbornly on guard next to the seed—a mistake they would pay for soon enough.

Padding softly through the mists, I inched closer to the stygians until they swam into view. Barely pausing to assess the situation, I blinked in, slaughtered my chosen victim, and fled again on wings of air.

You have killed a stygian weaver with a fatal blow.

Then, I repeated the maneuver twice more.

You have killed a stygian weaver with a fatal blow.
You have killed a stygian weaver with a fatal blow.
You have reached level 167!
Your nether absorption skill has reached rank 7.
Your shortswords has reached rank 15, allowing you to learn tier 4 abilities.

Chest heaving and standing over the body of my latest victim I stared at the remains of the six stygians. In the end, the strength of the weavers' magic had counted for little.

They'd been unable to adapt to my tactics and had paid for it dearly. Not only had the weavers failed in their duty to guard the seed, but they had gifted me with a generous amount of loot too. Extracting my alchemy stone, I placed it inside one of the weaver's bodies.

The stone activated, pulsing emerald. In response, the corpse shrunk, shriveling before my eyes, and in less than a minute, it vanished entirely. Picking up the object, I moved to the next corpse and repeated the process.

While I waited for the alchemy stone to collect the reagents, I attended to my other chores.

Your Magic has increased to rank 24. Other modifiers: +14 from items.
You have successfully stored the <u>cold sphere</u> spell in the ring, mage's surprise. This spell may now be trigger-cast when required.

In total, slaying the six weavers had earned me two levels, and advanced two more of my skills to tier four. A not-inconsiderable return, and in the process, I'd lost nothing except a little time and stamina. I smiled. A profitable exchange.

The alchemy stone finished harvesting the last corpse and I picked it up.

New ingredients acquired: 30 x lumps of necrotic plasma and 6 x vial of nether residue.

Idly, I wondered if there were weavers in the other fog banks too. If there were... But before I could pursue that thought further, a slip of motion around the corner of my eye drew my attention.

It was Ghost sniffing at the stygian seed.

"Get back, Ghost," I warned. "You don't want to mess with that."

Not retreating, the spirit wolf met my gaze. *"Why? Is it dangerous?"*

"I'm not sure," I admitted, "but there is no telling what the seeds are capable of."

"It is aware," Ghost mused, lowering her muzzle to the seed again.

It took me a moment to parse that. And when I did, my eyes widened in shock. Throwing open my mindsight, I searched the vicinity. But despite Ghost's assertion, I detected no consciousnesses nearby but my own and the spirit wolf's.

Still, when it came to such things, I trusted the spirit wolf's senses more than my own. "You're saying the seed has a mind?" I asked, needing confirmation that I hadn't misunderstood her.

"It does," Ghost replied. *"But it is tiny. Even from this distance I can barely make out the shape of his mind."*

I was growing more alarmed by the second. *"His* mind? You're saying it's a 'he'?"

Without looking at me, Ghost bobbed her head. *"He is inviting me in. He wants to talk."* She lowered her head farther, nose almost touching the seed. *"I just need to get a little closer..."*

"Get back, Ghost," I snapped.

Caught up in her fascinated study of the seed, the spirit wolf did not respond.

I rushed to her side, wishing she had physical form so I could wrench her aside. *"I mean it!"* I roared using my mindvoice and infusing my words with the lash of an alpha's command. *"GET BACK!"*

Ghost shrank back on her haunches, instinctively responding to my tone. It was not one I'd ever employed with her before.

"But you said it wasn't dangerous," she protested.

"I *said* I wasn't sure if it was," I ground out through clenched teeth. "Now, get back."

Meekly, the spirit wolf retreated, shoulders hunched and head lowered. I'd scared her, I realized and immediately felt guilty, but I kept my demeanor stiff and stern.

I was scared too. I had no evidence that the seed was dangerous— other than for the fact of its origin—but my own instincts were prickling, and they were telling me that to let Ghost commune with a mind born of the nether would be a mistake.

Her curiosity is going to be the death of me, I thought morosely, watching carefully as the spirit wolf backed farther away. Only when she was a good ten yards from the seed did I approach it myself.

Immediately, the putrid fragrance of spoiled flesh assailed my senses. *Damn, that's awful.* Wrinkling my nose, I brushed aside some of the tainted meat with the tip of my boot.

A deep furrow had been carved in the earth all around the small seed, and packed in its depths was the flesh of many creatures, not just the frost ent's. Some of the remains were desiccated and dried out—as if something had sucked them dry.

Hells, how long have the stygians been feeding this thing? Holding my nose, I crouched down to take a close look at the seed itself.

At the far reaches of my mind, I felt a faint... tickle. Not hesitating, I flung myself back.

The feather touched vanished.

Sitting on my rear, I exhaled a slow, relieved breath, not missing the irony of the situation. Not a moment ago, I'd been berating Ghost, but here I was behaving just as carelessly.

Reminded of the spirit wolf, I glanced back at her. "Raise your mind shield. As high as you can."

"*But—*" she began.

"No arguments," I said forcefully and maintained a hard stare on her, only relenting when her mindglow disappeared from my mindsight.

"Thank you," I murmured. Turning my focus inwards, I saw to my own defenses and transformed the pool of psi at the pit of my subconsciousness into steel bands that wrapped around my mind.

You have cast mind shield. Psi abilities are unavailable.

Then, I approached the seed again.

No foreign thoughts impinged on my own as I kneeled down. *Good.* Uncovering the seed fully, I studied it. The thing was smaller than the one in the rift, but in all other aspects, it was identical and burned with a blackness so thick not even the mists could obscure it.

I tugged on the seed, but fused to the rock beneath, it didn't budge. Sitting back, I rubbed my chin thoughtfully.

Ghost had said the seed had a mind. That bothered me. Why hadn't I felt anything from the *other* seed—the one I'd taken from the rift? I had carried it on my person for a considerable time, after all. Had it touched my mind and I'd simply not noticed? Or was there something different about this seed?

So much to learn, I mused. Reaching out with my will, I inspected the seed in the hope the Game would tell me more of it.

This is an artifact of unknown rank. You are unable to discern its properties.

I sighed. *So much for that idea.* I drew ebonheart. It was time to do what I came here for. Raising the black blade, I chopped down at the base of the seed. Once, twice, thrice.

It broke free.

You have acquired a stygian seed.

Rising to my feet, I turned about to find Ghost staring at the seed in my hands. "Can you feel anything from it?"

She shook her head mutely.

"Good," I said. "Keep your shield in place until I figure out what to do with this thing." The seed was valuable and would earn me a small fortune if I ever made it out of the dungeon. But I also didn't want to carry it on me, not knowing when it might invade my thoughts.

Maybe I can find somewhere to stash it.

"Let's head back to the plateau," I said. I glanced up at the looming cliffs I knew to be hiding beyond the nether. "The cliff walls here can't be any harder to—"

I fell silent, not sure if I could trust my eyes.

I could see the rock walls in question—not clearly as they were blurred by the intervening nether. Still, I could *see* them. What's more, they were growing more distinct by the second.

The fog bank is dissipating.

I glanced down at the seed in my hand, finally realizing its purpose. The stygians weren't using the seed to anchor a rift. They were using it to anchor the fog bank.

The void is using the seeds to spread its touch in the dungeon!

It was a wild leap, and one I made with not much to go on, but I was certain of my conclusion. And there was an easy way to prove it. If I was right, I would find a seed at each and every fog bank. And that meant...

I laughed.

If I was right, I wouldn't be leaving Draven's Reach with a small fortune, but a veritable mountain of gold in stygian seeds.

Ghost whined.

I looked up to find the spirit wolf studying me quizzically. My instruction that she keep her mind shields locked tight meant she couldn't speak to me with her mindvoice.

I opened my mouth to explain the source of my delight but was interrupted by the arrival of a Game message.

On behalf of Wolf, the Adjudicator has allocated you a new task: <u>Cleanse the Corruption</u>!

You have discovered one of the means by which the nether is spreading its touch in this sector. Find a way to cleanse the dungeon of the void's presence, and remember that, above all else, Wolf is a protector. Objective: Rid Draven's Reach of the nether's corruption.

"Well, well," I murmured. The arrival of the new task was all the confirmation I needed that I was on the right track in hunting down the stygian menace.

If I searched the fog banks, I could rid the dungeon of the void's touch *and* get rich in the process. I grinned happily. For once, things appeared to be going my way.

Ghost growled—loud and menacing.

"Sorry, Ghost," I said, thinking she was rebuking me. "I'm not ignoring you." I glanced at her. "The Game just sent me this new—"

I broke off.

The spirit wolf wasn't looking at me. Instead, her gaze was pinned upwards. Sensing something amiss, I lowered my mind shield halfway.

Immediately, Ghost's mindvoice broke through. *"Prime, look out! Incoming from above!"*

CHAPTER 322: HARBINGER OF DOOM

At the spirit wolf's cry my head jerked upwards. The fog bank had all but dissipated, leaving bare the purple sky above.

And the shape hurtling down.

Closing my fingers fast around the seed in my left hand, I threw myself out of the way.

You have evaded the attack of an unknown hostile.

Behind me rock shattered and stones flew, the ground itself shuddering as my mysterious attacker dove headlong into it. Rolling to my feet, I raced away in the opposite direction, not looking back.

I'd only a split-second to study the incoming hostile, but I'd seen enough to recognize the smokey outline of a stygian, and if the earth's shaking was anything to go by, it was one that had more physical form than most of the nether's creatures.

And that was bad.

Only the most powerful stygians had true physical mass outside the void. Tugging at the shadows around me, I attempted to conceal myself.

You have failed to hide.

I grimaced and ran harder. If hiding was not an option that only left fleeing.

An ethereal shape rushed up to my side. It was Ghost, with her mind shield up again. In a willful streak—one that I had more than a little reason to be grateful for—she had lowered her defenses earlier to give voice to her warning.

I waved her forward. "Go!" I shouted. "Run ahead. I'll teleport to you." Lowering her head in wordless acknowledgement, Ghost dashed away.

A roar split the air behind me. I was tempted to look over my shoulder but didn't. For now, all that mattered was putting a safe distance between me and the stygian at my rear.

"Coward! You flee? Face me!"

Startled, I stumbled and almost fell but caught myself in time. The stygian behind me was talking. Talking! *Since when can they speak?* I wondered inanely.

A gust of wind at my back. The half-caught flap of a wing.

My foe had gone airborne again, leaving me only seconds to spare. *Damn, and damn again.* My gaze darted to Ghost. She was twenty yards ahead, and cleverly hugging the right cliff sidewall. The shadows there would make concealing myself easier, but I'd hoped for greater separation from my pursuer before trying to hide again. Still, it would have to be enough.

I dropped my mind shield all the way.

An enormous mindglow appeared at my rear. He was closing fast and looked ready to swallow me whole. The size of my foe's mindglow reinforced my fear. Whatever the stygian was, he was powerful, and I was not about to attempt my mind tricks on him until I'd gained a better handle on the situation. Focusing on the spirit wolf, I spun psi.

The whisper of a fast-moving shape cut through the air.

He's diving. Ignoring my foe as best I could—a task all on its own—I rushed through my casting and completed it with only heartbeats to spare. Stepping through the aether, I shadow blinked away.

You have teleported 25 yards to Ghost.
You have evaded the attack of an unknown hostile.

The stygian hit the ground nearly as hard the second time as he had the first. Knowing he would recover soon, I wrenched myself to a screeching halt and sank into the shadows.

A hostile entity has failed to detect you! You are hidden.

That was too close, I thought, exhaling carefully. My heart was pounding, and my pulse still raced. Nor could I relax just yet. If I stayed where I was, my pursuer was sure to find me again. Dropping into a crouch, I padded away at the fastest pace I could manage while still maintaining my stealth.

Ghost appeared beside me, her lips pulled back in a silent snarl as she glared at the stygian. I placed a hand on her ethereal head, and she looked at me.

"Thank you," I mouthed. Glancing down at the seed I still held, I hesitated, then added, "Lower your shield."

The spirit wolf reappeared in my mindsight.

"Good work, Ghost," I said, speaking rapidly. *"Find me somewhere safer to hide. I'll wait here."*

"Yes, Prime," she replied and, spinning around, dashed away. I watched her go. As troublesome as Ghost could be at times, she'd never given me cause to question her loyalty.

"Do you think to hide, wolfling?" the stygian shouted, the words reverberating off the surrounding cliffs.

I flinched. It was not the volume of my foe's cry that startled me. It was his chosen epithet. *Wolfling?* It could not be a word the stygian had used by happenstance. *What is this bloody thing?*

"Oh yes, I know *what* you are." Feet pounded against the ground, heading unerringly in my direction. "And I know *where* you are."

A hostile entity has detected you. You are no longer hidden!

My face paled as the shadows concealing me were unceremoniously yanked away. How had the nether creature found me—and so quickly? Head whipping around, I looked directly at my foe for the first time.

The stygian was unlike any of his kind I'd faced before. He had the head of a crow, the body of a hyena, and the tail of a crocodile. An unholy chimera, if ever there was one.

The creature was huge too. Not as massive as the stone golems, but large enough to give even those colossal elites pause. With his midnight black wings unfurled and his beady eyes glaring balefully at me, the stygian horror rushed across the distance that separated us.

Unbidden, the wolf in me rose to the fore, and a snarl broke through my clenched teeth. Only, midway through, it transformed into a whine. My predatory self recognized what I had not yet: this was not a foe I could face and live.

Flight was the only option.

But despite the instinctive terror gnawing at me, I held my nerve. I could not flee blindly. I had to know what I faced. Reaching out with my will, I inspected the onrushing monster.

The target is a stygian harbinger of indeterminant level.

Well, that clinches it. My foe was at least level three hundred. The stygian charging me was on par with a minor Power. *There's no running from this. Better to—*

I reined in my burgeoning panic and drew psi. I had to change tactics. *"Ghost, turn around and get behind that thing!"*

I had just enough time to see the spirit wolf heed my words before my attention was snapped up by the approaching horror. The charging harbinger was less than ten yards away, his wickedly pointed beak leading the way. *He means to run me through,* I realized, eliminating me in a single disdainful strike.

I kept weaving psi. My spell would not complete in time but if I delayed the harbinger a touch…

The stygian closed the gap to five yards. I stood my ground, eyes fixed on the point of his beak.

Two yards.

Let's see how you deal with this. Dipping my mind into the ring on my right hand, I activated the spell waiting within.

Mage's surprise activated. Spellhold casting released.
You have trigger-cast cold sphere.
A stygian harbinger has failed a magical resistance check! 1 of 1 targets have been chilled.

The nether creature's beak hit the rim of the ice field, and in an eye blink his movement slowed. My gaze never leaving my foe, I waited.

The psi spell I had been preparing was completed, but I didn't release it just yet. Every heartbeat longer I kept the harbinger trapped in the cold sphere was a second more that I bought for Ghost to move into position.

The stygian's deadly beak swept closer.

I didn't bother attacking, either. A foe of the order of magnitude of a minor Power would have strong defenses, and no mere sword strike from me was going to kill him. Rather than triggering whatever nasty defenses the stygian hid, I watched and waited.

Fury burned in the harbinger's eyes. He knew I'd gotten the better of him, if temporarily. But anger aside, the stygian's gaze harbored no doubt or fear. He was eyeing me the way a predator did a prey that had performed an unexpected trick. His confidence in the hunt's outcome was unshaken.

I smiled mockingly in response, the only bit of defiance I could muster under the circumstances. My foe had every reason to be confident. I was outmatched, and I knew it just as well as he did.

Ghost's glowing shape rushed by.

Still, I did not act. I waited and waited, until the harbinger's beak was only mere inches from my face. Then, I met my foe's gaze. "Bye," I mouthed, and released the casting in my mind.

You have cast windborne.

I set down the windslide, not in the direction Ghost had fled, but in the opposite one, angling upward and around the harbinger.

Borne away on the currents of air, I zipped past the chilled stygian, taking the cold sphere with me and sadly freeing the nether creature from the bubble's frigid touch.

"You will not escape me that easily!" the harbinger screamed the moment his lungs were free to give vent to his rage. Beating his wings, the stygian flung himself aloft.

Paying my foe no mind, I sailed off the end of the windslide and dropped back to the ground. Landing lightly, I ran, feet pounding against the ground as I tried to widen the distance between me and my foe. At the same time, I kept my mindsight fixed on Ghost's receding form and wove psi. The gap between us was widening fast. Thirty yards.

The harbinger started his dive.

Forty yards.

The stygian opened his beak, giving vent to his anger and something else too. Thick plumes of an evil cloud rushed out and surged towards me. Whatever the cloud was, I knew I didn't want to feel its touch.

Forty-five yards.

Releasing the spell I held, I slipped out of the real...

You have teleported to Ghost.

... and back into it, *behind* the stygian.

The harbinger screeched in thwarted anger as my fleeing form disappeared from sight and flapped his wings hard to break out of its dive. Nearly fifty yards away, I rolled silently into the shadows.

You are hidden.

Nestled in the darkness, I stilled, gasping and short of breath. I could not stay where I was, though. The harbinger had found me once and might do so again.

Rising into a crouch, I crept stealthily along the cliff.

CHAPTER 323: SEEDS OF DESTRUCTION

It did not take long for the harbinger to recover from his dive. Less than a dozen seconds after I blinked away, the creature winged aloft and immediately began cutting a wide arc through the air.

"It's heading back this way," Ghost warned.

Looking over my shoulder and seeing the same, I nodded. My stealth was holding, but it might not when the harbinger drew closer.

I didn't have long to decide my course.

How does the harbinger know to turn around? I wondered. Both times that I blinked away, the stygian had picked the correct direction in which to head without hesitation. I was tempted to send Ghost racing ahead and to teleport to her again, but if the stygian could see her, that tactic would be useless.

Had the harbinger seen Ghost? Was that how he was locating me? If my foe could see the spirit wolf, then flight was useless. *Best I make my stand here.*

I drew ebonheart.

Glancing down, I saw the stygian seed still clutched in my left hand. I'd been holding it the entire time, and it was a wonder I hadn't dropped the thing. Hastily, I moved to stuff it in my pocket. There would be time enough to deal with the seed later.

Halfway through the motion, an errant glint caught my eye.

I paused. There was no light for the seed to reflect, which was why the flash struck me as odd. Perplexed, I stared at the thing.

A phantom thought flitted through my mind, too fast to follow. I chased after it but caught only the faintest of echoes. It had sounded oddly like a... mocking laugh.

A laugh?

Even then, for a split-second, I failed to make the connection. Finally, it dawned on me.

Of course.

It was the seed that was giving away my location.

My mind shield was down—it had to be for me to use my psi abilities—and in the intervening chaos I'd nearly forgotten about the seed's danger.

Or had been made to forget.

What if... the seed's first touch had been a misstep? What if the thing had been more careful the second time around? What if it had been subverting my thoughts all this time?

The fog clogging my mind burned away. And finally, I realized the truth. I was being manipulated, artfully so. Revulsion tore through me. The seed was truly insidious. *Gah!* I spat, almost throwing the thing away in horror.

But no, that was the seed's desires speaking again.

I wouldn't let it go. Not so easily.

"Prime?" Ghost prompted. "Whatever we're doing, we'd better do it quickly. The stygian is closing on us."

Glancing up, I saw that the harbinger had completed his half-circle and was heading directly for me. This time, the creature had declined to announce his approach, and was gliding in ominous silence.

"One second. I need to think." The urge to act was strong, but I feared if I didn't follow the thread I'd worked free, I never would.

When I'd been in the rift with Simone's party, the stygians had also found me time and again, and each time they had, I'd been holding a seed. It was only after I'd thrown it away that my stealth had held.

At the time, I'd not known how the nether creatures had managed to locate me, but now, armed with knowledge that the seeds were aware—and more than just aware—I had an inkling of how it had been done.

The seed in my hand had to be communicating with the harbinger, just like that other seed long ago had communicated with the stygian serpents.

The question now was what to do about it.

I glanced back at my foe. I had only seconds to decide the seed's fate—and my own. Unfortunately, I had no handy rift nearby to escape through, which left me only two options.

The first was to discard the seed. It wanted that. I didn't know how I knew that, but I did. Proof, if I needed more, that the seed was in my mind. The thing preferred me dead but would gladly accept its freedom. I was not about to give it what it wanted, though.

That left only the second option.

Unclenching my left hand, I dropped the seed and raised ebonheart. Before I could reconsider—or be made to reconsider—I took the black blade in a two-handed grip and stabbed downward.

Ebon-point met stygian-crystal and was rebuffed.

But not entirely, I thought, noticing a hairline crack along the seed's crystalline shell.

A cry rent the air behind me. "What are you doing? Stop, fleshling!"

I smiled tightly. The stark fear in the harbinger's words only encouraged me further. *"Go,"* I said, glancing at Ghost.

Understanding my intent, the spirit wolf dashed off, down the chasm and in the opposite direction from the stygian. I raised ebonheart again.

The harbinger roared in unbridled fury and flapped his wings, abandoning all attempts to conceal his approach. He *knew* what I was about to do. Something had told him.

My gaze dropped to the seed.

"Your minion is not going to save you this time," I whispered, not caring whether the thing understood me or not. Then, I brought my sword crashing down again, point first and squarely onto the weakened spot.

The seed shattered under the blow, exploding into dozens of little shards.

You had destroyed a stygian seed!

With a thunderous scream that set my ears ringing, the harbinger threw himself into a precipitous dive. He would miss me by a wide margin, I judged. Still, I had no desire to hang around.

Stepping into the aether, I shadow blinked to Ghost.

It took the harbinger a long time to calm down.

Nestled in the shadows, I watched intently as the stygian paced up and down the chasm, searching for me. He had passed my hiding spot multiple times already but without the seed's help was unable to pierce my stealth.

I could have fled outright, of course, and it would have been prudent to do so, but my foe ranted while he paced, and I was keen to learn what more of the stygians I could—and the harbinger in particular.

The creature was proof the stygians were more than simple beasts. Some of them at least were intelligent. Cunning. That made the void more dangerous than I'd originally assumed. And what I overheard of the harbinger's tirade only reinforced that notion.

"That was a mistake, wolfling," the harbinger raged at one point. "I'll rend you from limb to limb for this. I'll hunt you down to the ends of the sector."

A fairly standard threat as threats went, but he had called me wolfling again, setting to rest any doubts I had that the stygian knew what I was.

After another few minutes of name calling and vile curses he revealed something else of interest. "There will be no shelter for you, not anywhere! We own this dungeon. We control the safe zone and the portals. You are not getting out."

That bit was mildly concerning. I suspected my foe was exaggerating the extent of the void's influence, though. I'd seen enough of the dungeon already to know the nether didn't control it, but that the stygians knew of the safe zone troubled me.

"Do not think you can escape from whence you came, either," the harbinger hissed another time. "The overlord informed me of your coming, and I will warn the rest of my brethren! From now on, no sector will be safe for you. We will hunt you wherever you go."

And finally, most damningly, he added, "You can't hide your true self from us. I can smell what you are. The Adjudicator will not save you. The guardians will not save you. Awakening your blood cannot save you. Your Primes tried for eons to leash the void. They failed! You will be no different. We will feed on your blood just as we did theirs!"

* * *

Eventually, the harbinger left.

I remained where I was long after he was gone, pondering the creature's words. They did not a pretty picture make.

Not only were the nether creatures intelligent, they were coordinating their efforts across multiple sectors. They knew of the primes, their fight against the void, and were aware, too, of my own bloodline.

Then there were the stygian seeds. I was certain the thing had subverted my thoughts. Its touch had been so insidious, though, that even after knowing that to be the case, I was unable to pinpoint where my own thoughts ended and its manipulations began.

Do the new Powers realize what the seeds are capable of? I wondered. Given how freely seeds were traded and handled by players, I couldn't believe that they did. Loken and his fellows were many things, but I couldn't see them allowing their Sworn to be manipulated by anyone but themselves.

Another thing I hadn't figured out yet was the seeds' place amongst the stygians. That they were important was obvious. They appeared to play a central role in the void's spread, whether within a sector or between sectors. In fact, given what I'd witnessed, it wouldn't surprise me to find out that it was the seeds themselves that created the free-floating nether.

What was unclear though, was the relationship between the seeds and the stygian creatures. Was the harbinger and others of his ilk subservient to the seeds—and by extension, the trees that birthed them—or was it the other way around?

So many mysteries, I lamented. *So many questions still to answer.*

I rose to my feet. I was not going to figure out the answers sitting here, though. And as troubling as the bigger picture was, the immediate implications of smart stygians concerned me more.

The harbinger did not strike me as the type to give up.

I suspected the stygian Power would hunt me relentlessly, not stopping until he had made good on his threats. I sighed. On top of the elites and the nether itself, the harbinger was another headache I didn't need.

Moving slowly, I strode to where I'd last seen the seed and drew to a halt a safe distance away. The remains were untouched.

"What do you make of it?" I asked Ghost.

"*I can't feel anything from here,*" she replied. "*Should I go closer?*"

I hesitated, then waved the spirit wolf forward, making sure to stay by her side. I wouldn't have allowed this much, but the Adjudicator himself had reported the seed destroyed, and the harbinger hadn't taken the remains with him when he'd left. Both were proof the seed *really* was dead... but a little more confirmation wouldn't hurt.

Ghost lowered her head over the seed's remains, her nose wrinkling as she sniffed each piece separately. "*It's gone,*" she said with finality.

"You're sure?"

"*I am. Whatever mind occupied these pieces is either fled—or dead.*"

Finally convinced, I bent down and inspected the remains myself.

This is the remains of a stygian seed. You are unable to discern its properties.

I stared at the Adjudicator's response for a moment. To my surprise, the Game description implied that the broken pieces of dark crystal possessed whatever arcane properties the seed had before I'd destroyed it. Did that mean they were just as valuable?

Maybe they are, I decided, and swept up the fragments into my bag of holding.

You have acquired 1 set of stygian seed remains.

"Where do we go from here?" Ghost asked when I was done.

I glanced at her. "What did you make of our friend?"

The spirit wolf flopped down. *"Big. Ugly. And scary."*

My lips twitched. That was as apt a description of the harbinger as any. "To answer your question, let's head on up to the plateau." The stygian Power had left but there was no telling when he would return and with what forces.

"You're giving up fighting the elites?"

I shrugged. My curiosity about the dungeon's denizens had waned and any inclination I felt to pit myself against them was tempered by the thought of the harbinger intruding. Ghost had raised a valid point, though, and I *did* still have a stolen spell at my beck. I couldn't waste the opportunity to level.

"Let's head to the plateau first, then you can find me a suitable prey to hunt."

Ghost ears perked up. *"Suitable prey? Such as?"*

"Oh, I don't know. A fire giant maybe." If the dungeon harbored frost ents, it might contain elemental creatures of other types too, and what better foe to use my cold sphere against than one that would be especially vulnerable to its touch? "In the meantime, we'll keep heading north, towards those fires we spotted. I'll admit, after finding out there are stygians in Draven's Reach, I am more curious than ever about whose campfires those are."

And how they've managed to survive both the stygians and elites this long.

Chapter 324: A Heated Conversation

Hours later, Ghost and I were still traveling north across the plateau. I took the most direct route feasible, teleporting across yawning chasms when I could or skirting around the cracks in the plateau when I couldn't.

It was only for the fog banks that I made allowances. Whenever Ghost and I encountered one, we cut a wide circle around it, no matter how far off course it left us. Much to my relief, we encountered no more stygians. It implied that the nether creatures were not as numerous as I feared, and were forced to confine their presence to the immediate vicinity of the seeds.

While I hiked across the plateau, Ghost dipped in and out of the chasms, searching for an elite for me to fight. She found more than a few, but none that I considered suitable.

My appetite for risk had waned somewhat.

While I remained uncertain about the truth of the harbinger's words, I could not rule out the possibility that the stygians controlled the safe zone. It made dying an even more unappealing proposition.

I stifled a yawn. The day was growing late, and it had been many hours since I'd left the swarm viper's tunnel. Was it still only my third day in the dungeon? Raising my head, I measured the remaining distance to the northern gorge housing the campfires.

I won't reach it today. Perhaps it's time to break for the night.

Ghost floated out of a chasm. *"Found something!"* she sang smugly.

I turned disinterestedly towards her. This was not the first time the spirit wolf had returned thinking she'd found the perfect foe for me. "What is it this time?" I asked, covering another yawn with my hand.

"A dragon!"

I tried speaking, but only ended up sputtering. "A dragon," I gasped finally when I'd recovered. "Are you certain?"

"As sure as I can be without that analyze ability of yours," Ghost said, dancing around excitedly. *"It's big. Has wings and is on fire."*

"Breathes fire, you mean," I amended.

Ghost nodded. *"That too."*

I frowned. "How far away is it?"

"Not far," Ghost replied. *"Maybe a mile east."*

My frown deepened. I had maybe two hours left before I lost the cold sphere spell. It should be enough time, but... *a dragon?* Could I face such a foe?

"We better hurry, Prime," Ghost urged. *"Before it leaves."*

I sighed. "After you." At the very least, it was worth a look. After all, it was not every day that one got to see a dragon.

* * *

You have successfully stored the <u>cold sphere</u> spell in the ring, mage's surprise. You have fully restored your health, mana, and psi.

It was not a dragon.

But admittedly, I could understand how Ghost had mistaken the creature for one. The elite in the canyon below was half as large as the stone golems, possessed two colossal wings, clawed feet, a snaking tail, and an elongated face.

But its wings and tail were feathered, not scaled. It had two feet instead of four, a beak in place of a snout—and, as Ghost had said, it was on fire.

"A phoenix," I whispered in awe.

Ghost swung around to face me, her expression comically crestfallen. *"Not a dragon?"*

"Not a dragon," I confirmed, "but something just as spectacular."

From Ghost's disgruntled growl, I gathered she didn't agree. Ignoring the spirit wolf, I studied the elite. I was still on the plateau, stretched out flat on its smooth tabletop and looking down on Ghost's find.

The phoenix was curled around tight, resting its hooked beak on its tail feathers. With its eyes closed, the elite appeared to be sleeping. Tearing my gaze away from the reddish-gold creature, I studied the rest of the canyon. The stones and boulders in the vicinity bore scorch marks. Some glistened, too, as if they had been melted down and cooled again. All the phoenix's handiwork, I guessed.

It had been here a long time, I gathered.

"Are we going to kill it?" Ghost asked.

I eyed the avian doubtfully. As large as the phoenix was, there was no way the entirety of its body would fit within the cold sphere, but that should not be necessary. The harbinger had come under the sphere's effect the moment a tiny portion of its body had crossed the spell's rim, and the same should hold true for the phoenix.

If I teleported onto the phoenix's back, I could stab at it while it was slowed and unable to reach me with either its curved beak or clawed feet. The creature was clearly magical though, and likely had more than a few fire spells at its beck.

Not to mention it was wreathed in fire.

Would the cold sphere protect me against the flames?

I didn't know, but this was too good an opportunity to pass up. Ghost had been right. The phoenix was about as perfect a foe I would find against which to employ my cold sphere.

"Yes," I said at last. "I'll teleport onto its back, then attack with—"

"I rather you didn't."

I broke off.

"Who was that?" Ghost whispered.

I didn't answer. Except for me and Ghost, there was only one other mindglow in sight. Of their own accord, my eyes drifted to the phoenix and locked gazes with a single glistening orb of gold.

The open eye of the phoenix.

My foe was awake.

✳   ✳   ✳

I swallowed unhappily, caught for a moment between flight or fight.

"It's too late to run," the elite said, studying me from beneath a hooded gaze. *"Far too late."*

"Oww, it's the phoenix," Ghost exclaimed, seemingly ignorant of the threat in the burning bird's words. *"It can talk!"*

"Of course I can talk, dog. And it's 'he,' not 'it.'"

The spirit wolf drew up in affront. *"I'm a dire wolf,"* she snarled.

"Whatever," the phoenix yawned. *"Now shush and let the adults talk."* The huge creature popped open the other eye. *"Although, I'm not sure if your master can truly be described as one. How old are you, scion? Surely too young to be out from under your mother's skirts?"*

Ghost bristled at the insult, but I waved her to silence. In the wake of the phoenix's chatter, my nerves had quietened. The beast showed no sign of stirring from his rest, and despite his condescending tone, he seemed little inclined to violence—yet.

Even better, he spoke.

I don't know why that surprised me—after the dire wolves and the wyvern mother, sentient beasts were something I should be well-used to by now—but it did. And it changed the complexion of the encounter entirely, too.

In this dungeon, an unintelligent elite could never be anything other than my enemy. But a talking beast? *He* could be reasoned with, especially given that we shared a common enemy. Was there an opportunity here?

"You know what I am?" I asked carefully.

"Of course," the phoenix replied. *"Your beast Mark may be hidden, but I know the signs, and from the taste of your spirit, I can tell you bear a powerful Mark. Which House are you from?"*

I said nothing.

The phoenix laughed. *"Come, it's not so hard to figure out. As your companion has already so kindly pointed out, she is a dire wolf. That must make you a Wolf."*

"Then we are kin of sorts," I said, avoiding direct confirmation of his suspicions. "Maybe we can help each—"

"We are no kin, Wolf, and I don't need help from you," the phoenix replied, sounding amused.

I paused. "Then perhaps you can assist me. If you know who I am, you know my purpose. There are stygians in—"

"I am well aware," the phoenix interrupted again. *"The stygians don't concern me, however. Nor do I have any interest in resurrecting long-dead gods. I will not help you."*

I stared at the creature. "Then what do you want?" I asked bluntly.

The phoenix chuckled. *"So sure that I want something?"*

"You do," I said confidently. "Else why bother speaking to me in the first place?"

"Why indeed," the phoenix murmured. Tilting his head to the side, he seemed to consider this. *"Perhaps I am bored,"* he mused. *"Perhaps I wish only*

to find out if you are a worthy foe." Rising to his feet, the phoenix flared his wings, causing the air to spark with newly lit flames. "Now enough talking. To battle."

I scrambled upright, caught off-guard by the sudden shift in the elite's demeanor. Was he joking? "We're not enemies," I protested, backing away from the cliff's edge. "There's no need for us to fight."

"Oh, but there is," the phoenix replied. "There are no greater pleasures to be had in life than experiencing the joy of battle." He swayed dreamily, as if lost in the rapture of a memory. "Believe me, I've lived long enough to know."

I stared at the phoenix disbelievingly. Was he mad? It certainly sounded like it.

Ghost's eyes jumped from the elite to me, then back again. Upright and with his wings outstretched, the phoenix was a damn sight more intimidating. "Perhaps this was a mistake, Prime. Maybe we should retreat."

"I'd love to," I muttered, even while I began drawing energy to cast my buffs, "but I don't think *he* is going to let us."

The phoenix laughed, not missing the byplay. "Definitely not. I haven't fought a scion in..." He cocked his head to the side, thinking. "You know, it's been so long, I can't even remember. This should be entertaining!"

I had to keep the phoenix talking, if only until my buffs were in place. "You want to fight for... the uhm, fun of it?"

"Yes!"

You have cast load controller.

"But you could die," I said, pointing out the obvious. Although it was more likely that I would.

"You don't know much about phoenixes, do you?"

"I don't," I admitted and cast the next buff.

You have cast heightened reflexes.

"You are more ignorant than I expected, Wolf," the avian scoffed. "My kind are immortal. Kill me, and I will only be reborn in the ashes of my aviary."

"And where is that?" I asked automatically.

You have trigger-cast quick mend.

"In a sector far away from here," the phoenix replied smugly. "So you see, win or lose, I still win. Kill me, and I escape this wretched dungeon. If you die, on the other hand—a far more probable outcome, I may add—well then, at least I would have gained a brief moment of enjoyment in what has otherwise been a dreadfully boring incarnation."

You have cast fade.

"And what about me?" I asked. "What if I die? Will you kill an innocent without qualms—just for the fun of it?"

"What about you?" the phoenix repeated. "You may not be immortal, but you are a player, are you not? You have lives aplenty."

I had no answer to that. "I see," I murmured as my final buff fell into place.

You have cast piercing strike.

"Then I have only one more question for you. Before we begin, will you allow me to analyze you?"

"Go ahead," the phoenix said magnanimously. *"Where is the fun in fighting a foe whose power you do not comprehend? Inspect me and behold the true might of what you face."*

Wasting no more time, I reached out to inspect the avian with my will.

The target is Sunfury, a level 231 mature phoenix.

Phoenixes are undying creatures. Eternal and ever reborn. No phoenix is truly dead until their aviary has been destroyed and their sacred ashes scattered.

Like many elder species, phoenixes have few vulnerabilities. Their minds are strong, their bodies more so, and their command of fire is unrivaled. It is not unheard of for the firebirds to pit themselves against dragons and emerge victorious. They do, however, have one glaring weakness: cold. Most will do their utmost to avoid its touch.

My gaze narrowed.

The elite was more dangerous than anything else I'd faced thus far in the dungeon, but Sunfury was not so powerful that I didn't think I could slay him—especially given my secret weapon. Thankfully, during my conversation with Ghost, which it was clear the phoenix had overheard entirely, I had not made mention of the cold sphere spell.

Should I mention the spell? I wondered.

Would the phoenix be as eager to fight if I did? Would it cause Sunfury to back down?

I doubted it. As arrogant as the elite seemed, I suspected he would only consider the challenge all the greater and still believe himself able to overcome me. *Why warn him needlessly?* I thought, smiling tightly.

There was one final preparation I needed to make. Unsheathing my stygian shortsword, I dropped it onto the ground and replaced it with faithful.

You have equipped the sword faithful blade, increasing the damage you deal with your offhand by +40%.

"I'm done," I said, addressing Sunfury again. "Thank you."

"Good. Then shall we?"

"As you wish," I replied. I glanced sideways at Ghost. "Keep an eye out for the stygians."

Then, drawing ebonheart, I blinked into the canyon.

CHAPTER 325: A DANCE OF FIRE AND ICE

You have teleported into Sunfury's shadow.

I stepped out of the aether and directly onto the phoenix to be immediately assailed by flames.

You have failed a magical resistance check! You are <u>burning</u>.
Your void armor has reduced the elemental damage incurred by 40%.

I ignored the heat.

The flames rolling off the phoenix's body rose no more than knee-height and my void armor had already seen to it that much of their effect was blunted. Digging my boot heels into the phoenix's upper torso, I reached down and grabbed a tuft of his feathers in my left hand.

My wayfarer's boots and gloves were another thing I had to be thankful for. Both were impervious to damage. Anchored in place, I raised ebonheart and flicked my gaze upwards to measure my foe's response.

Sunfury's head was already snaking around.

If my sudden appearance atop him had caught the phoenix off guard, he was disguising his surprise well. But in letting me so close, Sunfury had made a fatal error—or so I hoped. Reaching into the ring on my right hand, I released the spell stored within.

You have trigger-cast cold sphere.
Sunfury has critically failed a magical resistance check! 1 of 1 targets have been <u>chilled</u>.

Despite his vulnerability to cold, Sunfury was not frozen.

That would have made for a short battle. Still, I was not about to complain. My foe had been slowed to half-speed. Even better, the cold sphere was having another unexpected, but welcome, effect.

Sunfury's aura of soothing flames has been extinguished. You are no longer <u>burning</u>.

In an instant, the flames licking the phoenix's form cooled, leaving me free of flames. Raising my eyes, I met my foes' twin blazing orbs. They drew steadily closer, if no longer at a pace that offered threat, and presently, they were widened in shock.

I *had* surprised Sunfury.

The phoenix's amazement did not last though. *"Excellent ploy, Wolf,"* he said a split-second later. Clearly, the chilling effect of my cold sphere had done nothing to slow my foe's thoughts. His mindvoice sounded natural and was devoid of fear or even anger. If anything, Sunfury appeared... delighted.

"Crazy phoenix," I muttered. I'd stolen the upper hand in the encounter and, still holding out hope for an amicable solution, saw no reason not to

indulge in further conversation. Sunfury was more valuable to me alive than dead. *"And it's Michael, not Wolf,"* I added.

Sunfury's beak—opening in increments—advanced closer. He'd not aborted his attack. Raising ebonheart, I held it aloft and pointed downward in naked threat. *"I told you we don't have to fight. Shall we stop this?"*

The phoenix's laughter rang loudly through my mind. *"We shall not. Not for my life's sake nor your own."* He paused. *"We fight to the death."*

I shrugged. *"Have it your way,"* I replied, and brought ebonheart crashing down.

The phoenix's feathers were not like any ordinary bird's. They gleamed red-gold and bore a distinctly metallic hue. But as hard as they were, ebonheart was forged of sterner stuff, and broke through after only a momentary pause.

You have injured Sunfury.

The black blade sank satisfactorily deep, all the way to the hilt.

But as large as my foe was, I could not tell if the damage was more than skin deep. Yanking out ebonheart, I inspected the wound. Blood oozed out in copious amounts. Not even a second later, though, the red rivulets dried out as the wound cauterized itself from the inside. It seemed that while the phoenix's flames were subdued, they were far from quenched.

I grimaced. I'd been hoping to inflict greater damage.

"Not what you were expecting?" Sunfury asked with unmistakable mirth and his beak almost fully opened.

In response, I rammed ebonheart downwards again.

You have injured Sunfury.

"Now, that was uncalled for. My turn."

Warned by the phoenix's words, I jerked my head up. Flames were growing inside his throat, ready to spill out of his open beak.

Eyes widening, I released my hold on Sunfury's feathers and threw myself flat against him. Bereft of my anchor, I slid down his torso, and out of the way of the newborn inferno he was about to unleash.

Sunfury has cast fiery breath. You have evaded your foe's attack.
Sunfury has hit himself with fiery breath. Your foe is <u>burning</u>. Duration: 5 seconds. Note, fire of all forms will heal a phoenix.

Urgh. Another self-healing foe.

I would have to damage Sunfury a lot faster if I wished to win the encounter. Scissoring open my legs, I pressed down tightly with the inside of my thighs against the phoenix. My descent halted and I sat up, secured in place once more.

Drawing faithful, I empowered my arms with stamina and stabbed downwards in a frenzy of motion.

You have cast whirlwind, increasing your attack speed by 100% for 3 seconds.
You have injured Sunfury. You have grazed Sunfury.
You have injured Sunfury. You have grazed Sunfury.

...
...

In out. In out. My arms swinging in tandem, I stabbed downward first with ebonheart, then with faithful. Over and over, I sank my blades into my foe, burying ebonheart hilt-deep every time. Faithful's wounds were shallower but still inflicted damage, and I kept striking with it, too.

Sunfury had no more to say.

He was either too pain riddled to mock me further or was finally taking the fight seriously. But that the phoenix was silent did not mean he hadn't reacted.

Tucking his head into his chest, the phoenix began furling his wings. As slowed as he was, Sunfury was not going to complete his maneuver in a hurry. Frowning, I kept hacking. What was Sunfury up to? Not for a second did I believe he was huddling in fear.

It was almost as if the phoenix was shielding himself from an expectant blow, one massive enough to cause even the colossal avian to seek shelter. *Is he casting a spell? But what spell could—*

Sunfury has cast supernova.

Flames flashed.

Fire blossomed.

And in the next instant, Sunfury transformed into a living bonfire. Heat and energy exploded outwards from the inferno—throwing me clear.

Sunfury has critically injured you!
Void armor charge remaining: 51%. Your health has decreased to 24%.
Quick mend triggered, restoring 20% of your health!

Flung off the phoenix, I sailed through the air, arms and legs flailing. Even within the protective bubble of my cold sphere, the heat was excruciating, but I retained enough presence of mind to weave psi.

My perspective was too skewed to get a lock on the ground, but I didn't need to see to know I was heading for a jarring and possibly fatal impact. Opening my mindsight, I searched for Sunfury.

But the phoenix was gone.

He, too, I suspected had been tossed aside by the explosion. Although I had no doubt he was weathering its effects better. *Well, that's one way to disengage.* Whatever the case, the phoenix was out of range of my senses. But another mindglow danced near the edges of my mind.

Ghost.

Completing my spell in a rush, I blinked to her.

You have teleported to Ghost.

I emerged from the aether in a tangle of splayed limbs, increasing my tally of cuts and bruises. I had no time to attend to them, though, nor my more serious burns. Limping back to my feet, I whipped my head around in search of Sunfury. "Where is he?" I rasped.

"Above us," Ghost replied.

I craned my neck backwards and, sure enough, saw the phoenix circling high overhead—well out of range of shadow blink.

"Had enough, have you?" I shouted.

Sunfury chuckled. *"Far from it. But I've decided I much prefer you at arm's length."*

"Don't tell me you're scared?" I goaded.

"Not at all," he replied. *"By the by, that was an interesting spell. I didn't mark you as a magic user. How did you cast it?*

"If you come down, I'll tell you," I said.

Sunfury laughed mockingly but did not deign to respond otherwise. Closing his wings, he dropped into a dive.

My lips turned down. The phoenix had begun an attack run. Had my taunts worked? Come to think of it, what had I been thinking, provoking him like that? It would have been wiser to flee.

"Shouldn't we run?" Ghost asked.

Even though I'd been contemplating the very same thing a moment ago, I bared my teeth in refusal. The wolf did not flee from a fight he was winning.

"No," I said, biting off each word, "he wants a fight; I'll give him one." Reaching out with my will, I inspected the descending phoenix.

The target is Sunfury. He is severely injured.

The Game's response was heartening.

I'd inflicted a significant amount of damage on the phoenix, but freed of the frigid touch of my cold sphere, the flames across his body had reignited, and even now I suspected he was healing.

If I hoped to win the battle, I would have to put an end to that.

The phoenix dropped to three hundred feet. Sheathing my blades, I crouched down and summoned psi. The moment Sunfury crossed into range, I would blink onto him and finish what I had started.

Sadly, my foe did not oblige.

At two hundred feet, the phoenix pulled out of his dive and opened his beak. Not waiting to see what would spill forth this time, I flung myself to the left.

Sunfury has cast heaven's fury.

A jet of concentrated fire boiled downwards. My quick thinking saved me, though, and I rolled back to my feet a few yards away—unharmed and untouched.

You have evaded Sunfury's attack.

My stomach queasy, I studied the once-solid patch of ground I'd so recently occupied. The white-hot bar of flames had turned the rock into a liquid, bubbling mess.

"Nice dodge," Sunfury commented, as he glided away on outstretched wings. The phoenix was already banking, and I knew he was going to circle back for a second go.

Sunfury was being chatty again, evidence enough that he believed he'd regained the upper hand—and he wasn't wrong. I ground my teeth in frustration. I'd lost the initiative.

As long as Sunfury hung back, there was little I could do to harm him with my swords or the cold sphere. I needed to draw him closer again. But first, I had to see how much the phoenix had recovered. Reaching out with my will, I analyzed Sunfury again.

The target is Sunfury. He is moderately injured.

Damn. The Game's feedback was hardly precise, but still served to confirm the phoenix was healing at an appreciable rate. I couldn't allow that to continue.

Time to change tactics. Letting the sphere spell lapse, I summoned psi.

You have deactivated a cold sphere.
You have cast slaysight.

Fixing my gaze on the flying elite, I sent strands of my will surging forward. They slipped easily past my foe's outer defenses.

Only to be summarily cut thereafter.

Sunfury is immune to mental manipulation! You have failed to sleep your target. Your mental intrusion has been detected!

"Ah, so you're more than a simple brawler," Sunfury said as he glided closer. *"You're a psionic too. Interesting."* Not waiting for my response, the phoenix went on smugly, *"But alas, you'll find your charms of no use against me."*

"We'll see," I replied tightly. The Game alert had said the phoenix was immune to mental manipulation—not *all* forms of mental assaults. Drawing psi again, I summoned two ethereal daggers into being.

You have cast astral blades.

The moment the violet psi daggers manifested, I cocked back my arms, took aim, and threw.

More than a few hundred feet separated me from my target—too far for any normal dagger to be thrown with accuracy, but the psi weapons were not 'real.' They lacked mass and were unaffected by gravity.

Once flung, they continued unerringly on their given course. And while Sunfury was a good way off, his trajectory was predictable and my aim true.

You have injured Sunfury.

"Ha! Got you!" I couldn't help but exclaim as both my blades hit their targets squarely.

"They're scratches, no more," Sunfury scoffed. But was that a hint of tightness I sensed in his tone?

"A scratch can kill as easily as a blade through the heart," I replied mildly. Drawing back my arms, I manifested two more psi daggers. *"Especially when struck by an endless tide of them,"* I added, hands flying forward to release the astral blades.

You have injured Sunfury.

"Pinpricks!" the phoenix jeered and dropped into another attacking dive.

I turned to Ghost, a command ready on the tip of my tongue, but before the words could emerge, she raced away in anticipation of the order. *"Repositioning,"* she called out.

Shaking my head ruefully at how fast the spirit wolf was learning, I turned back to the onrushing phoenix. Diving, Sunfury was an unmissable target, and I didn't miss the opportunity to riddle him with psi daggers.

You have injured Sunfury.
You have injured Sunfury.

...

The phoenix reached two hundred feet, and once more, pulled out of his dive. Flaring his wings and flapping them powerfully backwards, he brought himself to a wrenching stop. I kept hitting him with the astral blades, utilizing every second to maximize the damage I was inflicting.

Sunfury opened his beak.

Tensing, I readied myself. *Here it comes.*

Sunfury has cast fan of flames.

Hovering midair, the phoenix opened his beak and spewed out fire. But what emerged was not a single, white-hot bar of fire. Rather, it was a cone of destruction. Rapidly spreading, wild, uncontained.

And impossible to dodge with physical maneuvers alone.

It was too bad for the phoenix that I'd anticipated him—not the exact form his attack would take, but that he *would* change tactics—and had prepared accordingly. Before the first tongues of flames could hit the ground, I stepped through the aether and out again by Ghost's side, neatly sidestepping the spell.

You have evaded Sunfury's attack.

Fifty yards away from the boiling flames, I spun around and flung another volley of daggers at my stationary target.

You have injured Sunfury.

"Wha-?"

It took the phoenix a moment to realize I'd escaped the inferno. Flapping his wings, he turned around ungainly.

The lumbering maneuver caught me by surprise for a moment, then I realized that a creature the phoenix's size was not designed for hovering or sharp turns mid-air. *It must be taking a lot out of him.*

I smiled. Perhaps even without my cold sphere, the contest was not as one-sided as I feared. I flung another pair of daggers at Sunfury, then three more in quick succession.

All hit their targets squarely.

Across the distance separating us, Sunfury glared at me. Ghost had already raced away again, and the phoenix seemed to realize that trading blows with me from up above was a losing proposition. He might be able to stay out of the reach of my swords that way, but he was going to have a darn hard time hitting me with anything while airborne. *"I can do this all day,"* I mocked, to drive the point home.

"That hardly seems fair," Sunfury sniffed.

"When is battle ever fair," I retorted.

Sunfury said nothing for a moment, and I knew he was pondering his next move. The phoenix did not seem the type to goad easily, nor one to stick with a losing tactic.

True to expectations, Sunfury stretched out his wings and glided away. Not wasting the opportunity, I flung more blades his way. Treating the daggers like the pinpricks he claimed they were, the phoenix ignored the attacks.

He completed one circle around me, then another and another, flapping his wings every so often so that he spiraled ever upwards with each turning.

I lowered my hands. There was no point throwing my daggers anymore. Sunfury was so high that even the ethereal blades had no chance of striking him.

"What is he doing?" Ghost asked.

"Building altitude," I replied.

"Why?" she asked, puzzled.

"I have no idea," I replied honestly. Putting the lull in the battle to good use, I renewed my defenses and recast my buffs.

You have cast heightened reflexes, load controller, fade, and trigger-cast quick mend. You have successfully stored the <u>cold sphere</u> spell in the ring, mage's surprise.

Then, eyes narrowed, I watched the phoenix. He was little more than a distant speck now and even my enhanced sight struggled to make out any details. Still, I did not fail to note when he stopped spiraling.

Snapping his wings closed, Sunfury dropped like a stone.

The phoenix was high enough that it would take more than a dozen seconds for him to reach ground level again. Would he pull out of his dive again at the last minute?

But what point would that serve?

I would only harass him with my astral blades again. And Sunfury had to know that. He had something else in mind. But what?

He's not stopping this time. It was the only thing that made sense. Sunfury meant to follow through, striking the ground with the force of a small meteor.

The realization hit fast, and my pulse quickened. As rapidly as the phoenix was dropping, the impact would be catastrophic. The whole canyon could be torn apart—and me with it.

Teleporting onto Sunfury would make no difference. Nor would casting cold sphere. He was in freefall and it was not his own movements that needed slowing. How the phoenix intended on surviving the impact I had no idea, but I was sure *I* wouldn't—not if I was anywhere near its epicenter.

I have to get out of the canyon.

Dropping my head, I sprinted towards the nearest cliff wall. "Back to the plateau," I yelled to Ghost while I spun psi. "Quickly!" Not slowing my flight or stopping my casting, I reached into my backpack.

You have equipped a set of cat claws.

The rock wall was about fifteen yards away and my spell was ready. *Close enough*, I decided and manifested a windslide.

You have cast windborne.

I started the ramp of air a yard from my position and angled it sharply upward. My pounding feet carried me directly onto my creation and I rocketed up at an even quicker pace. Crouching down, I raised my hands and fixed my gaze on the onrushing cliff. I could afford no mistakes now.

Reaching the end of the ramp I leaped, springing off coiled legs to throw myself even higher.

I bridged the gap of empty space easily and crashed into the cliff wall with an audible thud. Paying my body's aches no mind, I pressed my clawed hands deep into the stone.

I fell a foot before they gripped.

As I was yanked to a halt, I risked a glance around. On my left, Ghost was already floating upwards. Soon, she would overtake my own position. Behind me, Sunfury plummeted downwards. Time was running out quickly.

Extending my right arm, I dug a clawed hand into the rock and pulled my body upwards, then I did the same with my left, scrambling up the cliff at the fastest pace I could manage. Ghost rushed past me, and still climbing, I silently urged her on.

Flames roared at my back.

Stealing another glance over my shoulder, I saw a super-heated jet of heat rushing downward from Sunfury's open beak into the ground directly beneath. Rocks caught alight, stone melted, and flames flowed.

A magma pool was forming.

So that's how he means to survive. I'd seen enough. Wrenching my head around, I kept at my desperate scramble. Ghost was nearly at the top. *C'mon, just a little—*

Sunfury has cast meteor dive.
Sunfury has critically injured himself!
Sunfury's impact has triggered an earthquake.

It was too late. The canyon's destruction had begun.

CHAPTER 326: MAELSTROM OF DESTRUCTION

The rock under my hands trembled, only slightly at first, then more violently. A boulder fell from above, passing scant inches from my face.

"Prime!" Ghost screamed.

"Keep going!" I shouted and reached upward with my right hand.

A jagged scar ripped across the rockface, and the entire cliff shifted, leaning inwards.

Uh-oh. I wasn't going to make it.

A huge chunk of stone, as large as two golems, broke off from the plateau and plummeted downwards. Making a split-second decision, I let go of the cliff and leaped onto the falling chunk.

It was a ludicrous maneuver and one almost certain to result in my death. But I had no good choices left. Clinging onto the cliff in the fast-fading hope that Ghost would reach the top before it fell was just as foolhardy.

In truth, I was likely dead already.

But the will to live was strong, and I would not give up until my last breath.

I made the jump easily. Landing on the falling piece of mountain, I scuttled across on all fours. My stone carriage would land soon and when it did, it would shatter into a thousand shards. Before that happened, I had to fly free.

Reaching the far end of the chunk, I spun psi and leaped again, making the jump blindly. Beneath me the ground bucked and heaved, rocks blew apart, and new chasms formed by the second.

You have cast windborne.

In freefall, I formed a ramp of air beneath my feet, and pointed it not towards the now-unsafe cliff walls, but at the bubbling magma in the canyon's center. Sunfury was there. And one way or the other, I had to bring the fight to an end.

Zipping along the windslide—and for once wishing I could traverse it slower—I glanced down. I hung about ten yards off the ground and was a fair distance still from the phoenix. There was no helping it. To reach the lava where Sunfury sheltered, I would have to make my way across the heaving earth.

Arriving at the end of the air ramp, I threw myself off.

You have injured yourself.

I landed heavily. And the ground did me no favors either, splitting apart anew beneath me and showering me with rubble.

A rock has injured you!
A rock has injured you!

...

Protecting my face with my hands, I searched for a safe path through the madness. There was none to be had. I couldn't stay put, though, and I forged ahead anyway.

A chasm yawned before me.

I leaped, relying on my agility to see me over. Legs pumping, I arced across the gap of empty air. Reaching the pinnacle of my jump, I descended.

But before I dropped too far, my searching feet found solid ground underfoot and I transitioned into a flat-out run.

A jagged stone shard clipped my right shoulder. Another my left. A third struck my temple.

You have been knocked down!

Bloodied and reeling from the triple strike, I staggered and fell. Beneath me, the ground rolled like an angry wave. The earth's heaving was about to get worse, I sensed. A lot worse.

I had to be gone before that.

Dizzy and with my vision blurred by splotchy patches, I climbed back to my feet. Turning about unsteadily, I spotted the bubbling magma to my left. It was still out of range, though. *Too far. Too damn far.* Ignoring the voice of pessimism, I gritted my teeth and resumed running.

Lava fountained upwards. Earth caved in. Boulders hit the ground.

Obstacles appeared apace, but with my gaze fixed on my target, I navigated past each with grim determination.

Then, the ground underfoot exploded.

A few dozen tons of earth and stone were hurled aloft, and me with them. A wretched passenger, I could do naught but let the explosion take me where it willed. Tucking in my limbs, I ducked my chin into my chest to wait it out. Windborne was not ready, and shadow blink had no target.

The storm of earth and rock carried me higher still. I had to have climbed more than twenty yards already. The fall, when it inevitably arrived, would be more than bone-jarring. *This is it,* I thought. *There will be no coming back from—*

A mindglow crossed the rim of my mindsight.

Sunfury.

Grasping onto the phoenix's mind like a lifeline, I spun psi. The explosion's momentum expired, and my course reversed. My fall had begun. But that was no longer of concern. My spell completed, and I stepped through the aether without hesitation.

You have teleported 49 yards to Sunfury.

I emerged on the phoenix's back, the tip of my boots dangling only a few feet from the bubbling lava pool in which he sat. The tremors here were milder, and after experiencing the violent eruptions elsewhere in the canyon, my mind was almost tricked into believing the pool to be calm. The ground continued to heave, but at the epicenter of the quake, it seemed like the worst was already over.

It was still blistering hot, though.

But I had a cure for that, and before the heat's touch could make itself known, I used spellhold.

You have trigger-cast cold sphere.
Sunfury has been <u>chilled,</u> and his aura of soothing flames extinguished.

The phoenix yanked his head out of the lava pool, finally sensing my presence. *"Wh...at? H-how?"* For a wonder, Sunfury's mindvoice was absent amusement, and he seemed in nearly as bad a state as I was. His dive, I suspected, had been a last-ditch effort.

I chuckled hollowly. *"Wolves are hard to kill; you should know that."* Unsheathing my swords, I plunged them downward.

You have injured Sunfury.

I drew both blades free in a rush and held myself still and ready. How would Sunfury counterattack this time?

The phoenix's only response was to bury his head in the lava again.

Clenching my swords in a white-knuckled grip, I waited. I was at the very ragged edge of my limits, and it was more than likely I would not survive whatever counter Sunfury planned. Still, I intended on fighting to the very end.

"Well... fought... scion."

The words floated into my mind slowly, as if merely voicing them took effort.

I blinked, momentarily confused. Was Sunfury saying farewell before he dealt his death stroke? But no, there was no triumph in the phoenix's tone. If anything, his mindvoice tasted of ash. And defeat.

He's given up.

I lowered my swords in the wake of the realization. There was a finality to Sunfury's utterance that made me certain it was no last-minute ploy or trick. *"You too,"* I replied at last.

"Fin-ish... it," Sunfury said.

I said nothing for a moment. *"It doesn't have to end this way,"* I said. *"I told you: we're not enemies."*

"That... may be, but I w-welcome death. You... will be... doing me a favor. I've been trapped in this dungeon... a long time. Free my spirit... I return to my aviary."

Still, I didn't strike. *"But if you remain, we could work together—"*

"No! I am... sorry, scion. You mean well... but I can't. Stay your hand and... I will do my damnedest to kill you. End it. Now."

I sighed. Even on the brink of death, Sunfury remained obstinate. *"Very well,"* I said and raised my blades. Bringing them down more reluctantly than I ever had, I struck the phoenix anew.

You have injured Sunfury.

Surprisingly, the phoenix survived the twin blows. He was tougher than I'd ever imagined. I didn't try to speak to him again, though. Respecting his final wishes, I prepared to strike again.

A Game message unfurled in my mind.

You have acquired a new spirit signature: the Mark of the Phoenix!

You have defeated a mature phoenix, a powerful fighter amongst the firebirds of the Kingdom, and he has acknowledged your merit, granting you the title of <u>Worthy Adversary</u>.

Any phoenix who beholds your Mark will be more kindly disposed to you than they ordinarily would be. Note, only firebirds can see your new spirit signature.

I halted my attack. *"What was that for?"* I asked, having no doubt as to the source of my new Mark.

"A... reward for a battle well-fought... and my freedom. When I breathe my last... make sure to take the c-central feather of my crest... you will know it w-when you see it. Consider it... a parting gift."

"Thank you," I said, not knowing what else to say. Bringing my blades down, I struck again.

You have killed Sunfury.

"Goodbye," I whispered. *"May you find peace."* I paused, considering what I knew of the phoenix. *"And an endless litany of battles,"* I amended.

✳ ✳ ✳

Long minutes after Sunfury's death, the canyon's heaving finally quietened.

Staying where I was atop the corpse, I waited it out. Beneath me the phoenix's body slowly sank. Now that Sunfury was dead, whatever magic that had prevented the lava from eating away at his flesh had fled and the smell of charred and burning meat filled the air.

I saw no sign of the feather Sunfury had mentioned—perhaps the flames had claimed it already—and with a shrug, I lay down a ramp of air and slid to safety on the solid ground beyond.

Sitting down cross-legged I turned my focus inwards and examined the results of the battle.

You have reached level 170 and rank 17!
For achieving rank 17, you have been awarded 1 additional attribute point.
Your two-weapon fighting has reached rank 13.
Your telekinesis and telepathy have reached rank 14.

My feelings about the battle's outcome were mixed.

I'd killed my adversary, true, but I still felt like I'd lost more than I'd gained. What I told Sunfury was true. He had not been my enemy, and if only he'd been inclined towards a less final end, I was sure he could have made for a powerful ally. With the phoenix by my side, defeating even the harbinger would have been possible.

I sighed. Still, what was done was done, and it was not like I'd come away empty-handed from the encounter. I'd gained three levels, four attribute points, and ranked up three of my skills. Not a bad outcome by any means.

Closing my eyes, I attended to my injuries and restored my defenses to working order.

You have fully restored your health, mana, and psi.
You have successfully stored the <u>cold sphere</u> spell in the ring, mage's surprise.

Sadly, my time knowing the stolen spell was nearly up. But thanks to spellhold, I would indefinitely retain one more instance of the casting. I would have to make certain to choose the moment of its next use carefully.

Lastly, I invested my new attribute points.

Your Magic has increased to rank 28. Other modifiers: +14 from items.

Witnessing the changes to my mana pool, I nodded in satisfaction. It had grown to the point where I felt further investment in Magic unnecessary, allowing me to refocus on the development of my Mind and Dexterity attributes.

"You killed him!" Ghost said, approaching from behind.

I glanced over my shoulder at her. "Don't sound so surprised," I said with a smile.

"I always knew you could," Ghost objected. *"I just didn't think you would go through with it."*

I raised one eyebrow. "Oh? Why's that?"

Ghost dipped her head in a lupine version of a shrug. *"You liked him."*

I opened my mouth, then closed it, shaking my head. Once more, Ghost displayed an uncanny knack for knowing my own mind better than I sometimes did. What she said was true. I had liked the phoenix, seeing in him something of a kindred spirit, and I regretted being forced to kill him.

Perhaps our paths will cross again, I thought, thinking about Sunfury's mention of an aviary.

Now though, it was time to move on.

Rising to my feet, I turned about in a slow circle. Behind me, the lava still bubbled, but the rest of the canyon had settled down—for all that it resembled an overwrought child's wrecked playpen.

"Did you see a loot chest anywhere?" I asked, frowning.

Ghost shook her head. *"No, and I made sure to look before rejoining you."*

My lips turned down. "That's a pity." Glancing around again, I looked for a place to camp. The canyon was likely unstable but that suited me just fine. Any foes that approached would not be able to do so soundlessly.

Spotting a shadowed crack in the ground that didn't seem too deep, I waved Ghost over. "Come, I think we have time for a few more lessons before I turn in for the night."

Chapter 327: Gifts of the Flame

You have slept 8 hours. Stamina, mana, and psi reserves have been fully restored.

I awoke early the next day. The night had passed undisturbed, and I was rested and refreshed. Yawning, I made my way to the entrance of my hidey-hole.

"All quiet?" I asked Ghost who sat guard there.

"All quiet," she agreed.

"Then let's get out of here." While Ghost floated upwards to the canyon floor I flexed my limbs, loosening them for the day's expected exertions. Today, I didn't plan on stopping until I reached the campfires in the north, and I estimated getting there was going to take the better part of the day.

Glancing upward, I saw Ghost was in position. Drawing psi, I blinked to her. The spirit wolf trotted off northwards, knowing our destination already.

"One second, Ghost."

Stopping, she glanced questioningly over her shoulder at me.

"Before we get going, there's something I need to check first." Turning about, I headed south. There was only one spot in the crater that Ghost and I hadn't searched for a loot chest yesterday—the crater left in the wake of Sunfury's cataclysmic dive.

Last night, it had been brimming with lava. Today, I was hoping things would be different.

Sure enough, when I neared the bowl-shaped hole, I found it empty of magma and flames. They had likely cooled overnight or leaked back into the earth.

That was not to say the crater was empty, though.

Sitting squarely in its center was a gold loot chest. And atop that was what looked remarkably like a phoenix feather.

Grinning in excitement, I dropped into the crater and rushed over to examine the waiting contents. First, I inspected the feather. It was about two feet in length and had a long central shaft that was light and flexible. The reddish-gold veins were at one time tough as steel and as soft as duck down.

"A magical feather indeed," I murmured, analyzing the item with my will.

The target is the rank 6 soulbound artifact: <u>phoenix's feather</u>. It is a mythical crafting ingredient that only the most skilled of enchanters can work with. Any item forged from the feather will be soulbound. Its other properties, however, will only be revealed thereafter.

Phoenix feathers can only be bequeathed, never looted. For this reason, they are nearly impossible to attain, and once taken up, will remain with the player even after death. With careful encouragement and magical manipulation, the artifact can be made to take the shape of a variety of

items, from a bow to a sword, from a vambrace to a glove, or from a buckler to an amulet.

The choice is yours.

"Wow," I exclaimed, awed by Sunfury's generosity. His gift was beyond anything I'd expected.

"Is that the phoenix's feather?" Ghost asked.

I nodded, not tearing my gaze away from the golden-hued object.

"Is it any good?"

"Better than good," I murmured. The feather's potential uses were limitless, but I already knew what I wanted to do with Sunfury's gift.

It was the perfect size for a shortsword. First though, I would have to find a suitable crafter. Reverently, I picked up the golden object.

You have acquired a phoenix's feather. This rank 6 artifact is only usable by the player Michael. Do you wish to soul-bind this item?

I replied in the affirmative and felt new bonds slip into place between the feather and myself.

You have soulbound a phoenix's feather. From this point onwards, this artifact cannot be stolen, lost, or kept from your hands except by the strongest of enchantments.

Stowing away the feather, I turned to the loot chest, feeling my anticipation rise as I flipped open the lid and peered inside.

There were four items, and I wasted no time in inspecting each.

The target is a piece of enchanted mosaic.

The target is an upgrade gem and allows you to improve any ability by a single tier.

The target is a greater attribute gem. It grants you 3 attribute points.

The target is the rank 5 longbow: quaker. It increases the damage you deal by 50%. Additionally, all arrows fired from this bow will bear the enchantment: paralyzing touch. Any target hit that fails a physical resistance check is stunned for 3 seconds. This item requires a minimum Perception of 20 to wield.

I sighed.

It was not that the chest's loot was not good—far from it—it was just that none of the items were on par with Sunfury's gift. *Too rich for rank five loot now, are we, eh?* I thought, poking fun at my reaction.

Shaking my head ruefully, I picked up the attribute gem, simultaneously activating the item and investing the new points.

You have gained 3 attribute points.
Your Mind has increased to rank 77. Other modifiers: +4 from items.

After a cursory study, I packed away the enchanted mosaic. Like the other one of its kind I'd found, it was an irregularly shaped stone tile with indecipherably scribblings and was identified by the Game as being another piece of the Emblem of the Reach. As yet, I had no sense yet of how many parts I would need to complete the Emblem.

The longbow I barely inspected. I couldn't use it and would either sell it or give it away.

Finally, I turned to the last item: the upgrade gem. The item would be used to advance one of my rarer abilities, and while I had more than a few of those, none were ready yet to progress to tier four.

But fade soon would be.

My sneaking skill was just three points short of reaching rank fifteen. Sure, my fade ability was still new—and unproven—but the invisibility it promised at tier five made advancing it more important than even my scion abilities.

Fade it will be, I decided, storing away the upgrade gem. Rising to my feet, I reoriented myself.

"Time to go," I said and climbed out of the canyon.

✳ ✳ ✳

The journey north took as long as I feared.

Most of the day passed with me and Ghost working our way across the plateau, ever skirting the nether fog banks and never dipping into the chasms and canyons, no matter how enticing some of the elite foes below appeared.

We kept our eyes peeled for signs of the harbinger and other winged stygians but didn't spot any nether creatures. Deciding to put the time to good use, I resumed Ghost's training. The spirit wolf was coming along nicely, and soon I expected she would be casting the astral blade spell on her own.

I was a bit concerned about what that would mean, though.

Except for her mind shield, Ghost lacked any real defenses. Her greatest protection had always been her invisibility—the fact that others did not realize she was around.

But if Ghost started launching spelled attacks, even the most thick-headed of foes would eventually realize they had an invisible enemy nearby, and once they knew to look for her, how many would be able to find her?

The possibility worried me.

I knew from my own experience in the Wolf mind trials that a damaged spirit was hard—if not impossible—to repair without a body. I didn't look forward to explaining any of this to Ghost either. I knew she would rebel against the notion of *not* acting, of doing nothing, in order to stay safe.

But despite my concerns, I wasn't going to shelter Ghost—even from herself.

I would not withhold knowledge from her. If the spirit wolf wanted to learn, I would train her. But I also would strive to teach her caution too. Hopefully, she learned enough of the latter to make a difference.

Beset by my worries—not just for Ghost but about the dungeon, the nether, the Pack, Safyre, and the twins too—the hours flew by and, in what seemed like no time at all, afternoon arrived. With it, the gorge that was our destination came into view, finally creeping over the horizon.

Almost immediately, I could tell I'd been wrong about the distant fires. They weren't ordinary campfires, but a dense grouping of smaller lights.

So dense that the settlement housing them could be nothing short of a city.

"A city in a dungeon," I muttered, marveling at the idea. The Endless Dungeon was said to house entire civilizations in its depths, but this was the first I'd run across any sign of such.

I wondered what sort of people would live in a dungeon like Draven's Reach. Were they giants? Probably. How else could they fend off the dungeon's colossal denizens?

"Is that where we are going?" Ghost asked, peering at the gorge.

I nodded absently.

"Will you be safe there?"

"Doubtful," I replied.

Ghost wrinkled her nose. *"Then I don't understand why we're heading there,"* she complained.

"For information, primarily." I glanced at her. "If we're fortunate, the city's inhabitants can provide us valuable information on the void, and perhaps about the elites too. And if we're very lucky, they might even tell us where the exit portal is."

"And if we're not... lucky?"

"Then they might try to kill me," I replied grimly.

My response did nothing to assuage the worry in the spirit wolf's eyes. Her concern sparked my own wariness. Experience had taught me to approach other people—whether they were players or not—with caution. "That reminds me." Setting my pack down I sat down cross-legged.

"What are you doing?" Ghost asked curiously.

"Attending to my disguise," I replied. Anyone living in this dungeon would know enough to be suspicious of a lone player wandering its depths. I couldn't do anything about that. But they would be even more suspicious if the selfsame player was under leveled. Conversely, they were less likely to react aggressively toward a player who was so far above them that toying with him would be dangerous.

And pretending to be that was something I could manage.

You have cast facial disguise, assuming the visage of Taim, a level 247 human explorer. Duration: 3 hours.

Ghost's ears turned down. *"What happened to your face?"* she whined.

I grinned. I'd altered the lines of my face subtly, giving myself a more rugged weather-beaten appearance. I gestured to the distant city. "Don't worry. It's only a little deception in case our friends there prove troublesome."

Rising to my feet, I unequipped ebonheart and stowed it in my pack. Now, my disguise was complete. Striding forward, I marched towards the gorge.

It was time to discover what manner of people it sheltered.

CHAPTER 328: THE WANDERING EXPLORER

It took Ghost and I just under an hour to reach the gorge's edge.

Two things became immediately apparent. One, the walled city at its center was huge, nearly the size of the plague quarter in Nexus.

And two: it was under siege.

The gorge nestled right up against the dungeon's protective dome and marked its northwestern corner. The city commanding the valley's center was replete with towers, ramparts, and ringed by walls so formidable that I doubted even the dungeon's elites would attempt storming them.

Not so the surrounding farmlands.

The entire length and breadth of the gorge outside the city had been transformed into farms, and it was not hard to see why. The city undoubtedly housed thousands, and that many mouths had to be a challenge to feed.

All the fields to the south, though, lay fallow and barren—courtesy of the two fog banks planted outside the city walls. And having learned what I had recently of the void, I was sure the nether clouds' placement was not happenstance.

The void appeared intent on capturing the city.

I crouched down on the plateau's lip. The drop to the bottom of the gorge was sheer, and the rockface beneath looked like it had been deliberately smoothened out. Gazing left and right, I saw that held true for all the encircling cliffs. There was no obvious entry into the gorge either, not that I could see anyway.

I rubbed my chin thoughtfully. Whoever controlled the gorge was both patient and meticulous, not to mention paranoid. Their precautions hadn't stopped the nether from invading, though.

My gaze drifted to the fog banks. Both nether clouds were about a few dozen yards across—no larger than the others of their kind I'd run across in the dungeon already—and by my reckoning, were just outside the range of the catapults and ballista on the city walls.

I pointed out the nether to Ghost. "What do you see?"

Narrowing her gaze, the spirit wolf scrutinized the first spot in question. *"Stygians,"* she growled. *"Lots of them."*

I nodded unsurprised.

Ghost's head turned farther right. *"Look there."*

Following her gaze, I saw a pack of stygians boil out of the second fog bank. They did not charge the walls as I half expected, but instead headed farther east, angling around the city walls. A moment later, I realized what they were about. The nether creatures were making for the still-farmed fields on the northern side of the city.

It's a raid, I thought.

Before the stygians could reach the crops, though, a horn trumpeted. Its cry rang across the gorge, and in response, the heavy metal gate along the city's eastern wall opened.

Horses thundered out, at least three full companies of them.

Each carried a heavily armored warrior covered from head to toe in plate mail. The knights had their helms closed, so I could make nothing of the features. The stygians saw the approaching warriors but did not break off from their own advance, and in short order, the two forces collided.

The resulting battle was short and brutal.

Miles from the action, and too far away to affect the outcome, I watched impassively, taking in as many details as I could. The knights were disciplined and well organized. The stygians less so. Surprisingly, the contest between the two forces was purely physical. There was no magic in evidence, meaning the knights had to be using stygian weapons. I saw no sign of anything else that resembled player abilities either.

When it was over, all of the stygians lay dead, but so, too, did a few knights. Picking up their dead and injured, the cavalry returned to the city.

Squinting to focus over the distance, I reached out and analyzed the soldiers at random.

The target is Tonka, a level 121 human.
The target is Wildbow, a level 126 dark elf.
The target is Hanya, a level 124 half-orc.
The target is Greenside, a level 118 dwarf.

"Huh." As expected, none of the knights were players. What I found baffling, though, was how *ordinary* they were.

All the soldiers belonged to species found in the aboveground world. In my mind, I had imagined the city owners as belonging to an exotic race, one adapted to life in a dungeon—rather than orcs, dwarves, humans and elves, ordinary everyday citizens of the Kingdom. I was unsure what to make of it.

Or what to do next.

Given the city's size and the apparent presence of humans, there was a good chance I'd been able to pass unnoticed amongst its inhabitants—just one more face amongst many. It gave me the option of trying to sneak over the walls and blending in. And while the vigilance of the soldiers made this a somewhat risky proposition, I foresaw no difficulty penetrating the city's defenses.

But once inside... what then?

It could take days to scout the city and learn anything of importance, days in which a hundred and one different things could expose me as a stranger.

And why even bother with any of that?

It was clear the void imperiled the city. I hadn't missed the fact that the knights had not attempted to enter the fog bank. It suggested they had no protection against the nether's touch. In which case, the city had every reason to welcome a player—someone who could not only penetrate the mist, but also destroy the seed inside.

I nodded thoughtfully. It made sense to approach the city walls openly and hail the defenders. A modicum of care was still required, though, and I would keep my disguise and false identity in place.

Decision made, I climbed down into the gorge.

✳ ✳ ✳

I crept through the southern farmlands wrapped in shadows. I had no intention of rousing the stygians en-route to the city and made sure to give both fog banks a wide berth.

"Are you sure this is wise?" Ghost asked. She disagreed with my plan, thinking it better for us to avoid the city altogether.

I shrugged. *"Wise? No. But necessary? I think so. I told you, it could take weeks if we have to search for the exit portal ourselves."*

There was nothing linear about the design of Draven's Reach, and I'd seen enough of the dungeon in the past few days to realize that finding the exit was going to be no small feat. If I didn't want to be stuck here for months, we needed help.

Multiple hostile entities have failed to detect you! You are hidden.

I drew to a halt. I was almost within bowshot off the city's walls and directly in front of its south-facing gate. I glanced at Ghost.

Knowing the plan, the spirit wolf bobbed her head in acknowledgement of the silent order and retreated fifty yards. Once she was in position I stood and let the shadows about me dissipate.

You are no longer hidden.

Cupping my hands around my mouth, I called out, "Hello, the city!"

For a drawn-out moment there was silence. Then the sounds of soft oaths and muttered curses carried to my ears. Smiling, I waited. More ordered chaos followed. Blades were unsheathed, weapons were taken in hand, and bows were drawn.

And in an impressively short time, a head popped over the parapets.

It was a soldier—an officer, I guessed—garbed in a similar manner to the knights I'd spied earlier. The helmed figure studied me intently, and I him. A second later, twelve more soldiers joined him, each staring down at me from the end of a shaft. Ignoring the drawn bows pointed at my heart, I analyzed the first figure.

The target is Algar, a level 120 human.

"Who are you?" he barked.

"My name is Taim," I replied easily.

Multiple hostile entities have failed to pierce your disguise.
Your deception has increased to level 112.

"I don't recognize you," Algar replied. "What are you doing outside the gate after curfew?"

I opened my mouth to reply but before I could, a second figure joined the first. He was tall, dark-skinned, and unarmored, yet walked with the quiet confidence of a warrior. A chain of office adorned his neck, and a plain but serviceable longsword was belted at his hip. Fine scars covered his hands, while an uglier larger one ran up his cheek to disappear beneath the hairline. *A veteran fighter.*

"Who's this?" The newcomer peered down, his steel gray eyes passing quickly over me, yet leaving me with the feeling he'd picked over every detail. "That's no farmer, Captain," the fighter whispered, lips barely moving.

"I agree, sir," Algar replied just as softly. "Do I order the archers to fire?"

Before that precipitous decision could be made, I faced the newcomer and said loudly, "As I told your companion, my name is Taim. I'm a visitor to your city."

The newcomer—a senior officer by the sounds of it—folded his arms across his chest. "A visitor? From where?"

"From beyond the dungeon, of course."

My answer was met with palpable silence, and I saw the fingers of more than one archer twitch. I did not fear their arrows, though. I held psi in my mind and was ready to flee at the least sign of aggression. While I waited for the officers' response, I took the opportunity to inspect Algar's companion.

The target is Elron, a level 151 dark elf.

I betrayed no reaction at the Game's feedback, yet I was startled. The dark elf was incredibly high leveled for a non-player. *He has to be some fighter.*

"You're a player?" Although the dark elf phrased the question neutrally, I could tell from his expression he did not believe this to be the case.

I nodded. "I am, *Elron.*"

Algar's eyes widened and his gaze darted sideways to his commander, but the dark elf's reaction was more controlled. "That's High Marshal Elron to you," he replied placidly.

I inclined my head. "I meant no disrespect." I had proved my point and there was no reason to be impolite, especially since I wanted something from these people.

Elron glanced from me to the farmlands beyond, eyes narrowing a touch at their emptiness. "Where is the rest of your party?"

I'd anticipated the question. "I'm alone." Before they could scoff at this, I added, "I'm an explorer, here to map the dungeon for my faction." Dungeon surveying was common practice in the Game and there was no reason my claim should be challenged.

Elron's face, though, stayed impassive. Did he not believe me?

"Assuming all you say is true," the marshal said, "why have you come to New Haven?"

I stared at him blankly.

"Our city," he amended.

"For information." I glanced pointedly in the direction of the two nether clouds. "And to find out what *they* are doing here. I've never seen their kind in a dungeon before." Which was true enough.

"What do you offer in return?"

"Well, I could always try helping you with your stygian problem," I said lightly. "Who knows? Maybe I can even destroy the fog banks."

"You know how to do that?" Elron asked, his face not even twitching in response to my remarkable proposal.

I nodded. "There is a seed at the fog's center. It must be destroyed."

Elron stared at me for another drawn-out moment. Then, he swung around to face Algar.

"Open the gates," he ordered.

Chapter 329: New Haven

As I ambled through the city gates, a squad of waiting soldiers surged forward to form a solid block around me.

Multiple unknown entities have failed to pierce your disguise.
Multiple unknown entities have failed to pierce your disguise.
Multiple unknown entities have...

...

Ignoring both the guards and Game alerts, I stood on my tiptoes and peered at the city beyond. The streets bordering the walls were devoid of civilians. That was not to say they were empty.

Armed warriors rushed to and fro, either climbing up to the parapets or descending. I counted one thousand soldiers in all, and those were just the ones I could see.

I whistled softly. New Haven had a sizable army at its command.

A tower door banged open, and Elron strode out to place himself at the head of my guard contingent. Not acknowledging my presence in the least, he waved the column onwards.

The marshal, I suspected, was trying to make a statement. *You are my prisoner,* his posturing seemed to say. And perhaps he even believed that, but it was far from true. Escape was only a short hop away, and neither the guards nor Elron's brusque treatment unsettled me.

If anything, I found it amusing.

"March!" the sergeant in charge barked.

The soldiers trotted forward, and I with them, craning my neck to take in the passing sights. For the first minute, there was not much to see, only more soldiers.

After nearly a dozen streets, I caught my first glimpse of a civilian. It was an orc, green-skinned and laughing as he chatted to his dwarven companion. A street over, we passed a mixed group of human and orc kids. Then a pair of elven merchants.

Ten minutes and scores of civilians later, it became clear that no one species dominated New Haven. It was equally home to orcs, dwarves, humans, and dark elves. I spotted other races too, but they were far more uncommon and, invariably, gathered together in tight-knit groups.

Interestingly enough, even though all the civilians were low leveled— beneath rank five—they were well-armed, and there was a pervasive sense of... readiness.

Like in any city, the watch patrolled the streets. But in New Haven, they were armed with pikes and shields, not cudgels. The children that played in the streets all had whistles slung around their necks and wore color-coded armbands—emergency spotters?

Houses were block-shaped and their insides as comfortable as any home. But each had an internal staircase running to their flat rooftops. In a pinch, they could be made to serve as a platform for archers to fire from.

Vendor stalls lined the city's many squares, with their owners proclaiming their wares' virtues like all merchants did. A second look revealed the sharpened poles decorating the sides of the tents, though. It would not take much, I suspected, to turn the stalls into makeshift barricades.

But the overt display of martial readiness aside, the city was...

...ordinary.

Our company drew more than a few stares, but no one looked too long or too hard. And those that did almost universally focused on Elron, nodding respectfully as he passed. The marshal, it seemed, was well-known.

"Do you know where we're headed?" Ghost asked.

I didn't glance in her direction. The spirit wolf was keeping pace with our company and hovered about thirty yards to my right. So far no one appeared to have noticed her. *"They must be taking me to whoever is in charge."*

"Isn't that the marshal?"

"He's just a soldier. A place this big, it must have a ruler of sorts."

"And once you meet them, what then?"

"He or she will ask lots of questions. And perhaps issue a few threats." I shrugged imperceptibly. *"But in the end, they'll come around. They'll have to. What I can do for New Haven is too valuable for the city's ruler to ignore."*

Ghost looked dubious, but all she said was, *"I hope you're right."*

✳ ✳ ✳

I was wrong.

Not about everything, hopefully, but about our destination at least. Elron's soldiers led me not to the palace I was expecting, but to a grim-looking building with a barricaded steel door and barred windows. There was no mistaking what it was.

He is taking this posturing a step too far, I thought and slowed my steps. "You're throwing me in jail?"

The marshal glanced over his shoulder at me but didn't stop walking. "Only temporarily and until we can ascertain you are no threat."

Not posturing then.

"I did not consent to being held prisoner," I growled.

"Nonetheless, you will comply," he said equably.

Wrong again. It seemed the threats were going to precede the questioning.

"Or what?" I asked bitingly. Grounding to a halt, I forced my escorts to stop as well.

Elron turned around to face me fully. "If you resist in any way—" he shot me a look as if to warn me not to—"or fail to comply with the orders of your jailers, no matter how beneath you you think them, then you can rest assured you will never find the sector's exit portal."

I'd underestimated the marshal. Without being told, he'd figured out what information I wanted. But did he know how badly I desired it? *I hope not.*

"I need the portal's location a lot less than your city needs saving from the nether," I retorted.

"I doubt that," Elron said. "Without our help you'll never find the exit." He smiled but there was no mirth in the expression. "Then you will be trapped here like the rest of us, and the void will be as much your problem as it is ours."

I didn't react, but internally, my anger subsided. Unwittingly, Elron had revealed two important tidbits of information. One, the city's population was stuck in the dungeon. Two, and far more importantly, New Haven knew the location of the exit.

And for the promise of that, I would go along with Elron's games—for now.

"How long?" I asked.

The marshal's brows crinkled. "How long can we hold you? For however long we wish—"

I slashed my hand downwards, deciding to do some posturing of my own. Elron could not be allowed to believe he could toy with me willy-nilly. "Not that. You cannot hold me if I do not wish it. What I meant was how long do you need to deceive yourself into believing I'm no threat?"

Elron's face hardened. "Two days."

I nodded. "Two days, then," I said and resumed walking. I did not need to say what would happen after that. From the expression on Elron's face he well understood my counter-threat.

✳ ✳ ✳

The next day passed slowly.

Every few hours, I made certain to renew my disguise. So far, none of the city's populace had been able to see through my deception, and I was determined to keep it that way.

The cell I'd been assigned was bare but clean. It was also unwarded, which I confirmed using the spectacles of ward seeing. Freeing myself would be trivial, only a matter of picking open the lock on the cell door.

I found the lack of magic interesting, and it made me all the more curious about how New Haven survived the dungeon's denizens. It could not only be due to strength of arms. Surely not?

Just as puzzling was that no one had attempted to take away my weapons or gear—not that I would have allowed it. It all pointed to my prison being one only in name.

Is that by design? I wondered. Or had one of Elron's minions erred?

With little else to do, I contemplated this and other mysteries. There was only so much thinking one could do, though, and before long boredom set in.

Toward nightfall, Ghost returned.

I'd set the spirit wolf to tailing Elron. She'd followed him all of last night and for much of today.

"Did you learn anything?" I asked, turning to face her as she walked in through the walls.

Ghost growled in disgust. *"Nothing. The marshal returned to the wall today, and stayed there all day, reinforcing the defenses."*

Elron had done the same last night too. And it is what I would have done if I suspected the strange visitor to be a decoy. What I could not fathom though, was what the marshal feared. It could not be that he believed I was working with the nether—what sane person would willingly cooperate with the void?

Perhaps that's it. Perhaps he thinks I'm insane.

"What about the rest of the city?" I asked, refocusing on my companion. *"Did your scouting turn up anything of interest?"*

Ghost lowered her head in shame. *"I'm sorry, Prime. But I could not find the city ruler you mentioned. This place is just so big."*

I sighed. *"It was always a long shot, anyway."*

"What do we do now?" Ghost asked despondently.

I sat down beside her. *"I guess we'd better see to your training."* At the very least it would keep me busy while I waited for the clock to tick down on the two days I'd promised Elron.

✳   ✳   ✳

With only hours to spare on his allotted time, the marshal made a reappearance. But he was not alone.

Accompanying him were two blue-robed figures, carrying an unwieldy device between them. The pair—youths, I thought—set down the item in the middle of the cell, taking pains to stay as far away from me as possible.

My gaze darted from the strange device to Elron. "What's that?" I jerked my thumb at the robed youngsters. "And who are they?"

"They are apprentices," the marshal replied, "and that is the device our mages have been preparing for the past two days."

So, the city *did* have magic. My gaze drifted back to the object, and without further ado, I inspected it.

This is a basic diviner, a tier 3 divining tool. It contains a single-use enchantment that will reveal a player's spirit signatures to the operators.

"Clever," I remarked and rose to my feet, having no fear of the device. "Let's get this over with."

Elron nodded to the apprentices, and they began chanting. Shortly, I felt the weaves of a spell settle on me. Staying motionless, I waited.

Diviner activated. Scanning commencing...

...

You have passed a mental resistance check.

Your secret blood trait has been triggered!

Scans completed.

Two unknown entities have failed to pierce your disguise and your awakened blood has been successfully hidden.

The older youth turned to Elron. "He is a player. The diviner has confirmed it."

The marshal took the news without any visible reaction. "What Marks does he bear?"

"A Mark of Lesser Shadow, Lesser Light, and Lesser Dark," the other apprentice replied.

Elron's eyes narrowed. "That's it?" he asked. "He has no other Marks?"

Both apprentices shook their heads. "None that the device can detect."

The marshal swung to face me. "Which Power are you sworn to?"

Tilting my head, I studied him curiously. "Why does that matter? Your device has confirmed I'm a player and thus capable of helping you."

Elron snorted, showing more emotion than he had so far. "My people may have been stuck in this dungeon for centuries, but we are not ignorant of the ways of your lot. Player though you may be, it does not mean you are *trustworthy*. There are some we will not deal with. If you wish for us to come to an arrangement, you must tell me who you serve."

I mused over Elron's words. He'd said 'centuries.' That was a long time for anyone to be stuck in a dungeon. Just how desperate were the New Haveners to get out? I forbore to comment, though, and answered his question forthrightly. "I serve no one. I belong to an unaligned faction. We serve no Force or Power."

The marshal did not relent, and I got the feeling he would not until he got the answers he sought. "I know of no such faction. Name it."

I shrugged. "The bounty hunters guild."

"The guild is not a faction," he retorted.

"True," I admitted, "but it operates very much like one."

The marshal was silent for a moment. "Show me your badge," he said at last.

I concealed my surprise. Elron was better versed in the ways of players than I expected, but I'd constructed my story carefully and had the proof he required on hand. Withdrawing my BHG ID, I showed it to him.

The dark elf scrutinized the card minutely before nodding slowly. "It seems you are truly what you claim." Not saying anything further, he strode out the cell's open door.

When I didn't budge, he tapped his foot impatiently. "Let's go."

"You will tell me where we are headed first," I said, not inclined to follow him blindly again.

"To the fortress," he replied. "The council is anxious to meet you."

CHAPTER 330: A CITY OF FOURS

DAY SIX IN DRAVEN'S REACH

An hour later, I found myself in one of the fortresses at the heart of the city. New Haven did not have anything like a main keep, but that did not mean its center was undefended. Four separate strongholds occupied the middle, each almost a fortified city on its own.

The inside of the fortress was decorated with tapestries, rugs, and artworks of wooded forests, green pastures, blue skies, and meandering rivers. The pictures were a stark contrast to Draven's Reach's purple horizon and barren mountains, and I suspected they were the memories of a homesick people. But despite the rich furnishings, the corridors we walked through were empty. Had they been cleared in anticipation of our arrival?

The marshal led me directly to a large hall on an upper floor. The entrance was guarded by four separate squads of soldiers, each bearing a different crest on their tabards, I noted. Waving me past the sentries, Elron guided me into the chamber and closed the doors behind us.

"Go ahead, they're waiting," he said, pointing towards the table at the hall's other end. Staying behind, he leaned against the doors, as if to ensure the meeting's privacy.

Two men and two women sat at the table—an orc, a human, a dwarf, and an elf. *The city's rulers.* At last, we'd come face to face, and I did not think it a coincidence that between them, the four represented the city's primary races. Before proceedings could begin, I analyzed each figure.

> The target is Cilia, a level 78 dark elf.
> The target is Sienna, a level 32 human.
> The target is Stormhammer, a level 43 dwarf.
> The target is Lorn, a level 47 orc.

The four were richly dressed in civilian clothes and crowned with silver circlets. The dark elf woman, Cilia, was the most interesting. She wore a gown of severe black and multiple pieces of jewelry, all of which had the telltale gleam of magical enchantments. *A spellcaster?* She was the highest ranked of the rulers too, and my gaze fixed on her expectantly.

It was the dwarf who rose to greet me, though. "So, you are the one," he rumbled, the words laced with derision.

I studied the dwarf curiously. His fine robes sat uneasily on him, and I guessed they were not his regular garb. His hands were rough and his fingernails short. *A fighter?* But no, his stomach bulged, and his arms lacked tone. *A crafter,* I decided. And one in a foul mood too, judging by his expression. Folding my hands behind my back, I waited for him to go on.

"Well? Aren't you going to answer?" Stormhammer demanded.

"You asked no question," I replied mildly.

The dwarf's face turned red. "Why, you insolent—"

"Stormhammer," Cilia interjected smoothly, "do not forget the player is our *guest.*"

"Yes, perhaps it would be wise to introduce ourselves first," the human added in a languid tone. *Her* clothes fit her perfectly. Elegantly dressed and manicured, Sienna was the epitome of human beauty.

"Bah," the dwarf muttered testily. Sitting down, he waved them to go ahead.

The elf rose. "I'm Cilia, first amongst the dark elves of New Haven," she pronounced. Sitting down, she glanced at the orc.

The tall, green-skinned figure did not bother getting up. "Lorn, orc chief," he rasped in a bored tone. His clothes, while no less finely made than the others, were festooned with primitive looking beads and feathers.

An affectation, I decided. The orc might play at looking the barbarian, but beneath his lidded gaze, I sensed a shrewd mind.

The human ruler inclined her head regally. "Sienna. High Lord of the humans of New Haven." A coy smile toyed on her lips and her gaze held more than a hint of promise.

Fighting the urge to look away, I didn't break eye contact. This was a woman well-used to the halls of power and intrigue, and I wasn't about to betray any weakness before her.

After Sienna finished, a small silence descended, and when it became clear the dwarf would not speak, the other rulers turned his way.

"What?" he growled, wilting under their stares. "He knows who I am already."

Cilia did not roll her eyes, but I could see she wanted to. "That," she said, pointing to the dwarf, "is Thane Stormhammer, ruler of the dwarves and current leader of the New Haven council."

Four fortresses. Four rulers. Four races. *A city of fours.*

I bowed respectfully. "And I am Taim, an explorer from the Nexus branch of the bounty hunters guild."

An expectant hush followed.

"Come now," Sienna prompted when I didn't go on, "you are surely more than that. You are an elite amongst your kind, are you not?"

"As well as an unsworn," Cilia added. "*And* beholden to no Power. All these things taken together mark you as one meant for greater things."

"Tell us, which factions support your rise?" Lorn asked.

Three inquisitive gazes pinned me, waiting for my response.

Now I know how the thane felt. Keeping my face smooth, I let no sign of my confusion show. Like Elron, the council members appeared well-acquainted with players, but more than that, they appeared to be drawing conclusions I had not intended—and quite frankly did not fully understand.

Stormhammer thumped a fist down on the table, saving me from answering. "Foolishness! None of that is here nor there." He glared at his fellow rulers with a surprising amount of heat. "Forget this useless prattle and let's get to the heart of the matter!"

The others' faces tightened at the dwarf's scolding, but none demurred. "As you wish," Cilia said, her lips thinning.

The dwarf swung back to me without acknowledging their acquiescence. "How did you get here?" he demanded.

I did not hide my confusion this time. "Here? If you mean the city, then through the south gate. If you mean this fortress—"

"Don't play the fool," the dwarf roared. "We want to know how you got into the dungeon!"

"Through the entrance portal, of course," I replied evenly, ignoring his ire.

Cilia's face fell, Sienna pouted, and even Lorn was moved to look disappointed.

"I told you!" Stormhammer crowed. "He is not what he claims."

"Is this a trick?" Sienna asked in a low-voiced aside to Cilia. "Is he one of *them*?"

Shaking her head, the dark elf whispered back, "He cannot be possessed. The diviner proved that. He *is* Marked."

My gaze jumped from one city ruler to another. It was clear they did not believe me, but what I didn't understand was why. "Possessed? Possessed by what?" I asked loudly, hoping to shake free a clue as to the reason.

Sienna and Cilia looked startled that I'd overheard them, but neither responded. I glanced at Lorn. His face had grown impassive again, though, and was of no help. Finally, I turned to Stormhammer.

The dwarf was staring at me with open hostility. "You are a liar," he accused. "The dungeon's entrance portal lies in the square at the center of the city, and since our exodus into Draven's Reach, it has remained shut." Just in case I didn't understand, he added, "The portal is dead and will remain so for all eternity."

I stared at him. I'd never heard of a dead portal before. The thane could be lying, but I didn't think so, and at least I now knew the cause of their disbelief. "How did that happen?" I asked softly.

My question was ignored—again.

"This audience is over," Stormhammer declared. "Take him back to—"

"I entered Draven's Reach through a hidden portal," I interjected. I wasn't ready to risk open hostilities with the council yet and if that meant sharing more truth than I planned, so be it.

Cilia stilled, and Sienna drew in a sharp breath, but Stormhammer was unmoved. "Guards!" he shouted. "Come, take—"

"This portal, is it two-way?" Lorn asked abruptly.

The thane shot him a sideways glance but didn't admonish the orc or call for the guards again.

They seek escape as desperately as I do, I thought. I shook my head. "Sadly, it's not."

"Convenient," the thane huffed.

"Not at all," I said, deliberately misinterpreting his comment. "It's proving most inconvenient. I urgently need to return to the guild—" I paused for emphasis—"which is why I need the location of the exit portal."

"Why is it that you are the only one to have come through?" Lorn probed, ignoring my oblique request altogether.

"Because the second entrance is *hidden*," I said with mild exasperation. "I'm the first to have discovered it."

Cilia studied her fingers. "Can we expect more players to visit us then?"

I hesitated. "I doubt it. The portal is in a sector in the throes of a nether invasion."

At the mention of the void the faces of all four rulers paled. "What the harbinger said was true then," Sienna murmured, tugging anxiously at her hair. "The void *has* spread everywhere. We will find no escape from its touch."

My curiosity was piqued by her words. That the city rulers knew of the harbinger was interesting, but not wanting to send them down another tangent, I ignored the reference.

"Not at all," I said, meeting the high lord's gaze squarely. "The void has not won, nor is it close to doing so." I did not know this for a fact but had no compunctions about overstating my case. "There are still many sectors in the Kingdom free of its touch, and I can help you rid your own sector of it."

"And in exchange for this... generosity, you want information on the portal's exit location?" Lorn asked.

"Yes," I said simply.

"This is all an elaborate trick," the dwarf scoffed. "Some sick ploy of the possessed. They toy with us again!"

Again, the mention of possessed. "Whatever the possessed are," I said, not flinching away from the angry thane's gaze, "I am not one of them."

"Prove it," the dwarf growled.

I opened my mouth to protest, but before I could do so, Cilia intervened, "We already *know* he is not one of the possessed, Stormhammer. And like it or not, Taim's explanation of how he entered the dungeon is logical. He *is* a player. Your stubborn persistence in believing otherwise is childish and beneath you."

She turned back to me. "But players can be just as dangerous as anything else in Draven's Reach. That Taim is one does not automatically make him our friend. It is time, I think, for our guest to prove his intentions." She glanced at the door, and in response, the nearly forgotten marshal strode forward.

"My men are prepared," Elron said. "If the player can do what he says, we are ready to sally through the south gate and see the deed done."

I glanced from the marshal to the First. I suspected I already knew how Cilia expected me to prove my 'intentions,' but I wanted the council to voice their request aloud. "What is it that you want of me?"

Cilia stared pointedly at Stormhammer.

The thane's mouth worked mutinously, but only for a moment. "The council has agreed that to prove yourself you must destroy one of the fog banks threatening New Haven," he said, shoulders slumping.

"Call it a gesture of good faith," Sienna added.

My interest quickened. We'd finally gotten to the meat of the matter. "If I do this... you will tell me where the exit portal is?"

"We shall," Lorn confirmed. "But only on the condition that you destroy the second fog bank thereafter."

I nodded. "Then we have a deal."

* * *

The moment the audience concluded, Elron strode purposefully out of the council chamber. Hurrying my own steps, I caught up to him.

The meeting with the city's rulers had raised more questions than it had answered, but now was not the time to deal with any of them. Things were finally moving in the right direction, and I was anxious to get started on my own part.

I glanced at the marshal. "So, what's the plan?"

He didn't slow down. "That depends on whether you can do what you say."

"You don't believe I can?"

"You are one man, even if you are a player." He shrugged. "There are dozens of stygians guarding each seed. Even if you could enter the fog bank and survive its touch long enough to reach the thing, I fail to see how you could defeat that many foes *and* destroy the seed before the nether killed you."

"How do you know that?"

"Know what?"

"You said there are dozens of stygian are hiding in the fog," I pointed out. "How can you know that?" I asked reasonably.

Saying nothing, Elron stared at me tight-lipped.

"You've already tried to destroy the seeds," I guessed. "You sent men into the fog."

Emotion, quickly suppressed, flickered across the dark elf's face. "I did," he admitted.

"How did they—" I broke off. "No one survived, did they?"

Elron nodded, his face impassive, but in his stony expression, I read bleakness. "I would've gone myself but the First forbade it."

I winced sympathetically. "How long did your soldiers last?"

Elron's expression did not change. "No one knows. Once they passed beyond the fog's edge, we lost track of them. But however long it was, it was not long enough to reach the seed." The marshal's frozen mask finally cracked. "They were good men," he whispered.

"I have no doubt," I said soberly.

The marshal drew to a halt and swung to face me. "I will not repeat my mistakes," he said, his tone hard. Taking a step forward, he placed his face an inch from mine. "I know you players don't value the lives of proles much, but I will not let my men suffer the nether's touch again—no matter what you, the council, or anyone else demands."

I didn't back away. "I won't ask that of them or you," I said quietly.

Elron scrutinized me for a drawn-out moment before retreating. "Then we understand each other. Now, let's discuss the plan..."

CHAPTER 331: KILLING FLIGHTS

"Do you trust them?"

Elron and I were back at the city walls. The marshal was readying his men inside the south gate while Ghost and I stood silent witness. The spirit wolf's question was an apt one, and I took my time reviewing what I'd learned from the council meeting before answering.

New Haven was not a new city, and its inhabitants were not in the dungeon by choice. Like me, they had entered Draven's Reach unwillingly, and like me, they were trapped here. Some of this was supposition, but I didn't think I was mistaken. And I could think of only one reason why an entire people would uproot themselves.

The void.

At some point, in the distant past, New Haven's citizens must have fled their home sector, escaping the nether's touch. It explained the fear I'd seen in the councilors' faces at the mention of the void, and it explained why the portal they had entered through was sealed.

What I did not understand, though, was why there were no players amongst the New Haveners. Surely, some at least had felt obligated to enter the dungeon and protect the city's populace?

Then there was the rulers' repeated reference to 'the possessed.' What were they—dungeon denizens or nether creatures? Whatever the possessed were, the councilors seemed to fear them almost as much as they did the void.

But despite these mysteries, I did not doubt that the New Haveners hated the void, or that most of them wished out of the dungeon—with the possible exception of the dwarven thane.

"I do," I said finally. "Some of them, anyway."

"You will do as they ask, then, and destroy the seeds outside the city walls?"

I nodded.

"Who are you talking to?" Elron asked, approaching me from behind.

The dark elf moved well. His footfalls had been so silent, I'd not heard him over the sound of the assembling soldiers. "Only myself," I said lightly.

He eyed me askance. "You do that often?"

I chuckled. "More often than you would believe." I glanced at the gathered company and whistled softly. "This is what you meant by a small force?"

There had to be nearly two thousand men in the square, all standing to attention in neatly dressed lines. Half the soldiers carried bows and wore leather armor. The other half were heavily armed and wielded pikes.

Elron shrugged. "They will suffice."

The marshal would know the capabilities of his own people better than I did, and if he believed the company was up to the task of defeating the ten score stygians in the fog banks, I was not going to question his judgment.

One thing bothered me, though. "No calvary?" They had been effective in the first battle I'd witnessed, and I was surprised Elron had scorned their use for this venture.

"The pikemen will do a better job of protecting the archers," he replied simply.

Before I could say anything, two aides rushed up with a pair of armored horses. Elron mounted the first and motioned me towards the second.

I shook my head. "I'll do better on my own two feet."

The marshal raised an eyebrow in polite disbelief but did not gainsay me. "Open the gates!" he barked.

A squad of soldiers raced to do his bidding, and Elron's horse surged forward. "Let's be about it," he called as he galloped away.

*　*　*

The plan was a simple one.

Our company drew up two hundred yards from the edge of the rightmost fog bank, and at Elron's command, the bowmen crouched down and raised their bows while the pikeman hefted their weapons in readiness.

"Are you sure you can see through the mist, Taim?" Elron asked.

"I can," I lied smoothly. It was not me but Ghost whose gaze would penetrate the nether cloud.

Looking back, I saw the archers were waiting on our command. Like the pikemen's weapons, the arrowheads at the end of their bows were formed from stygian ore.

Noticing the direction of my glance, Elron said, "The stygian arrows are irreplaceable. If they are lost, there'll be no recovering them."

"How do you make them?" I asked curiously.

"The same way you players do, I imagine," he replied. "We harvest the ingredients from the stygians we kill, but there is never enough to go around, and stygian weapons are always in short supply. If this doesn't work, the city will be weakened by the loss of the arrows."

I met his gaze. "Better lost arrows than lost men."

The marshal nodded reluctantly. The fact that this plan would draw the stygians to us—and not so coincidentally negate the need for Elron's men to enter the fog—was a large reason why he had agreed to it, even though he still remained skeptical of my claims.

"Sir, the men are ready," a captain said, running up to us.

The marshal glanced at me expectantly.

Nodding, I turned my gaze towards the opaque mists. It was time for me and Ghost to perform.

"There is a clump of three dozen stygians thirty yards from the edge of the fog and fifty yards to the left," Ghost reported, right on cue. *"The rest of the creatures are farther back and waiting to see what the soldiers do."*

"What type of foes are we facing?" I asked.

"Mostly crawlers, but there are a handful of weavers too."

Murmuring my thanks, I relayed the information to Elron, and the bowmen adjusted their aim.

"Fire!" the captain barked.

In the next heartbeat, one thousand arrows took flight, darkening the sky as they arched upwards to disappear into the fog. Besides me, I sensed Elron hold his breath, and I felt like doing much the same.

A second passed and another.

Then hisses and snarls of pain broke out, loud enough that even the marshal and his men could not fail to hear. Elron beamed, and I felt a grin spread across my own face.

"By damn, it worked!" Elron exclaimed.

"I told you it would," I murmured. Letting my gaze slide to the right, I waited to hear Ghost's report.

"The volley missed the center of the crawlers' formation," she said, all business. *"Only half are injured. Inform the archers. They must adjust their aim another twenty yards to the right."*

My lips twitched. "Yes, ma'am," I said and relayed her orders.

A second flight of arrows took wing, and this time the cries of pain were notably louder.

Ghost wagged her tail furiously. *"That's it! That bunch is finished."* She paused. *"The rest of the crawlers are moving forward. They're getting ready to charge, I think."*

"Incoming," I reported.

Elron's smile vanished. "Pikemen, ready up!" he ordered.

Striding five paces forward, the soldiers planted their pikes in the ground, angling their points upwards. I glanced at the other fog bank. It was a few hundred yards distant, but I did not doubt the stygians inside were aware of the impending battle. *"What's happening in there?"*

"Not much," Ghost replied. *"The second group of stygians have drawn closer to their seed and show no sign of advancing. I doubt they will attack unless attacked."*

That will make things easier, I thought, and told the marshal what Ghost had seen.

"Inform me if anything changes," Elron said. Dismounting, he joined the pikemen in the defensive line they'd formed. Behind them, the bowmen held their weapons ready—arrows loosely nocked—but didn't fire.

Wisely, the marshal and his captains had decided to wait for the crawlers to show themselves before loosing the next wave. Readying my own buffs, I drew my stygian sword and placed myself on the other end of the pike line.

A handful of seconds later, the crawlers boiled out of the mists.

In total, the survivors numbered about seventy, still a significant force. But before they covered more than a dozen yards, they were met by another blistering volley from the archers.

A stygian crawler has died.
A stygian crawler has been injured.
A stygian crawler has died.
A stygian...

"Rapid fire!" a captain yelled.

In response, wave after wave of arrows took to the air, with barely any pauses between.

More stygians fell. *Many* more.

It was a breathtaking display of marksmanship, and my mouth dropped open in awe as I watched the crawler formation visibly shrink with every yard they advanced. I lowered my blade. Judging by how quickly the bowmen were cutting down their victims, I judged barely a quarter of the stygians would live long enough to trouble the pikemen.

I snorted, thinking back on Elron's previous words. "Suffice, indeed." This was a far cry from that.

This was overkill.

*   *   *

My estimation turned out to be overly optimistic. Only six crawlers made it to the pikeman line, and they were quickly cut down. "Well done," Elron said as he rejoined me.

"And to you, too," I said. "Your men do good work."

Elron smiled. "They've had lots of practice." Swinging around, he gazed into the fog bank. "What's left?"

"Six weavers," I said, relaying what Ghost had already reported. The weavers appear to be the seeds' favored guards, at least in this sector.

Elron did not ask me what the weavers were, so he had to be familiar with the breed. "Let's finish this."

I nodded. "Let's."

Glancing over his shoulder, Elron barked, "Soldiers, advance!"

*   *   *

It was about thirty yards from the edge of the fog bank to the seed and the weavers, which was well within range of the bowmen once the company drew up fifty yards short of the mists. Once everyone was in position, Elron gave the command, and the archers raised their bows and fired.

Half found their marks on the first volley.

The weavers were smarter than the crawlers, though, and although gravely injured, they did what their fellows should have: they scattered quickly.

The archers released again. Only two weavers were struck.

A third wave took to the air but, like the second, it failed to trouble the six seed guards. To make matters worse, the weavers had already healed up using the same magic I'd witnessed days ago.

"This isn't working," Elron said, spitting in disgust, when I passed on Ghost's reports.

"I agree," I said. "I'll take care of it."

"*You?*" the marshal asked.

I smiled. "Still lacking in faith, Elron?"

The marshal grunted noncommittally. "What's your plan?"

"You'll see," I said mysteriously, not about to share my tactics unnecessarily. "Draw your men back and let them rest. This may take a while."

The marshal opened his mouth to protest, but I spoke over him. "You know what happens after I destroy the seed, right?"

"We return to the city."

I waved aside his words. "Before that."

Elron's brows furrowed.

"The harbinger shows up," I said in response to his confusion.

The marshal stared at me searchingly. "You sound certain," he said quietly.

"I am."

Elron's eyes narrowed. "How can you be so sure?"

"This will not be the first seed I've tackled in this dungeon. When I destroyed the other one, the harbinger turned up. Somehow, he knows when the seeds are attacked." I left my explanation at that, not wanting to rouse the marshal's curiosity further by voicing all my suspicions about the seeds.

"I see," the marshal said, accepting my explanation. "I'll prepare the men and warn the city."

"See that you do," I said, and strode into the fog.

✳ ✳ ✳

You have activated a scent concealment crystal.

Five minutes later, I was crouched in the mists, watching the weavers with my mindsight. I'd taken the time to renew my buffs and use an enchantment crystal to mask my smell. The last thing I wanted was the harbinger speaking to me as he had done previously and the too-curious marshal overhearing.

The weavers had only just returned to their sentry positions around the seed and, not surprisingly, were still on edge. Cloaked in shadows, and thirty yards away from my targets, I drew psi. Having only faced physical attacks so far, the weavers had not erected their mental defenses, and after my previous experience with the creatures, I had no intention of allowing them to do so.

Completing my spell, I sent tendrils of will surging into the minds of four stygians.

You have cast slaysight.
You have induced 3 of 4 targets to sleep for 20 seconds.
Your mental intrusion has gone undetected!

The mindglows of the three bespelled weavers dimmed, and though I could not see the creatures yet, I imagined they had sunk to the ground. Just as importantly, the other stygians did not react. Drawing more psi, I cast mass charm.

You have charmed 3 of 3 targets for 20 seconds.

"Excellent," I murmured as the remaining weavers fell under my spell. *"Wait here and keep watch,"* I ordered Ghost. Turning my focus inwards, I transformed the psi sitting at my mind's core into an insurmountable wall.

You have cast mind shield. Psi abilities are unavailable.

Then, I dashed forward.

Sadly, without access to my psi, I had to cover the distance on foot. Nonetheless, it took me only a handful of seconds to reach the seed's guards. The moment the first nether creature emerged into sight, I slashed down with my stygian sword.

You have killed a stygian weaver with a fatal blow.

Knowing time was of the essence, I empowered my arms, ramping up the speed and power of my attacks.

You have cast whirlwind and piercing strike.

Spinning left, I chopped down, cutting a sleeping weaver in two. Lunging forward, I plunged my blade through the maw of another. Taking ten paces to the right, I skewered two more in quick succession, then charged forward and rammed my sword into the last.

You have killed 6 stygian weavers.

Panting heavily, I surveyed corpses strewn about. My foes had died without fuss and without resistance. I smiled in grim satisfaction. There was only one more thing left to do.

Sheathing my stygian blade, I drew ebonheart and approached the seed. Even now, I imagined it was squawking to the harbinger for help or trying to worm its way into my mind.

"Not this time," I muttered. Recasting piercing strike, I brought the black blade flashing down.

You had destroyed a stygian seed!

It was done. Sweeping up the seed's fragments into my backpack, I raced out of the mists.

CHAPTER 332: A VISIT FROM AN UNWELCOME GUEST

I emerged from the fog bank to find Elron and his men on the move. I frowned. Just as I'd expected, the marshal's company had retreated to shelter beneath the city's walls, but they had not stopped there. Swinging further west, they were heading toward the second seed.

"What is he up to?" I muttered. Jogging forward, I hurried to find out.

Behind me, the nether was already dissipating, and it wouldn't be long before it vanished entirely. Catching up to the marching soldiers, I stormed to the fore. "What are you doing?" I yelled.

Elron glanced over his shoulder at me but didn't respond or halt the column. He had not bothered to remount his horse and was on foot like the rest of his men. Forced to keep pace if I wanted answers, I dropped into step with the marshal.

"You said the harbinger is coming," Elron replied when I drew alongside him. He added nothing further as if his words were explanation enough.

I stared at him blankly for a moment. "All the *more* reason to get your people behind the city walls. If the harbinger catches your company out in the open, your losses will be incalculable."

To my surprise, my words did not deter Elron. "My people know how to deal with that flying horror. We can hold him at bay—for a time."

My eyes narrowed. "How do you plan on doing that?"

Elron smiled mysteriously—in gentle mockery of my own prior response, I suspected. "You'll see," he said.

I ground my teeth in frustration, but let the matter be. After all, it was Elron's own people whom the harbinger endangered, not me. I could look after myself well enough. "You still haven't told me *why* you are marching west," I pointed out.

"To attack the second seed, of course," he replied deadpan.

I stopped short. "That was not the deal," I growled harshly.

Stepping out of the column, Elron waved his men on while he turned around to face me. "The deal's changed," he said, his own face hard.

I balled my hands into fists. I couldn't believe it. The marshal had decided to renege on our deal. I'd thought better of him. What had possessed him to such foolishness?

"It's not what you think," Elron said, sensing the direction of my thoughts. "I haven't betrayed you. But the harbinger's coming changes everything."

I was unmoved. "Why?"

"Don't you see? Once he arrives, he'll realize what's happened. The other stygians may be mindless, but not the harbinger. He'll make sure to reinforce the second seed, perhaps even guard it himself, and we'll have lost our chance."

My lips stayed drawn into a tight line, but inwardly I groaned. Much as it galled me to admit, Elron was right. Once the harbinger took charge of the seed's guards, it would be out of reach.

Taking out a single seed was never a viable plan.

I should have figured out as much myself before this. But what was done was done, and there was little point dwelling on my miscalculation. Right now, I had to decide how to move on.

I did not for a second contemplate withdrawing and leaving Elron and his men to fend for themselves, though. True, if I destroyed the second seed, I would lose my leverage and would be forced to trust in the council's honor.

I snorted, imagining how much—or little—that was worth.

Still, I had many reasons for aiding New Haven, and obtaining the portal's exit location was just one of them. Even if the council *did* back out of our deal, it did not justify alienating the city—as I surely would do if I refused to aid Elron now. And besides, when it came right down to it, I didn't have the stomach to stand idly by and watch the soldiers die.

"What's your plan then?" I asked, turning back to the marshal.

Relief flitted across the dark elf's face. "The same as before. You direct our fire; we kill the stygians."

Nodding sharply, I hurried forward. "Then let's be about it."

✳   ✳   ✳

The company deployed itself rapidly under Elron's guidance, the archers forming ranks and unshouldering their bows while the pikemen lined up in front of them.

Still, it was too slow.

Before the first arrow could even be fired, the harbinger made an appearance. "Damn it," I hissed, spotting a distant speck on the horizon.

"What is it?" Elron rasped, following my gaze.

His eyes were not as good as my own. "The harbinger," I replied.

Elron cursed. "You have sharp eyes for a human."

"I'm a player, remember." I looked from the stygian winging closer to the dressed lines of soldiers. "What do you want to do?"

"We keep going," the marshal replied grimly. His gaze darted to the city walls. "Let them worry about the harbinger."

Glancing over my shoulder, I spotted dozens of hooded, blue-robed figures lining the city walls. "Mages?" I guessed.

Elron nodded. "They'll buy us some time, but not much. We'll have to hurry things along."

I debated questioning him further but held my peace. If the marshal's confidence in New Haven's mages was misplaced, it was his own men who would pay the price. "As you wish." I pointed to where Ghost reported the crawlers to be. "That's where you men should aim."

Elron passed on my directions to his officers. "Give the order; tell the archers not to stop until I say otherwise."

"You heard the marshal!" a captain barked. "Fire at will and kill those bastards!"

The bowmen were eager to begin. Having seen the direction of Elron and my gazes, not a few of them eyed the sky tremulously, but despite weak knees and shaky hands, the archers held their lines and did as ordered.

A scant second later, one thousand arrows darkened the sky, and before they could even begin their descent, another thousand trailed after them. But given the hurried nature of the volley, the arrow fire was less concentrated and directed than it could have been.

The first wave killed five crawlers. The second, twice that. And the third, barely a dozen. Still, the unending arrow storm succeeded in its intent, and in response, the crawlers surged forward.

"Stop!" I barked as soon as Ghost reported the stygians' movements. "The crawlers have been baited into engaging." I glanced skyward. The harbinger was still far enough that the company could reach the walls before he arrived. "Have your men retreat."

"But why?" Elron protested. "We haven't killed the creatures yet."

"Killing the stygians is not the objective," I said. "Destroying the seed is. With the crawlers out of the way, I can sneak into the mist and kill the thing." I gestured at the onrushing harbinger. Even the weaker-sighted marshal could not fail to see him now. "Or do you mean to tell me your mages can protect your men when your company is this far out?"

Elron hesitated for a moment before conceding. "No, not easily, they can't." Spinning on his heel, he signaled to his officers.

"Company, retreat!" a captain barked in response. "Double time!"

"Eyes up, archers," another ordered. "Infantry, pikes forward."

Once more, the New Haven soldiers showed remarkable discipline. Pointing their bows skyward, the archers rose to their feet and backstepped in good order. The pikeman followed on their heels, eyes fixed on the onrushing stygian horde.

Seeing that Elron had matters well in hand, I gestured Ghost forward and raced after her.

*　*　*

I ran straight at the horde of charging crawlers, closing the distance rapidly. But Ghost outpaced me and before the stygians could reach attack range, *she* entered the fog bank. Weaving psi, I shadow blinked past the creatures.

You have teleported to Ghost. You are hidden.

I emerged, wrapped in mist and free of threat. Dropping into a crouch, I padded forward with half an ear trained on the situation at my rear. The fog muffled sounds but the angry hissing of the crawlers and the trample of the soldiers' feet still carried clearly to me.

The clash of steel and cries of men cut through the air.

"*Ghost, tell me what's happening,*" I ordered, unable to resist knowing any longer.

"*The crawler and pikemen lines have met.*" She paused. "*The stygians' charge has been rebuffed and the soldiers are continuing their retreat.*"

"*And the archers?*"

"*They watch the sky, waiting for the harbinger to draw closer.*"

I nodded. "*Can you tell the harbinger's destination yet? Is he heading for the seed or the battle?*"

This time, Ghost took longer to reply. "*He is flying to the crawlers' aid, I think.*"

That reassured me. If the stygian Power knew I was in the fog bank, he would have no compunctions about sacrificing the crawlers to save the seed. *He must believe the soldiers were responsible for the first seed's destruction,* I thought as I continued my careful advance. "*Where is Elron's company now?*"

"*They've nearly reached the city's wall. The crawlers continue to harass the pikemen, but they are holding them off.*" She paused. "*A dome of silver has sprung up around the city. It extends a few yards beyond the walls, too.*"

"*A dome?*" I asked, startled. "*And it's over the entire city, you say?*" I would not have thought any single player powerful enough to cast a shield around an entire city, much less a group of non-players.

"*Yes,*" she replied. "*What is it?*"

"*Probably a shield of sorts,*" I replied. "*What do the stygians make of it?*"

Ghost waited a breath to see how events would unfold. "*The archers have passed into the dome.*" She paused again. "*Now the pikeman.*" Another moment of silence. "*The crawlers have been rebuffed by the shield.*"

"*And the harbinger?*"

"*He's coming up to the shield now. It looks like he means to charge straight at it.*" A drawn-out breath of silence. I waited impatiently. "*The stygian has been rebuffed.*"

I exhaled in relief. "*That's good,*" I said. It appeared Elron's confidence in the New Haven mages was not unfounded. Still, I could not understand how the city wielded such powerful magics—and that being the case, why I hadn't seen evidence of it before this.

I reoriented myself on the seed. Now that I was sure the city could hold off the harbinger, it was time to see my own task done.

Padding forward, I crept deeper into the mists.

＊　＊　＊

The weavers were agitated.

With Ghost guiding me, I closed the distance to the seed but, to my dismay, found that the weavers had enabled all their defenses—including their mental ones. Whether it was the harbinger's coming that had caused this abundance of caution or the death of the other seed, I wasn't sure.

Whatever the reason, it complicated the job at hand.

Six hostile entities have failed to detect you! You are hidden.

Sitting about ten yards from the seed, and with the closest two weavers just within sight range, I considered my next steps. I wasn't sure if attacking the creatures would alert the harbinger, but with the stygian Power so close, I couldn't risk it.

"*What are you going to do?*" Ghost asked.

"*The only thing I can,*" I replied grimly. "*Sneak past.*"

"*Will that work?*" Ghost asked doubtfully.

"*Only one way to find out,*" I said, inching forward. The weavers had arranged themselves in a circle around the seed, with each of them facing in a different direction. It was a good tactic, except that the creatures had formed their guard circle too large.

There were gaps.

Only a few feet separated the stygians from each other, but that was enough for me to slip through. Bent nearly double, I crept forward. An ice bomb was in my right hand and, in my left, a stone. I held both ready but made no move to throw either as I approached my target.

Six hostile entities have failed to detect you!

At the Game message, I slowed my advance to a crawl. Lifting my right foot, I extended it forward and gently touched my boot down before slowly rolling my weight onto it and picking up my left leg. Another step taken.

Six hostile entities have failed to detect you!

Only six feet separated me from the two closest weavers. I rotated my left leg forward. *Make that five feet.*

I stretched out my right leg. Four feet.

I took another step. Three feet.

Six hostile entities have failed to detect you!

Sweat dribbled down my forehead. Ignoring it, I advanced again. The two weavers were now so close that if I reached out with my hands, I could touch their raised pincers. One more step, then a second, and I drew even with the stygian pair.

Little more than a handspan separated me from either. Another careful step—

Six hostile entities have failed to detect you!

—and I was through.

My shoulders sagged and the tension drained from me. I'd penetrated the guard circle, and the most difficult part was over. Still, that did not mean I was in the clear. Taking a moment, I renewed my buffs, then resumed my advance.

Six hostile entities have failed to detect you!
Six hostile entities have failed to detect you!

...

...

Despite the persistent Game alerts, I covered the remaining distance to the seed with growing confidence and reached it without mishap. Elated, I stood unseen over my target.

My mind shield was up, and the thing did not appear aware of my presence. Carefully stowing away both rock and bomb, I quietly unsheathed ebonheart. Once I destroyed it, things would speed up. I couldn't see Ghost, but I trusted she was in position. Raising the black blade, I took careful aim.

And struck.

You have cast piercing strike. You had destroyed a stygian seed!

A weaver hissed. Then another. All six, I imagined were turning about.

I had no intention of fighting them, though. Lowering my mind shield, I wove psi. From beyond the mist, an unholy shriek sounded—the harbinger's cry of rage. Undoubtedly, he too had sensed the seed's death and was winging my way at the fastest pace he could manage.

The weavers took aim and fired.

Making no attempt to dodge the magic projectiles racing my way, I kept casting.

A blight thorn has injured you!
A blight thorn has injured you!
...
Your void armor has reduced the nether damage incurred by 35%.
Void thief triggered! You have acquired the direct-targeted spell, blight thorn (stolen).

The spelled attacks slammed into me one after the other, causing me to stagger drunkenly, but my void armor lessened the impact, and more importantly, I held on to my concentration.

A heartbeat later, my spell completed, and I vanished.

You have teleported 45 yards to Ghost.

Emerging out of the aether, I dived into a roll and wrapped myself in mist.

The ground shook. Something large had landed—the harbinger. Stilling, I waited.

Seven hostile entities have failed to detect you! You are hidden.

I smiled. The winged stygian had landed next to the seed, and I was already out of his detection range. My task was done and now all that was left was to escape.

Rising into a crouch, I crept away.

CHAPTER 333: PARLEY BEFORE THE WALLS

I had killed two stygian seeds but gained no player levels. That did not mean the Game did not reward me for the day's efforts, though.

Your nether absorption has reached rank 8.
Your deception has reached rank 14.
Your sneaking has reached rank 15, allowing you to learn tier 4 abilities.

I was pleased with the progress of all my skills, but it was the advancement of sneaking that delighted me the most. It meant I could finally upgrade fade. First, though, I needed an update on the battle.

"*Ghost, talk to me,*" I said, stopping at the edge of the thinning fog bank. "*What's happening?*"

"*The crawlers are all dead and the soldiers have returned to the city, but Elron has remained behind. He is waiting for you outside the gates.*"

Considerate of him, I thought. "*What about the harbinger?*"

"*He and the weavers are still searching the area around the seed. They haven't seemed to realize you've fled already.*"

I had guessed as much myself from the persistent growls and angry hissing emanating from behind. More importantly, though, I didn't hear any threats uttered—which was a relief. "*What is our friend's mood? Is he angry?*"

"*More like spitting mad,*" Ghost replied, her voice hiding more than a trace of amusement.

I grinned. "*Excellent.*"

"*Do you think he knows it was you who destroyed the seed?*"

"*Hmm, probably not. He isn't ranting like he did earlier.*" The scent crystal must've worked, I decided. "*But once he calms down, he might figure things out.*" I wanted to be well away before that happened, and in preparation for my reentry into the city, I renewed my disguise.

You have cast facial disguise, assuming the visage of Taim. Duration: 3 hours.

I'd been wearing Taim's face the entire time I'd been in New Haven and had no intention of abandoning the ruse yet. It was especially important with the harbinger around. If the stygian Power inadvertently—or deliberately— revealed my bloodline, then at least my real identity would not be exposed.

Then, too, there were the New Haveners to consider.

I wasn't certain what sort of reception awaited me back in the city. I hardly thought the council was going to hail me as a hero, but I didn't think a display of gratitude would be misplaced.

I grinned wryly. *That's hardly likely either, Michael.*

During our first meeting, the city's rulers had been more than a little ambivalent. The thane, for one, seemed to dislike me intensely—for no reason that I could fathom. The orc, too, had been distant. Only the dark elf ruler had been openly friendly. But I had not had enough time to judge if her overtures were genuine.

Lastly, there was the marshal.

Of all the city's occupants, Elron was the one I knew best, but even with him, I didn't have a firm read. An hour ago, I would've said the marshal was well-intentioned towards me, but now...

Now, I knew without a doubt he would place the well-being of his men and city first.

So, while I was willing to give the New Haveners the benefit of the doubt in the hopes of forging a long-term alliance, I was not foolish enough to let optimism blind me.

The city might prove trustworthy.

Or it might not.

And I had to be prepared for both eventualities. With that in mind, I removed the ability upgrade gem from my backpack and activated it.

Creating ability tome...

...

You have acquired a greater fade ability tome.

The gem vanished, leaving a small leatherbound book in its stead. This time, the Adjudicator had offered me no choice of variants which was not surprising given the specialized nature of the fade ability. Wasting no more time, I opened the book and absorbed its knowledge.

You have upgraded the fade ability to <u>greater fade</u> which makes you 50% harder to see for 2 minutes. Greater fade is a master tier ability and requires 5 more ability slots than its expert variant. You have 2 of 58 Dexterity ability slots remaining.

I smiled. I'd gained my first master-ranked ability! And it was arguably my most powerful ability yet.

Greater fade required an incredible fifteen ability slots, but given its benefits, I thought the cost warranted. The ability's next tier was more expensive still, requiring a whopping thirty slots. I would get it anyway, of course. True invisibility was worth nearly any expense.

Still smiling, I crept out of the mists.

※　※　※

I found Elron and a robed figure waiting for me.

The city gates were closed, and the silver dome Ghost had spied earlier was still in evidence. The marshal and his companion were standing outside the magic barrier—an unnecessary risk, I thought. Drawing to a halt, I let the shadows concealing me dissipate.

You are no longer hidden.

The marshal's companion started. Elron's response was more subdued, with only the slight widening of his eyes giving away his surprise. "Stealth?" he asked.

I nodded. "A must-have skill for every explorer," I said lightly.

"Is that how you evaded the charging crawlers earlier?" Elron asked curiously.

Since I'd shadow blinked directly into the fog bank, none of the New Haveners would have any way of realizing I'd teleported, and I saw no reason to enlighten him. "Exactly right," I replied glibly.

Not wanting the conversation to linger over my abilities, I glanced at the blue-robed figure. From his garb, I guessed him to be a mage. His hood was pushed back, revealing a hawkish face. "Who's this?"

"Taim, meet Magister Avery. Magister, this is the player you've heard about," Elron said.

I greeted the mage, and he nodded back brusquely.

"How did you do it?" Avery hissed before I could say anything further.

I raised an eyebrow, surprised by his demanding tone. "Do what?"

Avery stepped forward, his eyes wide, and his expression hungry. "Find the seed in the fog. What trick did you use to locate it?"

I studied the mage carefully. He'd quite deliberately entered my space and stood quivering with suppressed emotion less than a foot from me. But was it passion that drove him or an ill-conceived attempt to intimidate? "Like I told Elron, I have an ability that lets me see through the nether," I replied evenly.

"Nonsense," Avery barked, his fetid breath washing over me. "There's no such ability!"

I folded my arms across my chest. "And how would you know that?"

The magister's expression cooled so quickly it could only be pretense. "Books," he replied vaguely. "The Game has always fascinated me, and I've studied it extensively over the years." His eyes darted to mine again. "Will you tell me the name of your ability? It must be a truly extraordinary spell to pierce the nether."

Elron saved me from answering. "There will be time enough to discuss such matters later. We need to get back to the city." He threw Avery a warning glance. "*Before* the harbinger arrives."

The magister's lips tightened but he stepped back without argument.

The marshal turned to me. "Speaking of the harbinger, where is he?"

I jerked a thumb over my shoulder. "Still hanging around the seed's resting place."

Elron looked behind me. "Then we better get moving. The fog is dissipating fast."

I nodded. "My thoughts exactly." I started to advance, but the marshal's next words stopped me.

"Hold out your hand," Elron instructed.

I stared at him blankly. "Why?"

He gestured to the shield that still enclosed the city. "You will not be able to pass through until Avery grants you access."

My brows furrowed, realizing that's why the two were waiting for me *outside* the dome, and why Elron had felt the need to bring the magister in the first place. "Why does he need my hand for that?"

"To etch the access sigil, of course," Elron said impatiently.

I eyed the magister. After my experience with Loken and his magics, I was wary of letting any mage touch me, and Avery did not strike me as exactly trustworthy.

Sensing my hesitation, the marshal added, "Every New Haven citizen has one." Pulling back his own sleeve, he showed me the small silver mark inscribed below his wrist. "The city's wards will not let you pass without it."

I shook my head. "No thanks."

Elron's brows drew down. "What?"

"I'm not going to let anyone mark me." I glanced at Avery. *Much less him.* I didn't voice the words, but I think Elron caught my meaning. "Lower the shield," I added, "and I'll pass through quickly."

"I can't do that!" Elron said, aghast. "It will endanger the entire city."

I shrugged. "Then don't. And I'll wait out here until the harbinger leaves." I paused. "I assume the barrier will be lowered once he's gone."

Dumfounded, Elron stared at me. But after the silence drew on unbroken, he seemed to realize I was serious. "Stubborn, mistrustful fool," he muttered. Pulling Avery with him, the marshal stomped back to the gates to confer with the mage under the protection of the battlements.

"So, you don't *trust them,"* Ghost said from behind.

"I don't trust them enough to let myself be marked with a magic sigil of dubious origin," I corrected. *"I think Elron means well but I'm not so sure about the city council."* My gaze drifted towards Avery. *"Or that one."*

I'd taken an instant dislike to the magister, finding his mannerisms both disturbing and annoying, and hoped never to deal with him again. I suspected, though, that I wouldn't be so lucky. *Oh well, best I learn what I can while I have the opportunity.* Reaching out with my will, I analyzed the magister.

The target is Avery, a level 158 human.

My brows drew down in surprise. Avery was even higher ranked than Elron. *Perhaps, that explains his... arrogance.*

My gaze flitted back to the pair. I could see them conversing, but none of their words carried to me. Keenly interested to know what they were saying, I stepped forward until my nose nearly touched the warding barrier. Still, I heard nothing.

"Damn," I muttered. Raising a hand, I touched the silver dome.

This is a protective barrier. Only those who have been granted access by the ward's owners can pass through.

It seemed Elron had been telling the truth about the sigil. Still, I was adamant about staying unmarked. Time was running out, though, and I had to make a decision. I glanced behind me. The harbinger wasn't visible yet, but the fog wouldn't hold for much longer.

Wait or go?

Before I could make up my mind, a thin section of the city's protective dome flickered, then vanished. "Quickly! Get inside," Elron said, gesturing at me frantically.

Without hesitation, I stepped across the rim of the barrier.

By entering into New Haven without an access sigil, I knew I ran the risk of imprisoning myself within the city, but the city was large and had hiding places aplenty. Eventually, I would escape.

And declining to enter the city wasn't an option either.

I needed New Haven. Not just for the location of the exit portal, but to serve as my allies. With Elron's soldiers backing me, many things became possible—including defeating the harbinger and the sector boss. With the New Haveners' support, I could do more than escape Draven's Reach. I could *conquer* it.

And that was only the beginning.

First, though, I had to convince the city council that their interests aligned with my own. To do that, I had to win their trust, which destroying both stygian seeds should have gone a long way towards accomplishing.

Behind me, the dome around the city reformed. Up ahead, the gates began to open. The die was cast and my path set. Inhaling deeply, I strode through.

It was time to find out just how deeply I could bind New Haven to my cause.

CHAPTER 334: THE MISSING PIECE

"Let's go," Elron said as soon as the city gates shut behind us.

I glanced around but failed to spot Avery. "Where's the magister?"

"He had other things to attend to," Elron replied, not looking at me as he strode away.

I hurried to catch up. "That's a pity. I had some questions for him."

The marshal looked at me sharply. "Questions? What sort of questions?"

I shrugged. "All sorts. Like why he and his fellows didn't participate in the battle. About how is it that he is so high-leveled—it can't simply be from studying! Oh, and whether I could have a peek at those books he mentioned." I paused. "Do you think he'll let me read them?"

Elron said nothing. His eyes, though, spoke volumes. They were not that of a man caught out by ignorance, but of someone faced with questions he didn't want to answer.

Smiling, I kept going. "Then there is the dome. I find it fascinating that non-players can create a shield powerful enough to keep out a minor Power, and at the same time, make it large enough to cover the *entire* city. You wouldn't happen to know how they accomplished that minor miracle, would you?"

Elron remained stubbornly silent.

"It's curious, that's all," I said mildly. But it was more than that, and we both knew it.

The marshal seemed to deflate. "Very well," he sighed. "I'll tell you."

I waited expectantly, not daring to say anything else lest he change his mind.

"We always knew this day would come," Elron said softly.

I looked at him in confusion. *Did he mean my arrival?*

He smiled. "Not your coming. The stygians. And we've prepared for it accordingly."

"Back up," I said. "You *predicted* the stygians were going to invade the dungeon?"

He nodded mutely.

I frowned. "Why would you—?" I broke off. "It was because your home sector was overrun by the nether," I said, answering my own question. "After that happened, you expected them to follow you here."

"That's right," Elron agreed. "But how did you figure out even that much?"

"It's because of what Stormhammer said. He mentioned the gateway your people entered through was sealed, and I can think of only one reason why a Game portal would shut itself."

"The void. Of course." Elron shook his head sadly. "It's true. My people are refugees. We were forced to flee the nether's coming once and vowed thereafter never to be caught unprepared again."

"But that must have been a long time ago," I protested. "This city looks *old*."

"It's been centuries," Elron agreed. "We didn't forget, though. For generations now, our Mages' Guild has directed their arcane studies towards defensive magics—to the exclusion of all else. Over the years, they refined their spells and expanded their repertoire, and today, our spellcasters far surpass the skills they possessed prior to our exile."

"Hmm. Is that why none of the mages accompanied your soldiers on today's raid? Or the one the day I arrived?"

Elron sighed. "I shouldn't be telling you this, but you guessed right again. Our spellcasters have no offensive magics. And besides, they're too valuable to risk outside the walls."

For a minute, we walked in silence as I chewed over Elron's words. The marshal's story made sense—as far as it went. "Still, even given all that, I find it hard to credit that non-players can perform magic on—" I gestured to the dome—"*that* scale."

The marshal's lips twisted, disdain flickering across his face. "We proles are more capable than you players think."

My brow furrowed. Was Elron right? Was my perspective skewed? Did I underestimate the New Haveners? *Perhaps.* I would have to think on it further. I turned back to him. "What is that word? It's the second time you've used it."

"What, prole?" he scoffed. "It's what you players call us non-players. The term was in common use before our exile. Don't tell me it's gone out of fashion?"

I shrugged. "I have no idea," I said honestly.

Elron looked at me skeptically but let my comment pass uncontested. He did not, however, resume speaking.

"What about my other questions?" I asked, prompting him.

He glanced at me. "Such as?"

"Such as Avery's level. He is *too* high-leveled, you know." I shot him a sideways glance. "As are you."

Elron laughed, his ire vanishing as quickly as it appeared. "Thank you— I think. I've been training since I was a boy. I joined the army young and have been in countless fights." He shrugged. "I've been lucky enough to survive them all."

It was my turn to look dubious. "And you're saying Avery is like you?"

The marshal's smile faded. "No, the magister is not the same. But before you ask what he is, I cannot tell you. I've told you too much as it is."

I stared at him, trying to parse the meaning behind his words. "You've been ordered not to answer my questions," I guessed.

He nodded.

"Then why did you?" I asked, genuinely curious.

Elron hesitated. "I broke our agreement, and I shouldn't have done that. I forced you to destroy that second seed at a grave risk to yourself. Consider this a small measure of recompense."

"I knew what I was doing," I said. "I could have refused you."

The marshal smiled. "But you didn't. And for that, you have my gratitude. You prevented many deaths, not just those of the men I would have lost today, but all those that would've followed had the void been allowed to continue its raids." Elron met my gaze. "No matter what happens from here on out, I won't forget what you've done."

He fell silent then, and I let the conversation lapse. Elron had given me much to think about.

* * *

A little later, Elron and I entered the inner city.

We'd resumed talking, but the marshal kept the conversation light and spoke only about nonconsequential things: what everyday life in New Haven was like and pointing out the sights. I didn't try to steer him to more important matters—I wanted a better grasp of the city's culture—and like any tourist, I craned my neck left and right as I grilled him about the shops, homes, and people we passed.

In a market square close to the city's central fortresses, one shop in particular caught my attention, and I ground to a halt.

Elron trailed to a stop. "What is it?"

"That shop, do you know it?"

The marshal followed my gaze. "Master Gamil's Bazaar of Antiques," he said. "I do. What of it?"

"Can we go in?"

Indecision flickered across Elron's face. "I was ordered to escort you directly to the council."

"This won't take long," I said.

The marshal sighed. "Alright, but let's make it quick."

I was already in motion. Dashing towards the store, I tugged open the stained-glass door and strode through, then held it open for Elron, who followed more slowly. As the door swung shut, I turned around to study the shop.

The inside of the bazaar was dusty and somber. Floor-to-ceiling shelves marched in narrow rows from left to right, each overflowing with all manner of junk—antiques, I supposed the owner named them—but no customers walked the aisles. Elron and I were the only ones present.

A curtained doorway at the far end of the room parted, revealing an aging human.

"Gamil?" I asked, studying the hunched figure limping closer.

"That's right," he rasped as he drew to a stop before us. Holding himself upright with a cane that was as gnarled and ancient as he was, the shop owner squinted at us. "Soldiers," he concluded. "Don't get many of your lot here."

"Master Gamil," the marshal interjected. "It's Elron."

The old man leaned closer. "Ah, my boy, so it is. It's been a long time."

"It has," Elron agreed.

"What can I do for you?" Gamil asked. "Have you come looking for more artifacts to—"

Stepping forward, Elron cut him off. "I'm not here as a customer today, I'm afraid." He gestured towards me. "It is my friend here who has taken an interest in your shop."

The shopkeeper turned my way. "I see. And what can I do for you, young fella? Forgive me, but you don't look like a collector."

I smiled. "Ordinarily, I'd agree. But your shop sign caught my eye."

Gamil appeared confused. "My sign?"

I drew an object out of my backpack. "Yes. It's etched with lines that bear a remarkable resemblance to the ones on this."

The shopkeeper's head creaked downwards to stare at the mosaic tile in my hand. "Ah, now I understand. I have some more pieces like that somewhere."

My eyes lit. "You do? Show me, please."

Gamil swung around. "Come with me," he ordered and shuffled off.

Elron and I followed in his wake, the marshal's gaze darting from my face to the Emblem of the Reach I still held. Ignoring the silent question in his eyes, I kept my own gaze fastened on the slow-moving Gamil.

As we walked, the shopkeeper rambled on. "Did you know the placard above this store was first erected by my great-great-grandfather? He was its original owner. And those stone chits you're looking for? They were amongst the first items he put on sale. Sadly though, there's never been much interest. He sold less than a handful."

"You have a lot of them then?" I asked eagerly.

"Oh, yes. An entire boxful." Coming to a halt, the old shopkeeper raised his cane to tap a box on an upper shelf. "This here is it."

Before he could ask, I reached up and pulled the box down.

"Thanks, my boy," he said.

I barely heard him, my attention focused on the container's contents. Gamil hadn't been lying. The box was filled to the brim with dozens of mosaic tiles. Before I could let myself get too excited, I inspected a few.

The target is an enchanted mosaic tile and part of the Emblem of the Reach.

The target is an enchanted mosaic tile...

...

"They what you looking for?" the old man asked.

"Yes!" Upending the box, I sat down on the floor and sifted through the tiles. The ones in Gamil's box were as irregularly shaped as those I'd found in the loot chests, and it took only a little bit of experimentation to figure out they fit together like puzzle pieces.

The shopkeeper grunted. "You won't find whatever answers you're searching for like that."

Pausing, I looked up to find both Elron and Gamil peering down inquisitively at what I was doing. "Why not?"

"The puzzle's incomplete. There's a piece missing."

I held up the two pieces I'd looted. "One of these might—"

He snorted. "They aren't. It's the center piece that's absent. But don't take my word for it. Go on and see for yourself."

Bending my head back down, I did just that, ignoring Elron's growing impatience.

✳   ✳   ✳

The old man was right.

Sitting back a few minutes later, I studied the nearly complete Emblem. The artifact was disk-shaped, and all told, was formed from twenty pieces—one of which was missing.

It turned out the box contained multiple duplicate tiles, and I could only imagine that over the years they had been discarded by players who had failed to complete the Emblem. Somehow, the pieces had found their way to Gamil and his ancestors.

Resting my palm on the Emblem, I felt out the round hole in the middle that—frustratingly—still needed to be filled. Without the missing piece, the artifact remained inert. Devoid of enchantments, it was just another pile of stone tiles.

I sighed. It seemed I wasn't going to get the answers I desired. I traced the flowing lines etched across the emblem. "What is it?" I muttered.

"It's a sigil," Elron guessed.

I nodded slowly. That could very well be true but didn't help me figure out what the Emblem did—what its *purpose* was. I glanced at Gamil. "Did you sell the center piece to anyone?"

He shook his head emphatically. "No. That tile has never been found. It always bugged my ancestor that he couldn't complete the puzzle. He searched high and low for it, but if that piece ever reached the city, it never fell into my kin's hands."

I hung my head in disappointment. "So, you have no idea where to find it?"

"None."

I gestured back to the puzzle. "How much for these then?" Not counting pieces I'd already found, I needed seventeen pieces from Gamil's collection.

The old man didn't answer immediately. "What's your interest in the tiles? As interesting as I find them, they are admittedly only bits of dead history. Relics of a bygone era and of interest to no one except—"

He broke off abruptly.

I smiled. Gamil might be old, but he wasn't stupid, and I could see understanding dawning in his eyes.

"You a player, boy?" he asked.

"I am."

The old man's eyes darted sideways, seeking confirmation from the marshal.

Elron nodded.

"Well, I'll be damned," Gamil whistled. "In that case, come round back. I have a few more items that may spark your interest."

CHAPTER 335: THREE-IS-ONE

Mouth agape, I stared at the objects lined up on the table.

I'd analyzed each in turn, and the results had left me deeply shocked. "Do you know what you have here?" I whispered.

The old man shook his head, grinning toothily. "None at all. Not even our mages have been able to identify these artifacts. But I reckon they're important—and expensive."

I nodded, not bothering to attempt convincing him otherwise. Gamil appeared too shrewd for that. "That they are." The five items the shopkeeper had laid out on the table was player gear, of course.

But they weren't *ordinary* equipment.

Each piece was part of a legendary set and likely worth tens of thousands to the right buyer. Sadly, though, the items did not belong to the same collection. I couldn't use four, but the fifth... on its own, it more than made up for the others.

"How did you come across this equipment?" I asked absently, still studying the legendary artifacts in fascination.

Even though I was distracted, I did not fail to mark the glance Gamil and Elron exchanged. *What does it signify?* I wondered.

"Let's just say that over the years more than one player fell afoul of the dungeon and failed to retrieve his gear," the old man said.

I nodded, having expected the answer to be something like that. The pair's stolen looks implied there was more to the tale than they were letting on, though. "What happened to the rest of the items?" I asked, letting them keep their secrets.

Gamil tilted his head to the side. "What makes you sure there was anything else?"

I snorted. "Of course there was. The fact that these five items are here tells me you kept the most valuable pieces for yourself and got rid of the lesser ones. Who did you sell them to?" *And what possible use could they have for them?*

It was Elron who answered. "They were taken apart."

"Taken apart?" I repeated in confusion.

The marshal nodded. "The guild took possession of the items. In an effort to reverse engineer the enchantments and create equivalent gear for our people, they broke down each into its constituent parts." He gestured at the table. "These five resisted their best efforts."

I winced, imagining the wastage. "Did it work?"

Elron grimaced. "Not to the extent the mages hoped. None of the enchantments could be duplicated. A handful, though, were successfully modified and made usable. But the entire process was complicated and nearly not worth the effort expended."

"Let me guess, the diviner you used on me earlier was one such item?"

He nodded.

I turned back to the shopkeeper. "I'll take them all."

Gamil smiled. "Perfect. Is there anything else you need?"

About to complete the transaction, I paused. "You wouldn't, by any chance, happen to have a stygian shortsword for sale?"

The shopkeeper shook his head. "I'm afraid I can't help you there. I don't stock such weapons."

"Oh, alright. I'll stick with the artifacts and the mosaic tiles then."

"And in exchange?" the old man asked. "What do you offer?"

I opened my mouth, then closed it, realizing I had only a few golds on my person. The rest of my money was in my bank account and presently inaccessible. "Will seventy gold do?" I asked weakly.

Gamil laughed. "Not nearly."

I sighed, aware that I would have to trade something from my backpack. After a moment's thought, I extracted the stygian seed fragments. "What about these?" I asked, holding them out in the palm of my hand.

Elron straightened as he caught sight of the glistening shards, and even Gamil seemed shocked. "Is that...? Are those...?"

I nodded. "They're the remains of two destroyed stygian seeds. I don't know much about alchemy, but I know the seeds are more valuable than the reagents your people harvest from the nether creatures. Will they suffice?"

Gamil licked his lips, eyes darting between the seed fragments in my hands and the artifacts. "The fragments are valuable," he allowed, "but..."

The shopkeeper required further persuasion. "There is another dead seed outside the city, too. I didn't have time to gather its remains, but as soon as the harbinger is gone, Elron's men can collect them for you as well."

Gamil shot the marshal a look. "Is that right?"

"The fragments are Taim's by right," Elron said slowly. "If he wishes you to have them, my men will gather the pieces and deliver them to you."

Gamil turned back to me. "Then we have a deal, young fella," he said, smiling.

✳   ✳   ✳

You have acquired a cache of 4 x legendary items and 17 x enchanted mosaic pieces.

You have lost 2 x set of stygian seed remains.

You have acquired the <u>Psi Bracelet</u>. This item is indestructible and is part of the legendary jewelry set: <u>Three-is-One.</u>

It was crafted by renowned Chi Master Yellen eons ago. The master held to the philosophy that all the body's energies—mana, stamina, and psi—were the same. He believed that, with appropriate manipulation, one could be transformed into the other.

Setting out to prove his theory, Yellen crafted the Three-is-One artifacts. Unfortunately, the chi master only managed to create one such set before his untimely death. No one has been able to duplicate his feat since, making each piece of the Three-is-One set unique.

The Psi Bracelet increases your Mind by +8 ranks and grants you the tier 5 ability: psi-feed, which allows you to refill your psi pool using either stamina or mana. To experience the full benefits of Yellen's creation, all 3 pieces of the legendary set are required.

I hurried out of the shop in Elron's wake, a new bracelet on my wrist. It was hardly my first legendary item, yet it captured my interest as much as the Wayfarer boots had—if not more so.

The Three-is-One held incredible potential.

If I could cross-feed power between my pools of stamina, mana, and psi, then I could conceivably reach a state of nearly limitless energy. My void armor could be replenished on the fly, and I would become a tireless fighter.

Although in some ways, I had been unlucky to find the psi bracelet first. Of my three energy stores, psi was by far the largest, and in recent times I'd hardly ever run short. In fact, I was hard pressed to imagine any scenario where I would need to replenish psi.

Still, the boost to my Mind was welcome, and knowing that there were two other pieces of the Three-is-One out there, I would do my damnedest to find them. *As soon as I get out of this dungeon, of course.*

"We're here," Elron said.

Lifting my head, I saw that we were back on the steps leading to the entrance of one of the city's four central fortresses. We'd arrived. I glanced at the marshal. Making no move to push through the sealed doors, he shifted uncomfortably from foot to foot. It was the most anxiety I'd seen him express yet.

"We're not going in?" I asked.

"We are," he replied. "But before we do..."

He hesitated further, and I studied him carefully. What had gotten into him? "Yes?" I prompted.

The marshal clenched and unclenched his fists. "Just be careful in there... things aren't as they seem." On those ominous words, he swung around and banged on the fortress' doors. "Open up. It's Marshal Elron, escorting the player, Taim."

I studied the lines of the dark elf's back as the doors creaked open. Elron was stiff—upset, I thought—and I guessed something had happened to make him so.

Or was about to.

"Ghost, scout out the inside of the fortress," I said. *"And be careful."*

The spirit wolf slinked forward. *"What am I looking for?"*

"Anything out of the ordinary," I said. *"Anything different from the last time we were here. Sorry, but I can't be more precise than that."*

"Don't worry, Prime. I'm on it."

She vanished into the fortress, and I turned back to the door to see the marshal and two guards studying me impatiently. I didn't know what awaited me inside, but if Elron was going so far as to warn me—even indirectly—I had to be prepared for the worst.

My gaze slid from the marshal to the guards. I didn't fear New Haven's soldiers. They were impressive in a regular fight, but any confrontation with me would be anything but ordinary. If more soldiers were waiting for me inside the fortress, I would deal with them. Harshly.

The mages were still something of an unknown. But they, too, were surely no threat. Unless, of course, they caught me unawares. "One second," I said, and dug around in my backpack until I found what I was looking for.

You have equipped the spectacles of ward seeing.

"What's that for?" the senior of the two guards—a sergeant, I thought— asked, studying the glasses quizzically.

"Fashion statement," I replied glibly and stepped forward.

The soldiers didn't move aside.

Folding my arms across my chest, I waited patiently. The sergeant glanced at Elron, but the marshal's face was impassive, offering no help.

Left with no other choice, the sergeant waved me forward. "Go on then," he said gruffly. "The council's waiting."

Nodding politely, I entered the fortress alongside Elron. His gaze slid sideways to my face, but he forbore commenting. The marshal knew I was up to something but seemed content to let me be.

The fortress' corridors were as empty as during my last visit. Still, I scanned them repeatedly, searching for any telltale pricks of light. The spectacles I'd equipped were designed to identify wards of tier four and below, and as non-players, New Haven's mages would certainly not be capable of casting anything beyond that.

If there was a spelled trap waiting for me, I would find it.

Halfway to the council chamber, Ghost returned. *"Turn back,"* she shouted as she rushed forward. *"It's an ambush!"*

* * *

"Slow down, Ghost," I said, not breaking stride. *"Tell me what you've seen."*

"There are two dozen mages lying in wait ahead."

Only two dozen? I mused. That number seemed a bit low for taking down an elite player—which is what they thought I was. *"Where are they?"*

"They're split between two antechambers. Each room leads directly into the council hall," she replied, dancing anxiously around me. *"We should go!"*

Ghost's report only calmed me further. Whatever was going to happen would only happen after I met the city's rulers. There was time yet. *"What makes you think it's an ambush?"*

"I overheard one of the leaders give the others their orders. They know you're on the way and want to take you alive."

Even better. I folded my hands behind my back, out of Elron's line of sight, and rubbed my thumb across the blue crystal on the wristband on my left arm. *"We're not running,"* I told her. *"If there is a trap, I intend on springing it."*

"You're not worried?"

"Oh, I am," I explained. "But finding out what is going on in the city is more important. Go back to the council chamber and keep watch on the mages. Return if you learn anything more."

While the spirit wolf hurried away again, I pondered her report. The city council could not have simple betrayal in mind. Keeping their end of the bargain—and telling me the location of the exit portal—would cost them nothing.

So why betray me?

There was Elron's behavior to consider too. The circumspect manner of his actions suggested he feared something... or someone. But what did the commander of New Haven's armies have to fear?

I recalled his earlier words again: *things aren't as they seem.*

I didn't know enough yet, I decided. That the council planned to betray me in some manner was clear, but that could not be the whole story. There was more at play here.

I have to figure out what is going on. Perhaps matters are not as dire as I fear.

But just in case, I would be ready—for anything.

Chapter 336: Things aren't as They Seem

You have passed a thieving skill check!
You have removed 4 trap-making crystals from your trapper's wristband. Remaining trap-making crystals: 128 of 200.

Elron and I drew to a stop as we reached the doors to the council chamber. In my closed fist, I held four crystals. I'd been tempted to trap the corridor but had decided against it. Even in my present circumstances, I couldn't afford to waste my traps, and I suspected the council chamber was where most of the action would take place anyway.

"Tell the thane we've arrived," Elron said, addressing the two guards outside the doors. One of them slipped into the room—closing the door behind him—and the marshal turned to me. "Here is where I leave you."

I was not surprised. More and more, I was becoming convinced that Elron did not want to be party to whatever his superiors planned. "Thank you," I replied, leaving unsaid exactly what I was thanking him for.

The marshal swung around, walking away without a backward glance.

I watched him go for a moment, then turned back to find the remaining guard watching me intently. Striding up to him, I leaned casually against the closed doors. "If you don't mind me asking, what do they do in there all day long?"

The guard's brows crinkled. "The council, you mean?"

Nodding, I opened my right hand—hidden by my body—and placed it flat against the door.

You have activated a single-use enchantment. You have concealed an explosive trap element.

"Ruling stuff, I suppose," he said.

"Huh, imagine that," I said, and stuck another crystal to the door.

You have concealed a second explosive trap element.

The door began to open, and I stepped aside.

"They want you now," the second guard said, emerging from the chamber.

"Then I'd better go in," I said and slipped past him.

* * *

The council hall was conspicuously bright.

Magelights hung from the rafters and lined the walls, making the room far brighter than on my first visit. I took a second to study the chamber. There was not a single shadowed area to be seen.

That was not by chance, of course.

Two closed doors were along the hall's left and right walls. I didn't let my gaze linger on them for too long, but I was certain they led to the antechambers Ghost had mentioned. There were no spelled wards to be seen in the hall, though. It surprised me, and I had to work to keep the troubled frown off my face.

"Have a seat."

Glancing down the hall, I saw the dark elf, Cilia, had risen to address me. The council table was set as before, but this time a single chair had been placed on its nearside—for me, presumably. From behind, I heard the chamber's main door close and the quiet turn of a key.

I had been locked in.

Opening my mindsight, I strode closer to the waiting council members. The five of us were the only ones in the room. I detected no mindglows in the adjacent rooms, and I should have; both were in range.

The mages had shielded themselves.

Drawing to a halt before the council table and about a foot from the chair, I opened my right hand and let the third enchanted crystal fall noiselessly to the carpeted floor.

"Sit," Cilia repeated.

Shaking my head, I placed my booted heel over the crystal. "I prefer to stand."

You have concealed a darkness trap element.

"What's that on your face?" Stormhammer asked suspiciously.

"Spectacles," I replied laconically. The thane clearly expected me to expand on my statement, but instead I took the opportunity to weave together the spelled strands of the disparate trap elements I'd placed.

You have connected 3 trap elements to a remote-control trigger.
Two explosive traps and a darkness trap have been successfully configured!

"Why do you need them?" Sienna asked, frowning.

I gestured to the magelights overhead with my right hand while keeping the trigger concealed in my left. "Those are bright enough to hurt. The spectacles help. But if you dim the lights, I'd be more than happy to take them off."

Unsurprisingly, no one took me up on my offer.

"We didn't assemble here for idle chatter," Lorn remarked mildly before the silence could become too awkward.

"Quite right," Cilia said, regaining control of the conversation. "Let's begin."

I pursed my lips, not missing the change in the council's leadership. Stormhammer was no longer in charge. Was that significant?

"You have our thanks and that of the city for what you've done," Cilia said. "By destroying the fog banks, you've ensured New Haven's continued survival."

I inclined my head. "You're welcome. Now, it's your turn. Give me the location of the portal."

Cilia waved aside my question. "We'll get to that in due time. First, we have some questions."

"Questions?" I repeated blandly.

"Yes, questions," the dark elf said, leaning forward on the table. "Nothing onerous, mind you. But we must be certain, you understand."

"Of course," I said, keeping my face expressionless. Inwardly, though, I quivered with anger. Cilia was up to something. I wasn't sure what, but it was time to see to my final preparations. Drawing psi, I cast my buffs.

"Excellent," Cilia said. "Now, tell us, how were you able to find the seed? And so quickly! You barely spent more than a few minutes in each fog bank."

"Avery asked me the same thing," I mused aloud. "Why all this interest in a matter of such minor importance?"

Sienna's lips thinned. "We're asking the questions, not you," she retorted before Cilia could respond. "Now, answer the First!"

"Give me the location of the exit portal first," I countered.

Sienna's face flushed but before she could speak, Cilia laid a hand on her arm. "You don't seem to understand the situation," the dark elf said with a smile that didn't reach her eyes. "You've lost your leverage. Unless you satisfy our curiosity, you will not get the answers you seek."

I folded my arms across my chest. "If that was supposed to convince me to share even *more* of my secrets," I said disdainfully, "then it was a mighty awful effort."

Anger sparked in Cilia's eyes and her mask of affability appeared in danger of slipping. "I apologize for Sienna's impertinence, and my earlier... rudeness," she said, managing to keep up the act. "But come, this is a small matter. You said so yourself. Only tell us, and we can move on from all this unpleasantness."

I stared mutely back at her, wondering just how gullible she thought me.

"This is a waste of time," Stormhammer muttered. "Just tell him what he wants to know so we can get this damn charade over with."

"Shut up, you imbecile!" Cilia hissed, pinning the thane with a furious glare. "You were warned not to interfere!"

The dwarf's face turned red, and he looked ready to explode. "How dare you!" he roared, jerking upright. "Don't you forget who you're—"

I stopped listening. Ghost had reappeared—and from her expression, things were about to get interesting.

"They're coming," the spirit wolf sang.

I tensed, my thumb on the button of the remote trigger. I was primed to escape, but I'd still not learned what I'd come here to. Remaining outwardly calm and, to all appearances blissfully unaware, I waited.

The doors to the antechambers blew open and two dozen mages charged in. Each sparkled with wards and protective shields, and all of them had staffs and wands in hand. The council froze, argument forgotten as they stared wide-eyed at the blue-robed figures.

Either they're wonderful actors, I thought, *or they've been caught as much by surprise as I was supposed to be.*

The mages formed up on either side of me. All of them had their hoods up, concealing their identities, but I was sure Avery was amongst their number.

A final figure strolled languidly out of the antechamber on the right. Unlike the other mages, he was not wrapped in spells and didn't carry any weapons. His head was uncovered, too, revealing a gleaming bald head.

"*That's the leader,*" Ghost whispered.

I nodded ever so slightly in her direction and turned to inspect this approaching figure.

The target is Castor, a level 208 human.
Your mental intrusion has been detected!
You have passed a mental resistance check! A hostile entity has failed to pierce your disguise and has been fed false analyze data.

Only by dint of will did I keep my eyes from widening in shock.

Not only was the approaching human an elite—*and how did an ordinary human manage to become so powerful?*—he'd used analyze on me, an ability I would have sworn only players possessed.

The strange mage's lips turned down, seemingly disappointed by the failure of his ability.

"Castor, what's the meaning of this?" Cilia demanded. "I thought we agreed—"

The human slashed a hand downward. "Silence!"

The dark elf's mouth snapped closed.

My gaze darted to the other New Haven rulers; all were similarly tight-lipped. Heads bowed and eyes downcast, they refused to meet Castor's gaze. My eyes narrowed, not missing the implications. Whoever Castor was, he was the one truly in charge—not Cilia, and certainly not the other council members.

"Better," Castor said, letting his gaze linger over the cowed rulers. "Now, like the thane said, this charade has gone on long enough." He looked at me. "We have what we want."

"What are you?" I asked. Castor looked like a mundane human and the Game didn't dispute that, but he had to be *more*.

"Have a seat, and I'll tell you everything," he replied.

"No."

Castor raised an eyebrow and glanced meaningfully at the arrayed mages in silent threat.

"I'm bored already," I said, faking a yawn. "Either you tell me what I want now, or I leave."

Anger flashed in the human's eyes but no sign of it showed when he spoke again. "We're the possessed."

This time, I did not manage to hide my start of surprise.

"So, you've heard of us," Castor said matter-of-factly. "And how might that have happened?" he asked, studying the rulers.

Sweat dribbled down Sienna's face and even Cilia looked worried. Lorn was implacable as ever, and the thane just as disgruntled. "I let it slip," Stormhammer said shortly. "I accused him of being one of you."

"You," Castor said, his lips turning down. "I should have known." He turned back to me. "Do you know what we are?"

We? My gaze slid from him to the rest of the silent mages in the room.

"That's right," Castor said. "All of us are the so-called possessed." He stepped closer. "I never liked that term myself, but what can you do? Some idiot mistakenly labeled us so centuries ago and the name stuck." His eyes held mine. "Now answer me, do you know what we are?"

I shook my head.

Castor spread his arms and smiled as if my ignorance amused him. "Come, can't you guess?"

"Why bother? I can see you're dying to tell me."

The elite guffawed, laughing so hard he had to clutch his sides in an effort to stop.

I watched him expressionlessly. "What's so funny?"

"That word," Castor wheezed, getting himself under control. "Dying. We don't do that anymore."

I frowned.

"We've escaped death more fully than ever before."

My frown deepened. *Before?* I wondered. *Before what?*

"I can see you're finally catching on," Castor remarked, still amused. "Go on, think it through. I'll wait."

Ignoring his condescending tone, I did just that. "You are players," I said at last. Perhaps Castor and his fellows could falsify their Game data. That all of them could do so and with such effectiveness as to defeat my own perception did seem unlikely, but it was the only thing that made sense.

"So close, but so wrong," Castor said, shaking his head in mock sadness. "We are..."

He paused theatrically.

"...*former* players. Only now, we're so much better. Undying and eternal."

I stared at him. Elites. Stygian Powers. And now former players claiming to be undying.

Just how much worse could this bloody dungeon get?

CHAPTER 337: WHAT RETIREMENT LOOKS LIKE

"How?" I gasped. "How is it that you can be what you claim?"

While waiting for his response, I went over everything I'd learned. Matters were no closer to making sense. If anything, they'd grown even more confusing.

Retired players? It sounded like an impossibility. How did a player even leave the Game? I'd never heard any mention of anything like it before. Nor did the moniker 'possessed' bode anything good. It suggested that Castor and his companions had used dubious means to achieve their new status.

Castor smiled as if he could see my scrambling thoughts. "Taim, isn't it?"

I nodded.

"You will get the answers to all your questions in good time. But for now, you *will* come with us."

It was a thinly-disguised order, and one I was little inclined to follow. "No," I said curtly.

"No?" Castor glanced at one of the mages on the opposite line. "You hear that, Avery? Taim here thinks I was asking." He turned back to me, his eyes cold. "I wasn't."

"Be that as it may, I'm not going anywhere with you," I said with no hint of give in my tone.

Avery flung back his hood. "You think you can take all of us?" he hissed.

I smiled with false pleasantness. "We'll find out, won't we?"

Avery matched my smile with one just as fake. "I'm going to enjoy this. When we're done with you, you won't—"

"You want to leave the dungeon," Castor said abruptly. "Don't you?"

I broke off from my staring contest with Avery to glance at him. "What does that have to do with anything?"

Castor laughed, at ease once more. "Didn't they tell you?" he asked, gesturing to the council. "*We* control the exit. You're not getting out of Draven's Reach without our help."

I frowned. It was a bold assertion, and one made with such confidence I could not bring myself to doubt it. Still, I glanced at the council, seeking some hint of confirmation.

Surprisingly, it was Stormhammer who nodded as our gazes crossed.

I turned back to Castor. "I see," I said, backing down from my confrontation with Avery as if it had never happened. "And what will your help cost me?"

"Your body, for starters."

I blinked. "My what?"

"Your corpse," Avery interjected, grinning maliciously. "Don't worry, we don't need *you*. Just your body. It's better, in fact, if you're not there to foul up the plumbing."

My lips twisted sourly in realization. "Right. Possession."

Castor chuckled. "See? You're finally getting it."

I rubbed my chin as if I was considering the offer. "So, just to be clear, you want me to die?"

Avery beamed with exaggerated cheer. "Not so stupid this one, is he?"

Taking his words as confirmation, I continued, "And in exchange for one of my lives, you will let me leave the dungeon?"

"For one of your lives and answering all of our questions, the boss just *might*," Castor allowed.

I nodded, filing away the information. There were more possessed elsewhere in the dungeon, and Castor, it seemed, wasn't the one in charge overall. *That complicates matters.*

"Two lives might be even better," Avery quipped. "How many do you have remaining, Taim?"

Ignoring him, I kept my gaze fixed on Castor. "What questions?"

"Nothing too difficult. Where you're from, how you entered the dungeon, what's going on in the Kingdom, and how you managed to locate the seed in the fog bank. Things like that. Simple, really. Now why don't you have a seat, and we can get started?"

Why do they keep trying to get me to sit? I wondered irritably. *It's almost as if—*

I broke off, eyes narrowing. Reaching out with my will, I analyzed each of the other players one by one. To my relief, Castor was the only elite amongst them. *"Ghost, sink down to the floor below. Find an empty room and wait for me there."*

Bobbing her head in acknowledgment, the spirit wolf exited the room wordlessly.

Castor meanwhile was waving his hand to gain my attention. "Taim, did you hear me? I said: sit down."

I glanced from the chair to the possessed. "Why?" I asked mildly. "So, your trap can snare me?"

Castor's face tightened almost imperceptibly.

That the chair was trapped was only a guess, but the possessed's reaction implied I wasn't wrong. Whether he spoke truly or not, Castor didn't intend on negotiating with me in good faith.

"You can see tier five wards?" he asked, his eyes resting consideringly on my spectacles.

"I can," I lied.

The possessed leader's gaze shifted towards Avery. "Go ahead. Take—"

Not waiting for him to finish, I pressed my finger down on the trigger in my hand.

A blot of darkness trap has been activated.
Two explosion traps have been activated.
Multiple hostile entities have failed to detect you! You are hidden.

Plumes of dense blackness mushroomed out from beneath me, enveloping me, the possessed, and the four councilors. Tugging gladly at the darkness, I vanished from sight. At the same time, twin explosions wracked the hall's main doors, ripping them off their hinges and blowing them apart.

Dagen has died.
Nestor has died.

The two New Haven sentries perished instantly. I regretted their passing; it was the possessed who were the true targets of my ire, but the guards' deaths had been unavoidable—and necessary misdirection on my part.

In the hall itself, chaos reigned.

The sudden shift to violence had caught the possessed unprepared and contradictory orders were shouted. The mages first scattered, then tried to regroup. The councilors wisely ducked under the table, then not so wisely began to shout or cry—I couldn't tell which—adding to the general mayhem.

Long seconds later, weapons were finally aimed to point at where I'd been, the chair, and everywhere I *wasn't*. I'd already repositioned and placed myself out of harm's way.

"Find him!" Castor screamed when he realized his quarry had flown. "And someone get rid of this bloody cloud."

Nestled in the corner farthest from the destroyed doors, I smiled. My foes were all blinded. I, on the other hand, could see perfectly well, and for one reckless moment, I was tempted to wreak further havoc in their ranks... but the possessed were too much of an unknown quantity to tackle just yet. And that was not even factoring in that Castor was an elite. I may have stolen the upper hand, but I was certain I would not retain the advantage for long.

"Guard the door!" Avery shouted. "He is going to flee that way."

He was only half right. I *was* going to flee. Only I wasn't going to do it using the door. Weaving psi, I shadow blinked.

You have teleported to Ghost.

I emerged beside my companion, transitioning between one second and the next from chaos and shouts to silence and calm. Glancing around, I saw I was in a storage room of some sort. *"Nice find,"* I told Ghost.

Rising to my feet, I drew psi and cast another spell, then pressed a stud on my belt.

You have cast facial disguise, assuming the visage of Dagen. Duration: 3 hours.

You have activated the simple mode enchantment of the belt of the chameleon. Your armor and weapons are now hidden.

None of the New Haveners knew I could teleport, and I hoped they would remain guessing about the manner of my escape for a long time yet. Wearing the face of the dead hall guard, I left the room.

It was time to make my exit.

❋　❋　❋

Fleeing the fortress proved easy.

Barely any of the castle servitors glanced in my direction as I made my way to the gate. The fortress at large had not been put on alert, and I was simply one more face amongst many. When I neared the keep's main doors,

I blinked out with Ghost's help, leaving the guards posted there none the wiser.

"Do we flee the city?" she asked.

I glanced up. The protective dome around the city was still active, and given that the possessed would almost certainly be hunting me, I expected it would stay in place a while longer.

"Not yet," I replied. *"We're only just beginning to untangle matters in New Haven. Before we leave, I want to understand the entirety of what is going on."*

"Where do we go from here then?"

I thought about the question for a moment. *"First, we return to the antique shop."*

Ghost's ears went flat in confusion. *"You want to talk to the old man again. Why?"*

"He'll know where I can find Elron. If anyone has answers, it will be the marshal."

✳ ✳ ✳

You have cast facial disguise, assuming the visage of Taim.
You have teleported to Ghost.

Swapping my face to one Gamil knew, I shadow blinked into the center of the shop. It was as empty as before. *"Where is he?"* I asked Ghost, who'd already scouted the building.

"In the back room," she replied.

Lifting my head, I called out. "Gamil? You here?"

Footsteps shuffled closer from the rear of the building, and the curtains partitioning the rooms split to reveal the old shopkeeper. "Taim," he remarked with mild surprise. "You're back." He limped closer. "Elron not with you?"

I shook my head. "The marshal is why I'm here, actually."

The shopkeeper tilted his head to the side and looked at me questioningly.

"I'm trying to find him. Do you know where he lives?"

"At work, where else?" Gamil chuckled. "That boy spends more than half his time in the barracks with his men. You'll find them near the city's southeast tower."

I shook my head. "I can't meet him there. I need somewhere... more private."

The amusement faded from the old man's face. "What's this about?"

I hesitated. I could placate him with lies, but sooner or later, I expected everyone in the city would know that I was a wanted man, and when that happened, I did not want Gamil running to the authorities.

Better to tell him the gist of what happened and learn now how far he can be trusted. "There's been trouble with the council," I said finally. "I'm being hunted."

"Is Elron alright?" he asked sharply.

"He is, or I think so anyway. The marshal wasn't with me during the council meeting. And before you ask, I don't mean him harm. But he is possibly the only one in the city still willing to help me."

"Elron left you alone with the councilors?" Gamil asked, still seeming to be puzzled by that bit.

I nodded.

"Huh," he grunted. "That's not like him. The only time I've known him to..." Falling silent, the old man scrutinized me for a drawn-out moment. "This business, does it involve the possessed?"

I drew in a sharp breath. "You know about them?"

He spat to the side, not hiding his disgust. "Unfortunately, I do."

"Does everyone in the city?"

Gamil shrugged. "Sort of. The possessed are an... open secret. Nearly everyone has heard of them, but few understand their true nature, and no one likes to talk about them." His eyes drifted towards the back room. "You must have guessed by now that the possessed are the source of the artifacts you purchased."

I nodded slowly. "Did you buy the items from them?"

"Not directly," he said. "But just like the rest of us proles, the possessed have no use for Game items, and over time they've abandoned them."

"After which they made their way into your hands," I concluded.

He nodded. "Are the possessed the ones after you?"

"They are," I said heavily. "Which is why I need to find Elron." I held his gaze. "Will you help me?"

"I will," he said with barely a flicker of hesitation. "Elron has a house in the southern city quarter. He doesn't leave the barracks often, but when he does, you will find him there." Pulling a map from a nearby shelf, he began scribbling on it. "Here, let me direct you."

Chapter 338: A Tangled Knot

The marshal's house was a small one-story building that overlooked the city walls.

After Ghost scouted the building and pronounced it safe, I slipped inside. Elron was not home. The dark elf had no servants and no family, and the place looked barely lived in. Sitting down in the nearly empty living room, I made myself comfortable. I expected I had a long wait in store before the marshal returned.

Two hours passed, and still Elron didn't appear.

I glanced at Ghost. Seeming just as bored as I was, she was sniffing disinterestedly at every dusty corner. I could feel my own eyes struggling to stay open.

"Keep watch," I said. *"I'm going to get some sleep."* Then, I lay down on the floor and fell into a deep slumber.

$$* \quad * \quad *$$

"Prime, he's coming."

My eyes snapped open. *"Alone?"* I asked, sitting up.

"Yes."

"How long was I asleep for?"

"Long enough for it to be the next day," Ghost replied.

Shifting my focus inwards, I checked the waiting Game messages.

You have slept 5 hours. Stamina, mana, and psi reserves have been fully restored.

You have lost knowledge of the stolen spell, blight thorn.

The lock on the door rattled. Rising to my feet, I turned around. Elron stepped through the doorway, and on seeing me, stopped short.

"So, this is where you've been hiding," he said mildly and locked the door behind him.

"I've been waiting for you, not hiding."

"Huh, same thing." Elron sat down heavily on a couch. "Thanks to you, Avery and his ilk have been grilling me for hours. For some reason, they seem to believe I know where you've gone."

"Will they check here?"

He snorted. "Hardly. I barely use this place. Besides, they don't think I'm hiding you, just that I know more about you than I'm letting on."

I sat down on the couch across from him. "And do you?"

He stared at me for a moment. "I know you are not the simple explorer you claim to be—or not only that. The possessed may not be players anymore, but they retain many of their former abilities, and I've seen what they are capable of. Not one of them, not even Castor, would consider venturing through the dungeon alone as you have."

He held my gaze. "You are more than you make out, Taim. You must be." A smile flickered across his face. "I *also* know you make Avery and Castor more nervous than I've ever seen. That alone is good enough for me."

My own lips twitched upward. It seemed I had read Elron right. "Is that why you've been helping me?"

The dark elf leaned forward. "Understand me, Taim. I love my city; I love my people. And if we are to survive, we need to get out from under the possessed's thumb." He stared at me, his face serious. "That's why I helped you. Not for any mere dislike of the possessed. But to save my city."

"And you trust *me* to do that?" I asked solemnly. "That's a tall ask from someone you've only met recently."

Elron bared his teeth, revealing a deep-seated frustration. "Believe me, I know. And no offense, Taim, but if I had a choice, I *wouldn't* trust you. I would rid the city of the possessed myself. It's been tried before, though—many times." Sighing, he sat back. "We've always failed."

My brows creased. "Maybe it's better if you start from the beginning."

Elron nodded, still looking glum. "I take it from the reports I've heard about what happened in the council chamber that you know what the possessed are?"

"I know what they *claim* to be," I clarified. "I don't understand, though, how they can be former players."

Elron shrugged. "I don't either. But however the possessed came to be, there's no question of their power. They've been in this dungeon for as long as my own people—longer, in fact. And they're the only reason we've survived this long."

I looked at him in surprise. "So, the possessed have been *helping* New Haven?"

"Yes," he said bluntly. "Even I will attest to that. The possessed helped build this city. For centuries, they've also helped train our armies and keep the dungeon's denizens at bay. And when the stygians arrived, it was the possessed that shielded the city from the harbinger. Without them, we'd be dead many times over."

I frowned. "All those dangers you've just mentioned—the elites, the stygians—they're all still present. Yet, you want to get rid of the possessed. Who will protect the city then?"

Elron nodded dourly. "That's the rub, isn't it? New Haven still needs the possessed. Simply killing them—even if it were possible—is not the solution."

My frown deepened. "Then I take it you believe their claim that they are undying?"

"I don't just believe, I *know* it for a fact. I've witnessed Castor's return from the dead." He paused. "Only, when he came back, he was wearing a different body."

I pursed my lips. "And they can all do this?"

"That's more... doubtful." Elron hesitated, then added, "I've gotten the impression that the possessed have a limited supply of bodies, and those that they have are reserved for the higher-ups, like Castor. It's why they don't risk the fog banks lightly themselves."

I looked at him, startled. "Are you telling me," I said slowly, "that the possessed can survive the nether's touch?"

The marshal nodded. "They can. Avery claims a possessed's body retains its inherent immunities and weaknesses. According to him, there's something in a player's blood that protects him or her from the nether. The possessed still take damage from the void, though, and they can die as easily as anyone. When that happens, they don't always come back."

My anger had been steadily mounting during Elron's explanation. "That still doesn't tell me," I said from between gritted teeth, "why your council sent *me*—and not the possessed—into the fog banks to kill the seeds."

"We had no choice," the marshal said softly. "After their last venture, Castor has refused to send any more of his people into the fog."

"Their last venture?" I asked sharply.

Elron did not flinch from the anger in my face. "There have been other seeds," he admitted. "Three of them, to be exact. The possessed destroyed them but it was not easy. Castor's people spent hours searching for the things in the fog, all while fighting off the crawlers and the harbinger. As you can imagine, their losses were significant." He paused. "That's why Castor has vowed not to send any more possessed into the mists. And that's why he is so keen on knowing how you navigate the nether so easily yourself."

I rubbed my temples. "So, your council used me," I said bitterly. "You used me."

"I had no choice," Elron repeated. "Castor claims it is unnecessary to kill the seeds. And, strictly speaking, he is right. As long as the possessed can maintain the dome around the city, New Haven will survive the fog's touch—in the short run, at least." His face curled with resentment. "But that doesn't stop the city from starving because half the fields lie fallow. And that doesn't stop my men from dying when we are forced to put down stygian raids."

Stubbornly ignoring Elron's story of woe, I continued my questioning. "The tale you fed me about losing men to the fog, that was a lie then?"

"That was no tale," the marshal protested. "After the possessed refused to help, the council ordered me to try without them. As you can imagine, it was a disaster."

"Huh," I grunted noncommittally. I thought about everything Elron had told me over the last few days, and something else occurred to me. "You knew, didn't you?"

"About what?"

"That the harbinger would come. You knew before I told you."

Elron looked away shamefaced. "I did. The mages were already on standby."

I bowed my head. Matters in the city were more tangled than I had presumed and even Elron had not dealt with me straightly. I wanted to be angry with him about that, but the truth was... I understood his motivations. I had done much the same to protect those under my care, after all.

Sighing, I set aside my bitterness and returned to the matter at hand. "So, to summarize: the possessed protect the city, even if they are less willing to risk themselves of late. What I don't get is what they get out of the bargain."

"Bodies," Elron replied simply.

"Bodies," I repeated, finally making the connection. New Haven enabled the possessed's undying existence, and in return they had to keep its population alive—or at least a good portion of it. A moment later, I frowned, remembering my conversation with Castor. "But not just *any* bodies?"

"No, not just any bodies, as you've rightly seemed to have guessed already. The possessed can only use player corpses."

"Hence their interest in me."

"Correct," the marshal said. "The agreement between New Haven and the possessed is centuries old. In exchange for their protection, the city is required to hand over any player born into the population." Elron stared morosely into the distance. "But of course, the game is rigged."

I tilted my head. "How so?"

"The possessed are the ones keeping my people in the dungeon."

It took me a moment to work out what he meant. "So, Castor was telling the truth? The possessed control the exit portal?"

"Yes."

My brows furrowed. "But... but why don't they just leave themselves?"

Elron shrugged. "That, I don't know. Perhaps they like it here, or it may be that they're afraid to."

I nodded slowly. Both of those things could be true. "And where is the exit portal exactly?" I held my breath, half-afraid he would refuse to tell me.

"In the southeastern quadrant of the dungeon," the marshal answered easily. "But if you are thinking of trying to sneak through, think again."

"Why?" I asked, even as I ran through plans in my mind to do just that.

"The portal lies in the heart of the lich's court."

"Lich? What lich?"

"I've never seen him myself, but according to the city records, the possessed's ruler is an archlich. Even Castor seems to fear him."

"Hmm," I mused, wondering exactly what an archlich was. "And how many possessed are said to reside in this supposed court?"

Elron shrugged. "I can only guess, but according to the archives, at one time, there were as many as a thousand possessed in Draven's Reach."

"A thousand," I muttered, suddenly a whole lot less enthused at the idea of visiting the lich's court.

The marshal eyed me carefully. "You're going to go anyway, aren't you?"

"I must," I said. "I have people on the outside depending on me."

Elron snorted disdainfully. "What, like the bounty hunters guild?" I opened my mouth to reply, but before I could, he raised his hand. "I know you misled me before about your origins. No more lies, please. If you don't want to tell me who you really are, then don't."

I said nothing.

"I thought so," Elron said, smiling thinly. Without missing a beat, he continued, "If you are determined to penetrate the lich's court, will you permit me a suggestion?"

"Go ahead."

"Seek out help first," he said.

"And where would I find that?" I asked sourly. "Your council has already refused, and from what you've told me, there's not much you or your city can do to aid me."

"New Haven can't help you," he agreed. "Not directly. But there may be someone else who could."

"Oh? And who would that be?"

"Another possessed."

I stared at him in amazement, but Elron held up his hands for patience. "Hear me out, please. The possessed have taken advantage of the city, but they are not all bad. And if the old tales are to be believed, they started out with the best of intentions. But more to the point—I've overheard Castor and Avery talking of an exile."

"An exile? Go on."

"This exile is said to have fled the lich's court and is rumored to be in the northeastern section of the dungeon. Not only that, Castor and the others believe she is nearly as powerful as the archlich himself. Apparently, the possessed ruler has tried on multiple occasions to assassinate her. She still lives, though, and he has long since given up trying. She may help you."

I nodded vaguely. "I'll have to think about it." Falling silent, I pondered my next steps.

"You know, all of this could have turned out differently," Elron remarked.

I looked up at him. "How so?"

"When you arrived, if you hadn't been so impatient, I could have kept the council from finding out about you."

I blinked. "Are you saying you were trying to hide me from them?"

"Oh yes," he said. "The jail might not have looked like much, but the men there are all loyal to me personally, as are the soldiers on the wall. No one would have talked."

I looked at him skeptically. "So, what went wrong?"

"*You* did. If you hadn't given me a two-day limit to finish my investigations, I wouldn't have been forced to call in the Mages' Guild to verify you were what you said you were."

"You're saying this is all *my* fault?"

He grinned unrepentantly. "Yes."

I let that pass and focused on something else he mentioned. "Are all the mages in the guild possessed?"

"Not all, but many among the upper echelons are," Elron allowed. "They find the cowled hoods useful. It helps disguise their deformities."

"Deformities?"

"Sometimes, the weaker possessed are forced to reuse the same body after they die. And as I understand it, any damage a corpse sustains can't be removed post 'death.'"

I stared at him in morbid fascination. "Can't they just heal themselves once they repossess the corpse?"

Elron shook his head. "Apparently, they can't. Any bodily injuries dealt pre-possession are considered permanent traits. It's what makes Castor and his fellows so eager for 'clean' bodies."

I shuddered at the thought of living inside a mutilated corpse. "It doesn't sound like a pleasant existence. But enough of that. Tell me about the Mages' Guild. Was any of that stuff about them specializing in defensive magic true?"

"It was, but *only* as it applies to the city-born mages. The apprentices I brought to work the device were two such." He sighed. "Involving them, though, was always a risk, and it clued their superiors that something was amiss. Eventually, Castor and Avery got wind of what I was up to, and they forced the council to summon you."

"I wasn't sure I could trust you," I said, defending my actions.

"I understand. And in your place, I would have likely done the same." He paused. "But enough of the past. Let's talk about the future. I assume you want my help to get out of the city?"

"I don't," I contradicted. "I can deal with Castor and the others myself."

Elron looked doubtful but did not gainsay me.

"It will be helpful, though, to know how long their protective dome will remain in place."

"A day more at most," the marshal said confidently. "As badly as Castor wants you, he won't risk tiring his people needlessly. Otherwise, he will be forced to call for reinforcements from the archlich, and he will want to avoid that at all costs."

"That's good."

"If you don't need my help escaping the city, is there anything else I can help you with?" Elron asked.

I looked at him speculatively for a moment. "That bit about wanting to save your city, did you mean it?"

"I did," he replied unhesitatingly. "But don't worry, I realize my aspiration is doomed to remain a dream. The challenge is too big for any one man—even if that man is a player—to surmount. Get yourself away from this dungeon and back to your own people and let me worry about how to take care of New Haven."

"No dream is too big," I said softly. "Actually, I was going to ask you: if you had the opportunity, would you save your city?"

"Of course." Staring at me with almost frightening intensity, Elron leaned forward. "You're saying the city can be saved? How?"

"Not the city," I corrected, not shying from his gaze. "But its people can be." I paused. "How do you feel about evacuating New Haven?"

CHAPTER 339: FORGING ALLIANCES

Elron and I spoke for hours.

I did not remove my disguise or share any of my own truths. There was no need to, and the possessed were already looking to the marshal for answers. I couldn't risk my secrets falling into their hands. For his part, Elron did not pry, and I was certain he kept his own council on many matters.

We came up with a half a dozen schemes for evacuating New Haven. But every plan was convoluted and fraught with peril, and more crucially, they all presumed the possessed could be dealt with.

Finally, we both accepted the obvious.

Sitting back, I said what we both were thinking. "This is no use. We can't finalize anything until we figure out a way to deal with the lich and the other possessed. And to do that, I must leave the city."

Elron nodded. "I agree."

"The first step will be to scout the archlich's court. I only wish there was a way to get there quickly." I sighed, thinking of the many miles of plateau I would have to trek across.

The marshal hesitated. "There *is* a way. But, like I said earlier, if you heed my advice, you will head east and find the exile before venturing into the possessed's domain."

"What are you talking about?" I asked sharply, ignoring the latter part of his statement to focus on the first. "What way?"

"There is a tunnel," he replied. "It was constructed centuries ago."

My brows rose in surprise. "A tunnel?" Elron had made no mention of this before. "Between the city and the lich's court?"

He nodded mutely.

I threw up my hands. "But why didn't you say so earlier? This changes everything!"

Elron shook his head. "It doesn't."

I narrowed my eyes. "Explain."

"The tunnel is vigilantly guarded." He leaned forward, his expression solemn. "Look, Taim, you know I'd back my men against any other prole army out there. But against the possessed? They stand no chance—*especially* in a small, confined space like the tunnel. Even Castor's gang could hold it indefinitely against us." He shook his head. "Until the tunnel is cleared of the lich's people, it is a death trap."

I inclined my head, acknowledging the point. "But perhaps *I* could sneak through..."

"I doubt it." He raised his palms before I could protest. "I'm aware you're more capable than you want me or the council to believe, and maybe, just maybe, you can perform the feat as you claim. I still think it's the wrong approach."

"You want me to seek out the exile," I accused. "That's why you didn't tell me about the tunnel."

"You're right," the marshal said evenly.

His lack of denial caught me off-guard, and in a fit of pique, I almost refuted his advice there and then. But I reined in my irritation in time and forced myself to think through the matter.

I'd doubted Elron more than once during our short acquaintance. And so far, that hadn't turned out so well for me. The marshal was a smart man, and he knew Draven's Reach and the possessed better than I did. Did I doubt he hated the possessed? *No.* Did I believe he would betray me? *No.*

Then perhaps it's time I heed his words.

"Alright, we'll do it your way," I said at last.

Elron exhaled heavily, making no attempt to conceal his relief. "Thank you."

I raised a cautionary finger. "But I want to know everything about this tunnel. Just in case."

"Of course," he agreed. "The tunnel is well-protected from external dangers and runs underground for its entire length, far below even the deepest chasm. It was constructed with two purposes in mind. First and foremost, to provide a means of quickly reinforcing the city during emergencies. And secondly, to evacuate New Haven's populace when the time came."

"Where is the entrance?"

Elron smiled. "In the lower levels of the same fortress you just escaped from."

I lowered my head into my palms. "The council's keep? Of course."

Elron nodded. "That fortress is not the council's though; it's Cilia's."

My lips turned down. The two of us had spoken at length about New Haven's rulers, and I was still irritated at myself for being so easily taken in by the dark elf. According to Elron, Cilia was the possessed's staunchest ally on the council. "What are we going to do about her?"

The marshal knew what I was driving at. "Leave it to me," he said grimly. "I'll take care of matters with the council. You find the exile and deal with the lich."

"Alright," I agreed reluctantly and rose to my feet. "Then I better get started."

Elron stood too. "Come this way first. I have something for you," he said and hurried out of the room before I could respond.

Following the marshal into the adjacent room, I found him ruffling through a chest. The room was an arsenal of sorts and overflowed with stygian weapons of all types.

"I know it's somewhere around here," Elron said, muttering to himself as he dug through the chest's contents. A moment later, he yanked something out. "Aha! Found it."

I studied the weapon in the marshal's hand. It was a stygian shortsword, well-used but serviceable.

Without further ceremony, Elron placed the blade in my hands. "Here you go."

You have acquired a basic stygian shortsword. This item is a well-crafted blade with no additional enchantments or properties.

"What's this?" I asked, examining the weapon. It was not as good as any of my other swords, but in the absence of anything better, would do well enough as an offhand weapon.

"I remembered you asking Gamil for a sword and thought of this one." He shrugged. "It's not much, but it works against the stygians."

"Thanks." Stowing the blade away, I clasped hands with the dark elf. "I guess this is farewell then."

"But only for now," Elron said.

"For now," I agreed.

✳   ✳   ✳

I left the marshal's abode cloaked in shadow and slipped unseen into the closest alley. Glancing upward, I saw the silver dome was still active around the city. It seemed I had yet more time to kill.

And I knew just where to do that.

Orienting myself with the map Gamil had given me, I headed in the direction of the Mages' Guild. Thanks to both the shopkeeper and the marshal, I'd gained a good grasp of the city's geography. As a result, it did not take me long to reach my destination. Wearing a new face, I studied the tower ahead.

Judging by the number of window slits, it consisted of seven levels. From what Elron had told me, I knew it to be the focal point of the city's protective dome. The mages who maintained it—whether they were possessed or not—would be gathered inside.

And the doors were wide open and unguarded.

Careless, I thought.

"You're going inside?" Ghost asked.

I nodded.

"To kill the possessed?" she asked.

"Only if I have to."

Ghost's face wrinkled in confusion. *"Why?"*

The spirit wolf had listened in on my conversation with the marshal, and she knew as well as I did that the dome around the city would be lowered soon. There was therefore no reason for me to seek out the possessed or enter their lair.

Except to get a measure of my foes.

"I'm going to have to go up against them eventually. Better I learn what they're capable of before I enter the lich's court."

"Oh," she said, understanding my reasoning immediately. *"What's the plan then?"*

I slipped the spectacles of ward seeing back on. Castor was an elite, but the rest of the possessed weren't. I would not be able to see Castor's spells, but the spectacles would do just fine against everyone else.

"I don't have one. This is only an exploratory mission." Wrapping myself in shadow, I crept across the street.

You are hidden.

I made it to the tower doors without incident. Bracing my back against the wall, I peered in. The entrance led into a large foyer area with two occupants: a human and an elf. From their speech and mannerisms, I marked both as young. Reaching out with my will, I inspected both.

The target is Noel, a level 65 human.
The target is Corin, a level 71 elf.

I frowned. Both youths were dressed in the ubiquitous blue robes of the Mages' Guild and had their cowls raised to obscure their faces, and for a moment, I debated whether they were possessed or not.

But neither bore any obvious scarring that I could see, and so far, I had no other means of telling the possessed apart from ordinary non-players.

Possessed, though, are unlikely to be manning the front desk, I thought. Ducking around the doorway, I snuck into the room.

Two entities have failed to detect you! You are hidden.

There was an open archway behind the two mages, and trusting in my stealth, I crept towards it. *"Check the next room,"* I ordered Ghost.

"Empty," she reported when I reached its entrance.

I stepped into the room. It was as brightly lit as the foyer and was lined with display cases along the adjacent walls, while up ahead, a staircase spiraled upwards to the next level. Through an open doorway on the left, I heard the clang of dishes and raised voices. *The kitchen.* To my right were three closed doors.

"Check those rooms," I ordered Ghost, staying put.

She slipped through the doors one after the other before reporting back. *"They're full of sleeping people."*

Dormitories, I decided. *"Are there any wardrobes?"*

Ghost stared blankly back at me.

"Cupboards full of clothes," I clarified.

"Oh, those. Yes, there are."

I nodded, pleased. *"And you say everyone inside is sleeping?"*

She bobbed her head in agreement.

I smiled. *"Then it's time for another disguise."* I murmured as I entered the first room.

✳   ✳   ✳

The guild clearly had little to fear in the city.

The dormitory was completely unwarded, and had I wished, I could have slain everyone inside, but by age and levels alone, I judged all the sleepers to be apprentices—and likely innocents. Still, the lack of protective wards was sloppy.

Their seniors should have taught them better, I thought. Shaking my head in disgust, I rifled through the closest wardrobe and soon found what I was looking for.

You have assumed the visage of Nell.

A few minutes later, I exited the chamber, garbed like a mage and wearing the face of one of the youngsters from the dormitory. Stealing the robes had been a breeze, and none of the sleeping apprentices had stirred.

Not removing the spectacles of ward seeing, I headed up to the second floor. With the robe's cowl pulled forward to hide my face, they would not be easily spotted.

Ghost had already run ahead to scout, and I found her waiting at the top of the stairway to greet me. *"It's a library,"* she reported without preamble.

I nodded. *"Is it occupied?"*

"Only by a few," she said.

"Lead the way to the next floor," I replied, even though I was tempted by the idea of exploring the library. *I'll have a peek on the way back,* I temporized.

The third floor was made up of workshops and laboratories and it, too, was sparsely occupied. The chambers were warded, but the castings were paltry things—easily avoided. In my stolen robes, I walked down the main corridor in plain sight of the preoccupied mages tinkering about in their rooms.

No one stopped me.

The fourth floor contained the sleeping chambers of the senior mages.

And it was where I ran across the first possessed.

Chapter 340: Enter the Lair

The fourth floor was a maze of corridors and after only a few seconds navigating them, Ghost and I were in danger of getting lost. Sending her ahead to scout, I followed more slowly.

"You there, stop!"

The shout had come from behind. I halted. I hadn't sensed my questioner's approach, which meant his mind was shielded.

Have I been found out already?

But no, the voice was relaxed—bored. Deciding to maintain my ruse, I pulled off my spectacles and, keeping them concealed in my palm, turned around.

The figure scowled.

The mage's head was bare, revealing a heavily pockmarked face. My interest quickened. *A possessed?* I wondered.

"Lower your cowl," he snapped.

Obediently, I did as I was told. At the same time, I reached out with my will and analyzed the mage.

You have passed a mental resistance check! A hostile entity has failed to pierce your disguise.

The target is Davin, a level 120 human.

On seeing my face, Davin's scowl deepened.

"How can I help you?" I asked with pretended meekness.

"It's how can I help you, *Master*," the mage sneered. "Or have you forgotten who you are addressing, boy?"

I bowed from the waist. "Apologies, Master. I meant no disrespect."

Davin stared searchingly at my face for a moment, then snorted, satisfied that I was sufficiently cowed. "What are you doing on this level? You know it's restricted."

No, I didn't know that. I thought fast. "I'm delivering a message, Master."

"A message? For whom?"

"It's for Magister Avery, Master. It concerns the player."

Davin's eyes gleamed. "Has he been found?"

I bowed again. "I can't say, Master. Forgive me, but I've been told the message is for Magister Avery's ears only."

The mage grunted in disappointment. "And I suppose you need someone to escort you through the wards?"

If that was what he supposed, then yes. I looked at him pleadingly. "Would Master be so kind? Thank you!"

Davin mouth twisted sourly as he realized he'd trapped himself into performing a menial task. Spinning around, he cut left through the corridors. "Don't dawdle!" he snapped. "Follow me!"

Bowing my head to conceal my smirk, I hurried after the mage. Finally, it looked like I was getting somewhere.

✳   ✳   ✳

Davin led me to another stairway—the entrance to the fifth floor. Coming to a halt three feet before the first step, he glanced over his shoulder and barked, "Stay there and don't move!"

I dropped my head in mute acknowledgment.

Swinging around, Davin began muttering to himself. I suspected he was lowering the wards he'd mentioned earlier.

The fifth floor, it seemed, had significantly more protections than the lower levels, and given that even the apprentices could not enter without assistance from a higher-up, it was clear that whatever occupied it was important.

I will find the possessed there, I thought.

"Should I go scout the floor?" Ghost asked from beside me.

I hesitated. So far, none of the possessed—not even Castor—had been able to perceive the spirit wolf. But would the same hold true for their wards? Sadly, I did not know enough about the mages nor their spells to determine the probability of that.

"Better not," I murmured. *"Things seem to be going well. Let's not needlessly trip ourselves up."*

Davin swung back towards me. "It's open. Go."

Without wearing the spectacles of ward seeing, I had to take the mage at his word. "Thank you, Master," I said and ducked past him.

Behind me, I heard Davin whispering to himself again. I cursed under my breath. If the mage was renewing the wards, getting out might be a problem...

But I would worry about that later. I had another floor to explore. Forgetting Davin, I hurried up the short flight of steps with Ghost by my side. At the top, I found a closed door and two mages. Holding staffs in their hands, they were facing the staircase and had their backs to the entrance. *Guards,* I thought.

Two hostile entities have failed to pierce your disguise.

Both mages stared fixedly at me. Careful to appear unthreatening, I approached slowly while studying them in turn.

The pair had their cowls lowered, revealing unmarked faces. One had a deep laceration on his right hand though, and the other, a curved gash across the neck. Both wounds looked raw yet did not seem to discomfort the mages at all.

The pair were undoubtedly possessed. Reaching out with my will, I analyzed both.

The target is Gagan, a level 153 elf.
The target is Orlock, a level 141 human.

"Name and business?" Gagan asked in a bored tone.

"It's Nell, Master. Here to deliver a message to Magister Avery."

Orlock opened the door. "Go on through. You'll find him in the casting hall."

197

"Thank you, Master," I said, a little amazed at how easy it was proving to penetrate the possessed's defenses. They seemed even sloppier than the players I'd encountered in Nexus. If this was the caliber of protections I could expect in the lich's court, then getting through would require no great effort.

Elron has overestimated them.

On that cheerful thought, I stepped through the open door.

Entrance denied! You do not possess the necessary access key to pass. Detection ward activated.

Scanning commencing...

...

Scans completed.

The subject has no Mages' Guild sigil and has been identified as a potential threat! 2 of 2 spell traps activated.

You have triggered a trap!

You have failed a magical resistance check! You are <u>quad chained</u>. Duration: 2 hours.

Quad chained is a tier 5 debuff that prevents you from accessing your mana, stamina, and psi pools, rendering any ability that draws from them inoperable. Additionally, it temporarily strips your enchanted items of their magics. Note, passive abilities and abilities already active are not affected by the debuff.

You have triggered a trap!

A Maizon Prison has been activated. Duration: 5 minutes.

Before my right foot could make contact on the other side of the doorway, bars of brilliant white erupted from the floor to encase me in a spelled cage. Shocked both by the plethora of Game messages and my sudden imprisonment, I staggered backwards, accidentally touching one of the glowing bars.

You have failed to damage a Maizon Prison. It is immune to all forms of damage.

The two guards spun around. "By the Powers! What's happening?" Orlock exclaimed.

"It's an intruder!" Gagan yelled.

Orlock swore. "How did he get this far?"

"Who cares?" Gagan retorted. "Get Avery."

Helpless, I spun around in a full circle, searching for any weaknesses in my prison. Barely two feet separated the opposite ends of the cage, trapping me in the doorway and leaving me almost no room to maneuver.

Orlock rushed past me into the corridor beyond. I watched him go, powerless to do otherwise. My abilities had been negated, and my magic items had gone dark.

For once, I was out of tricks.

Two hours, I thought, examining the Game alert again. That was a wretchedly long spell. Powerful, too. It could only have been cast by an elite. *This is Castor's work.*

I sighed. Even if I'd been wearing the spectacles, I would not have seen the spelled trap. *I underestimated the possessed,* I admitted glumly. Now, caught and stripped of my abilities, I was paying the price.

But I was not completely helpless.

My disguise hadn't been pierced, and I retained the use of my skills. Notably, that included stealth. My void armor should still work too; it was a passive ability, after all.

I can still escape, I concluded.

I scrutinized my surroundings anew. A corridor stretched beyond the doorway. About a dozen yards ahead was a left side passage, and a few more yards beyond that, there was another going right.

I examined the staircase behind me. The most direct means of escape lay that way, but Davin had probably already renewed the ward I'd come through. Returning to the lower floor would not be easy, and perhaps even impossible. I looked at the second guard who was scrutinizing me through slitted eyes.

"You're not Nell," Gagan spat. "Who are you?"

Ignoring his question, my gaze found the ethereal figure behind him. Ghost was still free, but from the wild look in her eyes, I could see she was panicking.

Would I be able to speak to her? I wondered. After all, mindspeech was not an ability but an extension of the telepathy skill. *"Ghost, can you hear me?"*

"Prime!" she replied, her voice heavy with relief. *"Your mindglow disappeared. I–I thought... thought you were..."*

"I'm alright," I assured her with false cheer. *"But I'll admit things aren't looking good."*

"Can't you teleport out?" Not waiting for my response, she turned around. *"Wait, let me find a safe spot. Then you can—"*

"No, Ghost. That won't work. My abilities have been disabled."

The spirit wolf swung back around. *"Then break through that cage. It doesn't look strong enough to hold you!"*

I shook my head minutely. *"Can't. It's immune to damage."*

Ghost looked crestfallen. *"You're trapped, then?"*

I nodded bleakly.

"What can I do?"

I wasn't sure anything could be done, but I sensed the spirit wolf needed something to occupy her. *"Scout this level and find me somewhere to hide,"* I replied. *"Return as soon as you can. I'll play for time until then."*

"Yes, Prime!" Ghost replied, rushing off immediately. I watched her go, a forlorn expression on my face. At least, she could still escape...

I shook myself, breaking free from the despair threatening to overcome me. The task I'd set Ghost wasn't completely without purpose. While the quad-chained debuff would take a ghastly two hours to dissipate, the Maizon Prison wouldn't last more than five minutes—less than four now—and when it fell, I had to be ready to act.

"Answer me!" the elf demanded abruptly. "Who are you?"

I turned back to the guard. He was still glaring at me. "B-b-but Master, I-I... am Nell," I said, maintaining my act.

"Liar," he growled.

I stared wide-eyed back at him, keeping my expression meek and pathetic. I didn't expect my pretense to work but if it delayed the guard from acting for even a minute, then the ploy would have served its purpose.

Before Gagan could respond, footsteps—many footsteps—heralded the approach of newcomers. Turning around, I spied nearly a full score of mages advancing down the corridor from deeper in the level. Leading them was Avery.

My gaze jumped from figure to figure, scanning faces, but I saw no sign of Castor and some of my tension dissipated. If the elite was absent, then even without my abilities, escape might be possible.

Avery drew to a stop an inch from the bars, so close I could feel his breath on my skin. His face was tight as he studied me from head to toe. "So... you are a deception player too."

I screwed up my face in affected befuddlement.

"You can drop the act," Avery said derisively. "You're not fooling anyone."

I didn't react.

"Is Taim even your real name? Or was the whole 'explorer' thing a ruse too?"

The possessed was perceptive, I granted him that. Still, I remained silent.

Another mage stepped forward, his motions hesitant. "Are you sure, Master? I know Nell. And this... person looks identical to him."

"Don't be a fool, Hedron," Avery snapped. "This is the player we're looking for."

"But—"

"Silence!" Avery roared.

As Hedron's mouth snapped closed, another mage advanced. "We'll be going then."

Avery's eyes narrowed. "Going? Going where, Horlick?"

Horlick gestured towards me. "You're certain he is the player?"

Avery nodded sharply.

"Then this is possessed business," Horlick said. "You have the one you want and don't require our aid. We will leave you to deal with him."

I studied Horlick and Hedron intently. Both mages were unscarred, and I realized they were city born. *Not possessed.*

Avery's mouth twisted, and I could see Horlick's words had angered him. Still, all he said was, "Go, if you must. Take the other fools with you, and tell Sevry he may lower the dome." His gaze found me again. "Our quarry won't be going anywhere."

Horlick nodded, seemingly unperturbed by the venom in Avery's tone. He returned the way he came, four other mages trailing behind him. Including Gagan, that left sixteen mages for me to deal with.

Avery looked at the guard. "Have you sent word to Castor?"

Gagan shook his head. "Not yet. He is in the fortress with—"

"See to it at once!" Avery snapped.

Mutely, the elf spun around and hurried down the stairs.

Inwardly, I smiled. Avery had just confirmed Castor was out of play. Now, all I had to figure out was how to deal with the remaining fifteen mages.

CHAPTER 341: BY SKILL ALONE

As Gagan scurried away, Avery ordered half the mages to circle around me. Retreating the way I'd come was definitely no longer an option. My gaze flickered forward. It did mean, though, that there were fewer obstacles between me and the rest of the fifth floor.

I eyed Avery and the seven other mages in the corridor. They were talking, but no part of their conversation carried to my ears, which made me suspect someone had raised a silence ward.

They're probably deciding how to hold me until Castor arrives, I decided. I didn't interrupt. For now, being ignored suited me just fine. Letting my gaze drift, I examined my surroundings in search of inspiration.

A short while later, a translucent shape appeared behind Avery's group. Ghost was back. *"Did you find anything?"* I asked, eyes latching onto her.

"Plenty," she replied eagerly. *"There are multiple storerooms on this level. Any one of them will make for a good hiding spot."* She paused. *"Some may be locked, though."*

"We'll figure it out," I assured her. *"What about other mages?"*

Ghost's ears turned down. *"There are lots of those, too. But most are gathered in the circular chamber at the center of this floor."*

Was that the casting hall Orlock had referred to? *Probably.* I checked the status of the spell imprisoning me. Less than two minutes remained. I'd bought enough time, I decided. Now, it was time to change things up and sow confusion.

Tugging at the seams of the blue apprentice's robe, I began ripping it apart.

Avery noticed. "So," he declared with a triumphant grin, "you've finally decided to abandon your charade and plead for mercy."

"Not quite," I said, not bothering to look at him as I rent the garment even further. "But it has served its purpose."

"And what purpose was that?"

I met his gaze as the blue robe fell apart. "It got me here, didn't it?"

"Nonsense," Avery said firmly. "You couldn't have planned this."

Saying nothing, I shuffled out of the rags, then stomped on them for good measure and set my hands on the hilt of my blades.

Avery tilted his head. "Don't tell me you're thinking of resisting?"

"It's better than the alternative." I grinned cockily. "And there are only fifteen of you."

Avery snorted. "You honestly expect to fight your way out of here?"

I smiled. "Oh, I hope to do more than that."

I didn't have many assets to deploy in the coming conflict. Avery and his fellows would know to expect my speed, stealth, and swords. My void armor, on the other hand, should come as a surprise. But there was one other advantage I had. Something less quantifiable.

I was a player.

And that made me unpredictable.

After all, who knew what Game-gifted skills I hid? It was something I was sure Avery and his fellow possessed were wondering right about now. If I was going to pull of an escape—which admittedly was unlikely—I had to play on that uncertainty. Deepen it and keep them guessing.

"I'm curious," I drawled, running my gaze nonchalantly across the mages. "How does possessing a headless corpse work? Is that even possible?"

"Your bravado is amusing," Avery said. "But we are too many and too strong. Or have you forgotten you've lost your abilities?"

I shrugged. "Abilities aren't everything. And *you* seem to have forgotten I've nothing to lose. Die here, and I come back in a shiny new body. You, on the other hand... you will have to make do with whatever disfigured carcasses I leave behind."

My gaze jumped meaningfully from Avery to the other possessed, many of whom bore scars of one type or the other. "I've got that bit right, haven't I? Any wounds I leave on a corpse will remain when you repossess it."

Avery's lips thinned. "Who told you that?" he demanded harshly.

Ignoring his question, I went on. "You will be hampered in other ways, too, of course. It's drearily hard to capture someone who has no care for his own life—did you know that? You will also have to do your utmost *not* to inflict any lingering scars on me in the process. I can't imagine the archlich being very happy with you otherwise."

For a moment, Avery said nothing, seething with anger. I was playing a dangerous game, I knew. But I was not taunting the possessed just for the fun of it. My words had deadly purpose.

"Who have you been talking to?" Avery hissed.

"The exile, of course." The words were uttered lightly, but there was nothing casual about the scrutiny I paid the possessed leader. From beneath lidded eyes, I watched him with hawklike intensity.

Avery's eyes widened. Not in surprise, nor in misunderstanding, but in dawning fear. Elron had been right.

There *was* an exile.

And judging by Avery's reaction, the possessed were terrified of her. *I guess my course is set now,* I thought. I would head east after I left the city—assuming I survived the coming fight.

"*She* sent you here?" Avery asked, sounding half-strangled.

I nodded mutely, no longer paying much attention. Only seconds remained on the spell holding me, and thanks to my little misdirection, Avery had lost sight of that fact.

"Impossible!" the possessed blurted.

"And why is that?" I asked easily. Inwardly, I tensed.

"Because—"

The luminous white bars surrounding me flickered, then died.

A Maizon's Prison has dissipated.

Already poised to react, I flew into action. My right leg shot out, kicking the robes gathered at my foot upwards, and directly into Avery's face. In the same motion, I dashed forward, hurtling towards the packed mages. Salvation lay past them, in the corridor beyond.

For a moment, chaos reigned.

Avery, temporarily blinded, had been neutralized, leaving his fellows rudderless. Some, attempting to take charge, shouted orders that were promptly ignored by the rest. Others lowered their weapons uncertainly, either for fear of their companions getting caught in the crossfire or because they were worried about damaging their 'prize.'

A few, though, enraged by my taunts, took their chances and fired.

I made no attempt to evade the disjointed volley of approaching magic. It would take the mages only seconds to recover and I couldn't waste that time dodging projectiles. I had to get *through*. Gritting my teeth, I raced on.

Your void armor has repelled a frost dagger!

The first attack landed, and to my surprise, was rebuffed. It was too early to celebrate though. Out of the corner of my eye, I spied three more spells approaching from behind.

You have failed a magical resistance check! You are <u>vine-trapped</u>. Duration: 4 seconds.

You have failed a magical resistance check! You are <u>frozen</u>. Duration: 3 seconds.

You have failed a magical resistance check! You are <u>burning</u>. Duration: 3 seconds.

You are no longer <u>frozen</u>.

Void armor charge remaining: 90%.

The searing waves of magic struck one after the other. One second, I was wrapped in strangling vines, the next, I was frozen, and the last, I was lit alight.

Unfortunately for the possessed, their spells worked at cross purposes to one another, and before the ice settling around my bones could truly set, it was melted away by the incoming firebolt. But sadly, my arms remained trapped in the vines, leaving stillborn my plan to disembowel as many mages as I could on the way past.

My momentum was unimpeded, though.

Letting my feet carry me forward, I barreled into Avery and his fellows before more spells could descend upon me. They scattered, mouthing imprecations.

"Don't use fire, you idiot! It will scar him!"

"He resisted my spell!"

"I got him! I got him!"

Shoved from multiple directions, and prevented by my trapped hands from catching my balance, I fell on my face. But the vine spell was nearly done, and I kept moving, wriggling across the floor like a worm.

Avery, meanwhile, had wrenched the rags off his face. "Coordinate your attacks, you fools!" he shouted. "Everyone hit him with slowing spells. Now!"

You are no longer <u>vine-trapped</u>.

My hands came free not a second too soon. Stretching out my arms, I threw my body over my head in a forward somersault.

You have evaded a grasping roots spell.
You have evaded a sinking mud spell.
Your void armor has repelled a lightning bolt!
You have failed a magical resistance check! You are <u>weakened</u>. Duration: 8 seconds.

I avoided all but one of the incoming spells, but the one that struck— wilting ray—had a long debuff, and already, I could feel myself slowing down as the energy was sapped from my limbs.
"Go left!" Ghost shouted suddenly.
Still rolling across the floor, I angled left as ordered.

You have evaded a cone of cold.

A blizzard of ice, sleet, and frost raged passed, missing me by scant inches, and it was only thanks to Ghost's quick thinking that I avoided its touch. With the danger past, I attempted to correct my trajectory, but my weakened body was slow to respond. *Damn*, I thought, realizing I was about to crash headlong into the left side of the passage.
But there was no wall.
Braced for an impact, it took me a second to realize what had happened. I'd entered the side passage.
"Don't lose him!" Avery screamed from the main corridor.
The shout galvanized me. Ghost had more than directed me out of the blizzard's path; she'd placed me out of the mage's direct line of sight—if only temporarily. Staggering to my feet, I braced my back against the nearest wall and cloaked myself in shadows.

You are hidden.

I squeezed my eyes shut. *Safe. I was safe.*
"Thanks, Ghost," I gasped, even as I sidled farther away from the intersection. *"Tell me what—"*
I broke off as the footsteps pounding down the corridor rounded the corner.

Eight hostile entities have failed to detect you!

"He's gone!" a shocked mage exclaimed.
"No, he is not," Avery retorted. "He's here. Hiding. Spread out and find him."
I bit back my disappointment. The mages had followed too soon. I was barely six feet from the closest and discovery was inevitable. The fact that my stealth was holding at all was surprising.
I have to do something.
I fixed my gaze on the nearest possessed. For now, he was looking the other way. Instead of drawing my blades—I was in no condition to fight yet—I extracted a stone flask from my bomber's belt and flicked my wrist forward.

Arcing past the mage, the tiny container landed in the T-junction. The magic inside was inert, but that did not stop the flask from shattering when it hit the floor as it was designed to do.

The sound grabbed the attention of all eight possessed.

Spinning around, they pointed weapons at the unoffending pieces of stone. It bought me a few precious seconds to inch farther away.

Fifteen hostile entities have failed to detect you!

Another seven mages had appeared in the intersection—the ones assigned to guard the stairs. Ignoring them, Avery pointed at the broken flask. "What is that?"

A possessed picked up the bottle and examined it carefully. "A dead bomb, I think. This was thrown." He looked down the main corridor. "Did he go that way?"

"No. It's a feint," Avery declared. He turned back to face in my direction. "Our quarry is in this passage. Advance." But despite the seeming confidence of his pronouncements, Avery hesitated to proceed himself. Glancing at one of the newcomers, he said, "Stone, cast revealing light. Just in case." He turned to another mage. "And you, Rice, ward the entrance to this passage. I don't want him fleeing back this way."

Avery's thoroughness did not bode well for me. Still, I was pleased with my own efforts so far. I had escaped certain death, and while I was by no means free, my chances of escape had improved immeasurably. Even better, the distance between me and the mages had opened to a comfortable gap.

I glanced at Ghost. *"Lead the way to the closest room."*

The spirit wolf hung her head. *"I can't."*

I frowned. *"Why?"*

"This passage is a dead end. There are no rooms to hide in."

CHAPTER 342: OUT OF TRICKS

Ghost's words hit me hard, and for a moment, I closed my eyes, tasting defeat like ash in my mouth.

Stone has cast revealing light.

Light blossomed in the T-junction, but I was already far enough away that the few rays that managed to reach my position failed to disrupt my stealth.

"I'm sorry, Prime. I didn't think there was any choice. That blizzard looked nasty."

I waved Ghost's concerns aside. *"You did the right thing. Staying in the main corridor was not an option."* I glanced over my shoulder. The possessed had split again, seven hanging back—presumably on the other side of the ward that Rice had erected—to guard the T-junction.

The other seven, under Avery's command, were advancing steadily toward me, strengthening their defenses with every step. They were in no hurry, and I easily outpaced them. Then again, they likely already knew I was trapped.

I faced forward again. *"This corridor must lead somewhere. What lies at its end?"*

"An open room with soft chairs, cushions, and tables," Ghost replied. *"I have no idea what purpose it serves."*

"It's a lounge," I murmured.

"Oh. What's that?"

"A room where you sit."

"Sit? Only sit?"

"That's right," I replied, amused by her confusion despite my grim circumstances. *"Sometimes you can talk too."* The lounge still hadn't come into sight, and I realized the corridor was a long one. Closing my eyes, I took a moment to get my bearings. *"The sitting room must be right up against the tower's outer wall. Are there any windows?"*

"A few," Ghost answered.

I smiled in relief. Escape was still possible, then.

A moment later, yet more good news arrived in the guise of another Game message.

You are no longer weakened.

The wilting spell had finally dissipated, and I straightened from the slouch I'd unconsciously fallen into. I didn't turn on my pursuers though. I had learned what I'd come to. And as much as it galled me to flee, now was not the time for more heroics.

Besides, the possessed mages were well-prepared for any counterattacks. Their buffs were cast, and their shields were up. Striking at them now would not be smart.

Quickening my steps, I padded down the corridor and into the lounge.

* * *

There were four windows in the room.

All were barred.

"Damn," I cursed, seeing my chance at freedom slipping away. Hurrying to the closest window, I inspected it carefully.

Three vertical rods were planted in the window frame, each a two-inch-thick bar formed from solid steel. I tested the gaps between. They were large enough to squeeze a limb through but not an entire body.

"Will you fit?" Ghost asked.

I shook my head. I could cut through the steel rods with ebonheart, but it would be noisy and take time—I glanced back at the lounge's arched entrance—time, I was sure, Avery would not give me.

That left only one option.

I sighed. *"We will have to deal with the mages first."* No easy feat, given how few tools I had at my disposal. I scanned the room.

It was brightly lit and held several large pieces of furniture: couches, tables, and chests mostly. At the very least, there were plenty of hiding spots, but beyond that, the room's contents were of no use.

I glanced up. The ceiling had been built high, presumably to accommodate the magelights floating beneath. I couldn't put out the glowing orbs, but the room's height gave me an idea. I had one other advantage not dependent on my abilities: my agility.

It gave me greater maneuverability than the possessed would expect. Reaching into my backpack, I pulled out my climbing gear.

You have equipped a set of cat claws.

Ordinarily, mages were at their most dangerous at range. If I was going to have any chance of surviving, I would have to close on them quickly and unseen. And the best way to do that...

...would be to drop down from above.

Soft whispers floated in from the corridor. The possessed were drawing closer, and my time had run out. Sprinting silently across the room, I launched myself onto a table. Weaving deftly through its clutter, I quickly reached its far end and leaped, hands extended.

My claws found purchase.

But my hold was far from secure. *"How far?"* I rasped, clinging tenaciously to the stone wall.

"You have a few seconds still," Ghost replied, not needing me to elaborate further.

A few seconds would suffice.

Extending my arms, I rushed diagonally across the wall in spiderlike fashion until I was directly over the lounge's arched entryway. Reaching my chosen perch, I scanned the wall quickly and spotted a deep groove between two bricks.

Good enough, I thought and jammed the claws on my left hand into the hole. Anchored in place, I peered down.

I was twelve feet above the floor and positioned directly over the room's only entrance. Pulling off my right glove with my teeth, I stowed it away and drew ebonheart.

I was ready.

✳   ✳   ✳

Eight hostile entities have failed to detect you!

It didn't take the possessed long to emerge from the corridor. They didn't immediately spread out, though.

"Where is he?" one asked in a hushed tone.

Avery rolled his eyes. "Hiding, obviously," he said, not bothering to lower his voice. The possessed leader scanned the room in predatory fashion, the tip of his staff glowing and ready to unleash whatever magics he had prepared.

He would have to die first, I decided, and measured the distance to the mage. If I threw myself to the left, I would land directly atop him.

"Rice, Lake, check the right side of the room," Avery ordered. "Johir, Sylver, start at the chests on the left and work your way to the windows. Gordon and Mikane, look beneath those tables. Haril, you stay here with me."

Eight hostile entities have failed to detect you!

I delayed my assault as the possessed dispersed to do Avery's bidding. So far, none of the mages had so much as glanced upwards, and I judged I would go undetected for a while still—leaving me with a few more precious seconds to time everything perfectly.

While I waited, I scrutinized my targets and prioritized threats. Thankfully, analyze required no energy and still functioned despite me being quad chained.

"Are we sure he is even here?" Haril asked. He was the lowest leveled of the possessed, and the most nervous.

"Where else would he be?" Avery snapped irritably.

Haril licked his lips. "Maybe he's—"

I stopped listening. The possessed had spread out enough. It was time. Slipping my left hand free of the clawed glove, I pushed off the wall with my legs and launched myself at Avery.

Mid-air, I drew faithful.

At the last second, the possessed leader sensed something amiss and spun around to look up. Barely a few feet separated us, though, and I bowled into him feet first before he could bring his staff up.

Your target's shield has blocked your attacks, absorbing its damage.

I struck Avery's defenses and not the man himself, of course. Still, the momentum of my assault sufficed to knock the possessed off his feet and send his weapon flying.

Behind me, Haril yelped.

209

Ignoring him, I leaped forward and onto the downed mage's shield bubble. The spelled surface was slippery, and its curvature made sitting awkward, but I was agile enough to not only maintain my perch, but to strike down at my shocked foe with both my blades.

Your target's shield has blocked your attacks.

Haril lowered his staff to point at me. The other possessed were also turning in my direction. Very soon, an avalanche of magic would be descending on me.

I had no choice, though, but to ignore the danger. Now that I had sprung my ambush, I had to finish off my prey. Leaving him alive would be to court even greater danger.

My swords a blur, I struck down repeatedly, each attack ricocheting sharply off Avery's defenses.

Your target's shield has blocked your attacks.
Your target's shield has blocked your attacks.
...
...

Avery raised his hands, magic boiling to life in his palms, but the possessed leader was already too late. My sword fighting skills had come a long way since I'd last battled a mage. Even unempowered by whirlwind or piercing strike, each hit from ebonheart and faithful inflicted huge swathes of damage.

Your target's shield has been destroyed!

Before Avery could finish his spell, his defenses collapsed, and I dropped down onto his chest, leaving him gasping for air.

"Don't do—" he began.

Not waiting to hear what he had to say, I buried my swords hilt-deep in his chest.

You have killed Avery with a fatal blow.

My triumph was short-lived, though, as the rest of the mages unleashed their spells near simultaneously and enveloped me in a storm of magic.

From behind, lightning struck.

From the left, jets of fire and poison.

And from the right, twin whips of light and darkness.

Haril and the others had finally rallied, and any inclination they might have had about leaving my corpse unmarked had vanished.

You have failed 4 magical resistance checks!

The lightning bolt fizzled, rebuffed by my void armor. Unfortunately, I was not so lucky with the remaining attacks.

A spray of venom has hit you. You are <u>poisoned</u>.
A fire lance has hit you. You are <u>burning</u>.
Death's touch has injured you.
A light ray has injured you.

Void armor charge remaining: 78%. Your health has decreased to 57%.

I staggered under the onslaught, alive, but dazed and reeling. Matters were only getting started though, and in the next instant, the toxins coating my body ignited.

You have detonated.

Contrary energies tugged at me, pulling me in multiple directions at once and threatening to rip my body apart. Bones splintered, sinew tore, and skin stretched, but just as it felt as if I'd reached breaking point, the explosive forces receded.

An explosion has critically injured you! Fire damage incurred reduced by 45%.
You are bleeding, befuddled, deafened, blinded, and crippled.

My void armor saved me.
Leeching away enough of the volatile magics, it had kept me intact. It did *not* prevent me from being treated like human flotsam, though, and I cannoned into an unyielding stone wall as if smacked aside by some giant uncaring hand.

Void armor depleted.
Quick mend triggered, restoring 20% of your health!
3 of 5 status effects healed. Remaining effects: crippled and blinded.

More of my bones fractured, but I barely noticed. My body was already a quivering mess. What was one more injury heaped upon the others? Nearly senseless with pain, I dropped bonelessly to the floor.

Warning! Your health is dangerously low at 13%.
7 of 7 hostiles have been knocked down.

Unconsciousness beckoned. I resisted its call.
I had to drag myself to safety, but where that was, I had no idea. The explosion had robbed me of sight. Blindly, I reached for the shadows and cloaked myself.

Multiple hostile entities have failed to detect you! You are hidden.

My skin was blackened and my armor was smoking, but I was alive. *I am alive,* I repeated, trying to distract myself from the searing pain riddling nearly every inch of my body.
I would not remain that way if I didn't act further, though.
Thankfully, the explosion had knocked back the possessed too—but they were shielded and would've weathered its effects better than I did. Rolling onto my stomach, I lifted my head and peered about.
I saw nothing, of course.
Until I healed myself fully, I would remain blind—I glanced down at my limp right leg—and crippled. But blind and broken did not mean senseless. I inhaled deeply.
And tasted ash.

The tower had shaken under the explosion, and I could only imagine that the room was filled with smoke. It would help, but I was under no illusions. Sooner or later, the mages would find me. Already, I could hear them picking themselves up and calling out to each other.

"Avery, you alive?" Rice shouted.

"H-he's... dead!"

"Haril, is that you?" Sylver yelled. "Where is the player?"

"I s-saw him... thrown."

"Is he still alive?" Mikane asked.

"I'm n-not... sure," Haril coughed.

"Find him!" Lake roared. "Castor will have our heads otherwise."

"Who put you in charge?" Gordon asked sourly. "I say we retreat and come back with the others."

"I agree," Johir chipped in.

"Shut up, you fools! Listen to Lake, or I'll take your heads myself," Rice threatened.

All seven mages were alive and at least some of them were determined to find me. *Not good,* I thought—which was an insane understatement.

My circumstances were dire enough that I would have downed a potion if I could. But, like my other items, they had also been stripped of magic. There was no getting around it. For the next two hours, I was going to be defenseless—and useless.

Perhaps it is time to give up the fight. I grinned evilly. It was not like any of the possessed would *want* my corpse now, anyway.

"Prime!" Ghost cried.

Both physically and telepathically blinded, I couldn't see her, which meant I couldn't respond without broadcasting my words to anyone in the vicinity with 'ears' to hear. So, I stayed silent.

"Prime, answer me!" she yelled frantically again. *"Please. Are you alright?"*

"I'm here," I gasped, ignoring the risk. What did it matter anyway? *"Still alive."* If barely.

"What should I do?" Ghost asked, sounding worried.

I had no cunning plan, though. I was out of tricks and disabled to boot. *"I don't know,"* I said honestly. *"Whatever you can."*

For a moment, the spirit wolf said nothing, and even without access to her mindglow, I could feel her frantic turn of thoughts as she searched for a way out of our predicament.

"It's alright, Ghost," I said, regretting my careless words. *"I don't think getting out of this one is possible."*

Ambushing the possessed had always been a gamble, and my assault had only been partially successful. Avery was dead and his followers left in disarray. But I had ended up blinded and crippled in the process.

Now, all that there was to do was hide and hope. Maybe the possessed wouldn't find me.

Maybe.

Resigned to my fate, I closed my eyes.

CHAPTER 343: DEAD IS NOT TRULY DEAD

It was difficult to imagine how I would escape this time. In fact, I was almost certain I wouldn't, and of its own accord, my mind wandered beyond my present circumstances to thoughts of the future.

When—if—I died here, how was I going to get back to the city? I hadn't even established where the safe zone was yet. Could I make it back without gear? Another concern loomed large. What would the possessed do with my equipment? *Maybe I should—*

"I'll save you!" Ghost yelled, interrupting my maudlin thoughts.

I winced at her loudness. *"Don't bother, Ghost,"* I replied tiredly. The mages were moving about, and at least two were already heading in my direction. *"It's too late for that."*

There was no response.

"Ghost?" I called, lifting my head off the floor.

More silence.

It took me a full second to realize what that meant. Ghost had already run off. *To try and save me?* Probably. It was the only explanation.

Sighing, I bestirred myself further. If Ghost wasn't giving up, I shouldn't either. Stretching out my arms, I felt out my surroundings. It was the only thing I could do at this point. On my left was cold stone—the wall—and on my right, empty space. In front of me, I felt something soft.

A couch?

It wasn't much of a hiding spot, but under the circumstances, it would do. Teeth clenched, I dragged myself across the floor.

My body screamed bloody murder and stars danced across my unseeing eyes, making every inch moved an exercise in torture. Still, I kept going.

Finally, the sounds of footsteps drawing ever closer penetrated the haze of pain surrounding my mind, and I stopped.

Two hostile entities have failed to detect you!

Biting my tongue to keep myself from venting the agony that demanded voice, I listened intently.

"He must be around here," Lake muttered. From the sound of it, he was circling around the right side of the couch. "I saw him thrown this way."

"Could he be hiding?" Rice whispered. He was behind me, approaching the front of the couch. I was caught between the pair.

Lake grunted. "It's likely. But the smoke is nearly gone. He won't be able to stay hidden much longer," he said, his voice getting louder with each word.

Two hostile entities have failed to detect you!

"Do you think the others are right?" Rice asked from nearly on top of me. Without waiting for a response, he continued. "I tell you, there is something strange about this player. Elite or not, he shouldn't have survived that explosion. You don't think he is a—"

A scream cut through the air.

Shouts and bedlam followed in its wake, and the two possessed froze. "What was that?" Rice asked anxiously.

"Our quarry," Lake crowed. "The others have found him! Quick, to the corridor."

"But—" Rice began.

Lake raced out of the lounge, sparing no thought for his companion.

Above me, Rice sighed. "Arrogant idiot," he grumbled before storming out as well and leaving me alone.

✳   ✳   ✳

My chance to affect a getaway had finally arrived.

If only my injuries hadn't seen to it that that was impossible. *No, not impossible. Difficult. Merely difficult.*

Favoring my right leg, I grasped the back of the couch with bloody fingers and rose to my feet. I wobbled but stayed erect. Using the couch as a crutch, I took a step forward.

My right leg quivered as my weight transferred to it. It held, though. The explosion had wrecked my knee, making every step excruciating. But I could still walk.

And despite the pain, I did.

Exhaling and inhaling in short sharp breaths, I tottered forward with my hands outstretched, blindly searching for the nearby wall I knew to be close by.

I couldn't give up—not after what Ghost had accomplished. It was she, of course, who had caused the commotion that spurred the mages' retreat. I didn't know how the spirit wolf had managed it, and with more important things on my mind—like escaping—I had little attention to spare the question. But I was determined to not let her down.

My left hand brushed stone.

I exhaled in relief. Now I was getting somewhere. Letting my fingers trail across the wall's surface, I circled the room. Sooner or later, I would run across one of the windows, and while getting there might take me longer, it was better than stumbling across the lounge.

"Prime, Prime! I've drawn them away!" an excited voice shouted in my mind.

That was Ghost. Still safe, thankfully. It was more good news, and right now, I needed all of that that I could get. I limped on.

"You have to escape," she added. *"Now, before they return there!"*

"I'm working on it," I rasped. *"What did you do?"*

"I cast astral blades!" she exclaimed.

I chuckled hoarsely, pleased that she had finally learned the spell. *"Tell me what happened,"* I said as I paused for breath. I'd taken a dozen steps around the room already, and my right leg felt like it was about to collapse beneath me.

"I manifested the dagger in my jaws and ran straight at one of the possessed. I passed through his body, of course, but the astral blade didn't! It lodged in his leg and left him limping."

I resumed my steady trek. Where were the damned windows? *"Well done, Ghost. I knew you could do it."*

Another bitten-off cry carried to me from the corridor. *"That's one of the possessed, I take it. What are they up to now?"*

"Jumping at shadows," Ghost replied smugly. *"They think you're hiding somewhere in the corridor and are firing blindly in random directions in hopes of hitting you."*

I smiled. She really had done well. *"Nicely done. But where are you right now?"*

"In the corridor, halfway between you and the possessed," she replied. *"Maybe if I kill one of them, they'll flee altogether,"* she mused.

"Don't do that. I need you with me."

"Why?" Ghost asked, sounding puzzled.

"They're mages," I explained. *"Sooner or later, one of them is going to cast a spell that will reveal you. And we can't have that."*

"But—"

"You've bought me enough time," I assured her. *"In fact, I'm already at a window."* And I was.

Unsheathing ebonheart, I started sawing at one of the steel bars. *"I need you here to guide me out. I lost my sight in the explosion."* I suspected that where certain danger would not convince Ghost, a cry for help would.

"Alright," she replied. Her reluctance was obvious, but she heeded my request nevertheless.

"Thank you," I said fervently. Breaking off communication with her, I focused fully on what my hands were doing.

Working without sight was difficult—but not impossible—and as tough as the steel was, it could not resist ebonheart's touch. The bottom of the bar came free, and soon after, the top broke off.

"Prime! You have company!" Ghost hissed.

"You're mistaken," I said absently as I positioned ebonheart at the base of the second bar. I might be blind at the moment, but there was nothing wrong with my ears, and I'd heard no one.

"I've just entered the room, and I'm telling you someone else is here!"

I stopped dead. There was no doubt in her voice. *"Here? As in this room?"*

"Yes!"

"Who is it?" I asked, slowly readying my blade. I had no idea how I would fight blind, crippled, and hovering near death, but I would try.

"He's... like me," she replied, alarm transforming into wonder.

"Like you?" I asked, my brows furrowing.

"Yes. A spirit."

For a moment, I didn't react, thinking I'd misheard. *"A... spirit?"*

"I think it's the possessed you killed."

"Avery?" I asked, still struggling to make sense of what was going on.

"Yes, him."

How could Ghost be seeing Avery? He was dead! *"Uhm, what is he doing?"*

"He is hovering above his body and staring straight at you." She paused. *"He doesn't look happy."*

I bet he wasn't. If it was truly Avery's spirit Ghost was seeing, given my spirit talker trait, he *should* be able to understand me if I spoke. "Avery, can you hear me?"

There was no response.

"I don't think he can hear you," Ghost said.

"Why not?" I asked, cursing the circumstances that had left my senses so debilitated.

"He's like me but not. His spirit is... incomplete. I don't think he is all there."

Had Avery become a wraith? I wondered. Some sort of half-mad spirit?

But as fascinating as I found the subject of spirit-Avery to be, I did not have time to ponder the mystery further. *"Forget him and come here. He seems harmless enough."* I pointed to the gap I'd widened. *"Will I fit through?"*

A pause. *"Yes."*

That was good enough for me. Returning ebonheart to its scabbard, I grasped the remaining bars in my hands and pulled myself onto the windowsill. Then, turning my body sideways, I squeezed through the window.

It was a tight fit, it hurt like hell, and I thought I passed out for a split-second or two during the process. Still, I managed to haul my entire body out and onto the tiny stone ledge that lay on the other side.

A breeze tugged at me.

Gentle though it was, the wind nearly yanked me off my perch. Gripping the bars tightly, I secured myself in place. I was five floors up and hopefully no more than a distant speck to those on the ground. But just in case, I wrapped myself in shadow.

You are hidden.

The wind pulled at me again.

I couldn't stay where I was. My position was too exposed, both to the elements and anyone who walked into the lounge. The moment the possessed found the sawn-off bar, they would know to look outside, and from such close quarters, not even my stealth would protect me.

I couldn't make my way down the tower, though. Not blind, with a bad leg, and a single climbing glove—its partner was still stuck in the wall above the lounge entrance. One glove was better than none, though, and I equipped the right hand cat claw.

"Ghost, talk to me. How far beyond the window does this ledge extend?"

A drawn-out silence. *"It doesn't."*

That wasn't promising. *"What about handholds? Do you see any to the left or right?"*

"The brickwork is smooth on both sides."

I winced. More bad news. Had I exceeded my quota of good news already? *"What about above?"*

"There is... something."

Anxiously, I waited for her to describe what she meant.

"A broken brick is within reach, and beyond that, another one is protruding out slightly. Above them is a row of gargoyle statues. You should be able reach them."

Some of my tension eased. *"Then I need you to be my eyes."* I raised my gloved hand. *"Guide me to those bricks..."*

✳   ✳   ✳

A few minutes later, I was about three feet above the window and nestled amongst the gargoyle decorating the tower.

Unfortunately, there were no more helpful irregularities in the tower's outer surface to assist my ascent, and not wanting to push my luck, I decided to stay put. The next one hundred minutes—the time remaining on the quad chained debuff—promised to be cold, excruciating, and boring.

But there was nothing for it but to wait it out.

"Something is happening," Ghost said.

"The possessed are returning to the lounge again?" I guessed.

The mages had already come and gone once during my climb. After peering out the window and failing to spot me, they had run back into the tower to search the floors above and below. According to Ghost, spirit-Avery was still in the room, but the possessed were either not able to see him or were ignoring him just like I was.

"No," Ghost said, surprising me. *"There is a procession approaching the tower."*

Instinctively, I glanced down, then realized I was still blind. *"A procession?"*

"It's the possessed from the council chamber. The one that was in charge." Ghost paused. *"There are over a dozen mages accompanying him."*

"Castor," I breathed. The elite had returned.

"What do we do?" Ghost asked.

"Nothing but watch and wait." And hope.

"Should I lure him away?"

"No," I said sharply. *"Castor is an elite. Risking yourself like that is too dangerous. Better I die instead."*

"But—"

"I'll come back," I said, overruling her, then drove the point home. *"You won't."*

Ghost subsided.

The seconds ticked by, and eventually I heard the sound I'd been dreading: the trample of many feet. Castor's party had entered the lounge. Straining my ears, I listened intently.

"Is this where it happened?" a familiar voice—Castor's—asked.

"Yeah," Lake replied.

"And you're sure my debuff tagged him?" the elite probed.

"He definitely didn't use any abilities that we noticed," Lake asserted confidently.

"That's not completely accurate," Rice interjected.

Robes swished, and I could imagine Castor swinging around to face the other possessed. "Explain," he demanded.

"We didn't *see* the player use any abilities, that's true," Rice admitted. "But then, how did he rebuff the spells we hit him with? And what was it that nearly crippled Haril?"

"Resistance skills could explain the first," Castor said. "And an unseen ally, the second. Didn't you say he appeared friendly with the marshal, Lake?"

"I did," Lake replied. "We should bring the dark elf in for questioning."

There was a pause as Castor considered this. "No," he said finally. "The marshal is too well-liked by the soldiers. We can't risk alienating them."

Footsteps approached the window.

"He escaped from here, you said?" Castor asked. From the sound of it, he had poked his head out the window.

"We think so," Rice answered.

Castor muttered under his breath, and a moment later, I heard a sharp bang.

I dearly wanted to ask Ghost what was going on, but with the possessed elite so close, I couldn't risk broadcasting my mindvoice.

Ghost anticipated my need anyway. *"The possessed has destroyed the remaining bars on the window and is climbing out,"* she said.

My alarm growing, I locked my limbs motionless.

Castor whispered the words of another spell.

"Now, he's standing on a platform of empty air outside the window," Ghost reported, sounding impressed.

Levitation, I guessed.

A hostile entity has failed to detect you!

At the Game message, I nearly fired a question at Ghost but managed to stay quiet.

"The platform has begun moving. Castor is circling the tower to inspect the area both above and below."

I stifled rising fear. I was about to find out just how good my stealth was.

A hostile entity has failed to detect you!

A minute passed, then another, and still the elite kept circling the tower. He mumbled to himself as he moved around, and I could only guess at the spells he was casting. But whatever they were, they weren't good enough to overcome my stealth.

"Find anything?" Lake shouted from the window. It seemed like he was getting impatient.

Castor came to a stop. "He's gone."

"Do we restore the dome around the city?" Rice asked, poking his head out of the window as well.

"No," Castor answered. "We don't have the numbers to maintain it long enough to matter. Have the soldiers search the city again, but I expect they'll turn up nothing. Our quarry is a slippery one."

"Alright, boss," Lake replied. He paused. "What about Avery?"

"Take his body back to court. The archlich will want to interrogate him, I imagine," Castor ordered as he reentered the tower and exited the lounge.

CHAPTER 344: SPIRIT GAMES

I waited a long ten minutes before risking mindspeech again. *"Are they gone?"*

"Castor is," Ghost replied. *"Some of the others are still poking around."*

"Alright, tell me if anything changes." There was no reason to move. My hiding place amongst the gargoyles was as safe a place as any, and until I removed my debuffs, I was too vulnerable to do much of anything.

With nothing else to occupy my attention, I reviewed the post-battle Game messages.

You have reached level 171!
Your meditation has reached rank 16, your elemental resistance rank 9, and your null life rank 1.

The encounter with the mages had netted me only a single level, a poor return considering the hurt they'd inflicted. But I had come out the other end alive and free and had no cause to complain. Besides which, it was not to fight but to acquire information that I'd ventured into the tower.

And in that respect, my mission had been a success.

I had confirmed the existence of the exile and gained a better understanding of the possessed's nature and their capabilities. It was knowledge that I was sure would stand me in good stead when we met again.

Which I was certain we would.

After investing my new attribute point, I wrapped my arms tightly about myself, and doing my best to ignore my body's cries of pain, set myself to wait.

The two hours took achingly long to pass, but pass it did.

You are no longer quad-chained.

My happiness at the Game alert knew no bounds, and I wasted no time in restoring my abused body back to working order.

You have healed yourself of all injuries. Your health is at 100%.
You have replenished 100% of your mana and psi.

My sight returned to normal, and my right leg functioned again as it should. Best of all, I had regained full use of my abilities. Shifting around carefully, I took a long look at my surroundings.

Everything was exactly as Ghost had described. Satisfied, I turned my attention to the room below. According to my mindsight, the lounge was empty, but there was something else I needed confirmation of. *"Is spirit-Avery still there?"*

"No, he's gone. He left when they took his body away."

Nodding, I took a moment to renew my buffs and disguise.

You have assumed the visage of Taim.

The possessed already suspected Taim was a false identity. But that was no reason to reveal my true form. Dropping back down to the window—a laughably easy exercise in comparison to my earlier tortuous climb—I slipped into the lounge again.

In the aftermath of the skirmish, it was a ruined, smoking mess and nothing seemed suspicious. But after being caught out by the possessed once, I wasn't about to take any unnecessary chances.

Ghost had observed Castor closely while he'd been in the room, and we both agreed he'd not tarried long enough to lay any further traps, which left only the other mages' spells to worry about.

Wrapped in shadow, I triple scanned the room, once with my physical sight, twice with mindsight, and thrice with my spectacles of ward seeing.

Finally, my gaze settled on my missing glove. The abandoned cat claw was still where I'd left it. Recovering it was the only reason I'd returned to the chamber. Weaving deftly through the debris, I tugged free the glove from where it was inset in the wall.

You have acquired a cat claw.

"Do we hunt the possessed now?" Ghost asked eagerly.

"We don't," I disagreed. *"Our work here is done."*

"But they almost killed you!" Ghost complained.

"They did. There is nothing further to be gained fighting the mages, though. It's time to head out."

Making my way back to the window, I slipped outside and began my descent to the street below. Now that I was nearly in the clear, I took the time to reflect on the nature of my foes.

The possessed certainly seemed to be aptly named.

After thinking matters through, I realized I'd learned how Castor and the others were maintaining their undying existence. I'd never seen the spirit of one of my victims before, nor had Ghost, and I could only imagine that the Game instantly whisked away the dead to whatever afterlife they enjoyed—or suffered.

Somehow though, the possessed had found a way to keep their spirits chained to their corpses after death, and it took no great leap of intuition to deduce they must also have a spell to reattach themselves thereafter.

Or, at least, some of them did.

Castor, I suspected, could not do it, or he would have restored Avery to life himself. It was, however, a good bet that the archlich could. It led me to wonder about other things too—like, for instance, what other spirit magics the archlich had. If the possessed leader could reforge spirit and body into a single whole after death, it was nearly certain he could also perceive free-roaming spirits.

That made the archlich a grave threat to Ghost.

I glanced at the spirit wolf hovering beside me. *"Again, are you sure that spirit-Avery did not see you?"* I asked for the third—or was it fourth?—time.

She nodded. *"He was focused entirely on you—probably because you were the one to kill him—and, like I said, he wasn't all there. I don't think he could see anything beyond you."*

I pursed my lips thoughtfully. I had no reason to believe Ghost was wrong, but I could not risk that she *might* be. If—no, when—I entered the archlich's court, Ghost would have to stay behind.

Somehow, I was going to have to find a way to break the news gently.

Reaching the base of the tower, I found the nearby streets free of mages and soldiers. My descent had gone unnoticed. Orienting myself in the direction of the closest city wall, I fell into a loping run.

* * *

We escaped the city without incident.

Taking to the plateau, Ghost and I made our way eastwards. Our destination: the exile Elron had mentioned. I'd been tempted to seek out the marshal before leaving the city but had decided against it. It would only put him in further danger—needlessly so. Nothing I'd learned changed the plan we had conceived.

After we put sufficient distance between ourselves and the city, Ghost and I broke for camp. I fell into a deep healing sleep while she kept watch.

Then, we resumed our hike east.

From what I'd learned of the dungeon's geography, I knew it would take us a few days to reach the northeastern corner of Draven's Reach, and I knew better than to rush things. In fact, just what to do with our time was a question that preoccupied me.

Ghost had no need for further lessons. She had mastered the astral blade spell and there was only so much Game lore I could pass on to her. That left my own self to tend to. Since entering the dungeon my desire to get stronger had grown, not shrunk. Even ignoring the dungeon's denizens there were a host of high-leveled foes standing between me and escape.

I had two choices then. Battle the dungeon's elites as we journeyed east. Or tackle the stygians hiding in the fog banks.

The former was riskier, but the rewards would be greater.

The latter would net me fewer levels but promised to provide more opportunities for training. Some of my skills were lagging far behind my player level, and I wanted to close the gap. And thanks to Elron's gift, I had two blades to use instead of the one I usually employed against the stygians.

Skill training first, I decided. *Then levels.*

Altering my course, I made for the closest fog bank a half-mile south of our position.

* * *

The fog bank in question swarmed with stygians.

Even from a hundred yards away, their chittering filled the air with a constant buzz. *"How many do you make out?"* I asked.

"Two hundred," Ghost replied.

That was a sizable number, but given that most were crawlers, they were well within my means to defeat. *"Do you remember the plan?"*

"I do," Ghost replied. *"But I can do more,"* she added, a note of pleading entering her voice.

I shook my head. *"Stick to what we agreed. Understood?"*

The spirit wolf nodded unhappily.

"Then let's go." Rising to my feet, I crept into the mist.

Multiple hostile entities have failed to detect you!

Warning: You have entered the nether! The nether toxicity at your current location is at tier 2. You are unprotected.

Your health, psi, stamina, and mana are degenerating at a rate of 9% per minute (damage reduced by 40% due to void armor).

I passed into the fog bank unprotected by a nether crystal and paused to orient myself.

"Five yards to your left."

I headed in the direction Ghost indicated and, a few steps later, came across six crawlers. They were milling about, as yet unaware of my presence. Drawing my stygian blades, I took a second to plan my strikes.

Then, I flew into action.

Creeping up behind the first, I stabbed down. Whirling, I cleaved through a second. Both creatures died without protest.

Darting forward, I cut left and right simultaneously. Two more crawlers fell.

The last two nether creatures, fortunate to be farther away than the others, sensed something amiss and turned my way. Catching sight of me, they opened their maws to sound the alarm.

I shadow blinked before their cries could escape them.

You have teleported 5 yards.

I emerged between the crawlers with my swords poised to strike. Extending my arms, I drove the point of my blades deep into my foes, killing both. With quiet sighs, the pair sank lifelessly to the ground.

You have killed 6 stygian crawlers.

Retracting my swords, I listened intently, but the slaughter had gone unnoticed. *"Anything?"* I asked, seeking confirmation.

Ghost shook her head. *"You're good."*

I sheathed my blades. Elron's gift had played its part beautifully, proving as true a sword as the one I'd gained from Jasiah so long ago. *"Perfect. Lead me to the next group."*

* * *

With Ghost directing me, I stalked along the rim of the fog bank, ambushing every clump of crawlers we found.

The creatures were largely oblivious of their surroundings, and ever so slowly, I whittled down their numbers, advancing both my sword skills and sneaking in the process. Eventually, of course, something went wrong, and the alarm was raised.

But I had a plan for that too.

As the cries of the remaining one hundred and fifty stygians rose to a fever pitch, I dropped into a crouch and huddled small. *"Lead them away,"* I ordered while drawing psi in anticipation.

Twenty yards to my right, a cry cut the air.

It was Ghost, using her astral blades. She had wanted to take a more direct role in the slaughter, but I had forbidden it. With her spirit unclothed, there was too much that could go wrong, and I was not about to risk her life unnecessarily.

Far better, I decided, that she play the same role she had in the mage's tower—that of distraction and feint.

With my mindsight, I watched the spirit wolf race away. Four dozen stygians were already dogging her heels. The creatures could not see her, but they could certainly feel the touch of the violet dagger she manifested—and they chased after it in the futile hope of snaring the caster.

Ghost kept up her spellcasting, drawing more of the crawlers to her as she fled the fog bank. I smiled. So far, everything was going according to plan. Rising to my haunches, I headed deeper into the mists.

Six mindglows appeared ahead.

I paused, assessing each. All were weavers of similar level as those I had encountered before. They were roused and alert, but their mental defenses weren't raised yet.

This should be easy, I thought and released the spell I held ready.

You have charmed 6 of 6 targets for 20 seconds.

Raising my mind shield, I advanced again.

✳   ✳   ✳

Void thief triggered! You have acquired the direct-targeted spell <u>blight thorn (stolen)</u>.

...

...

You have killed 6 stygian weavers.
You have destroyed a stygian seed!
You have acquired 1 set of stygian seed remains.

It was as easy as I expected.

Dual wielding my stygian blades, I killed the weavers quickly and efficiently while accepting enough blight thorn damage to steal the spell. Then, I destroyed the seed.

At its death, a mournful cry filled the air—the sound of over one hundred angry crawlers abandoning their fruitless pursuit and returning to their forgotten charge. Sheathing my swords, I put my head down and fled.

Before the first crawler could find me, Ghost entered the range of my mindsight. *"Follow me!"* she called. Without question, I did just that.

"He's here," Ghost cried a handful of seconds later.

I didn't have to ask who. Manifesting the spell I held ready, I shadow blinked.

You have teleported 48 yards to Ghost.

Emerging from the aether somewhere outside the fog bank, I rolled to a halt and wrapped myself in shadow. A few dozen yards to my left, the crawler pack surged into the mists. With Ghost's guidance, I had neatly avoided them.

A hostile entity has failed to detect you! You are hidden.

Raising my head, I watched a pair of mighty wings beat powerfully against the air. The harbinger had come. I had no intention of confronting the flying horror, of course. But I was admittedly curious to see what he would do.

The harbinger flew straight to the seed's former resting place, showing no awareness of me, the fragments in my pocket, or Ghost as he passed overhead.

A moment later, a roar of fury rolled through the air.

I waited.

More angry hisses and clicks followed, some from the crawlers, but most from the harbinger. Yet even after minutes had passed, the stygian Power did not speak as he had during our first encounter. Nor did he seek to address me.

Safe in the shadows, I filed away the information.

When we'd initially met, the harbinger had claimed he could smell me. To prevent that, I'd used a scent crystal when destroying the seeds outside New Haven. But this time around, I had not bothered.

For one, I didn't have nearly enough scent crystals to employ every time I entered a fog bank. For another, I was interested in seeing how the harbinger would respond when he realized who had been destroying the seeds.

His lack of reaction was puzzling at first.

Then I realized the harbinger had lied.

He could no more smell my wolf heritage than any other creature could. The seed had to have told him about my bloodline, the same seed that I had grasped in my hand for entirely too long.

My lips turned down sourly. I would have to be more careful when dealing with the things in the future.

A little later, after a cursory search of the area, the harbinger flew off. By then, the fog bank had largely dissipated, leaving behind only a few trailing wisps of nether. Through them, I could see the surviving crawlers.

Interestingly, the creatures' agitation had dissipated. The harbinger, I suspected, had given them new orders.

Forming up in a long column, the crawlers were making their way up the chasm. *To the next fog bank?* I wondered. *Or to a nearby elite?*

I glanced upward, studying the skies in the direction the harbinger had flown. I was curious, too, about where the stygian had gone. Did he have a nest somewhere in the dungeon? Somewhere he kept returning to?

"*Do we head back to the plateau?*" Ghost asked.

But I was not yet ready to leave the chasm. I eyed the retreating crawler column. They would make ideal training subjects, I decided.

"*No,*" I said at last. "*Let's take care of them first.*"

CHAPTER 345: A CLEANSING TOUCH

DAY EIGHT IN DRAVEN'S REACH

Ghost and I picked off the crawlers one at a time.

Using charm, I bespelled a single stygian and lured it away from the column for killing. It was slow and tedious work, but it sped my telepathy skill along nicely, and by the time the last crawler died, I'd achieved my training goal.

Your telepathy has reached rank 15, allowing you to learn tier 4 abilities.

In the process, I also advanced a few other skills and gained two levels—not a lot for killing over one hundred stygians. But I had reached level parity with the crawlers and a slowdown was to be expected.

You have reached level 173!
Your nether absorption skill has reached rank 10, your channeling rank 12, and your light armor rank 14.
Your Mind has increased to rank 80. Other modifiers: +12 from items.
New ingredients acquired: 130 x lumps of necrotic plasma and 56 x vial of nether residue.

The lack of levels did not bother me. What mattered most was that slaysight could be upgraded. Turning my focus inwards, I opened the Class advancement window. It was finally time to spend my last Class point.

Commencing Class upgrade...
...
Upgrade complete. Class points remaining: 0.
Congratulations, Michael, your voidstealer Class has advanced to rank 9!

You have upgraded your slaysight ability to <u>greater slaysight</u>. The fourth tier of the slaysight ability adds another mental manipulation to your arsenal: <u>shatter</u>. Additionally, the range, number of targets, and duration of the spell have increased.

With greater slaysight, you may detect any mind within 100 yards and <u>shatter</u>, <u>sleep</u>, <u>terrify</u> or <u>mentally blind</u> any 6 targets for 40 seconds. Shatter directly assaults a foe's mind shield, weakening it with every iteration applied. Note, after the spell's duration has lapsed, the targets' mental defenses will be restored.

This is a Class ability and does not occupy any ability slots.

"Well, well," I murmured as I scanned the Game messages—the changes to slaysight were impressive.

The upgrade had improved nearly every aspect of the Class ability. I was especially pleased by the new mental manipulation, shatter. It enabled me to accomplish what I'd not been able to do so far: strip a foe of his mind shield.

Even better, shatter's effects could be stacked, meaning that given sufficient time, I could destroy any enemy's mental defenses. Of course, the ability would not aid me against immune targets or those with high mental resistance. But that did not negate its potential.

"What now?" Ghost asked, interrupting my musings.

"Give me a moment to decide," I replied. The side trip into the fog bank had gone off without a hitch, and I could think of no reason not to continue hunting the seeds and its protectors to further improve my skills.

"We resume our journey east," I replied finally. *"But any seed we run across, we destroy."*

✳   ✳   ✳

It took us three days traveling by the plateau to cross the breadth of the dungeon. Thankfully we had not been forced to traverse the canyons or follow the winding chasms; otherwise the journey would have taken weeks longer. Along the way, we crossed paths with five more stygian seeds.

Ghost and I destroyed them all.

Each time, the spirit wolf lured away the bulk of the nether creatures while I snuck in, slew the remaining guards, and killed the seed. It was an efficient strategy, and even though I prepared multiple contingencies, none were called for.

The harbinger continued to respond to every incursion, but he was helpless to prevent the seeds' destruction. Time and again he winged away, only to return too late at the next fog bank.

Killing the seeds and the hundreds of stygians that guarded them netted me only six levels, but it was the improvement in my skills that made the side trips worthwhile. Nearly all of them ranked up, leaving me pleased with my progress when I finally pulled up my player profile and took a minute to study it.

Player Profile (Partial): Michael

Level: 179. Rank: 17. Lives Remaining: 3.
True Marks (hidden): Pack Alpha, Worthy Adversary.
Class: voidstealer IX (hidden).

Attributes

Strength: 21 (13)*. Constitution: 27 (19)*. Dexterity: 82 (58)*. Perception: 40 (36)*. Mind: 98 (86)*. Magic: 42 (28)*. Faith: 0.
* denotes attributes affected by items.

Active Buffs

Damage reduction: Life: 5%. Death: 5%. Air: 45%. Earth: 45%. Fire: 45%. Water: 45%. Shadow: 5%. Light: 5%. Dark: 5%. Nether: 55%. Physical: 54%*.

Additional resistance (excluding inherent resistance provided attributes): Life: 2.5%. Death: 2.5%. Air: 22.5%. Earth: 22.5%. Fire: 22.5%. Water: 22.5%. Shadow: 2.5%. Light: 2.5%. Dark: 2.5%. Nether: 27.5%. Physical: 0%.

Immunities: Entanglement: tier 2 spells*. Mind spells: tier 2 spells*.
denotes buffs affected by items.

<u>Skills</u>

Dodging: 155. Sneaking: 166. Shortswords: 165. Two weapon fighting: 144. Light armor: 145. Thieving: 118.
Chi: 151. Meditation: 182. Telekinesis: 156. Telepathy: 161.
Insight: 184. Deception: 147.
Channeling: 150. Elemental absorption: 90. Null force: 15. Null life: 11. Null death: 17. Nether absorption: 111.

<u>Backpack Contents (Key New Items)</u>

6 x set of stygian seed remains.
500 / 500 ingredients stored in alchemy stone.

With the notable exception of my void skills, most of my remaining ones had reached tier four, and I finally felt that they had caught up to my player level.

Truly, I was well on my way to becoming an elite.

Throughout the journey, the immense fog bank in the dungeon's center was a constant companion. I still didn't know what lay inside, but given what I'd learned from the New Haveners, I had no cause to explore it.

The dungeon's exit lay in the southeast quadrant, and the exile in the northeast. I had absolutely no reason to concern myself with the ominous nether cloud. No reason at all. Still...

I couldn't help wondering about it—and what the harbinger did there.

It had not escaped my notice that every time the stygian Power showed up, he seemed to be coming from somewhere in the central fogbank. Something there was keeping him busy. It was a distracting—if intriguing— mystery, but not one I was keen to investigate further. I had enough to deal with already.

On the fourth day of our journey out of New Haven, and my twelfth since entering Draven's Reach, the eastern edge of the dungeon's violet dome appeared on the horizon. I slowed my steps. We had finally reached our destination.

The dungeon's northeast quadrant.

Unfortunately, Elron had not been able to give me the exile's precise location. I only knew the possessed was somewhere in the vicinity and that I would have to search her out myself.

"We're here," I told Ghost.

She glanced from the shimmering curtain of violet that cut sharply across the plateau to the chasms below. *"We go down?"*

I nodded. The plateau made an ideal highway, but as deep as some of the dungeon's canyons were, it would be impossible to conduct a search for the exile from above.

Ghost gazed southwards. *"There's a fog bank close by,"* she said suggestively. Despite her initial unhappiness at playing the role of decoy, the spirit wolf had come to enjoy her own part in slaying the seeds.

I glanced in the direction she had pointed out. I'd seen the fog bank already, of course. It was half a mile away and was far enough that we probably wouldn't encounter any stygians while we searched the chasms. But, like Ghost had said, it was close enough not to be *too* far out of our way.

And every seed we killed helped cleanse the dungeon a little more.

"Alright, let's go kill it," I said.

✳   ✳   ✳

The fog bank in question stretched nearly one hundred yards across, filling almost half of the canyon it occupied. *Hmm, this seed must be one of the older ones,* I mused.

Given the nature of the seeds and the function they appeared to perform in a dungeon, I'd come to the conclusion that a fog bank's size was a good measure of a seed's age.

Larger fog banks meant older seeds, and invariably, more guardians. *"How many are there this time?"* I asked as we entered the shallow bowl-shaped canyon.

"Three hundred," she replied.

Her response barely gave me pause. Three hundred foes of any kind were a considerable number—if faced head-on. But, of course, we wouldn't be doing that.

Ghost led the way as we approached the fog bank. Neither of us spoke. We had done this enough times already that communication was superfluous. Following the spirit wolf's bright mindglow, I slipped into the nether and slaughtered the first of the seed's guardians—a crawler pack of six.

The creatures died as easily as ever.

Moving on, I tailed Ghost to the next pack and blitzed through them too. Then, the next. And the next.

Despite the ease with which I killed the crawlers, I did not let myself become lax. These were stygians I was facing off with, after all—and in an elite dungeon to boot.

My buffs were active, and my senses extended. Stalking silently, I killed mercilessly and efficiently, no blade stroke wasted, and making sure every second counted. I had become so practiced at ambushing the stygians, it was only after I completed a full circuit of the fog bank's rim that the alarm was raised.

"Damn," I muttered, easing into a crouch. *"How many does that make?"*

"Ninety-eight," Ghost replied nonchalantly. There was a split-second pause before she added smugly, *"I win!"*

I chuckled. *"That you did."* This time she'd guessed right.

We had taken to betting on how many crawlers I could kill before my presence was detected. A morbid game perhaps, but it helped me stay focused.

Oh well, I thought as the cry of alarm echoed from elsewhere in the mists. *"Time for phase two."*

Staying crouched, I waited while Ghost shifted roles from scout to decoy. Less than a dozen seconds later, the surviving crawlers broke south, following the enticing trail she'd laid down. With the path cleared, I headed deeper into the fog bank.

The seed was guarded by six weavers. The number had to have some mystical significance for the stygians because so far, every seed—no matter the size of its fog bank—always had the same number of weavers acting as its last line of defense.

And six stygians were far too few to stop me.

Drawing psi, I prepared to sleep the weavers. I'd been itching to try out my new slaysight variant, shatter, but had not had an excuse to do so yet. It was simpler to disable the weavers, then kill them and the seed. And I saw no reason to do otherwise on this occasion either.

"Prime, we have a problem."

I paused. *"What?"*

"The crawlers are returning."

I frowned. *"Already?"*

"Yes, they've ignored the last few daggers I manifested. I even killed one, but not even that drew a reaction from the others."

That was certainly unusual. *"Break off,"* I ordered.

Releasing the weaves of the spell I held ready, I did the same myself. If I hurried, there was still time to kill the seed, but I was not about to chance it. The sudden change in the stygians' behavior could not presage anything good, and I wanted to clear out of the canyon as soon as I could.

"Ghost, direct me. Where are—"

An unknown entity has detected you! You are no longer hidden.
An unknown entity has detected you!
An unknown entity has detected you!
An unknown entity has detected you!

CHAPTER 346: AMBUSHING THE AMBUSHERS

I couldn't believe it.

I had been found out. My mind turning frantic circles, I tried to work out what was going on. I had been discovered.

But by what?

Where were the foes that had detected me? And more importantly, in which direction did I have to flee to avoid them?

The only mindglows in range were the weavers behind me, and they weren't moving. Besides, I knew from experience that my stealth was good enough to deceive them. The crawlers couldn't be responsible either. They were too far away.

Whatever this is, it's something new.

The realization left me with a sick feeling in my stomach. While the 'who,' 'why,' and 'how' still eluded me, I was certain I had fallen into a trap—and its jaws were already closing.

Spinning around to face the way I'd come, I bolted.

But I'd barely managed a dozen steps before another Game message dropped into my mind.

You have failed to detect an unknown entity.

"Hells," I swore. Not only was my stealth too low to beat my mysterious foes' senses, but *their* stealth had no trouble defeating mine.

They are mind shielded and cloaked.

Having no other choice, I kept running. I had only one objective: to escape. Luckily, the canyon housing the seed was small and shallow—just over two hundred yards across. Getting out should be easy enough.

"Ghost, where are you?" I gasped, readying psi.

"Heading your way."

A few seconds passed, then Ghost appeared at the fringes of my mindsight. She was a hundred yards away, but still out of shadow blink range, and I adjusted my course towards her. *"Do you see them?"*

"Who, the crawlers? They're heading straight for the seed. Their path won't intersect with—"

"Not them," I interrupted. *"And not the weavers either. I mean the other four."*

A momentary pause. *"Prime, there is no one else in the canyon."*

Ghost's certainty could only mean she didn't see our new foes' mindglows either. This was bad. Very bad.

"You're safe," Ghost said, trying to reassure me when I didn't respond.

"Hardly," I retorted. "I've been spotted—many times over. We have visitors, Ghost. Four of them. And whatever or whoever they are, I can't pierce their stealth."

Grim silence followed. But no doubt.

Ghost believed me, even though her senses were telling her something else. "Are they constructs?"

"Perhaps," I replied, uncertain myself. "But we can ponder the mystery later. Right now, it's time to go." Releasing the spell I held ready, I shadow blinked.

You have teleported 49 yards to Ghost.

I emerged from the aether on the northern edge of the mists— Ghost had been circling the fog—and less than fifty yards from the canyon's edge.

The spirit wolf was not the only one nearby, though. The tail-end of the crawler pack was still outside the fog bank, and they spotted me instantly. Chittering in anger, the creatures charged my way.

I paid them no heed. The crawlers were comparatively slow and outrunning them would hardly tax me. Swinging about to face the canyon wall, I resumed my flight. Escape was within reach.

Wings flapped overhead.

My pulse quickened. Wings did not bode well. Wings, in fact, portended horrible things. Fighting back rising dread, I glanced over my shoulder and—

—spotted the familiar outline of an unholy chimera.

It was the harbinger. I squeezed my eyes, trying to choke back my panic. Worse yet, he had already crossed over into the canyon. Escape had just gone from probable to impossible.

Ghost had sensed the stygian too. "Prime—"

"I see him," I replied, regaining my composure. "Get to the plateau. Hurry!"

I didn't expect her to reach it in time, nor that I would survive long enough to teleport to her. But we had to try. Wordlessly, the spirit wolf broke left, arcing away from me and the rapidly closing harbinger.

I turned back to face the stygian. Now I knew the 'who' and the 'why.' This was retaliation for my campaign against the seeds. The 'how,' though, still baffled me. Where had the harbinger found allies capable of detecting me?

Dropping into a crouch, I attempted to recloak myself.

Four unknown entities have detected you! You cannot hide here.

Not unexpectedly, I'd failed. Sighing, I stood tall again. My fate appeared sealed. Drawing my blades, I readied myself to face the stygian.

The tip of the harbinger's shadow crossed mine.

Stilling, I waited for him to swoop down.

But the harbinger did not dive.

He flew past me, wings outstretched, and for just a second, I dared to hope I was wrong, that the harbinger hadn't laid the ambush and his presence here was only coincidence.

But no, behind me, the crawler horde had drawn up short too. And they would only have done that in response to some unseen command. My reprieve, I suspected, was going to be a short one.

I glanced to the left. Ghost was drawing closer to the canyon's west wall. Swiveling about to keep both the harbinger to the north and the crawlers to the south in sight, I summoned psi and backed away in her direction.

The harbinger, meanwhile, was landing. Stretching out his hyena-like legs, the stygian jogged to a halt on the plateau above before swinging around and drawing to a stop. I measured the distance between us.

He was sixty yards away—out of teleport range. My eyes narrowed. *Was that deliberate?*

"Well, well. If it isn't the wolfling," the harbinger said. Furling his black crow wings, he stared into the canyon and pinned me with a smoldering gaze that was at odds with his mild tone. "I suspected it was you all along. And now, I have you."

"Congratulations," I said sarcastically. Halting my retreat, I took a casual step forward. "But you will find me harder to kill than catch."

"We'll see," the harbinger replied, backing up a step.

So. It *was* deliberate.

The stygian must have guessed the range of shadow blink. "Afraid?" I sneered.

My words failed to rile. "Not at all," the harbinger said, chuckling. "But after all the trouble I went through to catch you, I'm not about to let you escape." His gaze shifted sideways. "And what do we have here? Another wolf. Such a strange one, too."

Ghost skidded to a halt.

I could feel the shock resonating from her in waves. My own astonishment was no less. The harbinger could *see* the spirit wolf— something I was sure he had not been able to do before. What had changed?

"Oh yes, I see her," the harbinger said, seeming to enjoy my confounded silence. Leaning forward, he sniffed the air. "She is pure spirit, isn't she? It explains much."

"How?" I ground out.

He ignored the question. "Did you really think you could slay the void's children with such impunity and get away with it? That I wouldn't respond?"

I paid the harbinger's question as much heed as he had mine. He was obviously in a mood to talk, but it was equally clear his trap was well-conceived. If there was any chance of me escaping, I would have to do something unexpected. *"Ghost, get out of the canyon. Don't wait for me."*

"But what about you—"

"This is no time for questions," I snapped harshly. *"Do it!"*

"I warned you what would happen if you destroyed the chosen, didn't I?" the harbinger continued blithely. "You ignored me. Now you will pay for your folly."

I didn't wait for whatever came next. Breaking into motion, I dashed forward, casting as I went.

You have cast fade, blurring your form and making you 50% harder to see for 2 minutes.

My other buffs were still active, not having expired yet after their initial casting. Fixing my gaze on the harbinger, I readied windborne. I would have to close the distance to him before he could withdraw, and that necessitated the use of both windborne and shadow blink.

Four unknown hostiles have negated your spell. Fade neutralized.

I ignored the Game message.

It was no less than I'd expected. But while my enemies had nullified my fade, they had not canceled the buff, and like with everything else in the Game, there had to be a limit to the range of their perception.

If I fled fast and far enough, I would escape their detection range, and fade would reactivate. Therein lay my hope.

The harbinger, though, was not in a cooperative mood. Observing my rapid approach, he took off running clockwise around the canyon and, in only a handful of steps, went airborne.

"Damn," I muttered, tracking his flight for a moment. The stygian was still out of teleport range and even if I laid down a windslide right now, it would do no good.

I would have to escape the canyon the hard way.

Spinning about again, I surged towards the closest canyon wall, feet pounding against the ground. Behind me, the crawler horde stirred to life and gave chase. The harbinger, too, it seemed, had decided the time for talking had passed. Weaving psi, I set down my windslide.

You have cast windborne.

I hopped onto the ramp of air and sheathed my swords. In their stead, I equipped my cat claws and measured the height of the rapidly approaching cliff. *Ten seconds,* I decided. That was all the time I needed to scale it and escape.

The harbinger did not give me ten seconds.

Or even five.

A stygian harbinger has cast void prison. Duration: 1 hour.

Before I reached the end of the windslide, glistening walls of ebony rose from the clifftops and shot skywards to encase the entire canyon in a dome of startling black.

Urgh. The harbinger had cut off my only route of escape. Not bothering to test the strength of the barrier his casting had erected—I expected it would be impervious to anything I could throw at it—I jumped off the windslide.

Unfortunately, the harbinger was not done casting. A second spell followed in the wake of the first.

A stygian harbinger has cast shackle spirit.
Ghost has been shackled. Duration: 5 minutes.
This spell binds a spirit entity with the same limitations as other physical beings, preventing them from passing through material objects and making them vulnerable to physical damage. A shackled spirit does not, however, inherit any of the advantages of being embodied. They cannot heal any damage they incur, nor deal physical damage of their own.

"There, much better," the harbinger shouted from where he circled above. "Now I have you *and* your pet."

I landed heavily but paid my bruises and the stygian's crowing no mind, having only thought to spare for Ghost. *"Did you make it out?"* I gasped.

She had to have made it out. She *had* to.

A pregnant pause. *"No."*

The blood drained from my face. The worst the harbinger could do to me was send me to respawn in the sector's safe zone. But Ghost... she faced final death.

And now she was vulnerable.

CHAPTER 347: A MULTITUDE OF DEATHS

"Prime?" Ghost asked, her mindvoice quivering with anxiety that echoed my own.

I had become careless, I realized, despite my steadfast resolution not to be, and had grown too sure of my own abilities. There was ample evidence that my stealth was equal to the challenge of deceiving the stygian Power but, foolishly, I had come to rely more on it than I should've.

And now that the harbinger had neutralized my stealth, I was at a loss on how to escape him...

Wordlessly, I stared across the canyon at Ghost, not sure what to say. How was I going to protect her? *"The shackles won't last long,"* I said finally, striving for optimism.

Five minutes.

That was all the time I needed to buy Ghost. Removing my cat claw gloves, I drew my stygian blades again. *I can do that.*

I didn't believe it, though.

Even ignoring the fact I had no stealth and over two hundred crawlers, six weavers, and four *still-unseen* watchers to contend with, there was also the harbinger to consider. He, on his own, was an insurmountable challenge. And every second I fought him, Ghost would be vulnerable. Even a grazing blow from any one of the stygians in the canyon would kill her.

Stop it! This isn't helping. It doesn't matter if you die. Only Ghost has to live.

Squashing my doubts, I took stock again. The harbinger was still circling up above, seemingly content to observe how events played out. Of the weavers and the unseen watchers there was no sign, while in front of me, the crawler pack was splitting, a dozen peeling off towards Ghost.

They would reach her soon.

And she was helpless.

A snarl crossed my face as, unbidden, the wolf in me rose to the fore. The Pack was imperiled. Ghost was in danger. I had to save her. Driven to act by instincts centuries old, I spun psi. I *had* to place myself between her and the impending threat. I had to.

But I couldn't.

Fighting back my bubbling rage, I forced myself to stillness. I couldn't act precipitately. If I did, Ghost was dead. With a brittle calm that threatened to abandon me at any moment, I looked past the crawlers and Ghost to study the rim of the canyon.

The base of the cliff walls was as scarred and pitted as everywhere else in the dungeon—and had hiding spots aplenty. Inspiration struck and an idea took shape in my mind.

The best way to save Ghost was not to place myself between her and the crawlers, but to draw the danger away from her. The wolf inside subsided.

It liked my plan, too.

Lifting my head, I found the harbinger's gliding shape. He was close enough to hear. "You will pay for that!" I bellowed with my hands cupped around my mouth. "You may have won here today, but your victory will not be without cost! Or have you forgotten? Your precious chosen is unprotected!" Not waiting for my foe's response, I sprinted back towards the fog.

My threat got the harbinger's attention, as I knew it would.

"No, you cur! Stop!" he screamed. Breaking off from his circling, he surged my way. Out of the corner of my eye, I noticed the crawlers—*all* of them—do the same.

Smiling tightly, I kept running. *"Ghost, find a hole to shelter in. Now, while the stygians are distracted."*

"But—"

"No, buts. You will *live,"* I said, infusing my words with the power of a Prime's command. *"Hide and don't come out until the harbinger is gone."*

Before she could reply, I broke off communication and refocused on the surroundings. My plan would only work if I lived long enough for Ghost to find refuge. And, eyeing the approaching harbinger, I knew I would need every bit of cunning to pull that off.

✻   ✻   ✻

I was less than ten yards from the edge of the fog bank when the plummeting harbinger attacked. Opening his beak, he spewed out a roiling cloud of nothingness.

A stygian harbinger has cast nether's cloying touch.

The darkness churned as if it were alive, individual trails of smoke darting and zipping through the air in a bid to outpace their fellows to their prey—me.

I didn't hang around.

You have teleported 50 yards. You have entered the nether!
You have evaded a stygian harbinger's attack.

I emerged out of the aether in the shadow of a crawler at the limit of my teleport range. Sensing me at its rear, the nether creature ceased the motion of its tiny legs and opened its jaws—perhaps to signal the rest of the pack, or maybe to latch onto me—but I didn't wait to find out. Chopping down with the sword in my right hand, I cut it in two.

You have killed a stygian crawler with a fatal blow.

Hurdling the corpse, I plunged my other blade through the torso of another nearby crawler, then spun around and skewered a third. Withdrawing both swords, I went searching for my next victim. But even as I slew the stygians with reckless abandon, I kept careful watch on the harbinger's mindglow.

Which was why I saw the moment he altered his heading to hone in on me again.

By rights, the harbinger shouldn't have been able to see me. I had teleported into the fog, and, even though I lacked stealth, none of the nether creatures—except the unseen watchers—should've been able to spot me from more than a few yards away. Yet somehow the harbinger had discerned my new location without trouble and was on course to intercept me.

As was the entire crawler pack, I realized.

Nearly every stygian mindglow in the canyon was converging on me. Granted, my mind shield was lowered, but this time around, I didn't think it was the seed that was giving away my location. I was too far away from the thing for it to be a factor yet.

It's the unseen watchers. It has to be.

Somehow, they were communicating my position to the others.

But regardless of how the stygians were doing it, I knew I couldn't stay where I was. I had to keep moving or the harbinger would make quick work of me. Sheathing my blades, I reoriented myself on the seed and dashed in its direction, weaving psi as I went.

I managed all of five steps before the next attack descended.

A stygian harbinger has cast death's cacophony.

A wave of discordant noise—loud, harsh, and ear-splitting— rolled over me as the harbinger cawed in imitation of the crow he partly resembled. I clamped my hands against my ears and kept running, but my efforts did nothing to keep the sound out.

You have failed a magical resistance check!
A harbinger has injured you.
Your void armor has reduced the death damage incurred by 5%.

Holding to my concentration, I kept casting, but the harbinger's spell was not done yet. More waves of sound followed, each building on the previous.

A harbinger has injured you.
A harbinger has injured you.
...
Void armor charge remaining: 70%. Your health has decreased to 76%.
Five stygian crawlers have died.

Blood ran down my nose, my eardrums ruptured, and the pressure inside my head built until it felt as if it was about to explode. But I remained standing—so I kept moving.

The crawlers behind me died, possibly because they were closer to the attack's epicenter. The creatures' deaths did not give the harbinger pause, though. Over and over, his screams amplified, dealing more damage with each new wave.

A harbinger has injured you.
A harbinger has injured you.
...
...

Void armor charge remaining: 45%. Your health has decreased to 55%.

Void thief triggered! You have acquired the tier 7 channeled spell, death's cacophony (stolen).

A conduit has been forged between you and a harbinger, allowing you to steal mana from your foe whenever he casts a spell at you.

Staggering and nearly senseless from pain, I nonetheless managed to complete my spell.

You have cast windborne.

Setting down the windslide, I threw myself on.

One second passed, two, then blessedly, the noise stopped. I was in the clear. For the moment, anyway.

The harbinger hadn't closed in for the kill, no doubt still wary of the cold sphere spell I'd used during our first encounter. Remaining airborne, he circled around for another attack.

Rising back to my feet, I stumbled onwards. The seed was close. Less than fifteen yards away, judging from the weavers I sensed up ahead. But the harbinger would be back. Of that, I was sure, and so despite my injuries, I kept advancing.

You have failed to detect a hostile entity.

The Game message gave me pause.

One of the unseen watchers had to be close. Would it attack? But given that the mysterious creatures hadn't so far, I felt safe in assuming it wouldn't. Drawing ebonheart, I raised my mental defenses.

You have cast mind shield. Psi abilities are unavailable.

In a flash, the mindglows of the weavers, crawlers, and harbinger disappeared, leaving me bereft of my second sight and near blind. It was far from ideal, but even in my current predicament, I dared not approach the seed with my mind exposed.

I didn't really need to destroy the seed, of course. I only had to make the harbinger believe I would. But my earlier threat had not been idle boast. I was determined the thing would die before I did.

And besides, the lack of access to my psi abilities would not hinder me as much as it should have. The harbinger had given me something *so* much better to use.

Drawing mana, I wove a magic spell.

You have cast death's cacophony. Mana remaining: 5%.

In a single burst, nearly all of my remaining mana disappeared, but the spell was worth it. Opening my mouth, I howled.

Sound erupted in a resounding, booming roar, the likes of which no wolf had ever given cry to. The mists shivered, vibrating in time to the wave of noise erupting from my mouth. Marching forward in ever-expanding circles, the pulses struck the weavers.

You have killed a level 180 stygian weaver.

You have killed a level 185 stygian weaver.
You have killed...

One after the other, the seed's six guards died. They were not the only ones to suffer the spell's wrath, though.

You have killed a level 5 stygian spore.
You have killed a level 4 stygian spore.

Stygian spores are amongst the most ephemeral of stygians with no consciousness to speak of and almost no physical form. They are indistinguishable from free-floating nether, and thus, impossible to detect when inside the mists. They do not travel far and rarely leave the vicinity of the void tree that spawned them.

The spores' lack of physical presence makes them harmless—or as harmless as any stygian can be considered. They have no means of attacking and only a single passive ability: truesight aura.

The aura not only gives the spores the ability to pierce all forms of illusion or concealment, it also grants the same to any stygian in the vicinity.

Well. That finally explained the 'how.'

The harbinger must have sown this, and perhaps other fog banks, with the spores in anticipation of an attack. And when I'd been found, the stygian seed had called him. *Simplicity itself.*

It lent me a measure of hope too.

Based on some of the initial Game messages, I was sure there were only four spores in the canyon, and I'd already slain two. *If I find the other two, perhaps surviving this debacle is not out of the question.*

An unholy shriek erupted behind me.

But as loud and painful as the scream of rage was, it was an ordinary scream, nonetheless. Still, it cued me to my foe's rapid approach.

Closing my mouth, and bringing an end to my own howl, I dashed forward, ebonheart at the ready.

"Stop, wolfling! if you—"

Ignoring the harbinger entirely, I skidded to a halt before the vulnerable seed and drove the blade through its black center.

You have destroyed a stygian seed!

I lowered my mind shield. With the seed dead, I had no more need of it, and I desperately wanted to know where my foes were.

A large mindglow surged closer.

It was the harbinger, swooping down, and he would reach me in only seconds. *Damn.*

I was out of time.

CHAPTER 348: OBLIVION

I took off at a run, needing to buy a few seconds to spin psi.

The harbinger adjusted his course the moment I did.

He wasn't slowing down either, and I could only guess he meant to run me through. The seed's death seemed to have infuriated him beyond reason, and cold sphere or not, he was coming to finish me off himself.

Unfortunately, I didn't have much mana to channel the frost ent's stolen spell for long, leaving me disinclined to meet the stygian Power head-on. Killing the weavers with death's cacophony—on top of stealing the spell in the first place—had drained my magic reserves. Staying out of reach of my foe's claws and spells was my best hope.

The stygian chimera darkened the mist above.

He was now close enough to see with the naked eye. Choosing a nearby nether creature at random, I shadow blinked.

You have teleported into a stygian crawler's shadow.
You have evaded a harbinger's attack.

I smiled as I stepped out of the aether, safely out of harm's way. I could do this all day if I had to.

The crawler flailed at me. Deftly avoiding the attack, I made no move to respond in kind and backed away instead. Focusing on the harbinger's mindglow, I waited to see what form his next attack would take.

But the stygian Power did not move. Or talk.

Retreating still further, I frowned. I could feel the hatred emanating from him. The harbinger wanted to rend me from limb to limb. So why was he sitting unmoving?

But if the harbinger wanted to waste time, I was content to let him do so. Using the opportunity afforded by the lull in battle, I scanned the area anew with my mindsight.

I failed to spot Ghost, though.

That both relieved and worried me. Was she safe? Had she found refuge? I didn't know, nor could I afford to seek out answers just yet.

I set aside further thought of my companion. As concerned as I was for her, I couldn't afford to dwell on her fate. If I was going to live, I had to find the remaining spores quickly.

Unfortunately, I had little idea where they were, and would have to rely on the Game alerts to notify me when I drew close to one. Then I would have to kill it—somehow. Choosing a direction at random, I began searching the fog.

The crawlers were no longer a threat. They still moved towards me, but in a lackluster fashion. That worried me, as did the harbinger's inaction. But I could do nothing about either.

"Killing the chosen was a mistake," the harbinger said abruptly, finally deigning to speak.

I rolled my eyes. Were we back to this again?

"Now, I have no reason to hold back," the harbinger continued.

My amusement faded. What did *that* mean?

A stygian harbinger has cast oblivion.

What spell is that?

I was nearly seventy yards away from the stygian Power and couldn't see him or the effects of the spell he had just cast. Was I its target? Drawing psi, I readied shadow blink—just in case I needed to reposition quickly.

A second passed. Then another, and still nothing came at me.

I frowned. *What is he—*

A stygian crawler has died.
A stygian crawler has died.
...
...

In the space of two seconds, half the remaining nether creatures were wiped out. My frown deepened. Was the harbinger killing the crawlers? Why would he do that?

The fog flashed black in front of my eyes.

Stumbling backward, I turned around and ran, knowing instinctively that the black flash was what had killed the crawlers. But there was no outrunning it, and a split-second later, darkness enfolded me.

Not a comforting, sheltering darkness of the type I'd grown accustomed to.

Not nearly.

This one stank of death.

You have entered an <u>oblivion field</u>. Oblivion is a death spell that destroys any living thing it encounters. Few can resist its touch, and for those that don't, death is instantaneous.
You have failed a magical resistance check!
You have disintegrated!

✳ ✳ ✳

My eyes and mouth snapped open as awareness returned with jarring suddenness.

Liquid splashed into my mouth, and I sat upright, choking and gasping. Panic-stricken, I stared at my hands. They were whole. But I remembered them being not; I remembered them turning into specks of dust before my eyes. Memory tickled, and my throat clenched.

The black flash.

Would it come again?

Heart racing, I surged to my feet, my right hand instinctively finding the hilt of ebonheart. Where was the harbinger? Was he closing in for the kill? I spun around and a flash of white caught my eye—my newbie shorts.

I jerked to a stop. *I am dead.*

Fragmented memories reconnected. *Was* dead, I corrected.

I was alive again—which could only mean I was in a rebirth well. I sagged in relief. The harbinger had lied, then. The sector's safe zone still stood free of the void.

Which was good. I would need every advantage at hand to extricate myself from my predicament. Raising my head, I studied my surroundings.

It was completely devoid of people. But in stark contrast to much of the dungeon, the safe zone was not barren. The soil was fertile and topped with grass, plants, and a smattering of trees. There was even a pond. It lay to my left, its waters still and clear. The setting was by no means idyllic, but compared to the rest of Draven's Reach, the safe zone was an oasis.

Unfortunately, the rest of the vicinity was less reassuring.

The safe zone was also home to a handful of buildings. They were log cabins, like those in the wolves' valley—but where those had been well-kept, these were ancient, their timbers missing or rotted, leading me to believe them long-abandoned.

It was what lay beyond the safe zone that concerned me the most, though.

To the left was a wall of mist. To the right, the same. Craning my neck upward, I beheld more mist. It could mean only one thing.

The safe zone is in a fog bank.

Crestfallen, I bowed my head. The harbinger had *not* lied then; he'd stretched the truth perhaps, but not lied.

"Welcome back."

I started at the words. The voice was familiar, *disturbingly* familiar. But how could he be here? Whirling around, I found myself staring into the harbinger's beady eyes.

Bloody hell!

The stygian was not in the safe zone, but I was sure he stood at its very edge, his forelegs and beak pressed up against the barrier protecting it. *Look at me,* his posture seemed to say, *the Game may be keeping me out for now, but for how much longer will that hold true?*

Not letting any glimmer of my despair show, I stiffened my limbs and stepped forward. My legs trembled, still shaky from my recent resurrection, but they held firm as I strode towards the harbinger with affected nonchalance.

The stygian watched me the whole way, his eyes gleaming with predatory intent. "How did you like being dead?" he asked as I drew to a stop three feet away.

I shrugged. "I can't complain. But as you can see, I'm back again. Your revenge, such as it was, counts for naught."

A throaty chuckle escaped the harbinger. "Your bluster will not save you, wolfling." Unfurling his wings, he battered them against the invisible barrier that separated us. "This is your new home. Come out and you die."

I raised one eyebrow. "What? You mean to tell me you intend on standing guard here the entire time? Don't you have anything better to do?"

"Oh, I have minions aplenty to watch you. You will not escape, rest assured. But don't take *my* word for it. Try to escape. You will die."

I said nothing. I was happy to let the harbinger talk in the hopes he would reveal something about the topic I was most desperate to broach—Ghost.

But so far, he only seemed interested in gloating, and I had no idea how the spirit wolf fared.

Was she alive? *Yes. Maybe.*

How far had the harbinger's oblivion spell reached? *Not across the entire canyon, surely.*

Had it seeped into her hiding place? *It couldn't have.*

Had the harbinger gone looking for her after I died? *Why would he, though?*

Could Ghost have escaped notice if he had? *Of course. I hope.*

Not knowing my companion's fate was driving me crazy. I *wanted* to ask after Ghost. But doing that would only let the harbinger know how important she was to me. She was a weakness he could exploit. And until I was free, I had to accept there was nothing I could do to protect her.

"Why is the void in Draven's Reach?" I asked suddenly, realizing I had been silent too long.

The harbinger looked taken aback by the question. It was a forthright demand for information, and quite unlike the back and forth sniping that had made up the better part of our exchanges so far. "What do you mean?" he asked slowly.

"What purpose does conquering this dungeon serve the void?" I asked. "Why come here at all? It's not like there are that many people to slaughter to begin with." I voiced my questions boldly despite knowing little of the nether or its objectives. But given my recent clashes with the stygians, it was high time I understood them better.

"The void goes where the void will," the harbinger said cryptically.

I waved aside his non-answer. "But why come *here*?"

"That is not knowledge I care to share with you, wolfling," he replied scornfully.

"Don't you know?" I retorted.

Stiff silence.

My eyes widened. "You don't, do you? Don't tell me the void's chosen have decided not to share the information with *you*?" I probed, hoping to shake loose any little nugget of information I could.

The harbinger lashed his reptilian tail angrily. "You are ignorant as a child, wolfling, picking and prodding at things you do not understand."

"Then enlighten me," I snapped.

"The void trees are beyond reproof!"

Interesting. So, the void trees were the 'chosen,' and if a being as powerful as the harbinger revered them, what did that make the trees?

Powers, I thought, shuddering at the realization. *It makes them Major Powers.* Beings on par with Loken and his fellows, and perhaps even the Primes.

"Where are we?" I demanded in another abrupt change of topic.

"Why? Are you thinking of returning to your corpse?" the harbinger countered.

I didn't say anything.

"You are smaller than I realized," he added. "Are you sure you're a scion?"

The questions threw me for a moment, then it left me wondering if the harbinger was starved of conversation. Now that my initial shock at his presence here had passed, I realized there was no reason for the stygian to be here at all.

In fact, the harbinger would have done better to ambush me anew when I left the safe zone. Instead, he'd given up the element of surprise. And for what?

To gloat.

To utter meaningless threats, and for no apparent reason that I could discern, he seemed intent on continuing the discussion. *Let's see how he handles rejection.*

Turning around, I walked away. "Goodbye, harbinger," I called over my shoulder. "We'll meet again. And next time, I promise you, it won't go so well for you."

For a drawn-out moment, silence reigned.

"We're in the heart of the dungeon, of course," the harbinger said suddenly, ignoring my parting words entirely.

I swung back to face him. "What's that supposed to mean?"

"Don't you know? We're in the central fog bank."

Of course. It made sense that Draven Reach's safe zone would be in its center. And it made sense, too, that that would be where the stygians would concentrate the greater part of their efforts.

But it also meant leaving the safe zone was going to be even harder than I expected. The central fog bank covered an entire square mile, I recollected. *All of it surely chock-full of stygians, too,* I thought, despair mounting.

This time, despite my efforts to the contrary, some glimmer of emotion escaped, and the harbinger spotted it immediately.

He chuckled throatily. "Ah, I see you understand your situation better now."

Not able to muster enough conviction for a retort, I swung away and headed back to the rebirth well.

I had a lot to consider.

CHAPTER 349: A MATTER OF PACE

It did not take the harbinger long to wander off. I guess watching me stare off into space wasn't much fun.

After the stygian left, I moved from worrying about the future to examining the waiting Game messages.

You have been reborn. Lives remaining: 2. Time lost during resurrection: 8 hours. Rebirth location: sector 73,102 safe zone. Two soul bond items have been restored.

You have lost knowledge of the stolen spell, death's cacophony.

Your null death skill has increased to level 21 and reached rank 2.

Not unexpectedly, I'd gained no levels from the encounter in the canyon and only a few of my skills had advanced. Interestingly enough, the spell the harbinger had used to kill me was from the school of death magic, which perhaps explained why I had failed so utterly to resist it. But it was not my player profile or the manner of my death that concerned me. It was my gear.

Or rather, the utter lack of any.

Morosely I stared down at the two items I'd placed on the ground: ebonheart and Sunfury's gift. The phoenix's feather was of no use just yet, which meant I had only ebonheart and my abilities to depend on to get me halfway across the dungeon to my corpse.

A mammoth task, and that was discounting the stygians that no doubt lay in wait in the nearby fog.

I sighed. *How am I going to do this?*

If Ghost was still alive, she was undoubtedly frantic with worry by this point. Would the spirit wolf remain in the canyon? And if she didn't, how would I find her?

I shook my head, setting aside the troubling thought before it could balloon into even more unanswerable questions. My first task was getting out of the fog bank. Then I would worry about Ghost and retrieving my belongings.

Strapping on ebonheart and sticking the feather in my belt, I rose to my feet and considered the encircling fog. I had no means of navigation either, but after my time in the tundra that was a state of affairs I was intimately familiar with, and I did not let it unduly trouble me.

Picking a direction at random I marched forward until I reached the edge of the fog line. The transition between the safe zone and the nether was startling. On one side the air was crystal clear, and on the other side it was opaque and tinged with a faint odor of decay.

Alright, time to find out what awaits me, I thought and opened my mindsight.

Immediately, a profusion of mindglows crowded my awareness. *Not unexpected,* I told myself, and patiently inspected them one by one.

The target is a stygian weaver.
The target is a stygian serpent.
The target is a stygian hydra.

...

There were over three hundred stygians, all of them gathered beyond the sixty yard line and at what, I suspected, the harbinger believed to be the limit of my telepathy skills. I was familiar with most of the nether creature types gathered, but it was not the stygians I could see that concerned me.

It was those I couldn't.

And there was only one way to determine if any of those were present. Calling on the shadows, I concealed myself.

Or, tried to.

An unknown entity has detected you! You have failed to hide.

I sighed. So, there were spores present. *Again, not unexpected,* I told myself. Swinging right, I set off clockwise to determine how complete the stygian cordon was.

But in my heart, I already knew.

✳   ✳   ✳

My suspicions proved correct.

The harbinger had completely encircled the safe zone with high-leveled nether creatures and an unknown number of stygian spores. There would be no sneaking past them.

I could try charming the visible nether creatures while secure in the safe zone and creating a gap in the cordon that way. But I suspected the harbinger would only plug the hole or shift the cordon out until the nearest stygian was out of mindsight range—and he had thousands to play with.

My jaunt around the safe zone had revealed a force of five thousand nether creatures, and those were only the ones the harbinger had deployed to imprison me. How many other stygians did the fog hide?

The next option would be to race through. I was fast enough to evade the stygians even if they knew where I was every step of the way. But this plan, too, was chancy, especially if the harbinger was close by and prepared to use his oblivion spell against me again.

And besides, once past the initial cordon, speed would be of no help. Since I couldn't see well enough to navigate, I would have to meticulously map out my path if I didn't want to wander in circles.

I can't sneak past. I can't charm my way through. And I can't outrun the stygians.

Where did that leave me?

Without a plan, I concluded gloomily.

I refuse to be dejected, though. *I will have to play it by ear,* I decided, altering my tactics on the fly depending on the stygians' response. And step one was leaving the safe zone.

Screwing up my courage, I stepped across the invisible barrier holding back the fog.

You have left a safe zone.

Warning: You have entered the nether! The nether toxicity at your current location is at tier 6. You are unprotected.

Your health, psi, stamina, and mana are degenerating at a rate of 16% per minute (damage reduced by 55% due to void armor).

Huh, that's another wrinkle, I thought, stepping back. The nether concentration was much stronger here than in any other fog bank I had been in. Why was that? It could be because the central fog bank was larger—but *why* was it larger? And why did this fog bank seem to feed the others?

There is a void tree here. Has to be.

It explained the presence of the spores, the seeds, the harbinger, and maybe even the nether itself. But why hadn't the Game warned me? It had done so when I'd entered the two other nether-infested sectors I had been to. Those had been Kingdom sectors, though. Did that account for the difference?

Perhaps, I thought, returning to the rebirth well. It was time for a rethink.

✳ ✳ ✳

The presence of the void tree complicated matters.

It guaranteed that there was a large stygian nest somewhere in the fog bank and it had ramped up the nether toxicity significantly. The increased degeneration rates of my mana, psi, and even health did not overly concern me. I could renew all three whilst in the nether with my abilities.

It was the stamina drain that worried me the most.

I had no way of replenishing it, and once I ran out, I would collapse into an immovable puddle—an easy target for any stygian. This, atop the other penalties I was laboring under, made getting out... impossible.

I had already lost eight hours, and a sense of urgency drove me. I knew Ghost. She was too curious to stay idle for long. If I didn't return soon, she would undoubtedly wander off in search of me—if she hadn't already.

She had no way to locate me, though, nor I her. And once Ghost left the site of my death, the chances of us finding each other dropped dramatically.

Of course, all of this assumed Ghost was alive. But I refused to believe her dead, and until I had incontrovertible proof otherwise, I would continue to act as if she was alive. Which was why I was so keen not just to get back to her, but to do so *quickly*.

That was impossible, though.

I could try anyway—take my chances and run the harbinger's gauntlet. In ideal conditions, it would take me less than a minute to cover the half-mile I estimated necessary to escape the fog. But these were less than ideal conditions.

For one, with no landmarks, I couldn't be certain I would be running in a straight line. And for another, I could expect to be under attack the entire time. There was also the harbinger to consider. He would undoubtedly turn up at some point, adding his own nasty share of surprises to the mix.

Lastly, there was the terrain to consider. I had no idea what I would be facing once I left the safe zone. There might be rivers to ford, or cliffs to scale, neither of which would be easy to do while racing against the clock. The cost of failure would be high, too. If I died, I would lose another eight hours and be left with only one life.

So, what will it be?

Slow and sure—well, not sure, but *surer*—and leaving Ghost to fend for herself for days on end?

Or fast and loose and returning to Ghost as quickly as possible?

I bit my lip, thinking. As much as I wanted to protect Ghost, she was not the only one depending on me. There were others who I had made promises to. Safyre, Anriq, Saya, Elron, and two entire wolf packs. I couldn't just roll the dice and let the chips fall as they may.

I had responsibilities.

I have to trust Ghost, I decided reluctantly. Since entering the dungeon, she had shown herself capable enough. She would manage on her own.

Slow and sure it is.

I rose to my feet. There would be no quick dash through the mist. I would be meticulous and thin the stygian numbers bit by bit. Five thousand stygians might be a lot, but by the time I was done, the harbinger would rue the day he gave me an unassailable base to operate from.

Hang in there, Ghost. I will find you—eventually.

CHAPTER 350: A SPATE OF TESTS

Before beginning my campaign against the stygians I had a few checks to conduct.

The first concerned my stealth.

I already knew from experience that the nether would not conceal me from the spores' truesight. What about other obstacles though? Would the spores be able to see through them?

I doubted it. But I had to be certain. *Time to test the theory.*

Standing in the center of the safe zone and in full view of any stygian that might be watching from beyond, I attempted to wrap myself in shadows.

Multiple unknown entities have detected you! You cannot hide here.

Right, that went exactly as expected. Sweeping my gaze from left to right, I studied the handful of ruined buildings in the safe zone. Almost none had four walls remaining, and what roofs they claimed were gutted and in imminent danger of falling. Still, for the purposes of my test, any one of the buildings would suffice.

Striding to the largest structure—a squat, low building that in its prime must have served as a great hall—I slipped inside and gingerly picked through the debris while trying not to disturb any of the structural beams still standing.

I came to a stop in the darkest corner I could find and turned about in a slow circle. I could see no part of the encircling fog, which meant no watching spore could see me either.

Dropping into a crouch, I drew the shadows to me.

You are hidden.

I smiled, pleased by the success of my test. The spores' truesight was not infallible. I could hide from the creatures, but to do so I would have to use the terrain to good effect.

It did not matter that I had little idea what the terrain outside the safe zone was like, or that my fog-impaired vision made figuring that out difficult, it was a surmountable challenge, and one I would overcome.

On to check number two.

Exiting the building, I strode to the pond next to the rebirth well. Kneeling down, I cupped my hands and took a tentative sip.

The water tasted clean and refreshing.

I exhaled in relief. I had drinking water—enough to last for weeks, if not longer. Standing anew, I turned my attention towards my next concern: food. All told, there were a dozen trees in the safe zone and each seemed to bear fruits of some sorts. The oblong-growing shapes on the bushes also looked promising. Walking over to the nearest tree, I plucked a fruit, and before I could reconsider, bit off a large mouthful and chewed with deliberate care.

The fruit was... delicious.

I smiled, ignoring the sticky juices dribbling down my chin. *An oasis indeed.* Thanks to the safe zone's bounty, I had a secure supply of both food and water and could stay put for weeks if necessary. Not that I wanted to. Finishing the fruit, I faced the nearest wall of fog.

It was time for my final set of checks.

✳   ✳   ✳

In plain sight and affecting a nonchalance I did not quite feel, I marched out of the safe zone.

Warning: You have entered the nether! The nether toxicity at your current location is at tier 6. You are unprotected.

The weavers had already disappeared from my mindsight, raising their mental shields the moment I slipped into the fog. The remaining stygians' mindglows were clearly visible though, and I watched them intently.

A minute passed and my health and energy reserves slipped downward. The stygians could see me, I knew that much. It was not enough, though. I had to know *more.* Folding my arms, I waited.

Another minute passed, and I felt myself weaken further, but still, no assault came. Certain now that the stygians wouldn't attack while I remained so close to the safe zone, I took three careful steps forward.

There was no response.

I covered another yard.

Still nothing. Resting my right hand on ebonheart, I continued advancing. The black blade was of no use against the stygians, but holding its hilt provided me with some measure of comfort.

A minute later, I was nine yards into the fog, but the stygians had yet to bestir themselves. I paused, wondering if I should go on. My energy levels had dropped substantially, and I could already feel myself flagging. Turning my focus inwards, I checked my status.

Health, stamina, and psi remaining: 49%. Mana remaining: 43%.

"Damn," I muttered. My mana was depleting faster than everything else, and for a moment I didn't understand why. Then, it hit me.

It was my void armor.

My armor was consuming mana in order to resist the void's touch. It was another unforeseen wrinkle and meant I could spend even less time in the fog than I'd originally imagined.

I glanced over my shoulder. The safe zone was already hidden from sight. *I have to return soon,* I thought. It was that, risk becoming lost, or worse. *I can manage another couple of yards at least,* I decided and took three more steps forward.

The stygians stirred.

I couldn't see the creatures themselves, of course. But across the distance that separated us, I heard the slither of serpentine coils and the stamp of heavy hydra feet. The creatures were charging.

That's it then, I thought. Fifty yards was as close as the stygians would allow me to approach before they reacted.

It was time to retreat, but I still had one more test in mind. It was the most difficult one and would require a live stygian to perform.

I knew the Game stopped players from harming one another when inside a safe zone, but I was less certain about its response to assaults made *across* a safe zone's boundary. Would the Adjudicator allow the stygians' attacks to pass through from outside? Or my own to reach them from inside?

I suspected not, but again, needed to confirm my theory. And there was only one way to do that.

The onrushing horde of mindglows drew closer. Not flinching, I drew psi and backstepped carefully. By the time I reached the edge of the safe zone, the stygians were less than twenty yards away. Tense, I waited for the first attack.

A projectile appeared in the mist.

The yellow ichor was hurtling on a direct course for my face. I had only a split second to observe it but recognized immediately what it was: a blight thorn fired from an unseen weaver. Not taking my eyes off the missile, I sprang backwards.

You have entered a safe zone.

Midair, the projectile stopped as if it had struck an invisible barrier—which it had.

I smiled tightly. So, the Game *would* stop the stygians' attacks. Now, to test the other part. Releasing the spell I'd woven in my mind, I targeted a random stygian.

Your spell has fizzled. Combat spells cannot be cast while you are inside a safe zone.

Huh. The Game response, while expected, was disappointing. Drawing ebonheart in one smooth motion, I flung it directly at the stygian in question. But just like the blight thorn had, the sword bounced off the invisible barrier and fell to the ground.

This time, there was no accompanying message from the Game.

Sighing, I sat down on the grass. My tests were complete, and I couldn't say the results were surprising. The safe zone would shelter and protect me, perhaps indefinitely. But beyond that I was on my own.

Like always. Closing my eyes, I began meditating.

＊　　＊　　＊

You have fully restored your health, mana, and psi.
You have replenished 30% of your stamina with an unidentified collection of fruits. Your stamina is at 64%.

After I recovered from my jaunt into the fog, I searched the safe zone's ruined buildings. Each of my upcoming forays into the nether would have to be planned meticulously, with the intent of not just killing stygians, but also mapping out the terrain.

Which was why before venturing out, I had to craft myself some equipment.

Creating the gear almost had me feeling nostalgic. I had done this before—or something similar—on the tundra, but this time the work went much faster.

The safe zone gave me more to work with too. The buildings, while not exactly treasure troves, had plenty of material to spare: rusted metal, frayed bits of ropes, pieces of wood, broken crockery, and so on.

While I worked, I wondered about the safe zone. It was readily apparent it had been abandoned centuries ago, perhaps the very day Elron's home sector had been overtaken by the void. From the marshal's own words, I knew that to be a long time ago, and I no longer had to guess what had happened to the players in the dungeon.

They had become the possessed—or had been taken over by them.

This, however, prompted a whole host of other questions. Just how old were the possessed? What had led them to become what they had? And what did this mean for my quest? After finding Ghost and regaining my possessions, I still intended on locating the exile. What sort of creature would she be? And could I secure her aid?

I had no answers to any of these questions.

In my present circumstances, all of them were unanswerable, and picking at the mysteries was fruitless. Still, since it stopped me from worrying about my lost companion, I did nothing to curb my wandering thoughts.

Four hours later I was done with my crafting.

You have created 10 x coils of rope, each made from debris, leaves, and branches.

You have created a primitive hammer. This item has been poorly crafted and will be prone to breaking.

You have created a simple shovel.

You have created a simple pickaxe.

You have created 90 x crude signposts.

You have created a crude bag.

Rising to my feet, I rolled my shoulders and cracked my knuckles, relieving the aches in my arms. I was finally ready, and the time had come to begin my campaign against the stygians in earnest.

CHAPTER 351: WAGING WAR

Three minutes.

That was how much time I decided I would spend outside the safe zone on each foray. Wrapping one end of my makeshift rope around my waist, I cast my buffs.

You have cast heightened reflexes, load controller, fade, and trigger-cast quick mend.

The other end of the rope was tethered to a beam in one of the ruined buildings. Serving as my lifeline, it would allow me to find my way back in case I got lost.

Strapping my makeshift bag across my back, I stepped onto my first marker. I had staked over a hundred small boards—each clearly numbered—along the perimeter of the safe zone and intended on using them to map the area beyond.

I inhaled deeply. I was ready. *Go time,* I thought and sprinted forward.

You have exited a safe zone.

Dismissing the Game message, I plunged onwards.

One yard. Two. Three... Nine.

Rocking to a halt, I scanned the stygian cordon. It remained stationary. *Perfect.* Pulling out a wooden stake from my bag, I hammered it into the soil.

The ground was hard, but luckily not as rocky as elsewhere in the dungeon, and the sharpened stick eventually went in. Returning the hammer to my bag, I focused anew on the stygians. *Time to get casting.*

Drawing psi, I advanced another yard and released my spell.

You have charmed 9 of 10 targets for 20 seconds.

The nether creatures fell easily under my control, and knowing the clock was ticking, I set them against their former fellows.

Surprised cries and angry hisses broke out amongst the stygians, prompting a spate of Game damage messages to scroll through my mind. Ignoring them, I wove more psi.

You have terrified 6 of 6 targets for 40 seconds.

The fight started by my nine minions had expanded to embroil their entire section, and the six terrified stygians only added to that chaos, with some of the other nether creatures mistaking their flight for aggression.

Unfortunately, that did not stop the rest of the cordon streaming towards me. Converging into a mass so tightly packed that their mindglows were indistinguishable from one another, the spear of living nether flew at me.

The charging horde did not daunt me, though. I had prepared for just this eventuality. Retreating, I wove psi again.

You have cast astral blades.

Twin violet daggers materialized in my hands, and I flung them forward, not bothering to aim. I could hardly miss.

You have injured a stygian hydra.
You have injured a stygian serpent.

Taking another careful step back, I cast anew. A split-second later my arms flew forward, releasing a second round of daggers. Then a third. A fourth.

I continued backstepping but didn't let up on my assault. My arms windmilling, I unleashed a near-endless stream of daggers at the charging nether creatures. By now, the closest stygian—at the tip of the spearpoint—was less than twenty yards away. Focusing all my attacks on it, I drove a slew of astral blades into it.

You have killed a stygian serpent.

The nether creature died ignominiously, trampled by its fellows even before my final blade could ram home.

Ten yards separated me and the stygians.

At my back, I could feel the comforting closeness of the safe zone. It was only inches away. I didn't step through, though. Holding my ground, I kept up my attacks.

You have critically injured a stygian hydra.
You have injured a stygian hydra.
You have crippled a stygian serpent.
You have killed a stygian crawler.
You have...

More stygians fell.

My minions were all also dead by this time, but they hadn't gone quietly and had claimed their own fair share of victims.

A blot of ichor appeared on my right, then another on my left. Disdaining to dodge, I stepped back.

You have entered a safe zone.

Letting the half-formed weaves of psi in my mind dissipate, I lowered my arms. They were trembling, I noted in surprise. As were my legs. My heart pounded too, and my mouth had gone dry.

Who would've thought that standing fast in the face of onrushing death could scare near one witless?

I laughed, releasing the last of my tension. The danger had passed, and I had survived. Lifting my gaze, I studied the opaque wall of nether ahead. Now, there was nothing to do but wait.

A second later, the horde appeared.

Unable to stop their charge, the heaving mass of stygians crashed headlong into the invisible barrier.

And were stopped cold.

Folding my arms, I watched as snarling faces and gaping jaws gnashed impotently at me from the other side. They would not get in, no matter how enraged. More stygians arrived. Spilling over the ends of the spear tip, they pressed up against the safe zone until a full quarter of its rim was coated in dark, smoky bodies.

Impassively, I waited.

Eventually the build up against the barrier reversed course, and the wave of nether creatures began to recede. Still, I didn't move. One particular stygian had yet to show himself, and until he did, I was not about to venture out of the safe zone again.

A bright mindglow dipped into range.

I smiled tightly. The harbinger had finally come. Turning tight circles in the sky—at a height of about three hundred feet—he waited as patiently as I did.

In anticipation of me leaving the safe zone once more?

I thought so.

Betraying no sign that I was aware of his presence, I resigned myself to more waiting. The harbinger still appeared ignorant of the true range of my mindsight, and I wanted to keep it that way.

Long minutes passed.

The stygian cordon reformed at its original position and the harbinger flew away. Still, I waited, unsure if the stygian Power had really left or had merely retreated farther back.

Five minutes later, I stepped back from the safe zone's rim, finally accepting that the skirmish was over. Withdrawing to the rebirth well, I sat down to review the results of the battle.

You have reached level 180 and rank 18!

For achieving rank 18, you have been awarded 1 additional attribute point and 1 Class point.

Your Mind has increased to rank 87.

By my estimate, perhaps thirty stygians had died in the battle. It was enough to gain me one additional level. None of my skills had ranked up though, not even telepathy nor nether absorption which had been in near-constant use during the skirmish. But that was alright. I expected both skills would get plenty of use in the coming days.

Days, I mused, lingering over the thought. I had no concrete plan for escaping the harbinger's trap—yet. Much would depend on how the stygians responded to my attacks in the coming days and the terrain itself.

I knew for certain, though, that it would take time.

Time to painstakingly survey the surroundings and reduce the stygians' numbers. Time during which I would steadily advance my nether absorption and telepathy skills. Sadly, with no usable weapon and my stealth negated, I couldn't train my sneaking and melee skills.

I eyed the new Class point, tempted for just a moment to invest it in void armor. But it made more sense to upgrade slaysight to tier five first—assuming, of course, I could advance my telepathy to rank twenty in the coming days. The increased mindsight range alone would make the upgrade worthwhile. Reluctantly conceding it was wiser to wait, I set aside further thought of the new Class point and, closing my eyes, began to meditate.

My opening strike against the stygians had gone exactly as planned. Now, I had to duplicate its success as many times as I could.

✳   ✳   ✳

Over the course of the next few hours, I executed six more assaults against the stygian cordon. Each attack was launched from a different marker, but the outcome was always the same.

I bespelled a few stygians. They surged forward.

I flung volleys of astral blades. They smashed into the safe zone's barrier.

Each and every time the harbinger responded, but always too late. Still, I made certain to note his reaction time. After my seventh successful foray, the stygian Power countered by pulling the cordon back another twenty yards.

The move pleased me.

I had been expecting a shift in tactics all day, and while the harbinger's response was not the most desirable outcome, it was one I could work with. All told, I had killed just over two hundred nether creatures and gained one level, and a rank apiece in telepathy and nether absorption. Satisfied with my handiwork, I called it quits for the day.

✳   ✳   ✳

The next morning, refreshed and hale, I began anew.

But instead of attacking the nether creatures, I spent the day exploring the area outside the safe zone. The stygian cordon was now at the eighty-yard line, and since they would only attack when I was within fifty yards, that left me a whole thirty-yard ring to explore.

With wooden stakes and handmade ropes in tow, I did just that, and by day's end, gained another two ranks of nether absorption. I also spotted multiple crevices deep enough to fit into should the need arise, and I carefully marked those. I didn't enter any though, aware of the unseen watchers.

The rest of my time was spent attempting to find the spores.

I could not see, smell, nor hear them, and had to rely purely on the Game alerts to figure out their locations. It was hardly precise work. Still, slowly but surely, I narrowed down the possible areas they occupied.

On the third day of my imprisonment, I resumed my campaign against the cordon. Traveling to the thirty-yard line, I launched my attacks like before—with almost identical results.

This time though, it took the stygians longer to reach me, giving me yet more time to bleed them with my astral blades. The harbinger was as slow to adapt as before, and it took eight successful forays before he responded.

His counter lacked imagination, though.

Repeating his earlier response, the harbinger pulled the cordon back again. The stygian's lackluster maneuvering left me puzzled. There were far more aggressive tactics he could have employed, including pushing the cordon right up against the invisible barrier— which might have stopped me from venturing out of the safe zone—or joining the cordon himself.

His responses smacked of afterthought.

It was almost as if the harbinger was distracted, as if he had other duties elsewhere that preoccupied him, and his only interest was to keep me pinned down.

Whatever the case, I took full advantage of my foe's folly, and by the end of the day, killed another three hundred-odd stygians, gaining one player level and ranking up both telepathy and nether absorption again.

✳ ✳ ✳

Day four.

Yawning, I opened my eyes and stared gloomily at the bank of gray fog peeking through the broken roof. It was only my fourth day in the safe zone, and yet already I felt myself yearning for the sight of open sky.

There was something about the nether... about the way it robbed my sight and filled my nostrils with its stale, sterile stink that left me desperate to escape.

I'll be free soon. Things are going well.

And they were. Better than expected, in fact, and with the harbinger's latest move, I had another busy day to look forward to. Forcing myself to my feet, I munched through a handful of fruits while I walked a slow circuit around the safe zone and inspected the stygian's latest cordon through my mindsight.

For the most part the nether creatures had pulled back to the hundred-yard line, leaving me plenty more ground to explore today. But near marker fifty—in what I had designated the eastern side of the safe zone—their line curved inwards to ninety-five yards.

Drawing to a halt at the marker in question, I frowned. *Hmm, why the deviation?*

However the harbinger induced obedience from the lesser stygians, it was effective, and I had yet to witness any signs of them deviating from his orders. And so far, the stygian Power had been extremely rigid in his formation of the cordons. The first and second ones had been perfect circles, but this one... it was misshapen on the east side.

Deliberately so.

It was almost as if the nether creatures on that side had been forced closer. What would cause that?

My eyes widened as realization struck.

The stygians had run up against a cliff—or something similar. Had I just found the east end of the safe zone's canyon?

Perhaps. Probably. I hope so.

That I was in a canyon, gorge, or some other form of indentation in the plateau was only assumption on my part, of course. But where else would the safe zone be located?

It made no sense for it to be atop the plateau. That would be inconsistent with the rest of the dungeon's design. The only question that had been plaguing me over the last few days was how big the canyon was. But if the stygian cordon had already run up against the eastern wall of the canyon, then the answer was: not so large.

Freedom was close at hand—from the stygians themselves, if not the nether.

I expected the central fog bank occupied multiple chasms in the dungeon's center, but crucially, I'd not encountered any stygians on the plateau so far, and except for the harbinger himself, I had no reason to believe the other creatures could reach the plateau's heights.

The chances of finding any spores atop the plateau were therefore low—which meant if I reached the clifftops, I would be safe from detection.

But before I could get too excited, I set aside my scheming.

There was the not-so-little matter of the spores *in* the canyon to take care of. Until I found a way to deal with them, I would not be scaling the cliffs. The other stygians would mob me the moment they saw me doing such. And I still had to confirm there actually *was* a cliff to be climbed.

But despite these challenges, I felt reinvigorated and strode out of the safe zone with a new spring in my step.

It was time to begin the day's explorations.

CHAPTER 352: SPORE HUNT

You have failed to detect an unknown entity.

At the Adjudicator's message, I paused. Taking a step back, a dozen to the left, then one more forward, I waited.

Two seconds passed.

But no further Game message arrived.

Advancing a single step, I waited anew. When I was sure I would receive no other alerts, I took a third probing step, then another, and another, until...

You have failed to detect an unknown entity.

That confirms it, I thought. I'd pinpointed the last spore.

Striding forward to what I judged to be the center of the circle of 'failed' detection messages, I bent down and drove a stake into the ground.

That's the last of them, I thought, wondering what the spores made of my antics—assuming they had enough mind to do so.

Straightening, I twisted from side to side to relieve the ache in my lower back. It had been a long day. In total, I'd uncovered ten stygian spores. All of them were strung along the forty-yard line, almost equidistant apart.

I shook my head ruefully. Even in deploying the invisible spores, the harbinger had maintained perfect symmetry. *A tendency that I can maybe exploit.* Raising my head, I studied the second cordon.

The stygian circle was no thinner, despite the numerous kills I'd scored on the first and third days. If anything, even more nether creatures surrounded me.

They had remained unmoving the entire day, not reacting to my antics at all, and I was sure they had been ordered to stay put unless I approached closer than fifty yards. The spores, too, had not moved—as far I could tell, anyway—which also suited my purposes perfectly.

Turning about, I headed back to the safe zone, following the markers I had laid down earlier. The day was drawing to a close and before I kicked off the next phase of my plan, I wanted to rest.

Two yards from the barrier, another Game message flashed for attention.

Your nether absorption has increased to level 160 and reached rank 16, increasing your chance of resisting harmful nether effects by 40% and decreasing the damage you suffer from the void by 80%.

Your health, psi, stamina, and mana are degenerating at a rate of 7% per minute (damage reduced by 80% due to void armor).

My lips curved upwards. The three days spent in the central fog bank—especially the two given over to exploring—had done wonders for my nether absorption.

The skill had advanced at a steady rate, increasing the time I was able to spend in the mists which, in turn, had allowed me to train my nether resistance even faster. In all, I'd gained five whole ranks in the skill.

I wonder what will happen when the skill surpasses rank twenty.

At that point, my nether damage reduction would exceed one hundred percent. Would the void replenish me then? Would it restore my stamina, mana, psi, *and* health?

I chuckled. *That will certainly be interesting if it does, but somehow, I doubt I'm going to be that lucky.*

Amusement fading, I considered if my nether absorption skill was high enough. I wanted it to be.

A stamina degeneration rate of seven percent gave me fifteen minutes— twenty-one if I ate some fruit along the way—but would that suffice? I didn't know how deep in the central fog bank I was, and even on the plateau without the spores to worry about, it could still take me days to win free of the nether.

I sighed, accepting the unpalatable truth. *I have to train my nether absorption further.*

As impatient as I was to escape, I was not ready to kick off the next phase of my plan. And it would be foolish to rush now when I was so close to success. I had to get the skill all the way to rank twenty. It might take a few more days, but without full immunity, time would always be hounding me.

So be it, I thought. Swinging away from the safe zone, I headed back into the mist to resume my training.

✳   ✳   ✳

It took a whole week.

Seven days of patiently slipping into the fog and out again. Seven days of standing still and doing nothing while my nether absorption skill slowly ticked upwards. And four days longer than I'd anticipated.

Over that entire time, the harbinger visited only once. He did a quick flyby over the canyon and didn't even bother to land or trade insults. Perhaps he wanted only to a certain I remained caught in his trap. Still, his disinterest pleased me. It would make things easier later on.

More than once I was tempted to break the monotony of my nether training by launching further forays against the stygians. But I was happy with the status quo; I had a plan that would work with the way things were, and I was not about to risk it—not just to relieve my boredom.

Still, eventually, the Game alert I'd been waiting for arrived.

Your nether absorption has increased to level 200 and reached rank 20, increasing your chance of resisting harmful nether effects by 50% and decreasing the damage you suffer from the void by 100%.

Your health, psi, stamina, and mana are no longer degenerating.

I hardly had time to enjoy the achievement, though, before a less welcome message followed on its heels.

Congratulations, Michael! You have advanced your first skill to tier 5. However, further improvement in this skill will not be possible until you reach player level 200, and you join the ranks of the Game's elite.

For a moment, I was stunned speechless. I had been unaware of the skill cap, and while it made a certain sort of sense, it smacked of unfairness to someone not elite-ranked yet.

At least it won't stop me from gaining tier five abilities, I grumbled. *Now that would be—*

I broke off, reconsidering my assumption.

There was in fact no reason to believe the Game *would* allow me to acquire an elite ability before level two hundred, especially not after it had so unexpectedly blocked further training of my nether absorption skill. I would have to assume the worst—meaning no invisibility and no tier five slaysight until I reached rank twenty.

Urgh. This is another wrinkle I don't need.

Sighing, I strode back to the safe zone. Despite my mixed feelings, I had achieved what I had set out to do and obtained full nether immunity. It was not without cost, though. Every second that my void armor worked to repel the nether's influence, a little bit of my mana would drain away. But I had grown sufficiently practiced at channeling that I could replenish my mana faster than my void armor could consume it—provided, of course, I found the necessary time and space to use the skill.

It was not only my nether absorption that had progressed over the last ten days, though. I had managed to train four other skills. While they had advanced at a slower rate than nether absorption, they had been at a much higher level to begin with and were now also approaching rank twenty.

Your insight is at level 197, your meditation at level 195, your telepathy at level 185, and your channeling at level 175.

Despite my lack of any elite tier abilities for the four skills, their levels made for pretty reading, and I imagined I would reap the benefits of their improvements soon enough.

But those were considerations for another time. Of immediate concern was the escape I still needed to execute. Slipping into the safe zone, I went straight to my makeshift bed in the ruined building.

Tomorrow was a big day.

✳   ✳   ✳

Eight hours later, I was awake, refreshed, and ready to start.

But before I began the day's adventures, there was one last thing I needed to do. I'd spent much of the previous night contemplating my remaining Class point. The best use for it would be to upgrade slaysight, but the more I thought about it, the more certain I grew that the Game would not allow me to advance the Class ability to tier five until I myself reached that tier.

In which case, the point was best spent elsewhere.

Sitting down cross-legged and turning my focus inwards, I willed my intention to the Adjudicator.

Assessing player's suitability for a Class upgrade...
Class points available: 1.
Player rank: 18.
Upgrade requirements met.
You may advance your Class to rank 10 by improving an existing Class benefit or by selecting a new one. Do you wish to proceed?

Taking a deep breath, I conveyed my response to the Adjudicator.

More Game text filled my mind. My gaze flitting from left to right, I sped over the options. Some of the new benefits on offer looked interesting, but I had already decided how I wanted to spend the Class point and nothing I saw convinced me to do otherwise.

Commencing Class upgrade...
...
Upgrade complete. Class points remaining: 0.
Congratulations, Michael, your voidstealer Class has advanced to rank 10!

You have upgraded your void thief ability to <u>superior void thief</u>. The third tier of this ability makes it easier for you to filch knowledge from your foes by reducing the damage that your void armor needs to sustain to trigger a theft from 40% to 30%.

The range of hostile spells that can be stolen has also expanded to include damage over time spells. Additionally, the memory capacity of your void armor has improved, allowing you to remember your stolen knowledge for 12 hours instead of 8.

Superior void thief also provides you with a third method, called <u>negate</u>, of disrupting your foes' attacks. After you perform a successful spell theft, your mana's understanding of the stolen spell is such that it can perfectly resist any further iterations of the same spell. Note, like its lower tier counterparts, negate is a passive ability and dependent on a successful void theft to function.

I chewed my lip thoughtfully. Negate looked interesting and would be particularly useful against foes with few offensive spells. But it was less for the new void thief variant that I'd upgraded the ability than it was for the improved performance of its core ability: steal.

I rose to my feet. It was time to get to work.

Striding out of the safe zone, I passed through the circle of invisible spores without pause and continued on until I was fifty yards from the stygian cordon.

There, I halted.

Peering behind me, I made sure the guide ropes I'd set yesterday hadn't shifted out of place. Forty yards separated me from the safe zone, a considerable distance if the harbinger caught me unawares. I didn't intend on letting that happen, though.

But I did intend on being caught — partially, anyway.

No use stalling, I scolded myself. *Let's get this show on the road.* Drawing in a deep breath, I wove psi and cast.

You have charmed 10 of 10 targets for 20 seconds.
You have terrified 6 of 6 targets for 40 seconds.

Having done this on multiple prior occasions, I knew how the stygians would react. As expected, the nether creatures broke out of their careful ranks and charged forward.

This time, though, I did not bother peppering them with astral blades. Turning around, I set off in a looping run — not straight back to the safe zone, but in a carefully planned path that bore all the hallmarks of someone confused and panicked.

Eyes trained on the ground, I followed the guide ropes. I couldn't afford to lose sight of them. If I did, I would truly become what I pretended: lost.

The seconds ticked by, and the stygian horde drew closer.

I paid them no mind. What attention I could spare was fixed on the sky. I had the harbinger's timings down pat, and I knew almost to the second when he would arrive.

He did not disappoint.

As punctual as ever, the stygian Power dropped into mindsight range. Now came the trickiest part of my plan. What would the harbinger do? Would he perceive that I was lost and take the bait? Or would he leave the horde to decide my fate?

The harbinger dived.

I grinned wolfishly, so giddy with excitement for a moment that I almost missed the next turn in the guide ropes. That wouldn't do. Cursing my carelessness, I locked my gaze on the ground.

The harbinger swooped into an attacking run.

I didn't look back, but I imagined he was skimming low to the ground as he closed in for the kill. I swerved left, still following the guide ropes — but now on a direct course for the safe zone. The maneuver was pre-planned but to the harbinger it would look like my luck had turned and I was about to escape his reach.

A stygian harbinger has cast death's cacophony.

Surging forward, I redoubled my pace, but *not* enough to escape the blast of sound emanating from behind.

I wanted the spell to reach me — partially, anyway.

The wave of discordant noise overtook me. I staggered, but already braced for the sonic assault, I retained my balance. If I fell now, I was dead, and all my careful preparations would have been for nothing.

You have failed a magical resistance check.
A harbinger has injured you.
Your void armor has reduced the death damage incurred by 10%.

Clamping my hands against my ears, I kept running even as successive pulses of sound overran me.

A harbinger has injured you.
A harbinger has injured you.
...
Void armor charge remaining: 68%.
Void thief triggered! Void siphon and negate activated!
You have acquired the channeled spell <u>death's cacophony (stolen)</u>.

Yes! I exulted. Releasing the spell I had held waiting, I set down a windslide and dove onto it. The wave of sound at my back built to a crescendo, but borne away by the ramp of air, I outpaced the peak for another five crucial yards.

It was enough.

You have entered a safe zone.

The harsh notes hit the invisible barrier and were reflected away, followed a split second later by the harbinger. Veering away, the stygian cawed angrily as he flapped his wings powerfully to build altitude again.

I paid him no heed. I was safe and had gotten what I wanted: a spell that didn't need to be direct-targeted.

Rolling onto my back, chest heaving, and pulse fluttering, I inspected my new spell. It was one I was familiar with, and even better, I already *knew* it could destroy the stygian spores. Stealing it was the entire reason I'd let the harbinger 'nab' me in the first place.

But before I could commence the next phase of my plan, I had to wait for the commotion the rest of the stygians were making to die down.

A smile on my lips, I closed my eyes and meditated.

✳   ✳   ✳

A little later, the stygian cordon reset itself.

The harbinger himself had long since left, disappearing to whatever tasks preoccupied him. With my mana and psi reserves full, I stepped out of the safe zone and approached the first stygian spore.

You have failed to detect an unknown entity.

I drew to a halt. By my reckoning, the spore was just over a dozen yards ahead of me. Drawing on my mana, I infused my voice with power and howled.

You have cast death's cacophony.

A roar erupted from my open mouth, shattering the fog's silence. I would have preferred a much quieter spell but there was no use complaining. I had to work with what I had.

A split second later, I snapped my mouth closed and waited. I had terminated the spell early, releasing only a single sound pulse, but it should more than suffice.

And indeed, it did.

You have killed a level 5 stygian spore.

I felt like grinning but curbed my excitement. My work was far from done. Watching both the sky and the cordon with my mindsight, I waited.

I was about to find out how comprehensive the harbinger's instructions were. There was no doubt the stygians in the cordon had heard my howl. But how would they react? Would they attack and summon the harbinger? Or would they do nothing until I crossed the fifty-yard line? I was prepared for either eventuality, but much preferred the latter.

Ten seconds later, the stygians had still not moved.

Sure now that they would remain unresponsive, I moved to the next spore. I had nine more invisible watchers to kill.

Then, I would have my stealth back—or so I hoped.

CHAPTER 353: FORCE MULTIPLICATION

You have killed 9 stygian spores.

Killing the remaining spores went smoothly.

Standing at the boundary of the safe zone with my energy reserves full and my bag packed, I was ready to leave—for good. There was just one last test to run. More anxious than I cared to admit, I drew on the nearby shadows and attempted to conceal myself.

You are hidden.

My breath escaped in an explosive rush. It had worked! I was halfway to escaping the harbinger's trap and could almost taste freedom. Best of all, my jailor remained blissfully unaware.

Let's keep it that way, I thought. That meant moving stealthily. Exiting the safe zone, I crept 'east' towards the indent in the cordon. The nether had grown strangely familiar and other than restricting my sight, inconvenienced me not at all.

Using the mindglows of the stygians as beacons, I snuck up on my targets. I reached the fifty-yard line and passed it without incident, keeping my eyes fixed on the terrain. Without my wayfarer boots, moving soundlessly was not effortless, and I had to constantly check my stride or adjust my footing.

I closed the distance to forty yards.

Thirty. Twenty. Ten.

Multiple hostile entities have failed to detect you! You are hidden.

Drawing psi into my mind, I slowed my pace further, then kept going. Nine yards. Seven. Five.

I stopped.

Through the thinning mists ahead, I spotted five hydras and three serpents. The eight creatures had their heads bowed. They were sleeping perhaps, and certainly not alert. There were dozens more stygians to my left and right, all still concealed from sight by the fog.

It was the eight in front that held my interest, though.

Beyond them lay a cliff and the path to freedom, hopefully. I couldn't see it, but that did not concern me just yet. Weaving the psi in my mind, I unleashed my will on the closest of the six.

You have cast slaysight.
You have induced 6 of 6 targets to sleep for 40 seconds.

The spell was likely overkill but the last thing I wanted was to slip up at this late stage. Neither of the two remaining stygians stirred. My casting had gone unnoticed. Drawing more psi, I shadow blinked.

You have teleported into a stygian hydra's shadow.

Multiple hostile entities have failed to detect you! You are hidden.

I emerged from the aether, still and crouched. Shifting around carefully, I turned around to find myself staring at cold, gray rock.

Gotcha, I thought with a happy grin. Inching forward, I placed the palms of my hands flat on the cliff and studied the portion that was visible.

There were handholds aplenty.

There was no guarantee the cliff would be scalable along the full distance, but that was why I had brought along some makeshift climbing gear.

Reaching up with my right hand, I got started.

✳   ✳   ✳

Scaling the cliff was hard, and on two separate occasions I was forced to employ windborne. Nevertheless, I managed the ascent without incident, neither showering the stygians below with loose rocks nor falling to my death.

Pulling myself onto the top of the plateau, I turned about in a slow circle. The mist was as opaque as ever, and I could see little farther than a few yards in any direction. But I had expected that.

More importantly, there were no mindglows to my left, right or up ahead. Exhaling heavily, I marched forward. Now, came the only part of the plan I had no clear strategy for: finding my way out of the fog.

My bag was full of rope and stakes, but while those would help to an extent, there was no way I was going to map the entire plateau, not if I didn't want to spend months roaming the fog bank.

My best bet was to find a chasm and to follow along. The cracks in the plateau ran deep and often meandered, but they generally did not turn full circle. If I followed a chasm, it would lead me out of the fog bank— eventually. But there was no getting around the fact that however long that took, would very much depend on luck.

Adjudicator, if you're listening, I can use a decent handful of that about now.

✳   ✳   ✳

Either the Game heard or my luck was not as bad as I feared.

Before an hour passed, I located a chasm, and after following it for two more hours, I found myself standing on a stretch of open plateau that was blessedly free of nether.

Coming to a halt, I rocked back on my heels and squeezed my eyes shut. "Thank you," I whispered, not sure—and not caring—who I addressed.

I was free. A whole ten days later than I wanted but there was no helping that. It was time to move onward again and find my companion. Running forward, I put some distance between me and the fog bank before pivoting in a circle to take my bearings.

It did not take me long to pick out a few unmissable landmarks. What I'd been thinking of as east while in the nether was actually north.

I had emerged somewhere along the central fog bank's northeastern edge, and if I was judging my position correctly, I was less than a day from the canyon in which I had died.

No point in wasting more time.

Orienting myself in the direction I needed to go, I fell into a jog at a pace I could maintain for hours on end. "Almost there, Ghost," I murmured. "I'm coming."

Please be waiting.

* * *

My passage across the plateau went by swiftly. As I ran, my mind churned with worry over my lost companion—in a seeming bid to make up for the many days of carefully suppressed fears.

I thought of Elron, too, and wondered if he had given up on me. The wolf packs and my other companions stranded on the tundra surely had. I couldn't expect them to wait for me forever, and by now I feared many would have gone their own ways.

Safyre will keep them together. I hoped that was true but couldn't be certain.

Plagued by these worries and more, I ran. I was draining my stamina more quickly than was wise, but with the end of my unwanted side trip in sight, I couldn't seem to care.

Eight hours later, I arrived at my destination.

My legs were straining, and my feet hurt—running in newbie shoes was definitely ill-advised. Dropping into a crouch and cloaking myself in shadow, I crept to the canyon's edge and peered down.

The fog bank was gone. As were the stygians.

But the canyon was not empty.

Sitting in the exact center, almost directly over the spot where the destroyed seed had rested, was a strange blocked-shaped creature. My gaze passed over it, barely pausing as I searched for someone else entirely.

But the spirit wolf's ethereal form was nowhere to be seen. "GHOST," I shouted. "WHERE ARE YOU?"

The silence was resounding.

Disheartened but not giving up, I called out again. No answer was forthcoming the second time either. Or the third. My eyes drifted back to the canyon's sole occupant. Did it know where the spirit wolf was? And what was it, even? Drawing on my will, I analyzed the creature.

The target is a level 201 Force Multiplier.

I frowned. *An elite?* What was an elite doing here? Had it wandered in after the fog dissipated? But the creature was too big to have squeezed through the narrow chasm leading into this particular canyon.

Perhaps it's a new spawn.

My frown deepened as I considered that. I'd not revisited any of the locations previously inhabited by the stygians. Did the dungeon attempt to reclaim the regions after the seeds' destruction? The presence of an elite here certainly suggested so.

What did that mean for Ghost, though?

Nothing.

Whatever the Force Multiplier was, it was unlikely to be able to perceive the spirit wolf, much less hurt her. Just as I'd feared, Ghost had left the canyon. The only other possibility did not bear considering. I had to search for her. There was no question of that. But where did I even begin? And how?

My gaze drifted back to the elite. Before I could launch any search, I needed to regain my stuff—which left me with a problem.

The Force Multiplier was nearly atop my corpse.

If I wanted my things, I would have to enter the canyon and quite possibly fight it. I couldn't afford to delay too long either. I had less than an hour left on the harbinger's stolen spell. Not to mention, this was likely the first place the stygian Power would look once he realized I was missing.

It was now or never.

Grabbing a handful of fruit from my bag, I chewed grimly. I would need my strength for the battle ahead.

✳ ✳ ✳

You have replenished 30% of your stamina eating an unknown fruit. Stamina remaining: 41%.

You have cast heightened reflexes, load controller, fade, and trigger-cast quick mend.

I dropped silently into the canyon; my gaze fixed on the weird looking elite ahead. I had no intention of fighting it, if possible, but given the creature's proximity to my corpse, I suspected I would have no choice. With that in mind, I studied my foe intently.

The Multiplier resembled a tall, monolithic structure, one with rectangular blocks attached at random points. The creature had no limbs to speak of or anything resembling facial features. In fact, I was doubtful it could even be described as living.

The elite lacked a mind, or its mind was so well shielded I couldn't tell the difference. Ghost would know. But she wasn't here. The Multiplier's torso—if it could be called that—looked impenetrable, and if not for the harbinger's stolen spell, I would be hard-pressed to find a way to kill it.

A hostile entity has failed to detect you! You are hidden.

I drew to a halt, then walking sideways, circled the unmoving elite until my corpse was directly ahead. Although it could hardly be dignified as such. My remains were more properly a pile of ashes. A trace of a smile flickered across my face. Not even Avery and his ilk would get any use out of it.

My gear, though, seemed intact. However, the harbinger's oblivion spell functioned, it seemed to have left inanimate things untouched. Ten yards separated me from the discarded items. Placing my feet with care, I inched closer.

A hostile entity has failed to detect you!

I advanced another step.

A hostile entity has failed to detect you!

Pausing, I lifted my gaze to study my foe. There was no change in its demeanor, and given the alienness of its form I could not tell how alert the elite was.

I took another step.

You have failed a magical resistance check!
You have triggered an alarm.
A Force Multiplier has detected you! You are no longer hidden.

"Damn," I muttered and, weaving psi, prepared to dash the remaining distance to my stuff. But before I could act, motion around the corner of my eye drew my attention.

One of the odd-looking rectangular shapes had detached itself from the monolithic elite and was falling to the ground in eerie silence. But other than for this lone change, there was no other reaction from my foe. Feeling sudden trepidation, I watched the falling shape intently.

A foot from the ground, it burst apart in a shower of light.

A Light mimic has spawned.
Acquiring target...
...
...
Target acquired. Mimic configuration complete.
Chosen template: the player named Michael, a level 182 voidstalker.

The dancing afterimages faded from my eyes to reveal a glowing white form that was my spitting image, right down to my newbie clothes and ebonheart, which was clutched tightly in my right hand.

"Bloody hell," I muttered.

CHAPTER 354: BATTLING ONESELF

The mimic did not give me time to recover from my shock.

Blinking out of existence, the thing reformed at my back, and if not for its startling inner light, I would not have realized it was there at all. Death would have followed swiftly.

As it was, I did not manage to avoid my foe's assault entirely.

A Light mimic's attack has grazed you.
You have failed a magical resistance check! Your void armor has reduced the light damage incurred by 5%.

The blade in the mimic's hand was no ebonheart. While it looked identical, it was formed entirely of Light—and unsurprisingly dealt no physical damage. It hurt just the same, though.

The mimic's sword snaked forward again in a maneuver I instantly recognized. Throwing myself to the left, I avoided the sweeping blade.

You have evaded a Light mimic's attack.

Huh, I grunted as I rolled back to my feet. *So that's why it's called a Light mimic.* My gaze darted to the elite that had spawned it. *And that explains the designation, 'Force.'*

Holding ebonheart at guard, I turned back to my foe, expecting to see it charging straight at me. What I beheld instead was the mimic curving around on a bed of air. Only then, did the true horror of what I faced sink in.

It doesn't just look like me; it has my abilities too.

The thought spurred me into action. Realizing I could expect another assault from the rear, I spun around in time to see my foe's blade bearing down on me. Reflexively, I thrust out ebonheart.

You have blocked a Light mimic's attack.

Light met black steel and light was turned away.

It was only a split second later that I realized my attempted block could have gone horribly wrong had my foe's Light blade truly contained no physical presence. Still, my maneuver had succeeded, and I didn't dwell too long on the matter. Darting forward, I counterattacked.

The mimic slid out of the way and slashed down with his blade. Stepping into the attack, I parried the blow with ebonheart, then smashed my left fist into the creature's all-too-familiar face.

You have injured a Light mimic.

So. I can hurt it physically. Excellent. Empowering my sword with stamina, I attacked in earnest.

You have cast whirlwind and piercing strike.
A Light mimic has evaded your attack.
You have grazed your target.

Your target has injured you.

...

...

It did not take me long to figure out that something was wrong. My foe was matching the pace of my attacks which meant it had cast whirlwind too. *Damn. Time to change things up.* Jumping backwards from the mimic's searching blade, I shadow blinked.

You have teleported into the shadow of a Light mimic.

I emerged from the aether on the back foot and immediately lunged forward in attack.

My foe vanished.

Realizing there could be only one reason why, I kept going forward, transforming my lunge into a dive.

It was not enough.

A Light mimic has backstabbed you for 5x more damage!
Quick mend triggered, restoring 20% of your health!

My quick action saved me from a fatal blow, and instead of plunging through my heart, my foe's blade slashed across my lower back.

The damage was still enormous. I lived but teetered on a very thin edge. And so, I did the only thing I could think of. I used magic.

Rolling onto my back and ignoring the blood pooling beneath me, I unleashed the harbinger's stolen spell.

You have cast death's cacophony.

The mimic, dashing forward to finish off his kill, was caught squarely in the pulsating waves of sound.

You have injured a Light mimic, dealing death damage.

My foe staggered back and attempted to flee the discordant noise, but turning my head to track his movements, I kept my gruesome howl centered squarely on him. If the mimic was truly a replica of me, then his null death skill would be as low as mine, and he would not survive the spell long.

You have injured a Light mimic.
You have injured a Light mimic.

...

...

A Light mimic has died.

Gasping in relief, I closed my mouth, cutting off the horrendous sound, and let my head fall back to the ground. I was still alive—if barely—but if I wanted to remain that way, I had to heal, grab my stuff, and get out of here. I *definitely* did not want to hang about to see what the elite did next.

Drawing psi in preparation, I let my eyes drift back to the Force Multiplier, wondering what it made of its spawn's death.

Two more rectangular shapes were dropping free from the elite.

I stared aghast. "More mimics? Already?"

The first block vanished in a blot of darkness, the second and a cloud of shadow.

A Dark mimic has spawned. Chosen template: the player named Michael, a level 182 voidstalker.

A Shadow mimic has spawned. Chosen template: the player named Michael, a level 182 voidstalker.

"You've got to be kidding me," I groaned.

✳   ✳   ✳

I shoved my emotions—shock and despair—in a box and promptly forgot about them. There would be time enough to deal with them later. Now, I had to focus on one thing only: survival.

The fight with the Light mimic had carried me away from the elite, giving me a couple more vital seconds to react to its latest spawns. I was in no condition to fight, obviously. That left only flight or stealth, but with my back the way it was, I wouldn't get far running either.

Hiding it is, I decided, and attempted to vanish.

There were no shadows in easy reach, but my fade was still active, and I was counting on it to make up for the lack.

It did not let me down.

Multiple hostile entities have failed to detect you. You are hidden!

The two mimics—one of glistening black, the other of eerie gray—paused in their advance. I paid them little heed. I was not done yet.

Stealth alone wouldn't suffice to conceal me. Reforming the pool of psi at the pit of my subconsciousness, I hid my mind too.

You have cast mind shield. Psi abilities are unavailable.

The mimics resumed their approach, but this time at a much slower pace as they searched for me. No doubt they had attempted to locate me with mindsight but failed. Exhaling silently in relief, I rolled onto my side and very carefully regained my feet.

Multiple hostile entities have failed to detect you.

The pain was excruciating, but thankfully quick mend had already closed the wound, and I did not leak blood. Gritting my teeth against the expected agony, I gingerly limped away.

Given my injury and the need for stealth, I moved slower than my foes, and the pair drew closer. I wanted to hurry but couldn't. That way lay certain death.

The two mimics reached the spot they'd last seen me. I'd only managed four yards in the interim. Expecting the worst, I braced myself.

Multiple hostile entities have failed to detect you.

I couldn't believe it. The two had failed to spot me. Even riddled with pain I found that strange. If the pair's senses matched my own, they should be able to find me.

Unless...

The earlier Game messages had labeled the mimics 'voidstalkers.' That was not my true Class, though. My real Class—the *hidden* one— was voidstealer. *It's my secret bloodline at work,* I realized.

The mimics were imitating my falsified Class, not my true one. The naming difference between the two was so small that in the chaos of the battle I'd missed it.

But while the naming difference was small, the Class difference was not.

As voidstalkers, the mimics would not have my Wolf-derived benefits. They would possess mindsight but not slaysight. They would be protected by void armor but lack the ability to steal or siphon my spells. Then, too, there was the wolfwalker trait that enhanced my senses. They would not have that either.

Which perhaps explains why they are struggling to find me. I grinned toothily. *This battle may not be a lost cause, after all.* But first, I had to get far enough away that I could heal up safely.

Limping on in torturously slow fashion, I headed towards the closest cliff wall.

✳   ✳   ✳

Nestled in the shadow of a cliff and out of what I knew to be my own mindsight range, I lowered my psi shield and chain-cast quick mend, before mediating and channeling mana.

You have healed yourself of all injuries. Your health is at 100%.
You have restored 100% of your psi and mana.

Fighting-fit once more, I glanced across the canyon to the elite and the two mimics. It was clear that the spawns were magical constructs, and I'd half expected them to have vanished by now.

But both remained manifested.

Killing the Light mimic had yielded no experience, nor had the Game reported a spell duration for any of the spawns. And I could not be certain they would *not* remain indefinitely.

My gaze flickered back to the Force Multiplier. There were over a dozen more rectangles spread along its central trunk. If they all spawned copies of me... I shuddered, not wanting to contemplate fighting a dozen versions of myself, even if they were only voidstalkers.

Besides, I thought, *there is no benefit to killing the elite's spawns.*

I had already analyzed the Force Multiplier and confirmed that the Light mimic's death had not hurt it at all. The spawns were purely a defense mechanism. If I was going to win the encounter, I had to attack the Force Multiplier directly and avoid getting drawn into a protracted engagement with the spawns.

And since the mimics were voidstalkers that was... doable.

I rose to my feet, a plan taking shape. After casting my buffs, I wrapped my mind in a psi shield again. Then leaving ebonheart sheathed, I crept closer to my targets. The two mimics were at the base of the Multiplier, standing guard together. My corpse lay a few yards to their left, but for now I ignored it.

Multiple hostile entities have failed to detect you.

I drew to a halt seven yards from my targets, making sure to place the spawns directly between me and the elite. *Here goes.* Opening my mouth, I howled.

You have cast death's cacophony. You are no longer hidden!

Discordant waves of noise rolled out of my mouth to strike the two mimics *and* the elite behind them. The spawns were caught completely by surprise. As for the Force Multiplier I couldn't say, but it sustained damage all the same.

You have injured a Shadow mimic.
You have injured a Dark mimic.
You have injured a Force Multiplier.

The two spawns tried to escape my banshee-like howl, but death claimed them before they could muster psi or advance into melee range.

Still screaming, I advanced.

You have injured a Force Multiplier.
You have injured a Force Multiplier.

...

...

My howl built to a crescendo as I passed the mimics' corpses, and I could only imagine the damage the elite was sustaining from the tier seven spell. Not letting up, I advanced closer still.

Two rectangular shapes fell downward from the monolith.

Snapping my mouth closed and cutting off my scream, I hurriedly wrapped my body in shadow and my mind in psi.

You are hidden.
You have cast mind shield. Psi abilities are unavailable.

Safe from detection, I reversed course and began my retreat. A second later, the new spawns burst into existence—this time they were both Light mimics—but finding themselves bereft of a target they stood around looking lost.

I smiled slyly. My plan was working beautifully. Continuing my retreat, I glanced at the elite. The Force Multiplier looked no worse for wear, but I was certain I'd hurt it. Seeking confirmation, I analyzed the creature.

The target is a level 201 Force Multiplier. It is barely injured.

Good enough, I thought.

✳   ✳   ✳

For whatever reason, the Force Multiplier could create only two spawns at a time. And against most foes, that would suffice, presumably.

Against me, however, it only served to delay the inevitable.

After replenishing my lost mana, I resumed my assault on the Force Multiplier and drained its health a little more. In all, it took four trips back and forth across the canyon before the elite finally succumbed.

You have killed a Force Multiplier.
You have reached level 185!

CHAPTER 355: PONDERING CARDINAL POINTS

Upon death, the Force Multiplier crumpled into dust.

It made for a sizable pile that for a few minutes, left me scrambling frantically for my lost gear. Thankfully, though, I found the equipment without much effort.

You have equipped a <u>ranger's kit</u>, gaining +40% physical damage reduction and +4 ranks in stealth.
You have equipped the sword, <u>faithful blade</u>, gaining...
...
...

A little later, I was fully dressed. I had double and triple-checked my equipment. Nothing had been lost or damaged during the intervening period. I'd also combed through the canyon thrice over—without uncovering any sign of Ghost.

I had found multiple hiding spots along the base of the cliff where she *could* have taken shelter. But being a spirit, Ghost left no physical marks. And I could not say for certain she had managed to hide from the spores or escape the harbinger's oblivion spell.

For a moment, I contemplated searching the canyon for a fourth time, then grudgingly dismissed the idea. It was no use. Ghost was not here.

Returning to the canyon's center, I considered the elite I had so recently slain. The battle had not been as hard as I had feared—for which I had my secret bloodline trait to thank. Nonetheless, I had gained three player levels, and after giving the matter only brief consideration, I invested my new attribute points.

Your Mind has increased to rank 92. Other modifiers: +12 from items.

Turning my attention inwards, I called up the rest of the battle report.

Your insight has reached rank 20. Note, you cannot learn tier 5 abilities until you reach player level 200.
Your sneaking has reached rank 17.
Your telekinesis has reached rank 16.
Your null force skill has reached rank 3.

"Huh, imagine that," I grunted on seeing the Adjudicator's warning regarding my insight skill. It confirmed my earlier suspicions and made me doubly thankful I'd not delayed investing my Class point.

Leaving the elite's remains behind, I strode to the inconspicuous looking box a few feet away. It was a gold loot chest, and I had left opening it for last. Crouching down, I flipped open the lid without ceremony and peered within.

The target is a piece of <u>enchanted mosaic</u>.

The target is a <u>greater attribute gem</u>. It grants you 3 attribute points.

The target is an <u>upgrade gem</u> and allows you to improve any ability by a single tier.

The target is the rank 4 soulbound artifact: <u>a pioneer's compass</u>. Unlike an ordinary compass, this item does not point to true north. Instead, it can be attuned to any discovered key point in a sector, after which it will point unerringly towards it.

For a second, I simply stared at the chest's contents. Finally, I picked up the compass, the main source of my befuddlement.

You have acquired a pioneer's compass. This artifact is presently unbound. Do you wish to soul-bind this item?

"Is this a joke?" I wondered aloud.

Had the Adjudicator finally tired of me getting lost?

I knew that a loot chest's contents were tailored—somewhat, anyway— to the player that had earned them, but still... had I really been lost so much that the Adjudicator believed I needed a compass to find my way?

"It seems so," I murmured.

But as strange as the loot item was, I would not turn it away. Replying in the affirmative to the Adjudicator, I held myself still as the Game forged unbreakable bonds between the artifact and myself.

You have soulbound a pioneer's compass.

A pioneer's compass is an essential tool of every budding explorer and has time and again saved many a scout from starvation, death, and even worse fates. With it, you will always be able to find your way back to any known safe zone or portal.

From this point onwards, this artifact cannot be wielded by any other, stolen, lost, or kept from your hands except by the strongest of enchantments.

Budding explorer, I mused, recalling that was also the name of the trait I'd earned by discovering the hidden sector.

So perhaps this 'gift' wasn't just my reward for getting lost. Perhaps I'd done more to earn it than that. Then again, 'explorer' was also what I had branded myself when entering New Haven. So maybe the Adjudicator *was* having a bit of fun at my expense.

Gift and joke, I thought. *I like that.*

Stowing away the compass and the upgrade gem in my backpack, I rose to my feet. I left the mosaic tile where it was, not needing the item. The greater attribute gem I used immediately.

Your Mind has increased to rank 95. Other modifiers: +12 from items.

One hundred was my target for my Mind rank—a nice round number. It would leave me with plenty of ability slots to expand my repertoire of psi spells. Thereafter, I would switch my attribute investments to Dexterity. And perhaps Magic, too.

Walking away from the chest, I surveyed the canyon again. It was time to leave, but for some reason I found myself reluctant to do so. This was where

I'd last seen Ghost and I couldn't shake the irrational feeling that by leaving, I was giving up on her.

I had to go, though. Ghost was not here, and the longer I delayed, the less chance I had of finding her. But where to begin?

I turned in another slow circle. Where would Ghost go? Back to our starting point? Or onwards to our destination? My gaze turned east. The exile was somewhere that way. I swung southwest. The hidden portal lay in that direction. I hesitated, then reluctantly considered a third possibility. South—the direction of the exit portal, and our ultimate destination.

I pondered my choices. They were not the only options, of course, but if the spirit wolf had headed in a random direction, my chances of finding her were nil. But I didn't think she'd do that.

Ghost was no longer the willful spirit I'd first met. Sure, she remained insatiably curious. But she had learned to restrain her curiosity and focus on the mission. And in this case, her mission was finding me. Just as mine was to locate her.

So, which will it be? South, east, or southwest?

After some consideration, I ruled out southwest. Ghost had never been one to retreat. She would move onwards, hoping to learn something of value to further our goals in the event she didn't find me. That left me with two options: south or east. Both were equally possible.

I turned eastwards. It was the closer of the two destinations. *I will begin my search there,* I decided, if for no other reason than that I could rule it out quicker.

Setting off across the canyon, I headed east to find the exile.

* * *

My search was disrupted almost immediately.

I was less than an hour out of the canyon when a familiar shape darkened the horizon. The harbinger had come looking for me, and sooner than I'd expected.

I scanned my surroundings, looking for cover. The plateau was barren, and the nearest pile of rocks was a few hundred yards away. Deciding against sprinting toward it, I cast fade and hid myself. Then I resumed my journey but kept one eye peeled skyward.

As the stygian Power drew closer, his destination became apparent. The harbinger was heading for the canyon I had just vacated. Turning around, I watched to see what he would do.

The stygian circled the valley a dozen times, swooping and diving to take a closer look at whatever had caught his interest, but he did not land. Then he headed east. In the very direction I watched from.

My eyes narrowing, I squinted at the dark shape growing steadily larger with every passing second. There could be no doubt. The harbinger was flying my way.

Why?

The harbinger couldn't know where I was. That was impossible. But if he *did*, there would be no fleeing. The very characteristics that made the plateau a perfect highway also made escaping aerial pursuit impossible. There was only one thing to do: trust in my stealth. Renewing my fade, I crouched down small and waited.

The harbinger drew closer, gliding on unseen currents of air. I tightened my hands around my blades. Would he dive?

A hostile entity has failed to detect you! You are hidden.

The stygian did not stop. Nor did he betray the least sign he was aware of my insignificant form huddled beneath his outstretched wings, and in only a matter of seconds, he flew past.

Turning my head, I watched him go. The harbinger was angling left. I frowned. Wherever he was going, it was not back to the central fog bank.

But what could be north?

We were almost at the northern boundary of the dungeon. The glistening violet protective barrier on my left was a reminder of that, and from what I could see, nothing lay between me and it except a spiderwork of narrow chasms.

Suddenly the harbinger dived.

What? Where is he—?

Before I could finish the thought, the stygian disappeared from view. He'd gone into the chasm, I realized. But why?

He must be after something.

Something like a spirit wolf, maybe? *Maybe.* Dropping my stealth in favor of speed, I jogged after the harbinger.

* * *

Chasing after a Power was not the smartest thing I'd ever done. On the other hand, it wasn't the most idiotic either.

My body was flagging, and I was mentally exhausted, too. I needed rest— if not urgently, then soon. Still, I persevered. Wherever the harbinger was going and whatever he was after, I had to know.

Borne up by wings of fear—or hope—I reached my destination sooner than I'd anticipated. Panting lightly, I drew to a halt. The near side of the chasm was less than a hundred yards ahead. A modicum of caution was called for.

Dropping into a crouch, I crept forward.

I had barely advanced six feet before a bright mindglow appeared ahead. A second later, I saw the harbinger in the 'real,' his wings beating energetically as he strived for altitude.

A hostile entity has failed to detect you.

Freezing in place, I watched silently as the huge stygian emerged from the chasm. Had he found what he'd come for? I couldn't tell from his demeanor. The only thing I knew for certain was that he was in a hurry. Arrowing straight south, the harbinger headed back to the central fog bank.

I waited a full minute, only turning back to the chasm when the stygian had disappeared entirely from sight. Weapons at the ready, I slipped closer.

CHAPTER 356: THE SPIDER AT THE CENTER OF THE WEB

The chasm was as deep and narrow as it had appeared from afar. Looking straight down, I studied its depths.

A little more than a jagged tear in the plateau, the chasm zigzagged from west to east before devolving into a network of even smaller scars that ran right up against the dungeon's northern boundary. Its two side walls marched in unison, so close together that no light penetrated to the rocky floor.

It must have been a tight fit, I thought, finding it surprising the harbinger had willingly entered the chasm. Fortunately, I was many times smaller than my counterpart and the darkness did not scare me. Equipping my cat's claws, I made my way down the sheer cliff wall.

The climb was no more difficult than others I'd performed in the dungeon, and shortly I reached the bottom of the chasm. It was pitch black— a problem for most, but not for me.

Both my mindsight and physical sight reported the surroundings to be empty. I was alone. Leaving my blades sheathed, I glanced from left to right, wondering which direction to explore first.

East, I decided. If something had come here seeking refuge from the harbinger, it followed they would choose the narrowest stretches to hide in, and those all lay to the east.

Setting out at an easy walk, I got going.

*   *   *

Hours later, I was still walking.

I had contemplated calling out for Ghost—either with my mindvoice or aloud—but had decided that would be unwise until I knew for certain the spidering network of cracks held no threat.

I was already in what I judged to be the chasm's narrowest passage, which measured about four yards from wall to wall. It was a space too tight for the harbinger or, for that matter, the majority of the dungeon's elite. But something like a swarm viper could still be lurking in the darkness, and I stayed vigilant.

Sss... eeuUuu... ssSss eeuuSss... eeuuw...

I rocked to a halt, startled.

During the entire time I've been in the chasm, nothing had disturbed the quiet. Until now.

The strange sound came again.

What was it? A hiss? A whistle? I wasn't quite sure. Whatever it was, it was too faint to hear clearly. It couldn't be the wind. There wasn't even a breeze to speak of. Deciding I needed to know, I turned down a side passage, following the sound.

I came to another fork in the path and once more chose the one from which the whistling seemed to emanate louder. I didn't worry about getting lost, knowing I could escape to the plateau any time it became necessary.

As I drew closer, the sound changed, or rather, became clearer. It was neither a hiss nor whistle but chanting. Chanting with words in a language I didn't understand.

In the middle of a passage so thin that two people could barely walk abreast, I paused and listened intently. There was only one voice. Which meant a single hostile.

Or did it?

Chanting implied sentience. Was it an elite up ahead or something else?

There was no way to tell. Casting my buffs, I advanced more cautiously. The sound had become progressively louder, and I knew I had to be close to the unseen chanter.

The passage I followed winded left and right, then suddenly ended. Drawing to a halt, in the center of the tiny cul-de-sac—barely a few yards across—I turned around in a slow circle. Had I chosen the wrong passage?

Should I return to the plateau?

I pivoted about again. The chanting was louder here than it had been anywhere else, and while it was difficult to pinpoint the sound's source, I thought it was coming from beneath me. Frowning, I went down on my knees and inspected the floor closely.

You have found an anomaly!

My brows drew down further. It was not the fact that I had found an anomaly that disturbed me, but that I had found *only* an anomaly.

My insight was at rank twenty, high enough to pierce the guise of most creatures. Whatever I was dealing with here, it had been set by a being of elite rank—or higher.

Is it a ward or a trap?

Putting on my spectacles, I checked the first possibility. Uncovering nothing, I drew on my stamina and cast lesser trap detect.

Energy rushed into my eyes, sharpening my gaze and causing glowing dust to swirl at the edges of my vision. I waited a beat, but the particles refused to coalesce.

You have failed to spot any traps.

The Game report was less helpful than I liked. There could still be a trap, only I was too unskilled to detect it. Sighing, I drew ebonheart and used its tip to brush aside loose gravel and pebbles from the spot that had attracted my interest. I knew I was taking a risk tinkering with a potential trap, but I could not walk away.

The harbinger had been interested enough in this area to investigate. The exile was supposedly also somewhere nearby. And then there was Ghost.

I did not see how the unknown chanter, or the anomaly, could lead me to finding my lost companion, but I could not ignore the possibility that they *might*.

No spelled ward or trap triggered.

Relieved, I leaned forward to inspect what I'd uncovered.

You have passed a Perception check!

You have pierced a veil of darkness. An illusion has been lifted. You have found a hidden trapdoor!

I sat back, rocking on my heels. *A trapdoor.* In the middle of nowhere, too. Where did it lead?

Not about to leave the mystery unanswered, I tugged open the wooden door.

* * *

Beneath the trapdoor was a flight of stairs.

They descended into an underground complex that, in stark contrast to the chasm's pitch-black dark, was flooded in light. More importantly, the chanting had grown in volume. After ascertaining there were no wards or traps lurking, I descended the steps.

At the base of the staircase, I crouched down to examine my surroundings anew. I was in a corridor tiled all around with chalk-white bricks that reflected the already harsh light tenfold.

I grimaced, realizing there were no shadows to be had. Nor was the source of light apparent. Neither of those things could be happenstance either. Recasting greater fade, I attempted to hide.

Prevailing light conditions prevent you from concealing yourself. You have failed to hide.

Urgh. I didn't want to venture down the white corridor, and I already felt too exposed, but I had to. Setting aside my misgivings, I drew my blades and crept forward.

* * *

Fifty yards later, the passage came to an abrupt end, terminating in a T-junction.

To the right it led to a handful of rooms, each hidden behind a closed door. To the left was another stretch of corridor, this one with only a single door set at its end. It was from there that the chanting was coming. Swinging left, I approached the door.

It stood slightly ajar.

I stepped up to the door but could make out nothing through the narrow slit. My mindsight, too, reported the room empty. Given the chanting that emanated from within, that was patently untrue, though. I would have to go in to find out more. Renewing my buffs, I tightened my hands around the hilt of my blades and gently pushed the door open further.

It did not creak.

Grateful to retain the element of surprise and not sure for how much longer that would still hold true, I slipped into the room.

You have entered a tier 6 concealment field. All entities within this field are hidden from outside detection.

I drew up short. It was not the Game alert, as troubling as it was, that gave me pause. Rather, it was the sight that greeted me.

The chamber was decorated in the same unrelieved white as the corridor. Even the tables and cupboards scattered along the edges of the room had been painted white—which made the two crimson circles in the center all the more eye-catching.

In the first circle was a misshapen pile of fur, meat, and bones that had been crudely strung together in something resembling a four-footed beast.

In the second circle was Ghost.

I had found her!

My elation lasted only a second, though, before concern marred it. Ghost did not seem to be aware of me. Lying on her side, the spirit wolf was to all appearances... unconscious. Her mindglow was small, wavering, and subdued. In the real, all was not right either. The lines of spirit defining Ghost's form were blurred. I didn't know what that signified, but it troubled me.

My eyes narrowed. In all the time I'd known Ghost, I had never seen her in such a state. My gaze shot to the motionless figure standing between the two circles with its—*her?*—back to me. The chanter. She had to be the one responsible.

Had she caged the spirit wolf somehow?

A snarl twisted my face and I almost charged forward before I could stop myself. But sense prevailed, and I remained as still as the figure I observed. The chanter didn't appear in my mindsight, which meant she was shielded, and whatever was happening to Ghost, it hadn't begun recently.

The chanting had been going on for some time, and I suspected Ghost's condition was related to it. The chanter was no ordinary foe, either. Given the ward around the room, she was powerful.

I have to move carefully, or I could end up as trapped as Ghost. And that would do no one any good.

My gaze drifted to the twin circles. They weren't just crimson, I realized; they had been drawn in blood. Tiny sigils, carefully etched in the white bricks, decorated the inside and outside of the circles. They, too, had been done in blood.

This is a ritual.

But to what end? My eyes darted from the unconscious Ghost to the meat-body. Was this a perverse attempt to create a pet? Or to raise an undead? I shuddered. Whatever was going on, I didn't think it boded well for my companion.

Finally, my gaze settled on the chanter. From the rear, she looked like an ordinary human. But looks could be deceptive, and I was sure she was one of the possessed *and* the so-called exiled. It was the only explanation that made sense.

My thoughts flickered back to the tier six ward enclosing the chamber. It could only be the chanter's doing. That put the silent figure on par with an envoy—for which reason, as much as I wanted to, I dared not attempt an analyze. I couldn't risk alerting my foe before I attacked.

And I *had* to attack, I realized.

That doing so would likely destroy the plans Elron and I had drawn up counted for little. This was a tier six foe I was dealing with. And she had Ghost at her mercy.

Attacking fast and without warning was the only chance Ghost had of living through the encounter. Even then, it might not be enough. *There is no other choice.* Settled in my decision, I drew psi and raised ebonheart.

The chanting stopped.

My heart sank. I had delayed too long. My spell was only half-ready, and it would take a few precious seconds to cover the distance to the exile.

But I lurched forward, anyway.

CHAPTER 357: BLOOD RITUAL

I managed all of two steps before a shockwave of air rippled outwards from the exile. Picking me up, it tossed me heedlessly into one of the white brick walls.

An unknown entity has trigger-cast repel-the-living.
You have failed a magical resistance check!
Your void armor has reduced the death damage incurred by 10%.

The exile turned around unhurriedly as I slid to the floor, and I caught my first glimpse of my foe. At some point, she must have been beautiful, but now her face bespoke only sternness and age—great age.

The exile's skin was papery, the lines drawn on her cheeks were deeply etched, and a milky film covered eyes that were pale and pupil-less. Her lips drawn in a severe line; she raised an arm to point at me. Forcing myself into motion, I threw myself to the right.

Not a second too early, either.

You have evaded death's finger.

Damn, why does she have to be a death spellcaster? I wondered as the white wall behind me dissolved into a puddle of decay and filth. Death magic was one of my bigger weaknesses. Rolling back to my feet, I resumed my interrupted spellcasting.

The exile watched me placidly, her expression unchanged. Moving with the same lack of speed she had earlier, she swung her arm back in my direction while renewed blackness gathered at the tip of her finger.

I didn't wait to greet the spell. My own casting was ready, and I shadow blinked.

You have teleported into the shadow of an unknown entity.

I stepped out of the aether behind the ancient woman, and without hesitation, plunged both my blades into her back.

You have destroyed the flesh golem of an unknown entity.

The corpse slumped lifelessly. In shock, I stared at it. It was a real body, not an image nor an illusion, yet obviously, it was not my foe.

"Who are you?"

My head whipped to the left to see the exile standing less than five yards away. She was the same, yet not. All signs of aging had fled. The person before me was young, beautiful, and in the prime of her womanhood.

But she was still very much my enemy.

Pivoting, I dashed straight at her, but before I could close the distance, black smoke spewed out of my foe's mouth. Once more, I was forced to take evasive action. The dark cloud was too widespread to dodge entirely, though.

A noxious vapors spell has grazed you.

You have failed a magical resistance check! You are _rotting_ (health decaying at 5% per second). Duration: 5 seconds.

I weaved past the trailing edge of the deadly smoke, then cut back to my foe, intent on resuming my assault. My foe was too powerful. I had to close the distance, and I _had_ to disrupt her casting. Diving beneath the last of the vapors, I came up in front of the exile and thrust both my blades upwards.

You have destroyed the flesh golem of an unknown entity.

The second corpse collapsed as easily as the first. It had looked so much like a real human and had even spoken. Could a construct do that?

"Why are you here?"

Turning around slowly, I saw the exile standing uninjured ten yards away. Once more, I spotted no mindglow. If it was another flesh golem addressing me, that was because it had no mind, but if it was my real foe then that meant her consciousness was shielded.

Let's find out which. Weaving psi, I thrust my will forward.

You have cast slaysight (shatter).
An unknown entity has failed a mental resistance check!
You have weakened your target's mind shield. Remaining: 90%.

That answers that. My mouth set in a grim line, I drew more psi and dashed forward.

The young woman watched me impassively, neither the mental assault nor my renewed charge seeming to faze her. But when I got to within three yards, she waved her hand in dismissal.

An unknown entity has cast wraith winds.

Tiny slivers of spirit, like shards of glass, flew at me, battering my face, arms, and legs. Ducking my head to shield my eyes, I pressed on into the spirit storm.

You have failed a magical resistance check!
You have been pushed back 1 foot. You have been injured.
You have been pushed back 1 foot. You have been injured.
...

The winds birthed from the exile's hands appeared unending, and for every foot I advanced, I was pushed back two, but my ineffective struggle against the casting was only a ploy to finish my own spell.

You have cast windborne.

I curved my windslide around and over the storm. Borne upon its currents, I shot forward to my target before she could redirect the winds my way again.

Launching off the ramp of air, I landed lightly behind the exile and lopped off her head with a single clean strike of ebonheart.

You have destroyed the flesh golem of an unknown entity.

I stared, confounded both by the Game alert and the fresh corpse at my feet. That it was a golem made no sense. The thing had had a mind, and I'd seen the spells it had woven. My foe had occupied it, I was sure of it, but she no longer did.

Is she somehow animating the golems from afar?

"Did Loskin send you?"

I turned, much slower this time, to face the exile again. Nothing I had done seemed to have troubled her. Her expression remained just as calm and her gaze unruffled. Even the killing spells she'd cast had been unleashed nonchalantly, like something one did every day.

I wasn't sure about the wisdom of talking to such a dangerous foe, not when she had my companion at such a disadvantage, but I conceded—reluctantly—my current tactics were not working.

I had to come up with a better plan and find out where my foe truly was. Until then, talking would suffice to buy me some time. I rammed my blades into their sheaths. "Let her go."

"Who?" was the mild reply.

I gestured at Ghost. "My companion."

The young woman frowned. "She is not yours. She is a free spirit."

I snarled, letting some of the wolf within me to the fore. "She is mine to protect. Stop this filthy ritual and let her go."

The young woman's eyes narrowed, and a moment later, I felt a telltale tickle ripple across me.

You have passed a mental resistance check! An unknown entity has failed to analyze you.

The exile's mouth twisted. "You are a player," she remarked dismissively. "That explains it. Now, begone. You will not have her." Then, she turned her back on me and resumed chanting.

It was an amazing display, made all the more astonishing by the fact that I didn't think it was an act. The exile really did seem to consider me too insignificant to pose much threat.

For a moment, my anger churned, and I contemplated cutting her down from behind—but I doubted that would work any better than it had the first three times.

Still, if the exile was going to ignore me, I would do the same to her. My gaze drifted to my companion. Besides, she was not the main reason I'd come here. Ghost was. But first, I needed to find out what exactly I was dealing with. Reaching out with my will, I analyzed the woman.

The target is Adriel, a level 261 lich.
Your analyze attempt has been detected!

A sigh escaped the young woman. It was uttered so softly between chants I was sure she didn't mean me to hear.

"You are a lich," I accused, hands dropping back to my blades in preparation for a retaliatory attack.

But Adriel did not break off from her chanting. In fact, other than that quiet, almost involuntary sigh, my words drew no other response from her.

Things were beginning to make a weird sort of sense. The exile was a lich—just like the possessed's ruler. It perhaps explained why the other possessed feared her as much as they did. But that realization did not concern me so much as knowing Ghost lay in the hands of one.

Lichs were rumored to hold vast sway over spirits and death, making Ghost particularly vulnerable to Adriel's brand of magic. My concern for my companion mounting, I rushed across the chamber and knelt beside the blood circle holding her. I didn't want to cross over yet in case doing so triggered something unpleasant.

"Ghost, can you hear me?"

There was no response.

"Ghost," I called again, louder and more urgently. *"Answer me, please."*

The chanting stopped.

Looking up, I found the young woman studying me quizzically. "What are you doing?" she asked slowly.

"Studying the circle," I lied.

Adriel snorted. "Why did you call her that?"

"Who?" My gaze drifted to the still-unmoving spirit wolf. The exile had overheard my mental call—another unpleasant surprise—and for a moment, I considered not answering. But, so far, open antagonism had not worked. Perhaps a more reasoned appeal might. "You mean Ghost?"

"Yes, the spirit wolf," Adriel replied testily. "But I told you, she is a free spirit, not a ghost."

"I know that!" I snapped back. "Ghost is her *name*."

She blinked. "Her name? You know her?"

"I seem to recall having said that earlier," I said evenly, managing to rein in my anger before I could blurt out an even harsher response.

"You claimed to be her owner," Adriel corrected.

"No," I refuted. "I claimed she was my *companion*."

"To a player that is one and the same."

I sighed. "I don't know what you mean by that and I'm too tired to play games. Ghost is my companion, and I'm duty bound to protect her."

Adriel fell silent for a moment. "Why did you attack me earlier?"

I shrugged. "Isn't that obvious? You are a possessed. You are holding my companion prisoner, and by the looks of it, you are performing a ritual most vile."

"Where did you hear that term?" Adriel asked sharply.

"What, possessed?" My lips turned down. "Let's just say I had the displeasure of meeting some of your fellows."

Adriel's eyes darkened, and between one second and the next the tiny woman grew in stature until she seemed to loom over me. I had no trouble believing she was indeed a lich now. "Was it Loskin? Was he the one? Did he send you here?"

Unable to match stares with her, I looked down. "I don't know who that is. It was Castor and Avery that I met."

"Ah. Those two."

"You know them, then." Still, not looking up again at Adriel, I stretched out my hand towards the comatose wolf.

"Don't."

An inch from the blood circle, my hand froze.

"If your hand crosses the circle now, you will cause irreparable harm."

I was not sure I believed Adriel, but I couldn't risk that she was telling the truth and retracted my hand. I couldn't just leave Ghost as she was in the hands of a lich, though. Focusing my thoughts, I yelled loudly, *"GHOST."*

"She won't hear you. She can't. She is too far gone."

Ignoring Adriel, I mustered every iota of command that being an alpha granted me and infused it in my mindvoice. *"GHOST, COME BACK."*

"You have a powerful voice, I grant you that," Adriel said. "But it will not work. Her spirit has deteriorated too—"

Ghost stirred. *"Prime...?"* she gasped weakly. *"Is that... you? How... d-did you find me? I thought—"*

A force like a hammer struck me from the rear, and before I knew it, I was splayed across one of the chamber's whitewashed walls—helpless to move.

Adriel stomped towards me, her eyes burning with a fury greater than I'd seen yet. "What did she call you?" the lich whispered in a tone that promised death.

CHAPTER 358: A SPIRITED DISCUSSION

I was a fly caught in a web of the lich's making.

My hands refused to budge, and even psi had been stolen from my reach. Still, I met Adriel's gaze unflinchingly. "Let her go," I growled.

"Answer me!" she demanded, paying my own words no heed.

"Release Ghost first," I insisted. "Then I'll tell you what you want to know."

"Don't toy with me boy," Adriel hissed. "I don't know which one of Loskin's sick sycophants dreamt up this ploy, but when I'm done with you, you will be begging to tell me their names."

I stared back at her, stubbornly silent.

"Adriel... let him go, please."

"Shush, wolfling," the lich replied, not looking away from me. "I see now how he bought your loyalty. But this one is a deceiver. He lied to you, little one."

"H-he... bears the alpha's Mark. The... elders have seen it. Please, Adriel... don't hurt... him."

The young woman's expression froze into a cool mask that was at odds with the fury that still danced in her eyes. Her rage had not vanished. It had only been shuttered—for Ghost's sake, I thought.

"Believe... he... Prime... one day."

Ghost's voice was growing more ragged with every word she uttered. Unable to ignore my concern any longer, I wrenched my gaze away from the lich's to study her.

The spirit wolf's being was fraying, the threads of herself drifting apart. *She is dying.*

In desperation, I turned back to Adriel. "Help her!" I begged.

The lich studied the spirit wolf for herself. "I cannot, not until the ritual is complete." She glanced at me. "You should not have awoken her. Every moment she's conscious drains more of her strength, leaving her less able to hold herself together."

I swore vehemently.

"Prime..." Ghost began.

"Hush, Ghost," I said, cutting her off gently. Then, infusing my words with the power of an alpha again, I ordered, *"Go to sleep."*

As weak as Ghost was, she could not resist the force of my command. *"Yes, Prime,"* she said meekly. *"Only... trust Adriel. She is a... friend. She can..."*

Before she could finish, Ghost's words ran aground as she fell into deep slumber again. Intently, I studied her spirit anew.

The dissociation had stopped.

In relief, I sagged against the invisible bonds that held me. Ghost was safe—temporarily, at least. Now that I'd seen what happened when she was awake, I understood the reason for her spirit form's fuzziness. What I did not understand, though, was why Ghost's spirit was unraveling in the first place.

Lifting my head, I stared at the lich. She was studying me the way one would an annoying insect. Somehow, the spirit wolf had won the strange possessed's trust and seemed to trust her in turn. She had advised me to do the same, but... after witnessing Ghost's condition, how could I?

Whatever was going on with Ghost, it had to be the lich's doing. I pinned her with a glare. "What did you do to her?" I hissed.

"Nothing," Adriel replied calmly. "The wolfling came to me as you see her." She gestured to the blood circles. "This is all at her own request."

My lips twisted in disgust. "That I don't believe. Whatever foul creature you plan on turning Ghost into, I cannot believe she asked for such a fate."

"Not even if it was to save you?"

My face stiffened. "What does that mean?" I asked slowly.

"The spirit wolf did not tell me much," the exile replied obliquely. "Only that her companion was in trouble, and she needed to save him. I thought she meant another wolf. But now I realize it must have been you she spoke of." She eyed me coolly. "It is you, not I, who forced her into this 'vile' ritual."

I opened my mouth to deny the accusation, then closed it with a snap. Adriel was correct. I *had* failed to protect Ghost, and knowing the spirit wolf, she would not flinch at the thought of performing a dangerous ritual if it meant being able to rescue me.

Trust Adriel, Ghost had said. Swallowing bile, I tried to do just that. "What is this ritual, anyway?"

"It is one meant to rehouse a lost spirit."

My eyes widened. "You can do that?"

Adriel nodded. "I don't, however, have many of the materials necessary for such a complex casting—" she gestured disparagingly at the meat body—"and had to do with what I could assemble on short notice."

I licked my lips. "Then you are not trying to enslave Ghost?"

Contempt sparked in Adriel's eyes. "Hardly."

I winced. I had misjudged the situation—badly. "So... Ghost *asked* you for a body?"

"No, but she needed one."

I frowned.

Renewed anger sparked in the young woman's eyes. "You can see her spirit, can't you?"

I nodded.

"Then you should know," Adriel said, her voice cold, "that her spirit is torn and tattered. It is so far gone she can no longer hold herself together. Why did you enter a dungeon with her in such a condition?"

"I didn't," I protested. "Ghost was whole when I last saw her. It must have been—"

I broke off.

"Must have been what?" Adriel demanded suspiciously.

I met her gaze. "I'm... sorry. I acted rashly earlier. I lost contact with Ghost days ago and feared I might never find her again. When I entered the room and saw the blood circles, I suspected the worst."

"That does not excuse your foolhardy assault. I would've been justified in killing you." Adriel's eyes glinted hard. "I would still be."

I hung my head. "That's true." I sighed, deciding to come clean. "It was the harbinger. He ambushed us. Ghost was shackled and I was killed before I found out what happened to her."

The exile grew still. "The stygian harbinger did this?"

I nodded mutely.

"That's why he has been poking around of late," she muttered. She paced back and forth. "Tell me exactly what happened."

"Release me first."

Adriel studied me wordlessly for a moment, then waved her hand. The bonds of magic holding me fell apart.

Falling heavily to the ground, I rubbed my sore limbs. But other than a few bruises, I was uninjured. Exhaling heavily, I began. "Right, where to start? It was ten days ago when the harbinger found us in a canyon not far from here. First, he..."

*　　*　　*

"That explains it," Adriel said when I was done.

"Explains what?"

"The harbinger is a death magic user." Her lips twitched in the first sign of amusement I had seen from her yet. "One nearly as practiced as a lich. Ghost must have caught the edges of his oblivion spell. That she is spirit herself would have offered her some measure of protection, but not enough. Now the spell is trying to complete its work."

"Alright... but how does knowing that help?"

Adriel's gaze flickered to the meat body. "Now I know I'm on the right track. Once her spirit is clothed anew, she will be stable enough for me to cast the necessary spells."

"Then you can heal her?"

Adriel nodded. "I can."

I slapped my hands together. "Excellent! Then let's get started," I said, and began to rise to my feet.

"Not so fast," Adriel said.

Mid-motion, I paused.

"Before we begin," she continued, "there are still matters we must resolve between us."

I had known this moment must come. Whatever anger drove the lich, it had not been forgotten. "Before? Can't it wait until—"

"No, it cannot," Adriel broke in. "We will settle matters now."

My lips thinned, not missing the implications of her timing. "You will leverage Ghost's condition to get the answers you seek?"

"If I must," Adriel replied evenly. "It's obvious you care for her, and this way, I can at least be sure you are being truthful."

For a moment, my mouth worked mutinously, then my gaze flickered to Ghost. "Will she be alright like that?"

Adriel nodded. "Sleep will keep her spirit contained. As long as she slumbers, she will be fine."

I disliked being strong-armed, but for my companion's sake, I would cooperate. "Very well," I sighed. "I will tell you what you want to know. Go ahead. Ask your questions."

Without ceremony, Adriel sat down opposite me, tugging in the hem of her robe beneath her legs. "Tell me she is mistaken," Adriel said. "Tell me you are not what she claims."

I stared at the lich for a long moment, sensing that much rested on my answer. Revealing the truth to a foe like Adriel could be catastrophic, but Ghost had told me to trust her. And even in the face of her own disbelief, I noted Adriel did not accuse Ghost of lying. Not only that, but I needed her help. For all these reasons and more, I would have to find a way to work with the lich—even if she did fly into a rage at my response.

"She was not mistaken," I said, holding Adriel's gaze. "I am an anointed scion of House Wolf."

The lich had her emotions well under control and betrayed no reaction at my response. "Explain," she ordered peremptorily.

I grinned faintly. "What's to explain? I awakened my blood and joined House Wolf."

Adriel did not find my response amusing. "Give me details," she demanded.

My grin faded. "What do you want to know?"

"Tell me when, where, and how."

I pursed my lips. "I acquired my Wolf mark early in the Game after I met a pair of dire wolves and their pups. 'Where' would be Erebus' dungeon. As for the how: the dire wolves' pack turned out to be gatekeepers for a Wolf Trials set up long ago by one of the Primes."

"This dire wolf pack, is that the same one the spirit wolf is from?"

"She told you about them?" I asked, striving to keep my surprise from showing.

"The wolfling did not betray any secrets. She is a careful one and was vague on the details. I chose not to pry."

"I see. Yet you pry with me?"

"You are something other."

Deciding not to tiptoe around the issue anymore, I asked bluntly, "Why is this of any interest to you? Why do you care if I am a scion or not?"

Adriel chose to ignore my question in favor of asking one of her own. "Who is Erebus?"

"What?"

"Who is—"

"I heard you the first time, but how can you not know who Erebus is? He is a Dark Power from the Awakened Dead faction."

Adriel's brows creased slightly before clearing again. "And the Prime whose Trials you entered, that was Atiras?"

I frowned. "You know of Atiras—a long-dead Prime—but fail to recognize the name of a Power like Erebus. Just how ancient are you, Adriel?"

"That is the wrong question," the lich responded dismissively.

My frown deepened. "The wrong question? What do you mean—"

"Why are you still alive?" Adriel interrupted.

I stared at her irritably. Was she going to ignore all my questions? "Because you haven't killed me yet?" I retorted flippantly.

"Besides that," Adriel replied, deadpan. "Why haven't any of the new Powers done so already?"

For a moment, I thought I misheard. Then I realized Adriel had not misspoken—or perhaps she had—and things finally began to click into place. "You're not a player!" I exclaimed.

"So glad you noticed," Adriel said dryly. "Now answer me, why haven't the Powers—"

"What I meant is you *never* were a player," I said, speaking over her unconcernedly. "You're a scion."

"Former scion," Adriel corrected. She paused. "What finally gave me away?"

I stared at her, still in shock. "You said 'new Powers.' No one calls them that."

"Hmm. I see."

My mind turned frantic circles, still racing through all the implications. Then another thought occurred to me. "Is that why you're an exile?" I asked, leaning forward eagerly. "Did the other possessed force you out because you are a former scion, unlike them?"

For a drawn-out moment, Adriel said nothing. "Oh, that's not it at all."

My brows creasing, I sat back. "It isn't?"

Adriel shook her head. "It isn't." She paused. "*All* the possessed are former scions."

CHAPTER 359: SHOCKING REVELATIONS

Bowing my head, I lowered my face into my hands. It was one shocking revelation too many, and I struggled to process Adriel's words. "All of you are scions?" I muttered, looking up a moment later.

"Former scions," Adriel corrected.

"Even Castor and Avery?" I persisted.

The lich's lips twitched again. "Even those two, yes."

"But... but that must mean you entered the dungeon millennia ago!"

"We did. Just right after the Primes' fall, in fact."

My brows creased. "What House are you from?"

Adriel made a shooing motion with her hand. "We can discuss that later. I'm still waiting for your answer to my question."

"What question?"

Adriel's gaze sharpened. "Why have the Powers let you be? Why are you still in the Game?"

"I am a deception player—" I began.

"Your deception may be high enough to deceive an elite, but that would not stop the Powers from divining the truth about your House affiliations."

Reluctantly, I nodded. "That is true. I have a trait that hides my Wolf heritage."

"What trait?"

"Secret blood."

"Secret blood?" Adriel mouthed. "I know it." She paused. "Did you choose the trait as soon as you awoke your blood?"

I nodded mutely.

"Bloody Wolves," she muttered. "Always hiding." But, despite the disparaging words, Adriel's tone was half admiring. "So, none of the new Powers know what you are?"

I hesitated a moment too long before responding.

"Don't start lying to me now, Wolf. If you want my help, you will tell me the truth. All the truth."

"One Power knows," I conceded. "He figured it out."

"Who?" Adriel rasped.

"Loken."

"Loken," she hissed. "Why am I not surprised?"

"You know him?" I asked, mildly alarmed at the notion.

"Unfortunately, I do. And he is no new Power. Loken is as ancient as they come."

I frowned. "I'm not sure I follow you."

"A discussion for another time," she said. "So, Loken knows who you are, yet he has decided to let you live? That can only mean he wants something."

I nodded. "You *do* know him. But Loken doesn't know everything. He is aware that I've begun treading the path of the Wolf, but he does not suspect that I have already awoken my blood."

"That's good," Adriel breathed. "Make sure you keep it that way."

I stared at her searchingly. "I will. It sounds as if you believe me. More to the point, it also sounds as if your cause is mine."

"Your cause," Adriel mused. "And what exactly is that?"

"I mean to raise House Wolf again," I said bluntly. "And from your words, former scion or not, I take it that is something you desire too. Is it?"

Adriel's hand lifted, no doubt to brush aside my question again.

I slashed my arm downwards first. "No. I've suffered your interrogation gladly. I've laid bare what I am and my own goals. It's time you do the same." I leaned forward. "Tell me, Adriel. Is bringing about a return of the ancients something you desire too?"

The lich leaned forward herself, her gaze roving over my face as if searching for weakness. I did not flinch as she inspected me minutely. "It is," she breathed finally.

I sighed in relief. "Then, you will help me?"

"I will," Adriel said, exhaling heavily. "But there is much you do not know yet. And I warn you, once you know the truth, you may not want my help."

Before I could inquire what she meant, the lich rose to her feet. "We will speak of it further. This is something your companion should hear, too. Let's see to her healing first."

I did not protest. As much as I wanted to unpack Adriel's cryptic statement, restoring Ghost was more important, and I stood with her.

✳   ✳   ✳

"So, what do we do?" I asked a moment later, standing with Adriel in front of the two blood-drawn circles.

"First, I transfer Ghost into that," she said, pointing to the mishmash of body parts in the second circle.

I stared at the meat pile dubiously. "And what is that exactly?"

Adriel looked at me. "Do you really want to know?"

I didn't particularly, but for Ghost's sake, I felt it necessary to ask. "Go on, tell me."

"It is a flesh golem," Adriel replied. "Crudely fashioned, admittedly, but I was pressed for time and had to use what I had on hand. As a body, it will serve Ghost poorly. She will do well to even walk in it."

"Then what is its purpose?"

Adriel shrugged. "The flesh golem may not look like much, but it will anchor Ghost's spirit and allow me to cast the mending spells necessary to re-knit her torn spirit. That part will take time, though. Days, perhaps, and much will depend on Ghost herself."

"When will she regain consciousness?"

"After she is clothed in flesh, she will be able to speak to us again."

I nodded, not knowing enough to question her further. "What do you need me to do?"

"Nothing. Just stay out of the way and deal with any unwanted visitors if it becomes necessary. Can you do that?"

"Of course." Placing myself against one of the walls that gave me a clear view of both the door and the lich, I crossed my arms and settled down to wait.

Turning back to face the blood circles, Adriel began chanting anew.

✳ ✳ ✳

Adriel chanted for hours.

I stayed vigilant the entire time, despite my own tiredness. It had been a long day, beginning with my adrenaline-fueled escape from the safe zone and ending with the lich's revelations.

Reflecting on those revelations gave me much food for thought and the hours slipped by almost unnoticed. That the possessed were scions opened up a whole host of questions: like what they were doing in the dungeon, how they had survived as long as they had, why they had abandoned the fight against the new Powers—and surely they must have—to finally, and most importantly, what had led them to become possessed.

This aspect troubled me the most.

It was not that the possessed were former scions, but the manner in which they had chosen to prolong their lives, that disturbed me. There were no two ways about it; the possessed were ruthless, oppressive, and in many respects, evil. According to Elron, the archlich had been oppressing New Haven for centuries.

How many young players' bodies had been stolen?

How many New Haveners had died because of the possessed?

Could I ally myself with such, even if they were scions?

I was not sure what I'd expected to find when I had set out to locate the exile. Admittedly, I hadn't given the matter much thought. I knew we needed allies, and on Elron's advice, had sought out the exile. Now I was faced with the reality of what allying with her might mean.

My gaze drifted to Adriel, recalling her earlier words. Her decision to cut short our conversation and see Ghost healed first was a wiser one than I'd grasped at the time. Knowing the truth, I realized I may not be able to stomach her help—even to save Ghost. Mercifully, Adriel had taken that choice out of my hands.

Do I want to know the truth?

I did. Ignorance was no excuse.

I had to know who Adriel was and what she stood for before I accepted more of her 'aid.' I walked a gray path myself, and there was not much I would not do to protect those I cared for, but there were some lines I refused to cross.

I squeezed my eyes shut. It did not matter that Elron had sent me here. It did not matter that many New Haven lives hung in the balance. If Adriel's path was one too black for me to follow, then I would have no choice but to refuse her help.

With these bleak thoughts for company, I watched both Adriel and the door with growing misgivings.

Six hours later, Adriel finally fell silent.

My eyes darted to the first blood circle. Ghost no longer occupied it. My gaze cut right to the second circle. The meat pile looked no different, but I could sense a familiar mindglow inside.

Kicking off the wall, I darted to the sagging lich's side. "It worked?"

She nodded tiredly. "It did."

I gestured to the circle. "Can I...?"

"Yes, the ritual is over, the blood sigils can be broken."

Not waiting any longer, I rushed to my companion. "Ghost... are you in there?"

Eyes that had been sewn into a head too small for them opened sleepily. *"Prime?"*

I smiled broadly. Even after everything she'd said, I had not been sure how far to trust Adriel. "I'm here. How are you feeling?"

"Strange... where am I?"

"In the body Adriel prepared for you."

Ghost's head quivered, and I guessed she was trying to raise it, but then her whole body began to shake, and she gave up. *"Did the spell work? Is it done?"*

"Only the first part is complete," Adriel said before I could answer. Coming up from behind, she knelt next to me. "There is more work to be done."

Ghost sighed. *"Thank you, Adriel. This already feels better."*

The lich patted Ghost's head, unfazed by its gruesome appearance. "You're welcome, little one. Rest now. We have a lot to do tomorrow." She glanced at me. "You should also get some sleep. The complex is safe. I have rooms in—"

"I'll stay here," I interjected.

Adriel did not try to convince me otherwise. "As you wish." Rising to her feet, she headed for the door. "Rest well. I will see both of you tomorrow."

CHAPTER 360: DEATH MATTERS

After Adriel left, Ghost and I spoke.

I filled her in on what had happened in the safe zone, and she told me her own tale. Ghost, it seemed, had managed to hide from the harbinger and the spores. That, however, had not stopped the oblivion spell from reaching her. It had not killed her outright, but like the lich had surmised, had hurt her badly.

Despite her fraying spirit, Ghost had ventured out to search for me as soon as the stygians had left. It was Ghost's mind cries that had attracted the lich.

A day after I'd been killed, Adriel had found the spirit wolf wandering lost and dazed. From what Ghost told me, she would not have survived without the lich's intervention. Adriel had taken her in and kept her alive with her spells and rituals.

Once her tale was done, Ghost fell asleep, unable to stay awake any longer. Leaving the exhausted spirit wolf be, I lay down and considered what I'd learned. It seemed that I had a lot to be grateful to Adriel for.

That, however, did not lessen my trepidation regarding her tale.

※　※　※

I awoke the next morning to the murmur of soft voices.

Turning around, I saw that Adriel and Ghost were already awake and chatting. Yawning, I sat up. I had slept longer than I'd expected and had clearly been more exhausted than I realized.

"*Morning, Prime,*" Ghost greeted.

"Morning," I replied, stepping closer to her. Sleep had done wonders for Ghost, and she sounded better than she had yesterday.

I glanced at Adriel, who nodded. "She is on the mend."

I smiled. "That is excellent news." I paused. "Does that mean your spells will not be necessary?"

The lich shook her head. "Not at all. Ghost still has some way to go."

"Oh," I said, deflating. I turned to Ghost, taking in the mismatched body she occupied. Even a day later, it looked no less appealing. "Looks like you're going to have to stay in there for a while longer."

"*I don't mind,*" she replied and strangely enough, she sounded as if she meant it.

"We'd better get started, then," I said to Adriel.

"We will," the lich replied. "After we finish the discussion we began yesterday."

I nodded, my good mood evaporating. "Go on," I said, sitting next to Ghost.

Adriel inhaled, nervous for the first time since I'd met her. "I guess I should start at the beginning." She exhaled slowly. "I am—was, rather—from House Death."

"House Death?" I murmured. It was not an ancient House I'd heard of, but that was not surprising given how little I still knew about the Primes. "Is that why you are a..." I gestured helplessly at her form.

Adriel smiled. "A flesh golem? Or do you mean a lich?"

I shrugged. "Either."

"Both came later." Her humor faded. "Believe it or not, but House Death does not look kindly upon lichs."

I frowned, puzzled.

"Why will become clear soon," Adriel said, seeing my look. "Given our earlier discussion, I assume you know of the conflict between the new Powers and the Primes?"

I nodded. "The new Powers overthrew the ancient Houses, and since then, they have been suppressing all knowledge of the Primes."

"That's about it in a nutshell," Adriel said. "My own tale began during the war." She gazed off into the distance. "I was in my home sector the day the insurrection reached House Death. By that point, there had been uprisings all over the Kingdom, but none of the major Houses had been affected yet and the Primes thought nothing of the threat."

She sighed. "That day, we learned the folly of our complacency. Despite being one of the biggest Houses in the Kingdom, Death fell swiftly. Our Prime was overpowered, and the sector sealed. Then the slaughter began. Every scion, regardless of age or strength, was killed, one by one, over and over."

"Couldn't you rally in the safe zone?" I asked quietly.

"We tried to," Adriel answered, still looking away. "But once you lose control of a sector, the last thing a safe zone is, is safe. The moment we were reborn, the rebels ejected us, and killed us anew." Her lips twisted in something resembling a smile. "It was—and I suppose still is—a proven tactic for slaying players. If you know beforehand when and where a player will resurrect, and have overwhelming force on your side, killing them is simplicity itself."

I nodded, realizing what she meant.

"That was when three of us decided to change the game. After dying and being reborn multiple times, we realized we couldn't escape—at least not in the normal sense. So, we did something unexpected. Slipping the rebels' leash, we took shelter in the wilds of the sector and managed to evade capture long enough to perform one of the most reviled rituals in House Death."

Adriel fell silent then, and not wanting to interrupt, I waited for her to go on.

"We severed the links between our bodies and spirits— permanently— and became lichs."

I felt Ghost's interest quicken, and my own did as well. "You mean you deliberately recreated an event similar to the one that transformed Ghost into a spirit wolf?"

Adriel looked from me to the spirit wolf then back again. "No, nothing like that. What happened to Ghost was a mistake. Her spirit survived the experience but was left vulnerable. A lich's spirit, on the other hand, is invulnerable." Reaching into her robe, she pulled out a necklace. Hanging on the end of it was a tiny glass vial. "This is my phylactery. It anchors my spirit. Until it is destroyed, I will never die."

I stared at the innocuous-looking bottle. "You weren't wearing that before," I deduced.

Adriel smiled. "Of course not. It is normally never on my person. I only brought it here today so you could understand the whole of what I am."

My gaze slid to the flesh golem corpses still in the chamber. Adriel had not bothered removing them, and unlike ordinary corpses, they bore no stink of death. "Then those were—"

"—all incarnations of myself," she finished for me. "Each time you slew one of my bodies, I slipped into another and returned."

"I see," I said. Then, screwing up my courage, I asked something I really didn't want to. "Who did those bodies belong to before you..."

Adriel's smile faded. "Before I stole them, you mean?"

I winced, but even knowing the matter was likely to raise Adriel's ire and possibly turn her uncooperative, I could not let it go. "Yes, whose lives did you steal?" I asked more bluntly.

"Prime," Ghost began. *"You're mistaken. Adriel would never—"*

"Shush, little one," Adriel interjected. "I appreciate your defense, but this is something for which I must answer on my own." Adriel held my gaze. "The flesh golems are of my own making."

I stared at her blankly. "What?"

"I mold flesh the way a blacksmith forges steel or a carpenter fashions wood." She gestured to Ghost. "That is how I formed Ghost's body."

I sagged, relieved to no end by her answer. "Then you didn't kill anyone to create your flesh golems?"

"I didn't," Adriel confirmed. "But." She squeezed her eyes shut. "You are not entirely wrong. Crafting a proper flesh golem is not the work of an instant. It takes time and material. Over the course of my long life, I have oftentimes found myself short of both and have stolen many a body."

"You possessed them, you mean," I said flatly, feeling suddenly sickened.

"I did what I needed to survive," Adriel said, not flinching from the accusation. "Can you claim to have done otherwise?"

I sighed, conceding the point. What Adriel said was true enough. I had slain no few to further my own survival. As repulsive as I found possession, in the end, it was no different than killing someone. Had I killed innocents? I didn't think so, but some of my victims would likely contest that. Where I in Adriel's place, would I have chosen differently? I didn't know the answer to that either, and it troubled me. It was something to ponder later on.

Letting the matter go, I returned to her tale. "How did becoming a lich help you escape the new Powers?"

"There is a reason the lich-making ritual is despised. Severing spirit from body also breaks the bonds between scion and House. In effect, after becoming lichs, we were no longer players."

"*How did that help?*" Ghost asked, sounding puzzled.

"It stopped her from resurrecting in the safe zone," I explained before Adriel could answer. "And likely misled the rebels into believing she suffered final death."

"Correct," the lich confirmed. "The next time we died, our spirits returned to these," she said, pointing to the phylactery on her necklace.

"You keep saying 'we,'" I said. "Who do you mean?"

"Two others performed the lich ritual with me. Farren, my brother. And Loskin, who was once a dear friend."

"You've mentioned that name before," I noted.

Adriel nodded somberly. "Loskin is the archlich."

"Ah," I breathed, not finding myself at all surprised.

"*Are the other possessed lichs too?*" Ghost asked.

Adriel shook her head. "The others are not like us. For one, none of them have the necessary skill in death magic. For another, the ritual for lich-making is one of House Death's most shameful secrets. Neither Farren, Loskin, nor I would ever share it with outsiders."

"So, if Avery and Castor aren't lichs, what are they?" I asked. "And how can they do what you do?"

"They can't," Adriel said. "Not entirely. But with their consent, a lich can affect a spirit jump—what you call possession—on their behalf."

"Which also makes them dependent on the archlich," I concluded.

"Exactly," Adriel said. "The possessed have no control over their own spirits and need Loskin to rehome them after death. It's how he maintains his power over the group."

I rubbed my chin thoughtfully. "But you said the others are scions too. Where do they come from, if not from House Death?"

"Getting back to my tale," Adriel said. "After we became lichs, Loskin, Farren, and I escaped the sector. By then, much of the Kingdom was in turmoil, and none of the other Houses could provide us with a safe haven. That's when the three of us hit upon the idea of entering a dungeon. Everyone was too caught up in the war to pay much attention to the Endless Dungeon.

"We selected Draven's Reach for our new home and headed here. Along the way, we ran across other refugees. Many were scared and desperate, and Loskin offered them what, at the time, seemed a magnanimous choice."

"Let me guess," I said, "stay and die at the hands of the new Powers or join you in the dungeon as possessed?"

Adriel nodded mutely.

"Why Draven's Reach, though?" I asked.

"For many reasons," she answered. "One, it was a high-tiered dungeon and therefore less likely to be heavily trafficked than other dungeons. For another, it had only a single entrance and exit, which made it easier to guard. Then, too, the dungeon would help us get stronger."

I frowned. "Stronger how? I thought you weren't players any longer?"

Adriel smiled humorlessly. "Being a player is the easiest path to power, but not the only one. Before our transformation, Farren, Loskin, and I were above rank twenty-five. We were destined for great things, which, incidentally, was why the new Powers' insurrection galled Loskin so much.

"He was determined to continue the fight against them but was realistic enough to know that we would have to get stronger first, and that meant *evolving* into Powers. As a non-player, that is infinitely harder, but still achievable."

"So, you came here for power," I said. "Then what?"

Adriel nodded. "We did, but only Loskin has stuck to the task. Both Farren and I lost interest after a few centuries. Loskin, though, is very close to his goal. Give him a few more decades, and he will be a minor Power himself."

"Where do the New Haveners fit in?" Ghost asked.

"They entered the dungeon centuries later," Adriel said, "after their sector was invaded by the nether. At first, we celebrated that fact, thinking it only made our refuge more secure. With the entrance portal permanently closed, no one else could enter the dungeon."

"But then the nether also came here," I said.

"It did." She eyed me carefully. "As have you. You still haven't told me how you managed to get into Draven's Reach."

I shrugged. "I entered through a hidden portal. From another nether-infested sector, funnily enough."

A frown marred Adriel's forehead. "I see. It seems the stygians want this sector more badly than I thought."

I could see the idea troubled the lich, but I was more interested in something else just then. "Back to the New Haveners. Is it true that the possessed are keeping them from leaving?"

Adriel's face went blank, but she did not shirk from the question. "Yes," she unanswered unequivocally.

"Is it also true that the possessed harvest the bodies of any player born in New Haven?"

"Again, correct," Adriel answered, her expression opaque.

My own face tightened. "And you allowed this?"

Adriel finally looked away. "I did. But you must understand, we began with the best of intentions. At first, we welcomed the New Haveners, and they, us. Our relationship was one of mutual dependence. We ensured their survival, and they eased the hardship the possessed were experiencing with their fraying bodies. Then the New Haveners completed their escape tunnel and wanted out of Draven's Reach. That's when things changed."

"But... but don't the rest of the possessed use flesh golems like you do?" Ghost asked, her own voice small as she realized the magnitude of Adriel's crimes.

Adriel sighed. "Sadly, little one, they can't. The possessed's spirits are not as fully separated from their bodies as mine is—or yours, for that matter—and they retain a certain attachment to their former physical forms. Because of this, they can only be spirit jumped into shells that are similar."

"Shells, you say," I said stiffly. "But you mean player bodies, don't you?"

The lich nodded impassively. "Or more correctly, those bearing the blood."

"You said things changed when the tunnel was built," I said, ignoring this aside. "How?"

"Loskin took over the escape route, pronouncing it was too early for the New Haveners to leave. By then, the city was well-established, and its people had already been in the dungeon for over a century. What were a few more centuries? he reasoned. The archlich believed it would be better if we—New Haveners and possessed—left the dungeon together as a unified force: one army under him.

"And was *that* when you turned exile?"

"No," Adriel whispered. "Even then, I remained Loskin's staunch supporter. Farren, Loskin, and I might not have had any need for the New Haven players, but the possessed did, and we needed *them* to defeat the new Powers in the coming war."

I bowed my head to hide my expression. Adriel's hands were stained with more blood than I could easily swallow. "So, what finally changed?" I asked softly. "When did you leave the archlich's court?"

"When the stygians came," she replied neutrally.

I looked up. "This was after the escape tunnel was built?" I asked.

"A couple of centuries, give or take," she replied.

"Why then?"

"At first, we helped the city fight the nether off," Adriel replied obliquely. "But when it became apparent the void would not relent, when the harbinger arrived, when they began sowing the sector with seed after seed, and our losses kept mounting, then Loskin withdrew his support. He claimed it was better Draven's Reach fell to the void than we whittle away our forces trying to stave off the inevitable. He believes the new Powers are the true threat. We had to stay strong to face them. I disagreed."

"Why?" I probed.

"Because Loskin is wrong," she said simply. "The new Powers are a... nuisance, compared to the void. It will swallow the Forever Kingdom whole if it is allowed to. And, more than most sectors, Draven's Reach is crucial to the Kingdom's wellbeing. It cannot be allowed to fall."

My eyes narrowed. "Why is that?"

"There is a reason the stygians came here. A reason why they have deployed so many resources to ensure its fall."

"And what reason is that?" I asked.

Not answering, Adriel rose to her feet. "That is a whole other conversation, and one we can entertain later, but I think it's time to resume Ghost's healing." She stared at me piercingly. "Assuming, of course, you still desire my aid?"

I disliked that Adriel was keeping things from me, but right now that concerned me less than the question she had just posed. Knowing about the lich's dark past, could I—we—accept her help? I glanced at Ghost. *"What do you think?"* I asked bluntly, despite knowing Adriel could overhear.

Ghost took her time answering. *"I... like Adriel. Her thoughts are open and honest, her mind bright,"* she replied. Despite this, she still sounded uncertain. *"But... I don't know. People can be confusing."*

I nodded. We could indeed. I rose to my feet. "I will have to think about it." Saying nothing else, I left the room.

CHAPTER 361: A CRISIS OF MIND

Sitting at the entrance of Adriel's underground complex, I stared out into the dungeon, pondering the path ahead.

What is the right thing to do here?

Adriel had killed hundreds, perhaps thousands, if not directly then indirectly.

Every one of Elron's soldiers that had died, every New Haven citizen that had perished because of the void, and every young player whose life had been stolen to feed the possessed's undying existence could be laid at the hands of Adriel and her fellows.

Why do you care what Adriel did, or did not do, in the past, Michael?

Her crimes were not my own. And it was not like I would be allowing the possessed's persecutions to continue. Just the opposite, in fact.

I pondered the question for a silent minute before the answer finally dawned on me. If I was not careful, my path could end up mirroring Adriel's. What troubled me was less what *she* had done than what *I* might be forced to do in the name of my own quests and those I protected.

Charitably, Adriel's actions could be described as gray. She had only done what she did to protect those under her charge. As I had in the past...

Perhaps her actions were more morally repugnant than mine had been — a debatable question — but who was to say I wouldn't be pushed to the same lengths in the future? Whatever choices I made as an alpha or Prime, someone, somewhere along the line, would get hurt. This was something I would have to accept.

A burden I would have to bear. Just like Adriel did.

I might not agree with the choices the lich had made, but did that make her evil? Ruthless and callous, certainly. But not necessarily evil. I did not discount Ghost's opinion either. She liked Adriel. That meant something. And the lich's own regret was plain to see.

There is no right choice here, only a least wrong one.

Healing Ghost was a good thing. As was securing Adriel's aid to free the New Haveners. And as long as I committed no atrocities in pursuit of both these goals, I could live with myself for allying with Adriel. The lich's past crimes were her own to answer for.

Settled in my choice, I swung around and headed back into the complex.

*　*　*

Adriel began Ghost's healing as soon as I gave her the go-ahead.

Sitting quietly by the sidelines, I looked on, but there was little for me to see. Since Ghost was reclothed in a physical form, I could no longer see her spirit, and therefore, could not tell how Adriel's efforts were progressing. One hour into the process, though, I got my first clue.

The lich was frowning.

I tensed, waiting to hear what she would say, but Adriel did not stop casting. She kept going, spinning spell after spell over the next few hours. All the while, though, her frown kept deepening.

Finally, around midday, no longer able to stand the suspense, I blurted out, "What's wrong?"

The lich glanced over her shoulder, her face smoothing instantly. "Nothing, but perhaps it's time for a break."

"It's not nothing," I began. "I saw you—"

Adriel held up a hand, cutting me off. "We can talk in the other room. Let Ghost rest."

I glanced at the wolf, and sure enough, saw her eyelids were already drooping despite the earliness of the day.

"She needs all the rest she can get," Adriel added and headed for the door.

Nodding in reluctant agreement, I followed her out.

✻   ✻   ✻

"Something's wrong," the lich said the moment we entered one of the rooms at the other end of the corridor.

"But you just said nothing was wrong," I protested.

"I lied," she said smoothly. "It is best Ghost does not realize something is amiss."

I frowned, not liking the idea of lying to my companion. "And why's that?" I asked, at least willing to hear her out.

"It's the spirit healing," Adriel said. "It is not going as well as I thought. Something is holding the spell back from working."

My alarm grew. "Is it the harbinger? Did he do something to—"

"No, nothing like that. It's Ghost, I think."

I blinked. "Ghost? You're saying *Ghost* is hindering the healing?"

Adriel nodded gravely.

"Why would she do that?" I asked, confused.

The lich did not answer directly. "Have you given thought to what happens after Ghost is healed?"

I frowned. "We haven't solidified our plans for the immediate future yet, but I suppose we would—"

Adriel brushed aside my words. "I don't mean *your* plans. I mean what happens to Ghost."

"Ghost?" I was growing more lost by the second. "Why, I expect she will leave that awful body and—"

"Exactly."

I still wasn't any more enlightened. "You'd better spell it out," I growled, finally out of patience, "because I'm not following you."

The lich smiled lopsidedly. "What happens next is that Ghost leaves that 'awful body,' as you called it, and returns to being a disembodied spirit."

"*And?*" I asked, when she said nothing else. "What's wrong with that?"

Adriel threw up her hands. "Everything! Existing as a pure spirit is not easy, especially when you have spent the greater part of your life as one.

Ghost has just been given a taste of what it's like to be a physical being once more, and she doesn't want to let go."

I stared at Adriel. "You're saying Ghost is scared?" I asked slowly.

She nodded. "I understand you may not realize what it is like to be disembodied yourself, but trust me, for the uninitiated, it can be disorienting."

"Actually, I do understand," I said absently, recalling my time in the Mind Trials. That experience had not lasted long, but I could still vividly recall my happiness at being rejoined with my body. Finally, I got an inkling of what Adriel was driving at.

"So, you're saying there's nothing actually wrong with your spells, only that Ghost doesn't want to leave her new body?"

Adriel nodded.

I bit my lip. "Where does that leave us?"

Adriel tilted her head to the side. "Other than hoping Ghost accepts the healing? We could rehome her in a more suitable physical vessel, I suppose. The one she is in now was never meant to last long."

"Rehome," I repeated stiffly. "You mean like you do with the possessed?"

"Ghost is nothing like the possessed," Adriel replied, not responding to the sudden anger in my tone.

"How is she different?" I demanded.

"If you remember, I said the former scions' spirits could not be fully severed from their bodies. A part of them still resides in their original bodies—a finger bone to be exact—making them less complete spirits than Ghost."

I stared at her blankly.

"As spirits, the possessed cannot see, move, or hear as Ghost does," she clarified.

I nodded slowly. That tallied with what Ghost had observed of the dead Avery. "Where do the possessed keep their... finger bones?" I knew I was getting sidetracked, but given what Adriel was proposing, I realized I needed to more fully understand the possessed's nature.

"The bones must be sewn into the possessed's new shells after they are spirit jumped," Adriel answered.

"Why?" I asked, fascinated.

"Because they act both as an anchor and vessel for the possessed's spirits. When their bodies are slain, the possessed's spirits do not venture off as they normally would but stay leashed to the physical plane by that portion of their spirit still residing in the bones."

"But since a 'dead' possessed lacks full awareness or the appropriate spells they cannot revive themselves without the aid of a lich," I deduced.

"Very good," Adriel said.

I rubbed my chin. "So, if the finger bone is destroyed, then so too, is the possessed?"

"Correct."

"Alright, I understand all that, but what does it have to do with Ghost?"

"It *means* Ghost can be rehomed in a flesh golem, whereas the possessed cannot," Adriel answered.

"I see. But a flesh golem?" I asked skeptically, not sure how I felt about the idea. "Like one of your human ones?"

Adriel shook her head. "No, no, those would not suit Ghost. A bipedal form is foreign to her whole identity and her spirit will reject it."

"Oh." I paused. "Then if not those...?" I trailed off, waiting for her to fill in the blanks.

"I could always craft her a dire wolf golem—" Adriel began.

My eyes lit at the suggestion, but she quickly dashed my hopes.

"—but I lack many of the proper materials, and I doubt we will be able to source them in this sector."

I sagged slightly. "Is there anything else we can do?"

Adriel glanced down at her phylactery. "I suppose I could create something like this for her."

I stared at the small, glass object hanging at the end of the lich's necklace. "How will that work?"

"Any physical object, properly prepared, can serve as a vessel for a free spirit like Ghost. She will be able to shelter within it whenever she feels the need. However, the vessel will not be a substitute for a true body. When Ghost leaves it, she will still manifest as a spirit."

"Still," I mused intrigued by the possibility, "surely that is better than leaving her as she is?"

"It is," she admitted. "But there are downsides too. The binding will be permanent. Ghost won't be able to roam freely as she once did. She will be forced to remain in close vicinity to her vessel." She held up her phylactery. "And if the object is destroyed, so too is the spirit within."

"Hmm," I said, less enthused by the idea now. "What about another form of golem? One made of stone perhaps?"

Adriel snorted. "I'm not an enchanter. I can't work with inorganic material. I can only mold flesh." She paused. "But there is something to what you say. Perhaps a bone wolf golem..."

I perked up. "Could that work?"

"It could, but it will require a lot of bones," she muttered. "Or maybe..." Falling silent, the lich eyed me.

No, not me. My backpack.

"What do you have in there?" Adriel asked suddenly. "Anything organic?"

Wordlessly, I upended the contents of my bags before her.

The lich frowned at the items that spilled out. "Yes," she said finally. "I believe I could make use of some of this."

I opened my mouth, but before I could speak, Adriel held up a restraining hand. "I advise not rushing. Permanently binding Ghost to a physical vessel is a drastic step—irrevocable too—and it's not one I'm sure we should take just yet." She picked through the contents of my backpack. "Leave these with me and let me think further on it."

Reluctantly, I conceded the point. I wasn't sure waiting would make any difference, though. Ghost was headstrong, and once she set herself on a course, she stuck stubbornly to it. But it *was* a big decision, and not one that should be rushed.

"Good," Adriel said. "In the meantime, I will resume Ghost's healing. Perhaps, given a bit more time, she will prove more cooperative."

She didn't sound any more hopeful than me, though.

*   *   *

The day passed slowly.

Returning to the casting chamber, we found Ghost in the same position we'd left her. After shaking the spirit wolf awake, Adriel resumed her casting, working through her repertoire of spells again.

I kept a close eye on Ghost the entire time and conversed with her periodically. There was no immediate sign that something was wrong, but now that I knew to look, I sensed a certain heaviness in the spirit wolf's responses.

Her cheer was forced, and she avoided talk of the future. Adriel was right. Ghost was depressed—or something very like.

Hour by hour, I could see Adriel grow more frustrated, but she remained patient with the spirit wolf throughout. Towards nightfall, she called a halt, and turning towards me, shook her head minutely—a signal that the healing had not worked.

I bowed my head, contemplating the unhappy news. Her confirmation was nothing more than I had expected after my own observations. Sensing she needed the distraction, I said, "Perhaps it's time we spoke further about Draven's Reach?"

Adriel glanced at the already-drowsy Ghost. "Let's talk in the other room."

"Go ahead, I'll be with you shortly." I turned back to my companion. Her eyes were closed, but her mindglow still flickered with activity. She wasn't asleep yet. "Ghost and I need to have a quick chat first."

Halfway to the door, Adriel paused to study me carefully. "Are you sure about this?"

I nodded. I knew the lich didn't want to confront Ghost on the matter for fear of making things worse, but I believed I knew Ghost well enough to know that a direct approach was best. "It's necessary, I think."

Inclining her head gravely in a gesture that I took to mean "good luck," Adriel left the chamber.

Once Ghost and I were alone, I strode up to her and kneeled before her. "We need to talk," I said gently.

"I'm tired, Prime," Ghost replied, not opening her eyes. "Can't it wait for the morning?"

"This won't take long," I said.

She sighed. "Alright. Go on."

I sat down cross-legged, and after contemplating her for a moment longer, began. "This is a conversation we should have had long ago, but for one reason or the other, the occasion never arose. Still, now is as good a time as any." I paused. "You've stuck with me all these many days in the dungeons when, truthfully, you could have left at any time. I've never asked before, but I am now. Tell me, Ghost: what is it you want?"

"To sleep," Ghost quipped.

I smiled at her attempt at humor. "I don't mean immediately. I mean in general. What do you want for your future, Ghost?"

The spirit wolf seemed to shrink from the question. *"I'm not sure what you're asking. I want what I've always wanted."*

"And what's that?" I asked.

She did not answer.

I went on. "Adriel says you've been rejecting the healing and —"

"I haven't!" Ghost protested weakly.

" —I believe her," I finished.

I waited to see if Ghost had anything to add, but she remained silent.

"You can't stay like you are now," I said softly. "The body you're in will waste away soon, and when it does, your situation will be even worse. Adriel has nothing else readily available."

I took a deep breath before going on. We had come to the crux of the matter. "As I see it, you have three choices. The first is to return to spirit form, but considering your resistance to Adriel's healing, I take it that is not something you want. Am I wrong?"

Ghost said nothing.

Taking her silence as agreement, I continued. "Your second option is to die."

Ghost's eyes finally creaked open. *"Die?"*

I nodded, doing my best to keep my tone smooth and my words matter of fact. "You've lived a long time as a spirit, and no one will blame you if you want to move on, Ghost." I paused. "Is that what you want?"

"I don't want to die," she whispered.

Not letting my relief show at this admission, I waited.

"You said three options... what's the third one?"

I smiled. "There is a chance that Adriel can craft you another body."

Ghost raised her head. *"A permanent one?"*

I raised a hand to rein in the sudden excitement I sensed bubbling in her. "I'm not sure. She has some ideas. Do you want to discuss them with her?"

"Yes!"

I rose to my feet. "I'll send her right in then," I said as I headed for the door.

"Prime," Ghost said, stopping me.

Pausing, I looked back at her.

"I know what I want," Ghost said.

"And what's that?"

"To serve. To help raise House Wolf again."

I smiled. "Then you'd best attend to your recovery. We have lots of work ahead of us."

CHAPTER 362: FIGURING OUT THINGS

I didn't intrude on Ghost and Adriel's discussion.

As alpha and scion, I already had too much sway over Ghost, and I didn't want to influence her choice unduly. The form she chose was hers to decide. I had already played my own part and reignited her will to live. The rest was up to her.

Two hours later, Adriel returned to the room I sat waiting in. "Has she decided?" I asked.

"She has," the lich answered, not elaborating.

I didn't pry. "Good. Then, let's—"

"I will need your cloak."

I frowned. "My cloak?"

"Ghost has made her choice, and given its nature, she will require an anchor. For these things, it's always best to use a legendary item. They are nearly indestructible."

"Alright," I said slowly, "but if a legendary item is all you need, what about one of the others I don't use?"

Adriel shook her head. "No. It has to be the cloak. Ghost and I agree it's the best option." Not explaining further, she waited.

Sighing, I removed my cloak and handed it over.

You have unequipped the <u>Magister's Cloak</u>, losing 8% physical damage reduction and 4 Magic.

"Thank you," Adriel said solemnly. Folding the garment neatly, the lich took a seat at the nearby table. "Now come, we have much to discuss."

I sat down opposite her.

"First, well done with Ghost," Adriel said.

"Oh?"

"I thought you took a big risk by confronting her like that, but you chose the right tack, I think. Her attitude has shifted remarkably."

"That's good to hear." I gestured to the cloak I had handed her. "How long will the process take?"

Adriel shrugged. "It's hard to say. A few days, perhaps. But once the ritual is started, both Ghost and I will be out of touch."

"Then we should settle matters between us before then."

"I agree," Adriel said, leaning back in her chair. "To begin with, will you tell me your plans for the future?"

I nodded. "On the most basic level, Ghost and I need to get out of Draven's Reach. We could use your help."

"Of course," Adriel said. "I have already gotten started on that."

I frowned. "You have?"

"We'll get to that just now. What else are you hoping to achieve in the dungeon?"

I sat back. "Do you know why Ghost and I were in this region of the dungeon?"

She shook her head.

"We were looking for you."

Adriel tilted her head to the side. "Why?"

"The New Haveners," I replied. "They want out of the dungeon, too. But evacuating the city is a mammoth undertaking and we can't do it without you."

"You need the possessed neutralized first," she deduced, "which explains your interest in the mechanics of spirit jumping."

I shook my head. "Not just neutralized. Dead."

"You want to kill them?" Adriel asked disbelievingly. "All of them?"

"I do," I said, not shying from her gaze. "That includes the archlich. The only way the city can be safely evacuated is if all the possessed are slain and the tunnel from the city to the exit portal is unblocked.

Rising to her feet, Adriel began pacing. "This changes things," she muttered.

I frowned in disappointment. After learning Adriel's history, I suspected she might be reluctant to help. Exile or not, one did not easily betray people one had known for centuries. "Then you will not help?"

She spun to face me. "I didn't say that. But it renders all my plans moot."

"Plans? What plans?"

Adriel sighed. "I have already arranged for you and Ghost to be snuck through Loskin's court and to the portal."

My eyes widened. "You have? How?"

Her lips twitched upward. "Loskin may have exiled me from his court, but that does not mean I am without contacts among the possessed."

I slapped my forehead. "Your brother. Of course. You're still in contact with him."

"More than that. Farren and I have been working for years to figure out how to unseat Loskin."

It took me a moment to parse that. "So, wait. You're saying you are *not* opposed to the idea of killing the possessed?"

"I'm not," Adriel agreed. "But slaying the possessed is not necessary. It is only Loskin we have to deal with. Kill him and the others will fall into line."

I frowned. "I'm not so sure about that," I said thinking of Castor and Avery.

Adriel smiled. "You forget. Without Loskin, the possessed cannot resurrect. They will need the help of another lich."

My eyes narrowed. "Which means they will have no choice but to turn to you and your brother."

She shook her head. "Not me. I've already burned my bridges with the others, and most would rather see themselves dead than deal with me. But Farren... Farren they will work with."

I rubbed my chin thoughtfully. "You and your brother have all of this neatly worked out already, don't you?"

She nodded.

"So, why haven't you acted before this?"

Adriel sighed. "Loskin is not stupid. He sees the same weaknesses we do and has plans in place to guard against an uprising from within." She sat back down. "The problem has always been getting to his phylactery. Loskin has a mountain of wards protecting it, many of which have been designed to keep out other lichs. Neither Farren nor I can get within a dozen feet of those wards without setting them off."

"The other possessed won't help?"

"We have allies amongst them too," Adriel admitted. "But none of them can get through the wards undetected either. The only option is an open assault. That, however, risks a pitched battle in the court—which we would lose. We've been trying to whittle down Loskin's supporters, but Farren and I are still years away from being ready to win any internal power struggle." She pursed her lips. "Perhaps with the support of New Haven's army we could pull it off."

"What if I could get through the wards?"

Adriel looked at me dubiously. "You?"

"I am not a bad sneak," I said modestly. "And I have a few other tricks that may let me bypass the wards."

Adriel studied me curiously. "Can you pierce a rank six ward? Or for that matter, even perceive one?"

I hesitated, then shook my head.

She held up her phylactery. "This may look like ordinary glass, but it is immune to physical damage and all types of lower magic. It will take a tier five spell to destroy this. Do you have such a spell?"

Again, I was forced to shake my head. "No, but—"

"I'm sorry, Wolf, but I don't think you sneaking in is going to work. The moment you enter the vault, Loskin will know. Unless you can destroy his phylactery before he arrives, you will be dead."

I suspected she was right and didn't argue further, but there was another matter I needed to address. "Call me Michael, that's my name, and before we go any further, I think it's time I told you my own tale."

Adriel nodded "Go on."

I took a deep breath. "It all began..."

*　　*　　*

It took me over an hour to share my story with Adriel.

I started with the first day I'd entered the Game, and I took her through everything, glossing over much—especially those aspects I was unwilling to share with anyone yet—but in the end, I told her most of it.

The lich was someone I felt I could trust. But, beyond that, I wanted her help—and not only to escape the dungeon. Adriel possessed a wealth of experience, and her knowledge of the Houses and the ancients surpassed that of anyone else I had access to.

Simply put, I needed her wholehearted support.

"That's quite the tale... Michael," Adriel said when I was finished. "You've had a most eventful entry into the Game."

I laughed. "That's one way to put it."

I leaned forward across the table. "I know you've already committed to helping me, but will you teach me too? About the Houses, the ancients, the Primes, and everything else I need to know?"

Adriel smiled. "Everything is a tall order," she murmured. "But I take your meaning and I will try." Her smile flickered, then died. "Assuming we have time, of course."

I frowned. "I'm not sure what you mean."

"We've talked about Loskin, and we both agree he must die. But there is another threat in the dungeon that we've not spoken of yet."

"The stygians," I guessed.

"Correct. The nether cannot be allowed to claim Draven's Reach."

"You said something similar the other day, I recall. What makes this sector so important?"

Adriel steepled her fingers before her. "You've met a guardian, correct?"

I raised one eyebrow, surprised by the turn the conversation was taking. "That's right, Kolath. What of it?"

"Draven's Reach is home to another guardian named, not-so-coincidentally, Draven."

I stared at her in astonishment while I began to connect the dots in my mind. "That makes... sense," I said finally. "Is Draven a giant stone statue like Kolath?"

Adriel nodded.

"I've not run across him yet, then. Where is he?"

"In the center of the dungeon, not far from the safe zone."

I frowned.

"That's right," Adriel said, seeing my expression. "You've been to the safe zone already. But you wouldn't have seen him because of the nether."

My eyes narrowed as I put those two facts together. "I suppose it's no coincidence either that most of the nether in the dungeon is concentrated around Draven's location?"

A fleeting smile touched Adriel's lips. "You're correct; it *isn't* happenstance. Draven is under assault by the stygians and has been so for decades."

I pinched the bridge of my nose. Things were beginning to make sense. That a guardian was present in the sector raised the stakes significantly. It explained why a stygian Power—a creature who's like I'd never heard of before, much less seen—was present in the dungeon, it perhaps even explained the harbinger's distraction and the unusual use the seeds had been put to.

What I did not understand, though, was why the void would choose to attack a fortified point like Draven's Reach. By all accounts, the guardians were the ones upholding the barriers around the dungeons—which meant Draven Reach's own defenses would be superior to most.

I looked up at Adriel. "Why would the void strike here of all places, though? Wouldn't it make more sense for the stygians to invade other weaker dungeons first?"

"What makes you think they haven't?" Adriel asked mildly.

I opened my mouth to protest that I would've heard if they had, then closed it with a snap as I realized how naïve that sounded.

"The void has assuredly already claimed other dungeons," Adriel said, unconsciously echoing my own thoughts. "But I am sure the new Powers have gone to great lengths to cover up such instances." She threw me a wry look. "Players may not care about the odd Kingdom sector disappearing, but dare a dungeon go 'missing'? That *would* have them up in arms."

I found myself nodding in agreement. Were all those 'locked' faction dungeons in Nexus truly locked?

"But to get back to your original question: why Draven's Reach?" Adriel said. "It is no coincidence that the void is also present in two of the sectors connected to this one."

My brows furrowed. "Uhm, I don't follow."

"The New Haven's home sector has fallen to the void, and the hidden sector you entered from has also been invaded. What does that tell you?"

I pondered the question for a minute.

It *did* seem improbable, given how many sectors there were in the Kingdom, that three so closely interconnected sectors would be threatened by the void almost simultaneously. And if it was *not* coincidence, it meant...

"The nether can somehow sense the ley lines joining sectors," I said slowly, "and it is using them to spread."

"You've got it," Adriel said. "That's exactly how the stygians extend their reach. They follow the ley lines. It's how the void found Draven's Reach in the first place, and it is *also* why it is so desperate to claim this sector."

I scratched my head. "You've lost me again."

Adriel smiled. "Understandable. This is not stuff you should know. In fact, I suspect many of the new Powers don't either. It all centers around the guardian. Draven is tasked with upholding the barrier around dozens, if not more, sectors. Which means he himself is an anchor point for multiple ley lines, one for each one of those sectors. If Draven falls—"

"—then the void can claim those sectors too," I finished for her in dismayed understanding.

"Not only that," Adriel added, "but the guardians are all interconnected. They have their own network through which they communicate. One of those myriad of ley lines inside Draven will lead to another guardian."

I didn't need the lich to spell out the rest. "So, taking Draven's Reach will give the stygians another attack point from which to assault the rest of the network." I shook my head in bemused horror. "Moving from guardian to guardian, the nether can quickly overrun the entire Endless Dungeon that way."

"Not quickly," Adriel corrected. "The network is not as fragile as that, and the guardians themselves are tough and difficult to overcome. Even weakened as he is, Draven has been holding off the void for years."

"And," I said, articulating my thoughts aloud, "the guardians may have already taken measures to protect the network."

"What makes you think that?" Adriel asked curiously.

"Something Kolath mentioned. He said his brethren were not responding to his hails. Could Draven have severed himself from the guardian network, disconnecting himself from his fellows?"

Adriel rubbed her chin thoughtfully. "Perhaps... he would have had to have done it when he was awake, though."

"Then, that explains—"

I broke off as the implications of the rest of what Adriel had said penetrated. "Wait, Draven is asleep?" I exclaimed. "Why? He is under assault!"

The lich sighed. "The guardians are wondrous creations, one of the greatest marvels in a world full of such. But as powerful as they are, Draven and his kindred share the same weakness all constructs do: they must be powered."

Adriel's words sparked another half-buried memory. What had Kolath said? Something about receiving energy from the amulet I'd given him... "They require tithes from players to stay awake," I realized aloud.

"Correct. Every dungeon that houses a guardian is configured to provide its construct with the necessary energy to keep him or her awake." Adriel shook her head sadly. "But the dungeons can't do so alone. Player intervention is required. Players go through the dungeon and collect artifact fragments which they offer to the guardian, who uses them to replenish his energy stores. In turn, the players get rewarded for their efforts by the Game. A happy symbiosis—when it works."

I nodded. "But since Draven's Reach entrance sector has been overrun by the nether, no player has come through the dungeon for centuries and no one has completed the Emblem of the Reach." Digging out my collection of mosaic tiles, I spread them out across the table.

Adriel's eyebrows rose in mild surprise. "You've been busy, I see."

I chuckled. "I didn't collect all these on my own. Most I bought in New Haven," I said and explained about Gamil's shop.

Adriel laughed. "Enterprising of him." She placed a finger in the unfilled space in the Emblem's center. "But there is still a piece missing."

I nodded. "And I'm guessing you know how to get it."

She smiled. "I do. The final piece can only be obtained by slaying the sector boss."

I perked up in interest. "And where would I find it?"

"Not 'it,' *he*," Adriel corrected. "The sector boss is Loskin."

CHAPTER 363: THE FINAL PIECE

I stared at Adriel aghast. "The archlich? You're telling me the sector boss is the archlich?"

She nodded.

"But how?" I demanded. "The possessed were once players. How does a former player become a sector boss?"

She laughed humorlessly. "We were as surprised as you. But as Farren likes to say, the Game cannot be tricked. The Adjudicator sees all and has his own way of punishing those who bend the rules too much."

"What does that mean?" I asked, confused again.

Adriel smiled sadly. "Have you forgotten? Loskin, Farren, and I became lichs. The other scions became possessed. By doing so, all of us abandoned the compact we'd forged with our Houses. It did not matter that we did it with the best of intentions—we tore free of the bindings the Game itself stood witness to."

"Alright, I see your point, but what does that have to do with Loskin becoming a sector boss?"

"When we entered the dungeon, we gave the Game its chance—not that we knew it at the time. We then proceeded to compound our error by slaying the sector boss. That allowed the Adjudicator to punish us in keeping with his own rules."

I was still lost. "How?"

"Simple, really. When a sector boss dies, the Game grants the Adjudicator some leeway in deciding how the dungeon is repopulated. And we were no longer players. So, what better way for the Game to replenish the creatures we had killed than by making *us* part of the dungeon?"

"Wow," I breathed. "That must have come as some shock."

Adriel nodded solemnly. "It did."

My brow furrowed. "Wait... what happens if Loskin leaves the dungeon?"

Adriel smiled. "That's the thing. A sector boss cannot leave his dungeon. The Game itself keeps him in place."

"So, the rest of you can leave, but not the archlich? That must irk him!"

"You have no idea," she murmured. "Of course, if Loskin can't leave, the others won't either. He is their ticket to eternal life."

"Which brings up another point," I said. "If the archlich can't escape the dungeon, how does he intend on taking the fight to the new Powers?"

Adriel's eyes twinkled. "He is still figuring out that bit."

I grinned. "Making Loskin a sector boss was certainly a dastardly play by the Adjudicator." A moment later, I grew more serious. "Coming back to the guardian. You said earlier that Draven is weakened. What did you mean by that?"

"It is not only Draven. *All* the guardians are weakening. And when the guardians wane, so do the barriers protecting the dungeons—which is the only reason the stygians managed to invade this sector in the first place." Her face grew morose. "I fear what is happening here could also be happening elsewhere." She shook herself. "That is only fruitless speculation on my part, though. But, regarding your question, the reason behind the guardians' deterioration is also tied to their nature. How much do you know about the guardians?"

"Only what I told you," I replied automatically. "That they are constructs." I paused. "If unusually intelligent and powerful ones."

"And do you know why they are so intelligent?" she pressed.

I shook my head.

"The answer lies in the manner of their creation. When the Primes made Draven and his brethren, they were somehow able to bond spirit to inanimate stone, marrying a living being with non-living matter."

I blinked in surprise. "Are you saying... there is a *person* inside each guardian?"

"I am, and not just any person. Every guardian is a former scion, one who willingly sacrificed themself to protect the Endless Dungeon."

"I see," I said slowly. "But what does that have to do with Draven being weak?"

"Stone and rock may be eternal—or nearly eternal—but people aren't," Adriel said. "People tire. People long for rest, which is exactly what is happening to the spirit in this dungeon's guardian. His will has faded. He has performed his tasks well beyond the time he should have and now longs for the afterlife."

"Hmm," I mused. Adriel had just told me everything I needed to know to complete the silent brethren task, but the solution she described was going to be far from easy. "So, to restore Draven, we need to find a scion willing to take his place?"

Adriel nodded. "Yes, but there is no need to find someone. I intend on replacing him."

I stared at her in shock. "You?"

"I may not be a scion any longer, but given the situation, I don't think Draven or the Game will refuse me." She looked at me gravely. "There is no one else, and this way, I can make up for a small measure of the harm I've done."

I wanted to convince her otherwise, but what she proposed made too much sense. If not Adriel, it would have to be one of the possessed—or me. I couldn't see *them* volunteering, and I still had too much left undone in the Game. "That is a brave thing to do," I said, acknowledging her decision. "How would we go about it?"

"Then you will help?"

"Of course."

Adriel bowed her head. "Thank you," she whispered. A moment later, she regained her composure and continued, "Before I can take his place, Draven will have to be awoken."

I glanced down at the Emblem. "Which means killing the archlich and completing this."

She nodded.

"Then what?"

"That's when things get difficult," Adriel said reluctantly.

"Really?" I asked wryly. "Because I thought killing the archlich sounded challenging enough."

Adriel smiled, but her eyes remained worried. "The void tree, the driving force behind the nether's invasion in the sector, has taken root next to the guardian, blocking access to him."

"Ah," I exclaimed sitting back. "I'd been wondering when we'd get to the stygians. I'm assuming the tree is a problem. Is it a young tree?"

Adriel shook her head. "No, it's a sapling."

"Oh? That doesn't sound too bad."

"It isn't," Adriel agreed. "Void trees are powerful psionics, especially the older ones. This tree hasn't matured enough to pose that much of a threat yet, though. As long as we stay outside of its mental range, we can deal with it easily." She exhaled heavily. "However, it is not the tree we have to worry about, but its protector: the harbinger. The stygian Power doesn't often leave his charge." Her gaze darted to mine. "And as you know, when he does, he returns quickly."

My eyes narrowed. "What do you know of the creature?"

"The void frequently uses chimeras like the harbinger to protect young trees in newly claimed sectors or where the threat level is high. It is, in fact, where the name 'harbinger' springs from. The chimeras are often the void's forerunners."

"I see," I said softly. "From your tone, I take it you don't think we can kill the harbinger?"

"We *can*, but not in the vicinity of the void tree where the nether is thickest. You've been to the safe zone. What was the nether toxicity there?"

"Tier six."

"There you go." Adriel frowned. "Even assuming we can rally all the possessed to our cause and get through the nest surrounding the void tree, the nether itself would kill us before we could take down the harbinger."

"Can't you and the possessed shield yourself from the nether?"

"We can," Adriel said, waving aside my suggestion, "but not long enough to take down a foe as powerful as a harbinger and the no-doubt hundreds of stygians nesting around the sapling. None of us have anything like your nether resistance skill."

"That is a problem," I conceded.

"An impossible one," Adriel muttered. "Farren and I have been worrying about it for years. To disperse the nether, we have to kill the sapling. But to kill the sapling, we have to survive the nether and its protectors long enough to reach it."

"Couldn't Draven help?" I asked, thinking of the power I had glimpsed in Kolath.

"There's no guarantee he could. Maybe if we woke him. But to wake him—"

"—we have to slay the void tree first," I finished for her. "Right, I see the problem." Bowing my head, I pondered the situation.

"So, to summarize," I said a minute later, "we have to kill the archlich—which we can't do because his phylactery is out of reach. And we have to kill the void tree—which we *also* can't do because of the harbinger. Yet, we must accomplish both to evacuate the New Haveners and restore the guardian. If we don't, the entire Endless Dungeon could be at risk. Is that about it?"

Adriel smiled humorously. "It is. The unfortunate truth is we cannot do this alone. We need help." She leaned forward across the table. "Which is why I think the best approach is still for you and Ghost to flee the sector. Farren and I could have you out in a matter of days. Find help and return. From what you told me, you are on amicable terms with at least two different Powers."

I stared at her. "You want me to seek help from the new Powers? Your sworn enemies?"

Adriel's mouth twisted unhappily. "I told you: the stygians are not a threat that can be ignored. I abandoned Loskin because of them. And, as much as it pains me to go begging to the new Powers, I will do it if it means keeping the Kingdom safe."

I rubbed at my temples, contemplating the lich's words. I didn't doubt Adriel's sincerity, and her conviction served to spell out how severe the situation was. She was right, too.

No matter how much it galled me, if we couldn't come up with a solution of our own, I would have to approach Tartar, or even Loken, for help. But something else niggled at my thoughts, and closing my eyes, I waited for my conscious mind to catch up.

"Michael? Are you listening to me?"

I held up my hand for patience as the idea in my subconscious slowly germinated. *Yes*, I thought, contemplating it for a moment. *That can work.*

I opened my eyes. "I think we're going about this all wrong."

Adriel frowned. "What do you mean?"

"What if, instead of treating this as two separate problems, we tackle them as one?"

Adriel looked at me askance.

I leaned forward across the table. "Here's what I think we should do..."

CHAPTER 364: THE BEGINNING OF THE END

I left Adriel's underground complex the next morning.

After much back-and-forth last night, the lich had finally agreed to my proposal, conceding it might work. But only after I promised Ghost and I would leave the dungeon and seek outside help if it didn't. It took us hours more after that to beat out the details, but when we were done, Adriel and I were both convinced that the plan stood a reasonable chance of success.

Before leaving, I said my goodbyes to Ghost. It was too dangerous for her to accompany me where I was going. Besides which, it would take the lich at least a couple of days to finish healing Ghost's tattered spirit and molding her new body.

I still wasn't completely certain what the outcome would be, though.

Neither Adriel nor Ghost had deigned to enlighten me, and all I knew for certain was that the ritual would see Ghost housed in a new form that both she and Adriel believed suitable.

In the meantime, I had critical tasks of my own to perform.

Traveling as fast as I could manage, I headed south, not stopping until I reached the closest fog bank—which was about a half-day south of Adriel's compound. Drawing up to the edges of the mushroom-shaped cloud rising above the plateau, I slowed my steps and peered into the canyon below.

The fog bank was small, and its base measured only twenty yards from one end to the other. I rubbed my chin thoughtfully. There had to be a seed in there, although it couldn't have many stygians protecting it. The fog could be easily avoided, but it did not cross my mind to detour around.

The plan didn't call for that.

In fact, the plan required me to do quite the opposite.

Swinging over the edge of the cliff, I made my way into the canyon.

*　*　*

The nether toxicity at your current location is at tier 2. Your health, psi, stamina, and mana are degenerating at a rate of 0% per minute (damage reduced by 100% due to void armor).

Multiple hostile entities have failed to detect you! You are hidden.

A few minutes later, I was crouched in the fog bank studying the dozen or so crawlers and six weavers milling about in the mists.

Without Ghost, I lacked eyes to see my targets. On the other hand, my rank twenty nether absorption meant I was free from nearly all time constraints. Drawing on my stamina and psi, I cast my buffs.

You have cast heightened reflexes, load controller, fade, and trigger-cast quick mend.

Eighteen stygians. *This is going to be almost too easy.* It did not preclude me from acting, though. Spinning psi, I sent strands of my will racing towards the weavers.

You have induced 6 of 6 targets to sleep for 40 seconds.

The biggest threat taken care of, I rose to my feet and dashed light-footed towards the closest crawler.

The stygian did not sense my approach. Two feet from the creature, I drew both my blades and struck.

You have backstabbed your target for 2.5x more damage!
You have killed a stygian crawler with a fatal blow.

Rushing past the corpse, I dove into the middle of the three crawlers beyond, the blade in my right hand arcing down while the one in my left thrust outwards.

You have killed 2 stygian crawlers. You are no longer hidden!

Retracting both blades, I sidestepped the snapping jaw of the fourth crawler, then plunged my swords through the top of its head as it passed by.

You have killed a stygian crawler with a fatal blow.
You have faded from sight. Eight hostile entities have failed to detect you!

The last Game alert came as a bit of a surprise before I realized it was my fade buff at work. I hadn't been depending on it, though. Retreating a few paces, I faced the onrushing crawlers.

Alerted by the deaths of their fellows, the eight creatures were rushing towards my location in chittering fury. Drawing psi, I waited for them. It was far simpler to let the crawlers come to me than to run them down separately.

It didn't take the creatures long to gather. That's when I struck, releasing the spell I held ready.

You have charmed 8 of 8 targets for 20 seconds.

The bespelled crawlers ground to a halt, robbed of agency and leashed to my will. Smiling tightly, I stalked forward. It was time for a bit of slaughter.

✳   ✳   ✳

You have killed 8 stygian crawlers and 6 stygian weavers.
You have reached level 186!
Your telepathy has reached rank 19.
Your Mind has increased to rank 96. Other modifiers: +12 from items.

A minute later, I was standing in front of the stygian seed. All its protectors were dead, and the thing was defenseless before me.

I did not strike, though.

I had something altogether different in mind for the seed and it would entail picking it up. But first, I needed to prepare. Retreating, I opened my backpack and retrieved the upgrade gem I'd gained from slaying the Force Multiplier.

Adriel had been the least enamored by this part of the plan.

After I told her about the stygian seed's ability to read a player's thoughts—which had been the first she had heard of such—she had thought it too risky for me to touch a living seed. I'd assured her that my mind shield would protect me, but she had been adamant that I employ additional safeguards, and in the end, I'd reluctantly agreed.

Which was why I was about to improve my mind shield ability. Holding the upgrade gem in my open palm, I activated it.

Creating ability tome...

...

You have acquired an improved mind shield ability tome.

The gem disappeared, replaced by a leatherbound book, and I wasted no time opening it to absorb the knowledge contained within.

You have upgraded the mind shield ability to improved mind shield, which, unlike its simple variant, allows you to employ mindspeech even while fully shielded. The tier 2 variant not only doubles the damage your mental defenses can absorb, but when active, it also protects your mental communications, ensuring they cannot be overheard.

Improved mind shield is an advanced ability and requires 4 more ability slots than its simple variant. You have 35 of 96 Mind ability slots remaining.

My eyebrows shot up in surprise as I read the Game's description of the tier two mind shield variant. The improvements were greater than I'd expected and made me doubly glad Adriel had convinced me to upgrade. Now, though, it was time to get what I'd come for.

Turning back to the seed, I reached into my subconscious and transformed the psi sitting within into an insurmountable wall.

You have cast mind shield.
Psi abilities are unavailable. Mental communications protected.

Taking a deep breath, I approached the stygian seed. Glinting a malevolent black, it looked no different from others of its kind that I'd slain. *Does it know who I am?* I wondered. *Or what I plan to do to its... kin?*

I hoped not. The plan would be in tatters if the harbinger got any whiff of what we intended. Ignoring the rotten smell of the flesh strewn all around the small black object, I drew ebonheart and knelt beside it.

Then I began to dig.

Not slash, nor cut, but dig. Raising the indestructible sword up high, I drove it down into the ground, once more, abusing the black blade and using it for a purpose for which it was never designed. I smiled wryly, thinking it was amazing how often I found myself digging holes in the ground.

I really need an adventurer's kit or something like.

Chuckling at the thought, I hacked downward into the rock to which the seed was fused, over and over, until, finally, it came free.

Sheathing ebonheart, I stared at the small object. It was time to pick up the seed. Even though I kept telling myself there was nothing to fear, I felt my trepidation rise. But also, at the back of my mind was the knowledge that even now the seed could be squawking to the harbinger and every second I delayed gave him time to draw closer. Banishing my misgivings, I thrust out my arm and closed my fist around the thing.

You have acquired a stygian seed.

I could sense no foreign thoughts impinging on my own. Nonetheless, I didn't delay opening the bag Adriel had prepared and thrusting the black object inside.

You have stored a stygian seed in a warded container.

Snapping closed the enchanted bag's drawstrings, I rose to my feet and dashed for the chasm leading away from the canyon. I was sure the harbinger was on his way and before he arrived, I had to get rid of my burden.

I covered the distance without mishap and, finding a likely crevice, shoved the bag inside. Backing away a full one hundred yards, I threw myself into a small nook at the base of the chasm walls and wrapped myself in shadow.

You are hidden.

Glancing upward, I surveyed the skies. There was no sign of the harbinger yet. I exhaled a relieved breath. I had done what I needed to—with time to spare, it seemed—and now all that was left was to see if the bag performed as expected.

Settling in, I prepared myself to wait.

✳   ✳   ✳

Five minutes went by, ten, then twenty. And still, the harbinger did not come.

I frowned. The stygian Power had never taken this long to respond before. My gaze dipped to the leather pouch a hundred yards away. Did that mean the wards Adriel had woven around the bag were working?

The lich had enchanted the pouch with her strongest spells of concealment and imprisonment. No psi or magic, she had promised, would be able to escape the bag.

I didn't doubt Adriel's wards, but I *had* expected the harbinger to know the general location of the endangered seed. The fact that he hadn't turned up at all meant either he didn't or—

The ground shook.

A hostile entity has failed to detect you!

My nemesis had arrived. Craning my neck carefully around the edge of the nook, I peered into the canyon. The stygian Power had landed on the exact spot the seed had *formerly* occupied.

His beady eyes narrowed to slits, the harbinger scanned the area. I watched him intently, but at no point did he seem particularly interested in my nook or the crevice I had stowed Adriel's pouch in.

I grinned. The bag was working. The harbinger's failure to sense the seed was conclusive proof Adriel's wards were performing as advertised.

"Are you here, Wolf?" the harbinger asked suddenly.

I didn't respond, of course.

"This is your handiwork," the stygian said, continuing the conversation on his own. "I recognize the signs."

Padding softly across the canyon on his hyena-like feet, the harbinger poked his beak randomly into its many cracks and crevices. "It was quite the feat escaping my cordon, but in the end, it will make no difference."

Pausing at a particularly big hole, the harbinger stuck his neck all the way in before retracting it. "Your childish attempts will not stop us. It does not matter if you kill fifty chosen, or even a hundred, the void fathers will only sow the sector anew. The void *will* claim the sector."

Oh, I think it does matter. I think it matters very much, I thought. *Or you wouldn't be here.*

The temptation to respond was strong, but I remained steadfastly silent. The harbinger's seeming indifference this time around was starkly at odds with his previous bouts of anger, and I was sure it was only pretense.

Returning to the center of the canyon, the stygian swiveled around for one last look before stretching his wings and taking flight. I followed him with my gaze, and only when I was certain he'd gone did I emerge from the nook.

The test had been a success. Now it was time to move on. Picking up the warded bag, I resumed my journey south.

CHAPTER 365: COURT OF THE DEAD

DAY TWENTY-SEVEN IN DRAVEN'S REACH

It took me two days to reach the southeastern corner of the dungeon, and by the time I did, I had five more stygian seeds stored in my bag. In the process, I'd killed hundreds of stygians—which advanced my skills greatly and gained me a few levels too.

You have reached level 190!
Your Mind has increased to rank 100 and your Dexterity to rank 59.
Your telepathy and meditation have reached rank 20.
Your sneaking and channeling have reached rank 18.
Your shortswords has reached rank 17.
Your dodging and chi have reached rank 16.
Your light armor and two weapon fighting have reached rank 15.

Unfortunately, I ran across no opportunities to train my void Class resistances and only managed to maximize two other skills. Still, I was pleased with my overall progress.

All my core fighting skills were at tier four or higher. Most importantly, my telepathy—which I had worked on improving with almost single-minded determination—had reached tier five. It would play a significant role in the forthcoming battles, I expected.

The harbinger had turned up at every one of my forays into the fog banks but had only bothered landing twice more. Wary of a repeat ambush like the one I had fallen victim to the first time, I made sure to vary my path and leave some of the seeds along my route untouched.

In the end, I reached my destination without mishap.

* * *

Waking up on the morning of my twenty-seventh day in the dungeon, I emerged from the cave in which I had rested overnight and peered southwards. An elegant compound sat there, a mile away from me and backed up right against the dungeon's rim.

It was the archlich's complex. The so-called Court of the Dead.

There were no walls, towers, or parapets. The possessed had little need for such. There was a fence, though. Only three feet high, its primary purpose appeared to be demarcating the court's boundaries. Hopping over it would be laughably easy, but I was not about to do that. According to Adriel, a tier six ward circled the entire compound.

My gaze drifted to the iron wrought gate at the main entrance. That would be my entry point. Removing my scabbards, I extracted a blue robe from my backpack—another gift from Adriel—and donned it over my leather armor.

Many of the possessed in the court were not mages, and even they usually went about without robes. But Adriel had assured me that newcomers to the court were typically seen wearing the New Haven Mages' Guild garb and I would go unremarked in it. The guards at the gate would still be suspicious, but they should already have been dealt with.

Taking out another bag from my backpack—an oversized mage's satchel—I shoved my backpack and swords inside, then slung it over my shoulder. I had only one final preparation to make. Closing my eyes, I drew on my stamina.

You have cast facial disguise, assuming the visage of Castor, a level 209 human. Duration: 3 hours.

The disguise shouldn't be necessary, but there was no point taking unnecessary chances. In case everything didn't go according to plan, I would at least have an alternative to fall back on.

Finally ready, I pulled the cowl of the robe over my head and marched across the canyon, making my way to the court's entrance.

＊　　＊　　＊

There were six guards on duty at the gate. Judging from their many deformities, they were all possessed. Four were heavy fighters and two were rangers. All six guards had their hands on the hilts of their weapons, but none had drawn steel yet.

I had approached openly, and while the appearance of a lone stranger would have raised the gate guards' suspicions, the blue robe I wore should have allayed their fears.

Multiple entities have failed to pierce your disguise.

"Stop right there!" a one-eyed orc growled.

Ten yards from the closest guard, I drew to a halt.

"Who are you?" the scarred elf next to him demanded.

I scanned the guards but didn't recognize any of their faces. *Damn*, I cursed, wondering if the plan was falling apart already. Where was my contact? With no other choice, I improvised. Drawing back the cowl over my head, I rasped, "Don't you recognize me?"

"Castor," one of the human fighters greeted in surprise when he caught sight of my bald head. "Aren't you supposed to be in New Haven?"

"It's a long story," I coughed. "Open the gates. I need to see Loskin. He is expecting me."

A ranger's eyes narrowed. "What are you doing out in the dungeon alone?"

You have passed a mental resistance check! A hostile entity has failed to pierce your disguise and has been fed false analyze data.

I kept my expression bland, showing no sign that I'd caught the ranger's attempt to analyze me. "Didn't you hear me?" I sneered in Castor's exact tone. "The archlich wants to see me."

Letting my gaze skip from figure to figure, I analyzed each in turn. None of the six were elites, and all were lower leveled than me. If this went pear-shaped, I knew who to attack and in what order.

"But why didn't you use the tunnel?" the orc asked in a puzzled tone.

I opened my mouth, ready with what I hoped was a plausible lie, but before I could speak, another intervened.

"Don't answer that!" a red-bearded figure ordered, striding *through* the gates as if they were not there.

A telekinesis ability or mage one? I wondered.

Closing my mouth, I studied the newcomer. Unlike the others, he was unscarred and, judging by his appearance, he was the one I'd been told to look out for. To be certain, I reached out and analyzed him.

The target is Regus, a level 179 human.

It is him, I thought, exhaling in silent relief. Adriel's contacts in the court had come through. Regus swung on the orc and elf. "Did I not tell you two knuckleheads to let any visitors straight through?" he yelled in their faces.

The two shrank back from the thickset man, too fearful to even wipe the spittle spraying on their faces. "You did, but—" the orc began.

Regus leaned closer to the orc. "And did I not *specifically* request that you not question him?"

The orc shrank even smaller, if that was possible. "You did," he said glumly.

"Then what are you waiting for, you miserable sods?" he roared. "Let him through!"

Accelerating into motion, the six guards rushed to the gate and threw them open. "Better," Regus growled. Throwing me an indecipherable look, he said, "Come, this way." Not waiting for a response, he stomped through the gates.

Pulling the cowl over my head again, I followed wordlessly on his heels.

You have entered a tier 6 protection field. Only entities who have been granted access by the ward's controllers can pass through.

On the other side, Regus paused and swung around to face the guards. "I will deal with you lot later," he said ominously.

The elf gulped audibly, and the others appeared too afraid to speak. Satisfied they were cowed, Regus swung around and headed away with me striding along next to him.

"Hopefully that will scare them into keeping their mouths shut," he muttered when we were far enough from the gate to not be overheard.

"Will they be a problem?" I asked.

Regus glanced at me sideways. "That was foolish."

"Not showing them my face would have been even more suspicious," I protested.

"Not that." He threw me a hard look. "I meant taking Castor's face. Whose daft idea was that? The elite is well known in the court."

"Mine," I growled. "Would you rather I wore Avery's face? I don't know any of the other possessed well enough to mimic their voices." Although in hindsight, I suddenly recalled there was one other possessed whose visage I could have used—Davin's. *Better keep that to myself.*

"Why wear anyone else's face other than your own?" Regus retorted.

I blinked. "Wouldn't a stranger have been more suspicious?"

"No," he bit off angrily. "A stranger I could have explained away more easily than a damn elite who is supposed to be on the *other* side of the dungeon!"

"Oh."

"Bloody deception players, always complicating things needlessly," Regus muttered under his breath, but still loud enough that I was sure he meant me to hear.

"Well, perhaps if you had been at the gate as you were supposed to be, there would've been no reason to show them my face!" I snapped back.

Offering no excuse in return, Regus merely grunted.

I forced down my anger. This was not the time to be picking fights with my allies. "Where are we going?" I asked in a more even tone.

"Somewhere we can talk," the red-bearded man replied, his tone less aggressive.

Refraining from saying anything else, I gave my attention to the surroundings. The compound was replete with expensive-looking villas, paved roads, and manicured hedges, and was nothing like what I expected of a lich's lair. Obvious care and attention had gone into its design.

Only one building was multistoried—the mansion in the very center of the court. That, I knew, was Loskin's residence. His phylactery was stored in the vault directly opposite and, from all appearances, it was the only structure that had been designed with defense in mind.

The squat stone building looked like it could withstand an all-out assault. Turning away from the buildings, I studied the passing people.

They contrasted sharply with the idyllic settings.

Nearly every person bore some form of deformity or scar. Some were missing limbs, others had open sores running down their faces or arms, and a few even looked... partially decomposed. Only a lucky few were as unsullied as my companion.

"Stop staring," Regus said. "It'll give you away."

I tore my gaze away from the court's gruesome residents to find that Regus had come to a stop outside a tidy-looking building. "Whose home is this?"

"Mine," he replied and pushed open the door.

After I followed him inside, the big man locked the door behind me, and turning to the large ornamental statue in the foyer, pressed a hidden stud on its rear.

You have been enclosed in a ward of silence that will prevent any sound from escaping.

"Now we can talk," Regus said with grim satisfaction. Leading me into the next room, he sat down on a large couch. "So, tell me, what is this plan that has gotten Farren and Adriel all fired up?"

Chapter 366: Red Beard

I sat down opposite my host. "What did Adriel tell you?"

"Everything," Regus said carelessly, his gaze not straying from mine. "But I want to hear it from you."

I took his measure for a moment. "I don't think that's necessary."

He snorted. "You think I'm trying to trick you?" Lurching forward faster than I would have thought a man his size could, Regus stared at me from less than a foot away. "I know you are not really Castor. I know you are a player. And I know you've been talking to Adriel."

He held up three fingers. "Those three things alone are enough to get you strung up by the archlich and tortured for days." He sat back again, at ease once more. "I have no need to trick you, Wolf."

"So, Adriel told you what I am," I remarked mildly.

"*She* trusts me," he said in a tone that implied I didn't.

Which was fair enough, I supposed. Because I didn't. Still, it was too late in the game to be questioning my ally's judgment. "Alright, I said, "I'll tell you. But I think we're wasting time. If you already know the plan, we should get going."

"We can spare the time," Regus assured me. Spreading his arms expansively, he added, "Just tell me. It's always better to double-check and avoid later misunderstandings."

Also true, I thought. A sharp mind lurked behind the thickset man's bluff exterior. Shrugging, I told him what he wanted to know.

✳   ✳   ✳

"Satisfied?" I asked when I was done.

"Very," Regus said, rubbing his hands in glee. "Loskin will finally get what's been coming to him these long years." He rose to his feet, and I with him. "Now, we should—"

A loud bang interrupted him.

It had come from the door. Someone was pounding on it with a heavy fist. I spun around, hands dropping to my waist in search of blades that weren't there.

"Regus! Regus, you in there?" a loud voice demanded.

"Damn," my companion spat.

"What is it?" I asked tersely.

"That's Gork, one of Castor's cronies. The gate guards must have talked."

My lips turned down. It seemed like I was about to pay for my mistake at the gate. "Sorry," I muttered.

"Open up, dammit!" Gork yelled.

Regus very graciously waved aside my apology. "Don't worry. We'll deal with it." He eyed my blue robes. "You're armed?"

"Always."

"Good, get ready. This might turn ugly."

Nodding sharply, I withdrew my sword belts from the mage's satchel and equipped them before following Regus into the foyer.

"I'm warning you! If you don't open this door, we'll kick it down," Gork threatened.

Standing next to the ornamental statue, Regus looked at me and held up a thick finger to his lips.

"Go," I mouthed, as I crouched down in the room's darkest corner.

You are hidden.

The red-bearded man's eyes widened slightly as I disappeared from his sight, but he did not remark on it. Pressing the hidden stud on the statue, he placed himself in front of the door.

"We know you're in there, you big oaf! Open up this bloody—"

Regus yanked open the door.

"What did you call me?" he asked ominously.

Someone tried to shove through, but Regus's big frame blocked them. From where I'd placed myself, I couldn't see who it was, but I suspected it was the loud Gork. Drawing on my psi and stamina, I began casting my buffs.

"Where is he?" Gork demanded.

"Who?" Regus asked innocently.

"Don't play the fool," Gork sneered. "Senak told us you escorted Castor in."

You have trigger-cast quick mend.

Senak, I recalled from my earlier analyzes, was the elven gate guard.

"Then he must have also told you it was on Loskin's orders," Regus growled. "Where Castor is, is none of your goddamn business."

You have cast fade.

"Come, Regus, be reasonable," another voice interjected. "You know who Castor is to us."

My hands tightened around the hilt of my blades. I recognized that voice. It was Avery. Twenty days had passed since I'd killed him, and I supposed it was no surprise he was back already.

"That's no concern of mine," Regus said, folding his arms across his chest.

You have cast heightened reflexes and load controller.

"It's only I scryed Castor two days ago and then he was still in New Haven," Avery continued as if Regus hadn't spoken. "There's no way he traveled overland across the dungeon in two days." The possessed paused. "Whoever you let in, it wasn't Castor."

Regus stiffened in a remarkable pretense at surprise. "What?"

It looked like things were going awry. Preparing to shadow blink, I opened my mindsight. If we killed Avery and Gork quickly, the plan could still be—

Twelve consciousnesses appeared in my awareness, all crowded around the door. Avery and Gork were not alone. *Hells.*

I couldn't kill that many on the open streets without being observed. I settled back down. Perhaps, my new ally would think of something.

"Someone has been lying to you, Regus," Avery said. "Whoever gave you your orders, it wasn't Loskin. I want to know who it was and where they told you to take Castor."

My eyes narrowed. Interestingly enough, Avery did not appear to suspect Regus of being the traitor.

"I let an intruder in?" Regus muttered, his shoulders sagging.

"Yes, you did," Gork chipped in smugly. "Regus the infallible has finally been fooled!"

Ignoring Gork, Regus moved aside from the doorway. "Come on in," he said, hanging in his head shame—he really was an admirable actor. "Let's talk inside."

Not suspecting anything amiss, Avery and Gork accepted the big man's invitation. Ten others trampled through after them. Gork was a half-orc, and the others were a mix of dwarves, elves, and humans.

Multiple hostile entities have failed to detect you! You are hidden.

I was tempted to burst out of hiding then and there, but my ally was handling things well so far, and I stayed put, waiting for his cue.

Regus closed the door. "Follow me," he said, pushing past the other possessed. "We can chat in the lounge." Just before he stepped out the foyer, his gaze paused—as if by happenstance—on my corner before flitting to the statue.

Getting the message, I nodded, even though Regus had no way of seeing my response.

* * *

After Avery and Gork's gang marched out of the room and into the next, I rose from my crouch and tiptoed to the statue. The stud on the rear was cleverly concealed, but having observed Regus earlier, I knew its approximate location and found it easily.

You have been enclosed in a ward of silence that will prevent any sound from escaping.

I turned to face the open doorway leading to the lounge. Gork and Avery were in the center of the room while their followers were bunched up near the entrance. The half-orc was yelling again. "I'm telling you this was the satchel he was seen carrying!"

I drew psi. The time to act had come. Focusing on the six rearmost of the hostile possessed, I flooded their minds with psi.

You have cast slaysight.
You have induced 4 of 6 targets to sleep for 40 seconds.
Your mental intrusion has gone undetected!

The sound of four bodies hitting the ground carried loudly to my ears. I paid them no mind. Drawing psi, I began a second casting.

Midstream, Gork broke from his rant. "What was that?" he asked, then, obviously spotting the prone fighters, he demanded, "What did you do to them?"

Regus snorted. "Did to who? Those idiots following you? You've been standing next to me the entire time. What could I possibly have done to them under your eagle eye?"

In the middle of my spell I was only half-listening, but even so, I didn't fail to hear Avery's response. "There's someone else here," he said tersely, not as slow on the uptake as Gork. "We're under—"

My spell completed before he could finish, and I released the casting, driving psi into the minds of the eight hostiles still standing.

You have cast mass charm.
4 targets have passed a mental resistance check!
You have charmed 4 of 8 targets for 20 seconds.

"—attack!" Avery snapped. "Draw your weapons and defend yourselves!"

Unsheathing my own blades, I dashed into the room. Only four of the twelve possessed were still a threat, Gork and Avery included.

But they did not remain amongst the living for long.

Before I could cross the threshold, Regus whipped his spiked maul around in an arc that ended at Gork's face, pulverizing the half-orc's head in a single, mighty blow.

Gork has died.

Avery spun on him in shock. "What are you—"

He didn't get to finish as Regus heaved his bloody weapon up and around before bringing it down in a two-handed chop that caved in Avery's skull— and kept going.

Avery has died.

Even from halfway across the room, I couldn't help but wince at the puddled mess. *Note to self: don't get on Regus' bad side.*

Staying by the door, my gaze flickered to the remaining two possessed. On observing the swift demise of their leaders, both turned tail and, obligingly, headed my way.

Perfect.

I let the first pass, and then as the second drew even with me, I struck.

You have backstabbed a level 168 human monk for 2.5x more damage!
You have killed your target!
You have backstabbed a level 155 elven ranger for 2.5x more damage!
You have killed your target!

Neither possessed saw my attacks coming and both fell without resistance. Stepping over the corpses, I entered the lounge. "Yikes," I muttered, studying Regus' blood-spattered clothes and the bits of gore all over his hands and face. "You look a sight."

Ignoring my remark, Regus casually wiped his face clean with the back of his hand. "What's wrong with them?" he asked, pointing to Avery and Gork's bespelled followers.

I gestured downward, "Sleeping—" then at the others—"charmed."

Regus grunted. "Nice work. I thought we were going to be in a spot of bother there." He hefted his maul. "Now, let's see to it that none of them can trouble us further."

CHAPTER 367: A DEAD BROTHER

You have killed a level 132 dwarf.
You have killed a level 143 human.
...
...
Your deception has reached rank 15, allowing you to learn tier 4 abilities.

When our gory handiwork was completed, twelve corpses littered the room. A ghostly presence hung above each—the possessed's shackled spirits.

I studied them in fascination. Ghost's description of the spirit she had seen all those days ago had been apt, I realized. The possessed's forms were less dense than hers—as if they were missing parts of themselves. Their eyes, too, were strangely vacant and empty. Lifeless.

"What a goddamn awful mess this is," Regus muttered.

Tearing my gaze away from the motionless spirits, I surveyed the hacked-up corpses, pooling blood, and drenched couches, and was inclined to agree. "That maul of yours certainly left an impression."

Regus snorted. "I'm not talking about the room. I'm talking about the situation. The plan has gone to shit."

I sighed. Unfortunately, I couldn't disagree with that statement either. "I think it's time to—"

Another knock sounded on the door.

Regus and I froze.

A split-second later, both our hands dropped to our sheathed weapons. Our reactions were so identical, in another situation it would have been comical.

"You expecting someone?" I asked sharply.

Regus shook his head. "You activated the silence ward, right?"

I nodded.

"Then, no one could have overheard—"

"Open up, Regus, it's me," a cultured voice whispered from the other side of the door. But, despite being softly spoken, the words carried clearly into the room.

The red-bearded giant next to me relaxed.

"Who is it?"

"Farren." He paused, then added, as if I needed to be told, "Adriel's brother." Exiting the room, he rushed to the door. "I'd better let him in."

* * *

The resemblance between the siblings was unmistakable.

Farren was an older, more aged version of his sister, but the lines on his face were less harsh, giving him a gentler mien. Stepping daintily over the corpses, the lich entered the room. "So," he remarked as he sized me up, "this is our savior-to-be."

Despite the gentle mockery behind his words, the lich's pale eyes glowed warmly. I inclined my head in greeting. "Adriel has told me much about you."

Farren chuckled. "She has? She must have taken a liking to you then. My sister has never been one to cultivate friends."

He, on the other hand, had friends aplenty, I could tell. "I like her, actually," I said with a shrug. "I found her honesty... refreshing."

Farren placed his hand against his chest. "Duly noted." Turning his gaze downwards, he acknowledged the corpses strewn across the lounge for the first time. "You've run into problems, I see," he said, addressing the remark to Regus.

The big man shrugged. "Nothing we couldn't handle."

Farren nodded, still running his gaze across the room. His eyes narrowed as they fell on one particular corpse. No, not on the corpse, I realized, but on the ethereal figure floating above it. "Is that... Avery?"

Regus nodded curtly.

The lich sighed. "I see he beat me here, then."

Regus frowned, as did I.

Catching sight of our expressions, the lich explained, "The gate guards didn't just carry the tale of Castor's return to Avery, they sent a report to the court too. Luckily, I was able to intercept the message before it got to Loskin." He sighed again. "But it's only a matter of time before the archlich hears." His eyes found mine. "We will have to accelerate matters."

My frown deepened, but before I could address his comment, I let my gaze drift to spirit-Avery. "Is it safe to talk in front of... them?"

Farren's eyebrows rose in surprise. "You can see—" He broke off. "Of course you can. I forgot about your spirit companion."

Regus straightened curiously at this, but Farren didn't enlighten him. "Don't worry about the dead," the lich said. "They will not remember anything they see in this form." He rubbed his forehead. "Still, they are why we will have to move things along."

The original timetable, as conceived by Adriel and me, only required us to kick things off tonight during the possessed's sleep cycle, when their guard would be at its lowest. That would have left me with ample time to get a feel for the court's layout and complete my own preparations. But now, Farren wanted to hurry things along.

"Why?" I asked bluntly.

"Loskin will realize the impossibility of Castor showing up as quickly as Avery did," Regus said, answering in the lich's stead. "He will suspect an intruder, or worse, a dungeon party."

I blinked in surprise. "The archlich is worried about an invasion of players?"

Regus nodded. "Loskin knows you are in the dungeon; Avery made sure of that. And where there is one player there is always the chance of more. The entire court has been placed on high alert." His lips turned down sourly. "It is why, despite my orders, the gate guards questioned you as they did." He shook his head. "Anyway, when Loskin finds out 'Castor' was brought here—and he *will* find out—he will launch an investigation."

"I see," I muttered.

"It is not only the false Castor that will worry Loskin, though." Farren glanced at my companion. "When he hears of Regus' involvement, his concern will grow tenfold."

"Because Regus is the court's head of security?" I guessed.

The red-bearded man nodded. "I've served Loskin faithfully for centuries, acting first as his bodyguard, then as his security chief. I know all the guard routines, every passcode, and all the safeguards."

"As far as Loskin trusts anyone, he trusts Regus," Farren said. "Which is why the first thing Loskin will do when he learns of Regus' betrayal is change everything." He paused. "He might even move his phylactery to an alternate location."

I winced. That *would* be a disaster. I rubbed the side of my face unhappily. There seemed to be no end to the problems created by me wearing Castor's face, and I regretted the impulse that had spurred the decision.

Farren turned to Regus. "You will have to flee."

"I agree," Regus said, with no regret showing on his face. "I have a hideout prepped and waiting outside the canyon. I will leave immediately."

"Not necessary," Farren said. "One way or the other, this will all end soon. You can take shelter in my mansion."

Regus hesitated then nodded. "Thank you."

Farren looked at me. "Are you ready to begin?"

I nodded. "Do you have the stuff Adriel promised?"

The lich waved his hand, and a black leather bag materialized on the floor. Leaning forward, I inspected the contents.

The targets are 6 x piles of raw meat, 1 x set of finely-made black robes, a simple shovel, and a steel key.

"You included a shovel, too?" I asked with a lopsided grin.

Farren looked at me strangely, no doubt wondering at my sudden bout of amusement, but he didn't remark on it. "I thought it might come in handy."

"It will," I assured him.

"Is that everything you need?"

I nodded. "What about the protection field? Will you be able to bring it down early?"

Farren tutted unhappily. "I arranged for my people to be posted on duty tonight. Changing the roster at this late stage is not possible." He sighed. "The mages maintaining the shield at the moment are not friendly to our cause. I'm afraid we'll have to kill them." He paused. "I will do it myself."

"But that will compromise the rest of the plan!" I protested.

Farren grimaced. "I know. But we don't have any choice."

"There must be another way," I growled. Bowing my head, I began pacing. In order for the plan to work, the court's defenses had to stay down for at least a few minutes *and* Loskin had to continue trusting Farren—as much as he did anyway.

Even then, things could get dicey. But to proceed with neither of those things was suicide.

I ground to a stop and faced Farren. "What about Adriel?" She only intended on arriving later tonight, and while we didn't need her just yet, her presence was essential for the finale.

"I've contacted her already," Farren said. "Adriel will be here when we need her."

That at least was a relief. I resumed pacing. "What if I kill the mages on duty?" I asked a moment later.

Regus laughed. "Killing the mages is not the problem. The shield's focus stone is in Loskin's mansion and is triggered to sound an alert the moment it goes down. The archlich will respond to the alarm. He will kill you without even breaking a sweat. Farren at least has a chance of surviving his wrath long enough to escape."

"And if the archlich wasn't there?" I persisted.

"You mean what if we draw him out?" Regus asked. He tugged at his beard, thinking it over. "Loskin almost never leaves his mansion. I don't think—"

"What if I tell him about the bodies I found?" Farren interjected. He looked around meaningfully. "In this house."

Regus frowned. "You mean to inform him of my 'treachery'?"

"Yes." Farren's eyes twinkled. "It might even allay some of Loskin's suspicions about me."

Regus grunted. "It might work. Or it might send Loskin hurrying to the vault to relocate his phylactery."

My gaze flitted between the two. "I don't understand. Why would telling the archlich about Avery and Gork's dead gang make him come here?"

Regus looked at me. "Interrogating the dead is the quickest way to get answers, and for obvious reasons, Loskin won't trust Farren to spirit jump them. He'll come himself."

It wasn't obvious to me, and I looked inquiringly at Farren.

The lich smiled wryly. "Ever since Adriel's exile, I've been living under a cloud of suspicion. Loskin would have gotten rid of me long ago if he dared, but he needs me too much to risk that."

I bit my lip, pondering the information. "So, the only way for Loskin to learn the truth about the dead possessed is to question them himself?"

Regus and Farren nodded.

"But if he suspects Regus is behind the deed," I continued, thinking aloud, "he might not bother with that and instead seek to secure his phylactery."

Farren grinned wryly. "Oh, he will bother, but only after he is satisfied his spirit is safe."

"And we can't hide my involvement, if that's what you're thinking. Too many people saw Castor with me, and by now the news has spread."

I waved aside his suggestion. "What if you don't flee?"

The big man stared at me blankly. "What, you mean stay here and wait for Loskin?"

"That's exactly what I mean," I said.

"Are you mad?" he asked, appalled. "I've served the archlich for centuries. I know the dark measures he uses to extract information from his victims." He shuddered. "There's no way I will voluntarily subject myself to his torture."

"I'm not asking you to let him torture you," I replied. Before he could respond, I spun to Farren. "How long does it take to rehome a spirit?"

The lich's brows creased. "Regus is right. The moment Loskin sees him here alive, he won't wait to raise the dead—he will torture Regus for the answers he needs."

"Just tell me, please," I said, only a little impatiently.

The lich stared at me impassively for a moment. "Two hours usually," he said finally. "One hour at best."

"One hour," I murmured. "I can work with that."

"But that still leaves the problem—" Farren began.

"—Of Loskin torturing Regus. I know." I held the red-bearded man's gaze. "But he can't do that if Regus is dead."

Regus's eyes widened. "Dead? As in, really dead?"

"Correct," I said. "If Farren reports you dead alongside Avery and Gork's men, he won't have a reason to suspect you of treachery, would he?"

Regus nodded. "Hmm. Yeah, I can see that, but—"

"Of course, Loskin will still suspect foul play, but to confirm those suspicions, he will have to raise you from the dead first, won't he?" I asked.

Regus nodded again. "But still... you want to kill me?" he asked in a half-strangled voice.

I shrugged. "It's not like you won't come back. You are a possessed, aren't you?"

The big man had no answer to that.

"And this way we buy the hour we need," I concluded.

Farren clapped his hands. "I like it," he laughed.

Regus glared at him. "Of course you do," he muttered. "*You* won't be the one dying."

The lich ignored him. "Adriel did say you were a tricky one. I see she was right."

"So, are we agreed?" I asked.

"We are," the lich replied.

I turned to Regus.

He sighed. "All right, let's do it."

Chapter 368: Drawing out the Subject

"So, how do you want to die today?"

Regus stared at me blackly, unamused by my glib question. "One quick strike through the heart," he said finally. "That's the cleanest."

I nodded. "As you wish."

"Ready?"

"I'm ready," he confirmed, squeezing his eyes shut. "Make sure you—"

Lunging, I thrust ebonheart forward.

You have killed Regus with a fatal blow.

The big man's eyes snapped open in momentary shock before the light in them faded, and he slumped lifelessly to the floor.

Farren chuckled. "You don't waste time, do you?"

I turned around to face him. "How would that have helped? He was already struggling with the idea. Better it was done quick and clean."

"I don't disagree," the lich said. He tilted his head to the side. "Is that what you want, too?"

Farren was referring to another key element of the plan—at least that's what I hoped he was referring to. Gritting my teeth, I spread my arms wide and exposed my chest. "Do it."

The lich did not need to be asked twice. A split second later, a jagged scar of darkness rushed across the room to strike me dead-center.

You have failed a magical resistance check! You are <u>stunned</u>. Duration: 6 seconds.

A darkness bolt has injured you!

The black bolt sent me hurtling across the room to crash against the far wall. "Owff," I exhaled as the air rushed out of me, and I sank to the ground in a parody of Regus. For a few seconds, helpless to do otherwise, I sat there dazed and incoherent.

"Ouch," Farren remarked when the stun wore off. "That looked like it hurt. Did it do the trick?"

Now I know how Regus felt, I grumbled. Ignoring the lich's inquisitive gaze, I staggered upright and checked the waiting Game messages.

Void armor charge remaining: 73%. Your health has decreased to 47%.

Farren had attacked me with a tier six dark magic spell. But since I was not in actual combat, my null force skill had not advanced. The Adjudicator could not be fooled that way. That lack, though, would not stop my void armor from functioning.

"Not quite," I admitted. "It'll take one more hit."

The lich raised his hand.

"Wait!" I said, gesturing frantically for him to stop. "Let me heal first."

"Oh, right," Farren said, hiding a grin as he lowered his arm. "Go ahead."

Glaring at the lich for good measure, I summoned psi and set about restoring my lost health.

I had not attempted to use my void armor in this way before for obvious reasons. Doing so risked revealing my Class. But too much rested on the outcome of the forthcoming battle to let secrecy hamper my efforts. The whole purpose of abusing my void armor this way was to gain a spell capable of destroying the archlich's phylactery. There was more to it, though.

Farren had deliberately used dark magic and not a spell from his primary magical discipline, death, against me. All three lichs—and the harbinger, for that matter—were immune to death magic. So, not only would the stolen spell help me destroy the lich's phylactery, but it might also come in handy against my nemesis.

You have healed yourself of all injuries. Your health is at 100%.

I was ready again, and before I could reconsider, I gestured for Farren to proceed.

A second bar of blackness flashed across the room.

A darkness bolt has injured you!
Void armor charge remaining: 46%.
Void thief triggered! Void siphon and negate activated!

"Goddamn, that hurt," I cursed as I picked myself up six seconds later. Farren waved away my complaints. "But did it work?"

You have acquired the direct-targeted spell darkness bolt (stolen), from the lich, Farren and will retain memory of it for the next 12 hours.
Darkness bolt (stolen) is a tier 6 piercing spell that will bypass shields and magical wards of tier 4 and lower. It is especially difficult to resist and will deal pure Force damage. Targets struck by the spell may be stunned.

Wiping away the bloody smear from the corner of my lip, I smiled at Farren. "Got it."

The lich shook his head in rueful admiration. "That's a powerful ability you've got there. Imagine what you could do in the right party."

I nodded, having the very same thought. It was too bad I didn't have more higher-leveled allies with whom I would voluntarily share knowledge of my void thief ability with. Still, stealing spells from my allies at opportune moments was something to keep in mind for the future.

Now, though, it was time to see to my final preparations. Removing the mage's robes I'd used to get here, I inspected the faces of each of the corpses closely.

"What are you doing?" Farren asked curiously.

"Looking for a new disguise," I replied offhandedly.

"Ah," the lich exclaimed. He pointed out a brown-haired human ranger. "Use him. No one will think it odd seeing him near Loskin's mansion."

I didn't bother asking why. "What's his name?"

"Bartimus."

"Thanks." I peered intently at the dead ranger's face for a moment, memorizing its lines and curves, then took it for my own.

You have cast facial disguise, assuming the visage of Bartimus, a level 138 human ranger. Duration: 3 hours.

Re-equipping my swords and backpack, I strode across the room and picked up the bag the lich had brought for me. I was finally ready.

Farren's face grew serious. "Before you go, I have one last gift to impart."

I looked at him questioningly.

Not explaining, the lich stepped forward and rested his hand on my shoulder. My arm began to tingle at the point of contact, and from there the sensation spread rapidly to encompass my entire body.

Farren has cast reaper's shield on you, granting you the buff: <u>death's favored</u> (+75% death magic resistance). Duration: 1 hour.

"Wow," I exclaimed. "That's some buff."

The lich smiled. "It might just save your life if Loskin catches you unawares." He grinned lopsidedly. "Or at least, let you survive his opening salvo."

I chuckled. "I'll do my best to not let it come to that."

"You do that," Farren said, patting my arm. He stepped back. "I guess it's time we part ways."

I nodded. The clock was ticking, and soon someone else would come to investigate. "Good luck," I said, and turning about, strode towards the door.

"The same to you, Wolf," Farren called back.

✱　✱　✱

I exited the building but did not immediately leave the vicinity. There was one more thing I needed to do before I could head to the court's center.

Glancing left and right, I checked both approaches to Regus' house. It was 'morning' in the compound and the streets were busy, but no one appeared to be paying me any particular attention.

Satisfied, I turned right into the street, walking casually, until I was a couple of villas away, then crossed over and concealed myself in an inconspicuous cranny.

You are hidden.

Less than a minute later, a familiar figure materialized outside of Regus's house. Farren. Swinging left into the street, he cut left again at the first crossroads. Heading for Loskin's mansion.

If everything went to plan—the *new* plan, I thought wryly—the archlich would soon be making an appearance. Folding my arms and bowing my head, I settled myself to wait.

It would not be long now.

Less than ten minutes later, a large procession turned onto the street, heading in the direction of Regus' house. Two black-robed figures were at their fore. One was Farren.

The other had to be Loskin.

Straightening, I studied the archlich intently. Loskin was gaunt and, judging by appearance, his current flesh golem was even older than Farren's. His colorless eyes were deeply sunken, his hands skeletal, and his head and hands were completely hairless. Not even eyebrows troubled his face.

He was a grim-looking figure indeed, and one I felt no little trepidation in observing, but Adriel had assured me Loskin had not invested heavily in Perception. My surveillance should go undetected. Reaching out with my will, I inspected the rail thin figure.

The target is Loskin, a level 292 archlich.

Pursing my lips, I whistled soundlessly. Adriel had been right; the archlich was close to becoming a Power. He would not be an easy foe to tackle alone—but I had no intention of doing that.

My gaze skipped from Loskin to the rest of his party. My analyze had gone undetected, and no one had glanced my way. Without pause, the entire retinue—made up of an untold number of hangers-on and bodyguards—strolled into Regus's house.

That was my cue to leave.

Slipping out of my hiding spot, I dashed onto a side street and, affecting a nonchalance I didn't quite feel, headed for the court's center. Loskin was temporarily out of play, leaving me an hour to complete my tasks. It should be enough time, but I'd had no chance to scout the terrain beforehand and was unhappily aware of the risks that entailed.

I would have to rely completely on Adriel's information and deal with any unforeseen complications as they came. Still, I was as prepared as I could be given the circumstances.

As I walked, I swept my gaze from left to right. None of the passersby gave me a second glance—which was good. So far, it seemed the deaths of Gork, Avery, and Regus had not troubled Loskin enough to sound a general alert.

Shortly, I reached the large central courtyard in the middle of the archlich's compound. Standing on its rim, and partially concealed in the shadow of a building, I scanned the area.

To my left was the archlich's mansion. To my right, and directly opposite Loskin's home, was the vault. The two buildings contrasted sharply with each other.

Where the mansion was all elegant lines, tall, and replete with open windows, the vault was a squat, brooding structure with only a single reinforced door to serve as an entrance. A statue fountain lay between the two buildings, its edges trimmed with hedges and flowers, and I made straight for it.

There were three possessed nearby, chatting idly amongst themselves, but they were on the other side of where I needed to be. Heading directly to one particular bush—made distinctive by the unusual color of its roses—I peered down casually.

Three hostile entities have failed to pierce your disguise.

From this close, I could see where the ground had already been softened. *Excellent*, I thought. It had to be the doing of Farren's people and made my own task easier. *I might not even need the shovel.*

Sitting on the bench next to the rose bush, I placed Farren's bag directly in front of the loosened soil. With the spot in question concealed from casual observation, I used the toe of my boot and reopened the hole—not a lot, but just enough for its intended cargo. Leaning down as if to rub my leg, I placed Adriel's pouch within.

Now came the most crucial and perhaps the most dangerous part. After doublechecking that my mental defenses were in place, I upended the pouch.

You have lost 6 stygian seeds.

The small black objects glinted evilly, and freed from their imprisonment, I could only imagine what the tiny minds inside were doing. *Probably yelling for their protector to come save them*, I thought. Not that it would do them any good yet.

According to my lich allies, the court's protective shield would prevent any of the seeds' communication attempts from reaching the harbinger—which was one reason the barrier had to be lowered. The other reason, of course, being to let the harbinger in.

But first, the seeds needed fertilizing.

After a quick look around to ascertain that neither the nearby possessed nor anyone else was watching me, I reached into Farren's satchel and removed a pouch of raw meat. Wrinkling my nose at the smell, I poured its contents over the seeds then quickly swept soil over with my boot.

Chore done, I sat back in relief. The seeds and their food had been successfully planted.

The original plan had called for me to bury the seeds in six different locations. That way, there would've been less risk of them being discovered prematurely. Unfortunately, time was now at a premium, but what I'd done should work just as well. Picking up the satchel, I stood up and looked around for somewhere to hide.

It was time to change outfits.

CHAPTER 369: SUBTERFUGE

You have lost a backpack.

You have successfully concealed the small weapons: ebonheart and faithful.

You have cast facial disguise, assuming the visage of Loskin, a level 292 archlich. Duration: 3 hours.

Stashing my bags in a secluded hedge, I strode openly towards the main entrance of the archlich's mansion wearing his face and the robes Farren had provided.

Two armored brutes stood guard at the door. According to Adriel, the possessed's tendency to switch bodies made detection wards problematic, forcing Loskin to rely on manned security posts everywhere *except* where no traffic was expected.

Two hostile entities have failed to pierce your disguise.
Your hidden weapons have gone unnoticed.

No suspicion sparked in the guards' gazes as I drew closer. "Back early, boss?" the one on the right asked.

I nodded brusquely. I hadn't heard Loskin speak so I couldn't mimic his voice. Brushing past the guards, I entered the mansion unchallenged.

I didn't pause in the entryway. With the direction I'd received from the lichs memorized, I strode confidently across the entry foyer, turned right at the first corner, left at the next, then crossed over the next two branches before coming to a halt.

Casually, I looked around.

I was alone.

The entrance to the casting chamber was not much farther, and before I barged in, I had to prepare. Removing my scabbards from where I'd concealed them beneath the robes, I buckled them on the outside.

No doubt the swords would draw attention if anyone spotted me, but for the next bit, I planned on relying on my stealth. Armed, I cast my buffs.

You have cast heightened reflexes, load controller, fade, and trigger-cast quick mend.

Ready, I dropped into a crouch and crept forward.

* * *

Two hostile entities have failed to detect you! You are hidden.

A pair of fighters had been posted outside the entrance to the casting chamber. Sitting twenty yards away in the corridor leading up to the entrance, I observed them silently for a minute.

The two, while obviously bored, stood stiffly at attention and the door they guarded was securely bolted. Neither of those things would be a problem, though. Opening my mindsight, I surveyed the room beyond.

Just as Farren had promised, there were four mages on duty in the casting chamber, the minimum number required to maintain the shield around the complex. If the court was ever attacked, more mages would flood the room to reinforce the defenses.

But for now, it was only the four I had to deal with. Drawing psi, I reached into the minds of the two fighters.

You have cast slaysight.
You have hidden your presence from 2 of 2 targets for 40 seconds.

Rising to my feet, I spun more psi. I had given myself forty seconds to slay the mages—ample time for four unshielded targets caught unawares. Completing my spell, I shadow blinked to the strongest of the possessed.

You have teleported into Maligen's shadow.

I stepped out of the aether, unseen and undetected, and with ebonheart already descending.

You have backstabbed Maligen for 2.5x more damage! You have killed your target. You are no longer hidden.

The four mages were standing close to each other, forming a small circle around the glowing artifact at their center. Spinning on my heel, I thrust faithful into the next possessed.

You have killed Suktar with a fatal blow.

The third mage's eyes widened. "Loskin? What are you—"
Bringing faithful around in a sweeping arc, I decapitated him before he could finish.

You have killed Yaris with a fatal blow.

The last possessed whirled around. "By the Powers!" he screamed, making a dash for the door. "Guards, help! There is an impos—"
Darting forward, I plunged ebonheart through the back of his throat.

You have killed Canevar with a fatal blow.

The creaking of bolts heralded the door's opening, and the arrival of the two fighters.

"My God!" the first exclaimed. "What the bloody hell happened here?"

"This is bad," the second said, biting his lip. "Loskin is going to blame us!"

The guards could not see me, of course. Killing the four mages had taken less than a handful of seconds and I still had time yet before their mental blinding faded.

Raising ebonheart aloft, I approached the glowing artifact that had been the focus of the mages' channeling. It would run out of mana soon, and then the court's shield would fall of its own accord, but I was not inclined to wait. Bringing the black blade crashing down, I shattered the artifact.

You have destroyed a tier six shield focus crystal.
You have triggered an alarm!

A siren wailed from somewhere deeper in the mansion.

I didn't panic. According to Regus, the alarm had been set to sound the moment the shield was lowered. Disabling it would have required sneaking into Loskin's chambers, one of the most protected areas in the mansion. Venturing there would have been ill-advised, especially when simple subterfuge might serve instead.

"Did you see that...?" the first fighter asked, his face a mask of confusion. "The crystal just broke on its own!"

"No, no, no," the second guard cried, burying his head in his hands. "Loskin is definitely going to kill us now."

Ignoring the pair, I dashed out of the room. Less than twenty seconds remained before the guards would be able to see me again, and I was sure others were also hurrying this way.

I didn't go far, though. Drawing to a halt outside the two fighters' immediate line of sight, I raised ebonheart to my throat and scored a thin line across—just deep enough for it to bleed profusely.

In the distance, I heard the pounding of approaching footsteps. I was almost out of time. Sheathing my swords, I hid both blades beneath my robes once more.

You have successfully concealed the small weapons: ebonheart and faithful.

Blood, meanwhile, flowed unchecked down my robes. Clamping my right hand around my throat to hide the shallowness of the wound, I staggered drunkenly back into the casting chamber.

Two hostile entities have failed to pierce your disguise.
Your hidden weapons have gone unnoticed.

Both guards whipped around.

"Loskin!" the first fighter greeted in relief. But only a moment later, his expression grew horrified as he spotted my bloodied throat. "What happened? Are you alright?"

"I swear boss, we don't know what happened," the second stuttered nervously. "We came in and found them like this. Please don't—"

"Sh-hut-t up, you f-fool!" I croaked, deliberately mangling the words. "Th-h-here is an... i-intruder in the mans-s-sion."

"Yes!" the second guard said, nodding emphatically. "He did this! Not us."

I glared at him but ignored his babbling. I doubted the real Loskin would've paid his excuses any heed either. "You-u," I said pointing a trembling finger at the first guard, "go and t-t-turn off the damned alarm."

He looked at me doubtfully. "You sure? You don't sound too good, boss. Shouldn't we stay here and—"

"Go!" I growled. "Don't need... p-protection."

He went.

The alarm was loud, but its siren call wouldn't extend farther than a few villas. Chances were that Loskin and his retinue—all the way across the complex in Regus' house—wouldn't hear it. The longer they stayed ignorant, the better.

Multiple hostile entities have failed to pierce your disguise.

More figures rushed into the room.

Ignoring them, I turned to the second guard. "You. I-idiot. Guard thissh room. M-make sh-sure no one... enters."

He nodded vigorously.

I rounded on the other guards streaming in. "W-what... y-you fools doing here? The intruder... n-not here! Sh-s-spread out and... s-search the mansion!"

"Yes, boss!" they sang in chorus.

Safely wrapped in my disguise, I stomped out of the chamber.

✳   ✳   ✳

I made it out of the mansion with no one the wiser about my deception. As an added bonus, the alarm shut down before I left, and I smiled in genuine pleasure. My ploy had worked beautifully.

Now, I only had one last bit of subterfuge still to enact. Wrapped in shadow, I returned to the secluded hedge and retrieved my belongings.

You have acquired a backpack.

Before moving on, I spared a moment to review the waiting Game alerts.

You have reached level 191!
Your Dexterity has increased to rank 60. Other modifiers: +24 from items.

Other than rewarding me with another player level, the battle in the casting chamber hadn't yielded any significant benefits. My deception had improved nicely but not enough to reach the next rank.

Dismissing the Game messages, I surveyed my surroundings.

The vicinity around Loskin's mansion had grown busy, with multiple possessed running in and out. Not a few glanced upward, but the sky looked no different in the absence of the shield.

Not yet anyway.

My gaze sought the buried seeds.

There had been much debate between Adriel, Farren and me about them, specifically around how long the seeds would need to establish a fog bank. Given everything I had told her, Adriel had been certain that they would, and I saw no reason to doubt her.

Since the seeds remained unbroken, the minds within them were still whole, which meant that sooner or later they would start attracting—or was it gathering?—nether from the void sapling. The only question none of us could answer with certainty was how long it would take. And in the end, we had decided to give the seeds a single night.

Of course, my mishap at the gate had changed all that, and now, the seeds would have minutes instead of hours. Still, even if they failed to draw in the nether in that time, a few minutes would suffice to bring the harbinger, and in the end, that was all that mattered.

He should be here soon, I thought, breaking off from my musings. I glanced again at the spot where I'd buried the seeds. Nothing had changed since the last few seconds I'd been studying it. Shrugging, I slipped out from behind the hedge and tiptoed towards the vault.

The squat building was tightly sealed, and I would not be getting inside anytime soon. But its outside was less protected, and I rather thought the vault's flat rooftop would serve as an ideal platform for what I intended next.

Slipping from building to building, and timing my movements to avoid passing possessed, I made it to the rear of the vault without being detected.

Here, things were less busy. Staying crouched, I weaved psi.

You have cast windborne.

I glanced around. *What will the possessed think if they spotted Loskin hopping about like a rogue?* I wondered, chuckling at the thought. But no one was close enough to observe—which was almost disappointing.

Time to move. Setting the windslide against the side of the building like one would a ladder, I hopped on and shot aloft. As I reached the end of the ramp of air, I extended my hands.

My fingers found the roof's edge, and flipping myself over, I dropped lightly into a crouch on the roof.

You are hidden.

I smiled. I had made it to my perch unseen. Craning my neck upward, I turned my gaze northwest.

It won't be long now.

CHAPTER 370: THE NETHER'S NEWEST CREATURE

It took the harbinger another five minutes to arrive. During that time, none of Loskin's retinue reappeared, and I could only assume the distraction we'd arranged was working.

The focus crystal I'd broken was a valuable artifact, and according to Farren, the possessed had only one other replacement—which happened to be stored in the very same vault on which I stood, a vault that only Loskin could get into.

In the interim, the movement of possessed into and out of the mansion had only grown. But, without Loskin or any of his immediate lieutenants to direct them, the other possessed appeared at a loss on what to do.

The conflicting report on the archlich's location added to the chaos. Some possessed insisted he was at Regus' house while others claimed he was overseeing matters from the mansion. A few had nonetheless run off in the direction of the security chief's house, but now that I'd spotted the harbinger on the horizon, I no longer cared what messages they carried.

We'd passed the point of no return. And whether they liked it or not, the possessed would soon be battling the harbinger—without a shield to hide behind.

I slinked to the northern end of the vault's roof, the side directly bordering the courtyard. None of the possessed below had spotted the approaching stygian yet. A silent, ominous shape gliding on outstretched wings, the harbinger was homing in on the buried seeds.

Drawing mana, I waited.

A second passed, then another, before one of the possessed finally spotted something amiss.

"Hey! Look at that!"

"Look at what?"

"That smudge in the sky. It wasn't there before."

"Pppft, you're jumping at shadows. That's nothing."

"No, she's right. I see it too. And it wasn't there before."

"Is it a cloud?" someone asked doubtfully.

"Can't be, it's growing too quickly for that."

"Well, what is it then?" a sergeant snapped impatiently.

"Damn, where are Loskin and Farren?"

"I k-kn-ow wha-at that is," the spotter added, her voice trembling.

"What?" a chorus of voices barked.

"It... it's the... harbinger," the sharp-eyed possessed replied with undisguised fear.

Silence—profound and disturbing. And for all of five seconds, the possessed were shocked into inaction, neither moving nor tearing their gazes from the sky.

"She's right," an archer whispered finally. The confirmation galvanized the possessed into action and chaos erupted. In the space of a single breath, conflicting orders, accusations, and even panicked screams were voiced atop one another.

Smiling, I rose to my feet. The harbinger was close enough now that no one could mistake him for anything else. Likewise, he could not miss *me* on the roof of the vault.

Multiple unknown entities have failed to pierce your disguise.

"Look! There's Loskin."

"He'll save us!"

"What are your orders, boss?"

Ignoring the possessed below, I kept my eyes pinned on the harbinger as I raised my right hand languidly to point, not at him, but at the buried seeds.

The stygian Power must have had some premonition of what I intended because he broke his silence then to snarl in wordless rage. My grin broadening, I released the pent-up mana gathered in my hand.

You have cast darkness bolt.
You have destroyed a stygian seed!
You have destroyed a stygian seed!

...

...

In the blink of an eye, all six seeds were turned to dust.

Satisfied with my work, I glanced upward at the harbinger. I'd timed things perfectly and he was still too far away to retaliate effectively. That did not stop the stygian from attempting a response, though. Magic, dark and malevolent, gathered in his open beak.

Preparing my own counter, I waited.

A split-second later, the harbinger's spell boiled out of his mouth. In the same heartbeat, I released my own casting.

A stygian harbinger has cast nether's cloying touch.
You have cast windborne.

I set the ramp of air on the roof, directing it back the way I'd come. It would have been simpler to jump off the building into the courtyard below, but I'd not forgotten the watching possessed. From afar, my deception might go unremarked, but from up close, someone was sure to notice my un-Loskin-like behavior.

You have evaded a harbinger's attack.

Zipping along the windslide, I somersaulted off the far edge of the roof to land lightly on the ground below, and without hesitation, wrapped myself in shadow.

Multiple hostile entities have failed to detect you! You are hidden.

I chuckled quietly, imagining the harbinger's fury at my escape. Whether or not the stygian knew who Loskin was, I had no idea, but I was certain he would give the archlich a warm welcome when he eventually did arrive. Rising into a half-crouch, I tiptoed away.

My part in the battle was done.

Now, it was up to Loskin to save his people—or not—and, more importantly, to show up and defend his phylactery.

✳   ✳   ✳

I felt the harbinger's landing. The entire court did, I suspected.

The ground rumbled and shook, knocking many of the possessed off their feet. As if that were not enough, the harbinger threw back his head and cawed, an angry announcement of his presence.

That will certainly catch Loskin's attention, I thought, snickering in delight.

"Lich, show yourself!" the harbinger bellowed.

I paused in my retreat. There was really no reason for me to hang about, and every reason not to, but I couldn't resist the temptation to witness the coming confrontation.

Just a few seconds, I temporized. *Then I'll go.*

Tiptoeing to the corner of the nearest building, I peeked around. The harbinger had landed in the center of the courtyard, next to the fountain, destroying it in the process. His hind legs stiff and erect, the stygian stood protectively over the dead seeds' remains.

An armored fighter rushed in from the side, his axe raised, but the harbinger barely glanced his way. Extending his right wing, the stygian battered the hapless possessed aside.

"LOSKIN!" the stygian roared again.

So, I thought, *the harbinger and archlich do know each other.*

A gaunt figure materialized in the courtyard, a hundred yards away from the angry stygian. "I'm here, beast," the archlich said, his voice as dry as parched paper. Sweeping his gaze over the chaos, he asked, "What is the meaning of this?"

"You murdered the chosen!" the harbinger screamed. "You and the Wolf! He is your creature, he must be."

Loskin frowned. "I have no idea what you are on about, nor do I care to know."

"LIAR!" the harbinger screamed. "It makes sense now—how he escaped my trap, how he killed the chosen." Lowering his head, the harbinger pinned the archlich with a furious gaze. "It's been you all along. You are the one who orchestrated this!"

Just shut up and fight, why don't you? I thought, rolling my eyes.

The harbinger's penchant for throwing tantrums could ruin everything. It was well and good he had fallen for my ploy, but the longer he went on speaking, the more chance there was that Loskin would realize the truth. Thankfully, though, the archlich paid the stygian's accusations no heed.

"I do not care if you believe me, wretched thing," the lich replied mildly. "What I do care about is that you've invaded my compound." His eyes glinted. "You've damaged what is mine. For that, you will pay."

"Bold words!" the harbinger spat. He sneered derisively at the possessed surrounding him. "And who do you expect to help you? These? They cannot stand against me."

"But we can," another said.

Glancing to the left, I saw Farren's slim figure appear in the courtyard. A dozen others stood behind him. Analyzing each in turn, I realized they were all elites. Loskin must have sent his fellow lich for reinforcements while he delayed the harbinger. *Clever.*

"You and your kind have no place in this world," Loskin said. "It is time I scrubbed the dungeon of your foulness." He raised his hands. "We are undying, beast. You cannot kill us."

"Undying? Bah!" The harbinger's gaze slid to the vault. "Do not think I don't know about your tricks, lich. When I destroy your precious golems, you will taste death. Forever."

Loskin's lips tightened fractionally, the only sign he gave that the harbinger's words perturbed him.

Then he attacked.

* * *

Between one second and the next, the courtyard was transformed into a maelstrom of destruction as first Loskin, then Farren and the others unleashed a deluge of spells.

The harbinger was not slow to act either and flung his own magic right back.

An errant blob of darkness—flung by who, I couldn't tell—landed less than ten yards from me. "That was too close," I muttered. It was time I left. Wrenching my gaze away from the combatants, I crept away.

My retreat, like everything else, was part of the plan, which—despite its rocky start—was back on course. The next step was meeting Adriel, who should already be at the rendezvous point.

Orienting myself towards the villa in question—the exile's old and apparently still-abandoned manor—I slipped unnoticed towards it. The building was not far and overlooked the courtyard, which suited our needs perfectly.

For what came next, we needed a clear line of sight to the vault. Breaking into the building would have to wait, though. Until both our targets—harbinger and archlich—tired themselves out, or better yet, killed each other outright, we couldn't act.

The harbinger's earlier words had not been an idle boast. For all Loskin's power, Adriel was convinced the archlich could not overcome the stygian Power alone. It was the entire reason Farren still stood by Loskin's side. He was the instrument by which we would control the tide of the battle.

When the time was right, he would betray Loskin.

Hopefully by then, the harbinger would be dead and Loskin on his last legs. At that point, Adriel and I would enter the fray and put an end to the lich—once and for all.

That was the plan, anyway.

But I doubted everything would go perfectly. Still, for now, there was nothing for me to do but watch and wait. Reaching my destination, I slunk up to the main door.

✳   ✳   ✳

Even though Adriel's villa was abandoned, it was well-kept. The possessed had maintained the mansion, but for some reason, no one else appeared keen to move in. Placing my ear against the door, I tapped quietly in the agreed pattern.

Silence.

Frowning, I raised my hand to knock again.

"Enter," a familiar voice called from within.

Relieved, I pushed open the door and slipped inside. Adriel was sitting at a table strategically placed in the entrance foyer. Sipping tea, the exile stared out the oversized windows at the magical lightshow. "Pretty, isn't it?" she remarked.

Turning around, I looked out myself. The sky bloomed with magical fire of all stripes: purple lightning, chromatic fireballs, meteor showers, howling rain, and ominous clouds of black.

I rolled my eyes. "That's not how I would choose to describe it, but yes, it's a spectacular display."

Adriel set down her cup. "What kept you?" she asked with a smile.

"Nothing much," I said, still maintaining my tone of false gaiety. "Only starting a war."

Adriel chuckled, but only a moment later, her humor faded. "You did well to get us this far. I freely admit, I didn't think you could pull it off." She sighed. "But now it's out of our hands."

"What's wrong?" I asked, spotting the troubled look that flitted across her face.

"Farren reports that the battle is not going well."

I stared at her disbelievingly. "Really? Two lichs, a dozen elites, hundreds of possessed, a favorable battleground, and *still* the battle is not going well?"

Adriel winced. "When you put it that way, it doesn't sound good. But yes, the possessed are losing. It seems all of us, Loskin included, underestimated the strength of this particular harbinger."

I turned back to the door. "Should we help?"

Adriel shook her head. "Not yet. The battle is still young, and while momentum is with the harbinger right now, that could change at any point. Farren will warn us if things turn dire."

I nodded reluctantly. I knew the two siblings had their own means of talking. It was not mindspeech, but a form of magical communication similar to the farspeaker bracelets I'd used before. It allowed the pair to communicate even when they were half a sector apart.

"Besides," Adriel said, "I'm sure you don't want to go out like that again."

Glancing down, I realized I was still wearing the archlich's robe—and face. Removing the black garb, I let the illusion wrapped around my face unravel.

Your facial disguise spell has dissipated.

"Better," Adriel said approvingly. "Even after all these years, I can't stand looking at that face."

The pair had a history, I knew. Adriel had not filled me in on the details, and I had not pried. "So. What now?"

"We wait," Adriel said simply, gesturing to the seat opposite her. "For however long it takes."

Reluctantly, I sat. Waiting, especially in a situation like this, did not sit well with me, but I knew Adriel was right. If we intervened too early, either the archlich or the harbinger—if not both—would sense the trap closing around them and break off.

And that we couldn't afford.

For a minute, I gazed out the window, but as dazzling as the spells being flung were, I could get no real sense of how the battle was going and eventually turned back to stare at Adriel uncertainly.

There was something I'd been meaning to ask, a topic I was almost too afraid to broach, and telling myself we were in the middle of a battle was the only way I'd been able to stop the matter from playing on my mind. But now... we appeared at loose ends.

I licked my lips. "Since we seem to have some time on our hands, tell me, how did it go with Ghost?"

Adriel chuckled. "I've been wondering how long it would take you to bring that up."

Now that I had broached the subject, impatience drove me on. "And?" I asked, leaning forward.

"Relax, Wolf. Everything went smoothly." She smiled mysteriously. "Even better than expected, actually."

I wasn't quite sure what she meant by that but focused on what was important. "Where is she?"

Withdrawing an item from her pack, Adriel placed it on the table between us. "Here."

My head jerked downwards.

The item on the table was my magister's cloak. Only, it looked different now. The legendary item had been a dull black before, so faded it could've almost been called dark gray. Now, it shone with a darkness so intense it was reminiscent of the void... or the darkness at the heart of a stygian seed.

I shuddered, a premonition of dread rising to the fore. "What's wrong with it?"

"Nothing," Adriel said dryly. "In fact, my handiwork has gone a long way in improving the cloak."

I was barely listening, though. "And what do you mean Ghost is 'here'? I don't sense her. Where is she?"

Adriel smiled that annoying smile again and pointed downwards at the cloak itself.

I finally took her meaning. "She is in *there*?"

The lich nodded. "I've transformed your cloak into a spirit vessel capable of housing Ghost." She tilted her head. "That's what we discussed, wasn't it?"

"Sort of," I muttered. "But you also said you were going to craft Ghost a new body, not just anchor her spirit in an object!"

"And I have," Adriel said, her smile broadening. "The cloak is home to both Ghost's spirit *and* her new body."

My brows drew down. "What?"

"Ghost is inside. All of her. Body, mind, and spirit," Adriel repeated patiently. "But don't just take my word for it. Inspect the cloak and see for yourself," she said, pushing the item towards me.

Still doubtful, I raised my hand and touched the garment.

You have acquired the <u>Cloak of the Reach</u>, a unique soulbound spirit vessel crafted by the lich Adriel.

The Cloak of the Reach is a former legendary item forged anew using the crest feather of a mature phoenix, raw essence stolen from the void, and the spirit of the entity known as Ghost. Under the lich's guidance, all the constituent parts have forevermore been bound together using the strongest of death magic spells.

The cloak both protects and hides the entity known as Ghost. She may at any time leave her shelter and manifest as a <u>stygian pyre wolf</u>, the fabric of whose form is woven into the cloak.

Due to the nature of the crafting ingredients employed in its making, the Cloak of the Reach is an indestructible soulbound artifact only usable by the player Michael.

In addition to housing the <u>stygian pyre wolf</u> Ghost, this item increases your Magic by +10 ranks, your nether resistance by +20% and your fire resistance by +20%. Note, the artifacts' full properties can only be seen by you, its true owner.

I stared at Adriel, my eyes wide in shock. "A stygian? You've turned Ghost into *a nether creature?*"

CHAPTER 371: THE CLOAK OF THE REACH

Adriel bobbed her head, looking too pleased with herself to pay much heed to my astonishment. "And not just any stygian. A stygian *pyre* wolf."

Closing my eyes, I squeezed the bridge of my nose. "And what exactly," I began slowly, "is a stygian pyre wolf?"

"I'm not entirely sure," Adriel said, a quizzical look on her face.

My eyes snapped open.

"Ghost's new form is unique," Adriel continued blithely. "There's never been such a creature as a stygian wolf before, much less a stygian pyre wolf! What Ghost will be capable of, I don't know, and I admit I'm more than a little curious to find out."

I groaned. The lich seemed to be too besotted by her creation to see the obvious downsides. "But a... stygian, Adriel? Really? What if the void calls to her? Or can somehow control her?"

Adriel shook her head. "You misunderstand, Michael. Ghost is not like other nether creatures. She is something this world has never seen before: a *free* stygian, one unbound by the void fathers. The trees cannot control her. The nether cannot call her. Her allegiance belongs only to you and House Wolf."

"I see," I said, still not sure what to make of Adriel's assurances. "And what does Ghost think of her new form? Is she pleased?"

Adriel chuckled. "I would say so. But you can find out for yourself. Put on the cloak."

Rising to my feet, I took the cloak up in my hands and studied it intently from all sides. On the outside, the garment was uniformly black, so dark it seemed to absorb the surrounding light.

It was the same on the inside too, except for one spot that would rest against my left breast. There, fiery red-gold lines had been stitched into the shape of a wolf's face, and not just that of any wolf—but Ghost's.

"It is a remarkable likeness," I murmured.

"Thank you," Adriel said, sounding pleased by the compliment. "I did my best."

Touching the snarling wolf, I felt the heat coming off the fibers. "You made this using Sunfury's feather?" I guessed.

"Correct," Adriel said with a grimace. "Working with the phoenix's feather was not easy, but it was worth it in the end. Which reminds me..." Drawing out another item, she placed it on the table. "This is yours."

It was the central shaft of Sunfury's feather.

"I couldn't use it, but I'm sure a skilled enchanter will be able to do something with it."

The lich, Adriel, has returned a phoenix's feather shaft.

One of the items the lich had asked for back at her complex was Sunfury's gift. At first, her request had caught me by surprise. I hadn't even known leaving a soulbound artifact with anyone else was possible, but Adriel assured me it was.

As long as I voluntarily willed the item into her keeping, it would stay with her. She wouldn't be able to wield the artifact, of course, but she would be able to employ it for crafting purposes. This, Adriel had told me, was a necessary allowance the Game made to enable crafters to work on players' soulbound items.

"Thank you," I said, returning the artifact to my backpack.

The other things I'd left with Adriel were my stygian ingredients, and all the seed fragments I'd collected. She had obviously used a good quantity of both. "What about the nether reagents?"

She waved aside my question. "None of that remains."

I stared at her. "You used *all* of it?"

Nodding, she handed me another object.

You have acquired a hunter's alchemy stone. Stored ingredients: 0 / 500.

"Right," I muttered. Holding out the cloak, I prepared to equip it.

"Hold on," Adriel said, raising a hand to stop. "I almost forgot, but before you put that on, there's a few things you should know."

Mid-motion, I paused. "Go on."

"First and foremost, now that Ghost has a body, she is as mortal as any other creature."

"I know—" I began.

Adriel cut me off. "No, you don't. Even in a body as powerful as the stygian pyre wolf's promises to be, Ghost is still only *a level one creature*. If she dies, her spirit will not return to the cloak, it will vanish forever into the afterlife." She pinned me with a hard look. "I take it you don't want that?"

I shook my head mutely. "I don't."

Adriel exhaled. "And neither does Ghost. Which is why you cannot let her manifest—"

"What? Not at all?" I blurted.

"Let me finish," she said in mild exasperation. She waited a second to see if I would interrupt again. When I didn't, she went on. "Like I was saying: you should not let Ghost manifest *until* you can make her your familiar."

"My... familiar?" I asked in confusion. "But I'm not a mage!"

Adriel chuckled. "Oh, but you are."

I stared at her, still puzzled.

"What do you think your third Class makes you? You told me so yourself: you're a void mage. Granted, you may use your magic in an atypical fashion, but make no mistake: you're a mage. And as far as the Game is concerned, that qualifies you for a familiar."

"Alright... I can see how that's true. So, what do I need to do?"

"It's not complicated," Adriel said with a shrug. "First, you will need Ghost's consent, which will not be an issue. She wants this too. Second, you need to meet the Game's requirements."

"Which are?"

"One, owning an item with a bound creature—in this case Ghost—and two, possessing a mage Class."

I smiled. "I meet both those requirements, don't I?"

"You do," Adriel agreed, smiling back. "So go ahead, put on the cloak, spend a Class point, and let's see Ghost in her new form."

My grin faded. "I need a Class point?"

"That's right," Adriel confirmed. "Familiar binding is a Class trait that the Adjudicator makes available to every mage meeting the requirements, which you do. You will find it amongst the new benefits the moment you begin the Class upgrade process." Seeing my expression, she paused. "What's wrong?"

I opened my mouth to answer, but before I could, Adriel's head whipped around in the direction of the open window.

✳   ✳   ✳

"What's wrong?" I asked, throwing her own question back at her.

Adriel rose to her feet. "We have to move. The harbinger has just blown away half the vault, which has Loskin panicked." She turned expressionless eyes on me. "Farren believes he is minutes away from calling for a retreat."

Cursing, I began casting my buffs. "What about the harbinger?"

"He's severely injured and shows no sign of backing off. But if Loskin grabs his phylactery and flees—"

"—we lose anyway," I finished.

Adriel nodded, then her gaze fell on the cloak. "Put that on. It will be safest on you." She paused. "Just remember what I said," she warned.

"Got it. Don't let Ghost manifest," I said, shrugging into the cloak.

You have equipped the <u>Cloak of the Reach</u>, gaining +20% fire resistance, +20% nether resistance, and +10 Magic.

You have soulbound the Cloak of the Reach.

From this point onwards, this artifact cannot be wielded by any other, stolen, lost, or kept from your hands except by the strongest of enchantments.

"Prime!" an excited voice cried in my mind.

Despite our dire circumstances, my lips twitched upwards. With the cloak on, I could hear Ghost as clearly as ever before. Although, now, she was only a disembodied voice. I couldn't see her spirit, only her mindglow. And a few minutes ago, I hadn't even seen that much. The cloak had to be masking both from sight—a good thing, I thought.

"Ghost," I greeted. *"It's good to have you back."*

"I missed you too, Prime!" She paused, then went on more tentatively, *"Did Adriel explain about... the familiar binding?"*

"Could you not hear our conversation?"

"No. While I'm in the cloak, I'm blind to the world."

"Oh," I said, absorbing the implications of that. *"Don't worry, she told me all about it."*

"Great! So, will you perform the binding now?" she asked, almost quivering with eagerness at the thought. *"Then I can show you my new form!"*

"I'm sorry, Ghost. I can't."

"You don't want to?" she asked in a small voice.

"It's not that," I assured her. *"I just don't have any Class points at the moment. But I promise I will get right to it when I can."*

"Thank you, Prime!" Ghost exclaimed, exuberant once again.

"You're welcome," I said with a smile. *"But we're about to head into battle. I'll fill you in on the details later."*

"Oh, alright," Ghost said, her consciousness fading from awareness.

Turning my focus outwards, I saw Adriel watching me patiently. "Chatted to her, have you?"

I nodded. "And you're right, she's excited about the whole thing."

"Good." Adriel flexed her hands. "Now, let's go. Farren is waiting."

✳   ✳   ✳

The courtyard had undergone a radical transformation in the few short minutes since my absence.

The cobblestones were pockmarked by craters and deep furrows had been dug through the street. Some villas were smoking ruins, icicles rimmed the sides of others, and a few had been obliterated entirely.

Everywhere I looked, there were bodies and vacantly staring spirits. Dozens of possessed had perished, some decapitated, others turned to ash, and more looked as if they had been boiled alive.

Half of the vault's stout walls were gone too, but that did not mean its contents were exposed. Lines of wards so thick they blurred the air still shimmered in place of the missing stone.

The battle had not abated either, but it had degenerated into a stalemate. Loskin and Farren, accompanied by six elites—all spellcasters by the shield bubbles encapsulating them—faced off across the breadth of the courtyard against the lone harbinger. Lines of magic colored the air as the two opposing sides slung an endless array of spells at one another.

Like his foes, the stygian Power was wrapped in a shield. His, though, stank of the nether, and given the multitude of bodies lying outside the gray rim, it was just as toxic. The other surviving possessed, meanwhile, had fled to the fringes of the battle, only occasionally darting in to strike when they could. They, too, seemed to be primarily magic slingers.

I whistled in wordless appreciation of the devastation. "Is this what the war looked like?" I asked Adriel softly.

"This?" she scoffed. "This is child's play compared to what the Primes and Powers did to each other and those unfortunate enough to get in their way."

The two of us were hidden behind a villa on the southern edge of the courtyard. The vault was directly in front of us. The ground appeared deceptively empty of threat, but I knew the moment we broke cover we'd be spotted by the combatants.

Still, we would have to cross the distance—and soon.

According to Farren, the archlich had already passed a series of whispered commands to the closest of his confidence. Soon, he would retreat, presumably abandoning Farren and the other less favored possessed in the process.

"How do you want to do this?" I asked Adriel.

"I will go in first," she said.

"You're sure?" I asked, studying her through the shimmering haze of her defensive castings. For this battle, Adriel had sheathed herself in multiple layers of buffs, wards, and shields—something she had not bothered doing the one time I'd been foolish enough to attack her.

But then, this time around, Adriel did not have a near infinite supply of 'bodies' close by. Other than the one she wore now, the lich only had one other flesh golem in the canyon.

"You will need me to take the vault's shield down," Adriel said. "Once it falls, Loskin will respond immediately. I will hold his attention while you destroy the phylactery." She glanced at me. "Do you remember its location?"

I nodded. "I do."

"Good. Remember, whatever happens, you destroy that phylactery. Understood?"

"Understood," I said grimly.

Saying nothing further, Adriel stepped out of cover and marched boldly across the street. No one saw her at first, and when they did, their reactions were not what I expected.

"Hey! Look there!"

"Who's that?"

"It's the exile, you moron. She's back!"

"Let's get her!"

"It's the *exile*, idiot! You would do better to run. I'm outta here!"

"She is heading for the vault. Quick! Someone warn Loskin."

"You do that. I'm getting out of here. Nozk was right. This is bad."

In bemused wonder, I listened to the cries of the nearby possessed and unclenched my hands from the hilts of my blades. I had been half-expecting I would need to leap out and save Adriel from being mobbed. But it seemed that, despite her comparatively low level, Adriel commanded as much fear—if not more—than the harbinger and Loskin.

It seems I don't know my ally as well as I thought I did.

"What's that?" Ghost asked, responding to my inner musings.

"It's Adriel. She has the possessed scared near witless."

"I told you she would make a good friend," Ghost said smugly. *"Didn't I?"*

I smiled. *"That you did."*

Adriel, meanwhile, had reached the vault. Ignoring the frantic shouts of the nearby possessed, the exile stretched out her arm.

Cold, gray fire leapt from her fingers to the vault's glowing wards and when they met, the results were cataclysmic.

Adriel has cast Death's righteous fury.
A tier 6 ward has been destroyed.
A tier 5 ward has been destroyed.

A tier 6 ward has been destroyed.

...

...

A kaleidoscope of colors exploded from the vault, so bright and harsh I had to squeeze my eyes shut for fear of being blinded. Nonetheless, the avalanche of Game messages scrolling through my mind left me in no doubt of the havoc Adriel was wreaking with a single spell.

Bloody hells, I thought, flabbergasted.

A second later, the fireworks show ended, and I dared to open my eyes again. The vault had vanished, completely obliterated in the wake of Adriel's casting—as were its untold number of wards. But a new obstacle stood between us and our objective.

Loskin. The archlich had come.

Ignoring the sudden pounding of my heart, I rose from the crouch I'd unconsciously fallen into. The time had come to play my own part. Stepping out from behind the wall sheltering me, I crept towards the vault, plotting a wide arc around the two lichs facing off against one another.

A hostile entity has failed to detect you! You are hidden.

"Adriel," the archlich rasped disdainfully.

"Loskin," Adriel greeted evenly.

"You used a blood spell to destroy my wards? That was beyond foolish."

A blood spell? I wondered, only half listening to the pair's conversation as I advanced on my objective. *Did he mean a blood memory?*

"It smacks of desperation," Loskin continued. "Are you desperate, Adriel?"

"You're a fine one to talk, *Archlich,*" Adriel sneered. "It's a damnable mess your court is in.

A hostile entity has failed to detect you!

Sneaking a peek beyond the two lichs, I saw that the battle between the harbinger and the others still raged on, but the odds had turned even more in the stygian's favor with Loskin's sudden withdrawal.

Only four elites remained standing with Farren. No longer launching any attacks of their own, the five were firmly on the defensive. All the nearby possessed had also scattered, even the few loudmouths that had advocated for attacking the exile.

Loskin's eyes narrowed. "Is all this your doing, Adriel? Did you orchestrate the stygian beast's arrival?"

Adriel laughed. "And what if I did? It's high time someone ended your bloody rule."

"And for the sake of that you will see what we built together destroyed?" the archlich asked disbelievingly.

"Yes!" Adriel spat angrily. "You've corrupted *everything*, Loskin. We—" she spread her arms to encompass all the possessed in the court—"no longer fight for justice, merely power. Power for your benefit. And that, I can no longer allow."

"A bit melodramatic of you, isn't it?" Loskin remarked, unbothered by her words. "But you were always one for moral grandstanding."

"As you were for self-serving rhetoric," Adriel retorted. For a split second, her gaze leaped from the archlich to sweep the empty streets. She couldn't see me, of course. Still, I read the message in her gaze. Adriel was buying me as much time as she could.

"How can you hope to defeat me now?" Loskin asked idly. "You've already expended your strongest spell."

"As have you," Adriel replied coolly. "Or don't tell me you've been holding back against the harbinger all this time?"

Loskin had no response to that.

Adriel smiled. "You shall fall, Loskin. I will see to it, even if it's the last thing I do."

The archlich lips tightened. "We shall see." Turning up his palms, he sent snaking lines of darkness racing towards Adriel.

The fight had begun in earnest. Fixing my gaze on my objective, I redoubled my pace.

CHAPTER 372: THE DEATH OF A LICH

I made it into the vault with Loskin none the wiser.

Thanks to the harbinger and Adriel's spells, the inside of the vault was exposed and unguarded, leaving anyone free to plunder it. Although, after seeing the contents, most would-be thieves would be disappointed.

The archlich's most-guarded treasure house was less a vault than it was a mortuary. From one end to the other, the building was lined with bodies. Rows and rows of them, each meticulously preserved. Or they had been. Many had since been tossed about and buried under the weight of broken shelves and collapsed walls.

I was in the very center of the vault, concealed by the ruined mess around me and crouched next to one particular shelf. Behind me, lich and archlich battered away at each other's shields, their animosity fueled by a centuries-old feud, while ahead, Farren and the remaining elites fought a losing battle against the harbinger.

My own focus remained riveted on the dusty steel box in my hands. It had been hidden beneath the shelf, and in every way, it was an ordinary looking box—not something one would ever believe to be the repository of an artifact as important as an archlich's phylactery.

It was Loskin's final defensive measure.

A last bit of subterfuge. An ordinary-seeming box opened by an ordinary-seeming steel key held by his chief of security. Formerly held, anyway. Taking in hand the key Farren had given me, I inserted the unassuming bit of steel in the lock and sprung it open.

The key turned with an audible click.

My actions triggered no Game messages—for which I was more than grateful. According to Regus, the box was covered in traps set by a master thief. No powerful spells would gain me access. Only the steel key would—of which there were only two copies. One that was kept by Loskin, and the other which had been left with his security chief for safeguarding.

This is it, I thought. Inhaling deeply, I cracked open the lid.

The phylactery was inside as promised.

It was a near replica of Adriel's. Wasting no more time, I wrapped my hand around the thin glass vial and summoned mana.

You have cast darkness bolt.
You have damaged an archlich's phylactery.

The vial cracked but did not break. "Damn it," I cursed and drew more mana.

A slim black shape materialized in front of me—Loskin.

My head jerked up, but my hand remained wrapped around the vial, and I kept casting. Somehow, the archlich must have sensed the box's opening or perhaps the damage dealt to his spirit vessel.

It didn't matter. Either way, the construct of living flesh in front of me was only a distraction. The *real* Loskin—the archlich himself—was in the tiny vial I held. And only by breaking it would I kill him. "Your time's up, Loskin," I whispered. "It's over."

Loskin did not so much as twitch a finger or bat an eyelid. "Die," was all he simply said.

The word was no ordinary word.

In the very instant that Loskin vocalized the word, I knew that. It was a primal thing, a spell targeted at the core of who I was.

The word held power. The power of Blood and the power of Death. And it was rushing toward me with palpable force. There would be no dodging. No clever evasive maneuver to escape. The spell was centered on my being. It would follow wherever I went.

And it had just ordered me to die.

In obedience to the primal command, the strands of myself frayed and split apart. My spirit began devolving; my flesh started melting; my mind lurched towards oblivion.

But then my void armor intervened.

And something else too: Farren's almost-forgotten buff.

The dissolution of my being reversed course. The shards of my spirit knit back, flesh firmed, and my mind escaped the pull into darkness.

You have passed a magical resistance check!
You have resisted the self-dissolution command of a power word!

I shuddered. The battle for myself had only lasted a split second, yet it felt like an eternity. But in the end, the efforts of my void armor and Farren's buff sufficed to repel the brunt of the power word's assault.

Unfortunately, the spell was not done with me yet, and a more mundane attack followed.

Power word second spell-stage triggered!

Gray, sickly tendrils of energy materialized between me and Loskin. Fat, wriggling worms, they flung themselves at me. There were thousands of the things, and as high as my death magic resistance was at the moment, the tendrils were too numerous to fend off entirely. Some still snuck through my defenses.

You have partially resisted the life leech effects of a power word!

'Some,' though, were still a lot, and in the next instant, near a score of the gray energy worms plunged into my torso, sucking me dry.

You have been life drained! Remaining health: 95%.
You have been life drained! Remaining health: 90%.
...
...
You have been life drained! Remaining health: 5%.

Quick mend triggered, restoring 20% of your health!
Void armor charge remaining: 61%.
Void thief failed to trigger! Your mana is currently not capable of learning power word spells.

In an instant, my health plummeted, emptied nearly to its dregs. But nearly was not good enough. I lived yet. Rocking back on my heels, I dropped the steel box but managed to retain hold of the phylactery—and my concentration. Raising my eyes, I found the archlich.

Loskin was staring at me, thunderstruck. "How?" he demanded.

I didn't bother answering. My own spell was ready, and I released it without hesitation or remorse.

You have cast darkness bolt.
You have destroyed an archlich's phylactery.
You have killed Loskin! The final sector boss has been slain.

That, sadly, was still not the end of the matter.

The vial in my hand exploded, but contrary to my expectations, the shards did not behave like ordinary glass and my wayfarer's gloves did nothing to stop the tiny slivers from slicing into my skin.

A destroyed archlich's phylactery has injured you.
A destroyed archlich's phylactery has injured you.
...
...

I stared at my hand in wordless horror. Each cut, while small, bit deep and eked away a little bit of my life.

Loskin's final revenge? I wondered, a sickly dazed grin pasted on my face. I knew I should do something—*anything*—to stop the ongoing damage, but my thoughts were foggy and for a moment I was at a loss as to what.

Quick mend... cast... quick mend, I thought. Gathering my scattered concentration, I tried to do just that, but my mind had suffered one shock too many, and my maligned body had had enough. My limbs giving way beneath me, I slumped to the floor.

✳ ✳ ✳

"Prime! Prime!"

Slowly, I came to. *"I'm... awake, Ghost."* I paused, my thoughts moving as slow as molasses. *"What... happened?"*

"I don't know!" Ghost exclaimed. *"It seemed like you were out forever, but locked up in this cloak, I can't tell how long it's been,"* she moaned. *"This wasn't a good idea. I should never have let Adriel put me in this thing. What was I thinking?"*

"Slow... down," I rasped, struggling to follow her.

"Sorry," Ghost said contritely. *"Did you... did you die?"*

I shook my head. *"I don't... think so. At least I don't remember that happening."*

"If you say so," Ghost said doubtfully. *"But maybe—"*

Another voice interrupted. "Michael? Are you awake?"

I knew that voice. It was Adriel. *"Adriel is here, Ghost. We're alright, I think."*

"Thank the Wolf!" she said fervently.

"*I'm going to need to talk to her,*" I said, feeling my thoughts begin to sharpen. Whatever had knocked me out, it seemed its effects were dissipating.

"*I know, I know. But make sure you tell me everything afterwards,*" Ghost said, retreating to the back of my mind.

"*I will,*" I promised her fading awareness before turning my attention outwards.

"Michael, are you in there? I saw you move."

I opened my eyes, then groaned as the harsh white light of a mage globe hit my eyes.

"He's alive," a relieved-sounding Adriel said.

"What happened?" I muttered.

"Told you he'd be too stubborn to die," another more caustic voice remarked.

I turned my head to the right, tracking the familiar sounding voice and saw a stout-looking dwarf. He was not anyone I knew, though.

Then I spotted the unforgettable maul across his back. "Regus?"

The dwarf grinned broadly. "Looks like he is all there, too," he said in an aside to Adriel. "This one is sharp as a tack. Can't sneak anything past him, can you?"

"What happened?" I repeated, ignoring Regus' mockery.

"Well, what with the battle," the dwarf said, "there's been a sudden shortage of bodies, and this was one of the few undamaged ones available—"

"Not to you," I interrupted. "To the harbinger."

"Oh. Right," Regus said with a sly smile. "I'll let Adriel answer that."

The security chief, I suspected, was extracting his own measure of revenge. No doubt he blamed me for his latest incarnation—as a dwarf, of all things.

Deciding to get in a jab of my own, I said glibly, "I like your new body. It suits you."

Regus' eyes narrowed to slits, but before he could retort, Adriel appeared in my line of sight, her face grave. "The harbinger is gone. He fled not long after Loskin perished."

My amusement died. That was not good, not good at all. I wanted to demand all the details there and then, but first, I had to see to my own body. Sitting upright, I took stock of my surroundings.

I was in a luxuriously appointed bed, in one of the villas, presumably. Looking down, I examined my limbs. Nothing was wrong with them, and according to the Game, my health was full. Someone had healed me while I was unconscious.

So, why had Adriel sounded so worried? "Is something wrong with me?" I asked.

Adriel smiled. "Nothing. You're fine."

"But?" I asked, knowing there had to be one.

"But," Adriel conceded, "you just endured a power word. You seem to have shrugged off its effects, but sometimes the survivors of such spells don't always emerge fully... intact."

"She means your mind's not turned into a puddle," Regus chirped in helpfully. "Your limbs appear to be fully functional, and your spirit is whole. We were afraid one of those might not be true."

"How nice to see you care," I said with a hint of a smile as I swung my legs off the bed. I glanced at Adriel. "What's a power word?"

"A blood memory, a formidable one," Adriel answered.

I nodded. It confirmed my own guess. "Was the spell you used on the wards also a blood memory?"

"Correct."

I stood up and flexed my limbs while I considered the implications. Both spells had been exceedingly powerful. "What about the possessed? Do they also retain their blood memories?"

Adriel shook her head. "No. Only us lichs do. The possessed lost theirs when they swapped bodies."

"Ah, I see." Letting the matter drop, I checked my gear. Nothing was missing. "How long was I out for?"

"Twenty minutes, maybe less," Adriel said.

I exhaled a relieved breath. "Then there's still time."

"Time? Time for what?" Farren asked, stepping into the room. Before I could answer, he looked me up and down and added, "I see you made it through in one piece. Congratulations. That was good work with Loskin."

"Thank you," I said. "You didn't fare too bad against the harbinger either."

"Other than for letting him get away," Farren said. "That's what you're leaving unsaid, right?"

"That's not what I—" I began.

Farren smiled, a twinkle in his eye. "Relax, Wolf, I'm only teasing. But go on. What were you saying before I came in?"

"I was saying, there's still time to catch the harbinger." I paused. "And kill him."

Regus barked out a laugh. "Ridiculous!"

He was the only one amused, though. From their grave expressions, the lichs were taking my suggestion more seriously.

"It's been twenty minutes. He will be back in the nether by now," Adriel said quietly. "And is likely already nesting by the void tree as we speak."

"I realize that," I said. "But we can't give up. Not when we're so close to achieving what we set out to. We have to kill the harbinger now."

Farren shook his head. "It can't be done."

"It can," I insisted.

The lich held up a hand. "Don't get me wrong. I'm not saying we shouldn't take the fight to him. We should. But we must marshal our strength first. We tried a quick strike. It failed. Now it's time to revive the dead and gather allies from New Haven. Only *then* should we march on the stygians."

"Farren is right," Adriel added gently. "I want to see this done as much as you do, but the wisest course right now is to regroup."

I shook my head stubbornly. "How badly was the harbinger injured?"

Farren and Adriel exchanged glances, then the male sibling answered. "I couldn't tell exactly, but I would say he wasn't far from death. But before you get too excited, that may only have been wishful thinking on my part."

I frowned, struggling to reconcile Farren's report with what I'd seen myself earlier. The harbinger had been winning. What had changed? "So, it wasn't just Loskin's demise that spurred his retreat?"

Adriel shook her head. "After Loskin died, I joined Farren and the surviving elites using my... other form. Together, we turned the tide."

Farren chuckled. "My sister is being too modest, and at times, I think she doesn't know her own strength. There is a reason the possessed are terrified of her. When she is roused, Adriel's wrath is fearsome to behold."

Rolling her eyes, Adriel jabbed an elbow into her brother. "Now, you're just making fun of me," she said before turning back to me. "Tooth and claw seemed to do more damage to the harbinger than either Loskin or Farren's spells could manage." Her look turned thoughtful. "It is perhaps something to remember. The harbinger appears to shrug off ranged spell attacks more easily than he does melee ones."

"That rings true," Farren said, his eyes narrowing. "And goes a long way to explaining why he was particularly harsh in his response to our own fighters."

"But Michael," Adriel said, returning to the original subject, "no matter how close to death the harbinger was, he would have healed himself by now."

"Perhaps," I conceded. "But do the stygians recover in the same manner we do?"

Farren frowned. "What do you mean?"

"I mean, do they need sleep to replenish their lost psi, mana, and stamina? Look at your own energy reserves, Farren. You too, Adriel. How depleted are they? Won't the harbinger's reserves be as low—if not lower?"

The two fell silent, thinking it over.

"The Wolf has a point," Regus interjected. "The harbinger is weakened, and if he was here right now, I would support a renewed assault." He shook his head. "But he isn't here. The stygian is in the nether and surrounded by a swarm of minions. He will be impossible to defeat there."

The two siblings exchanged another round of long glances. "You may be right about the harbinger, Michael," Adriel said. "But as you just pointed out, our own reserves are similarly low. Neither of us has had time yet to channel mana and recover. How can we take the fight to the stygian like this?"

Mutely, I removed a double handful of items from my backpack and placed them on the bed one at a time.

You have lost 6 x rank 4 nether protection crystals, 2 x full mana potions, 6 major mana potions, 2 x minor mana potions, 1 moderate healing potion, and 2 full healing potions.

"Are those...?" Farren asked, his eyes widening.

"They are. This first pile consists of nether protection crystals. They will reduce the nether toxicity you suffer in the fog to tier two." I pointed to the next pile. "These are mana regeneration potions. You can use them to replenish your mana before *and* during the fight. The last are health potions—for emergencies."

The lichs said nothing for a moment, but I could see the sparkle was back in Farren's eyes and Adriel was smiling again. Still, her next words dashed my hopes. "It's a good idea, but it won't work."

I stared at her. "Why not? There is nothing stopping you from using the potions, even as non-players."

"That's not it," Farren said. "The potions and crystals will definitely help. But aren't you forgetting about the void tree? It's not as powerful as its elder kin, true, but is still strong enough to keep us from venturing too close. It will serve as a secure base for the harbinger to retreat to if he starts losing, something, mind you, that we ourselves will lack. No, it can't be done the way you mean."

"But—" I protested.

"We can still kill the stygian Power," Adriel interjected, her smile broadening. "But it will require some careful maneuvering."

My eyes flitted from her to Farren. "Then you'll do it?"

"How long will it take us to get to the void tree?" Farren asked, shooting his sister a sideways glance.

"About as long as it took the harbinger... twenty minutes."

Farren smiled as he turned back to me. "Then yes, we'll do it. But the harbinger already has a twenty-minute head start. So, if we mean to do this, we have to move *now*."

"Agreed, but what about—" I began.

"We can discuss the details on the way over," Farren cut in. "You've got what you wanted, Wolf. Now, hustle. We leave immediately."

CHAPTER 373: HOT ON THE TRAIL

Immediately meant five minutes.

It did not take us long to reach consensus on who exactly would pursue the harbinger. Only three of us—Adriel, Farren, and myself—would go. While the lichs saw to their last-minute preparations, Regus led me back to the vault. There was something waiting for me there.

It was a loot chest, of course. A gold one.

"Go ahead," Regus said, gesturing towards it. "We've been keeping it under guard, and no one has looked in yet."

Ignoring Loskin's corpse, which I noted no one had bothered removing yet, I crouched beside the chest and flipped open the lid.

The target is a: <u>sorcerer's coif</u>. This is a rank 6 item that allows you to perceive wards of tier 6 and below. It requires a minimum Magic of 24 to use.

The target is a piece of <u>enchanted mosaic</u>.

The target is a <u>greater attribute gem</u>. It grants you 3 attribute points.

The target is an <u>upgrade gem</u> and allows you to improve any ability by a single tier.

I grinned lopsidedly on reading the description of the first item. It was an artifact I would much rather have had *before* facing the archlich. How much simpler would matters have been if I'd been able to sneak through the vault's wards in the first place?

Still, the item would not go amiss, and it was sure to come in handy in the future. Removing my ranger's leather helmet, I fitted the coif around my head, then re-equipped my headgear.

You have equipped a sorcerer's coif. Effects: ability to detect tier 6 spelled wards.

The chest's other three items were identical to those from the previous one I'd looted; nonetheless, I welcomed them—especially the enchanted mosaic piece. It was not just any piece, but the central cog of the entire artifact. Reaching into the chest, I picked up the mosaic tile.

A Game message unfurled in my mind.

You have acquired all parts of the Emblem of the Reach. Do you wish to combine the pieces?

Replying in the affirmative, I watched the enchanted mosaic disk in my hand grow, as one by one the other puzzle pieces materialized to slot in around it. I didn't have to look into my backpack to know where they had appeared from.

When the process was completed, another Game alert arrived.

Congratulations, Michael! You have created the artifact: the Emblem of the Reach. This item grants the bearer +10 to all attributes.

It was a nice item, but ultimately not one I would keep for long.

"So that's what it looks like," Regus said, looking over my shoulder. "Keep it safe. You don't want to lose that now."

Nodding, I stowed the artifact in my bag of holding. When I glanced up again it was to find Regus peering into the chest inquisitively.

"Is that an upgrade gem?" he asked.

"Yeah."

"And a lesser attribute gem?"

"A greater gem, actually."

Regus grunted, then chewed meditatively at his beard. "I'm guessing you've also gained a few levels from killing Loskin?"

Too preoccupied with thoughts of the harbinger, I hadn't actually reviewed my Game alerts from the battle yet, and I did so now.

You have reached level 195!

My eyes widened slightly at the Adjudicator's message. I'd earned four whole levels, for what in the end had only been a simple bit of thievery and sabotage.

"I did," I murmured, absently answering Regus while I considered the rest of my player profile. My skills had hardly advanced during the encounter.

"You want my advice?" he asked abruptly.

I looked up at him again, almost retorting that I didn't, before I swallowed back the words. "I'm always open to advice," I said mildly.

The dwarf grinned sardonically as if he didn't quite believe that. "All those tasty attribute points you've just earned," he said, sounding a little envious at the notion, "if I were you, I would invest them in Mind."

I stared at him thoughtfully. "Why's that?"

"You haven't met a void tree yet, have you?"

I shook my head.

"I thought not," Regus said, "or you wouldn't ask that. The trees are powerful telepaths." He held up his hands. "I know, I know. According to Adriel, you are none too shabby in that regard either. But if you're going to be battling the harbinger in the vicinity of one of those things, trust me, you want your mind as sharp as possible." He gestured to the other gem. "I'd use that, too, to upgrade any mental defenses you have."

I nodded slowly. "That makes... sense. Thank you." Adriel's advice had been of a similar vein.

"You're welcome," he rumbled. "Now, grab your items and let's go. Your ride should be here any moment."

✳   ✳   ✳

I took Regus's words to heart and put the gems to the exact use he recommended.

Your Mind has increased to rank 107. Other modifiers: +12 from items.

You have upgraded the mind shield ability to <u>fortified mind.</u> Fortified mind is a significant improvement over its lower tiered counterparts. This mind shield variant grants you full access to your offensive psi abilities without compromising your mental defense. When fortified mind is active, one half of your psi pool is used to shield your mind while the other half stays available for psicasting.

Fortified mind shield is an expert ability and requires 5 more ability slots. You have 65 of 107 Mind ability slots remaining.

I found the benefits of the tier three mind shield to be particularly delightful. When it came to matters of Mind, I would no longer have to choose between defense or offense. Fortified mind allowed me to employ both simultaneously.

It was perhaps overkill improving my Mind as much as I had, but I was palpably aware that we would have only one shot at taking down the harbinger and the void tree. If we failed, I could not see us making a second attempt without weeks of preparation.

And that was time I simply could not afford.

Others of the Pack needed me.

It had been close to a month since I'd entered Draven's Reach, and with the exit portal no longer barred to me, I felt a renewed sense of urgency to quickly wrap up my remaining obligations in the dungeon.

Wings flapped overhead.

I looked up to find myself obscured by a shadow nearly as large as the one the harbinger cast. But it was not the stygian Power. It was Adriel.

My ride.

Or rather, our ride, I amended, seeing Farren stride over to join me where I waited on the edge of the courtyard.

Regus had already disappeared, citing some task or another he had to perform, but from the darting looks the dwarf had cast skyward, I thought it might have been disquiet that drove him. The possessed seemed even less comfortable with Adriel in her alternate form. Still, his excuse might not have been entirely fabricated.

In Farren and Adriel's absence, the former security chief had been left in charge and tasked with keeping the other possessed in line. Not that, that appeared necessary.

Farren had wrested control by the simple expedient of not reviving any of the dead except Regus, whose own revival had mostly been completed by Loskin anyway. The threat of not just permanent death, but an eternity spent as a disembodied spirit—one forced to haunt the bones of its former body—was enough to secure the cooperation of even the most recalcitrant of the surviving possessed.

"Impressive, isn't she?" Farren remarked as he reached my side.

I nodded vaguely, avidly watching the dragon descend. It wasn't a real dragon, of course, but rather a flesh golem shaped in the form of one. However, the likeliness and attention to detail was so astonishing that if I hadn't known better, I would have believed it to be a real black dragon instead of what Adriel called it—a dracolich.

"Every time I see Adriel like this, I can't believe she is my little sister."

I turned to him. "You can't do this?"

Farren snorted. "I can't. Neither could Loskin. Adriel is one of the finest flesh sculptors ever to emerge from House Death," he said proudly. "What she can do, the rest of us can only dream of."

He gestured to the landing drake. "Adriel built that almost from scratch. Starting with the skeleton of a dead dragon, she added muscle, sinew, flesh, and scales. It was the work of a lifetime and her finest work ever." He looked at me sideways. "Although, from what she tells me, I think she may have surpassed herself with your companion's new body."

I nodded, even more impressed by my ally. I'd known of Adriel's alternate form—it was how she had traversed in minutes terrain that had taken me days to cross—but this was the first time I'd seen her in it.

"I don't know how I'm going to let her go," Farren mumbled in a voice so low I doubted he expected me to hear.

"She told you what she intends then?" I asked him, not pretending to not have overheard.

The lich nodded somberly. "I offered to take her place, but she won't have it. She believes it is her right and her path to redemption."

I didn't know what to say. I'd known Adriel for only a short time, but I, too, would miss her. "It will save this sector and many others," I said finally, as if that was compensation enough.

"I know," Farren whispered, "but I don't consider it a fair exchange."

"Stop nattering, you two, and hop on," an exasperated voice said in my mind.

Farren laughed and turned to me. "Ready?"

I nodded, and he pulled me forward towards the dracolich.

*   *   *

Flying across the dungeon atop a dracolich was both exhilarating and frightening.

Other than for a terse, "hang on," Adriel made no allowances for her passengers. Climbing to altitude had been scary, but my agile hands and feet had kept me in place. Farren had struggled more, but he appeared more experienced with our strange manner of conveyance, and I was soon following his lead. Once Adriel leveled out, though, things became more pleasant, and I relaxed enough to enjoy the experience.

But my leisure did not last long.

"We'll enter the central fog in ten minutes," Adriel said in my mind.

Glancing ahead, I saw that she was right. The fog bank was an ominous presence on the horizon, and as rapidly as the dracolich was flying, it grew perceptibly larger with every stroke of her wings.

"Have you activated the crystals I gave you?" I asked, projecting my words in both their minds.

"We have," Farren said. *"Our nether protections are active. What about you?"*

"Breaking my crystals as we speak," I replied.

You have activated 3 single-use enchantments, increasing your Strength by +8, your Magic by +8, and your Dexterity by +8. Duration: 1 hour.

I didn't have many attribute-enhancing enchantment crystals and had been saving the ones I did have for when I really needed them. If any time was that, then this was it.

"*It's time we told you the plan,*" Adriel said.

"*That sounds... ominous,*" I said.

"*Nothing so bad as all that,*" Adriel said with a chuckle. "*But it will require sacrifice from each of us.*" Her voice grew quieter. "*Are you prepared for that, Wolf?*"

"*I will do what's necessary,*" I said determinedly. I'd come this far, and I was not about to back out except for the most dire of reasons.

"*Good,*" Farren said, tapping me on the shoulder. "*Take this.*"

Glancing back, I saw he held a necklace clenched in his fist. Grabbing it quickly lest it fall to the dungeon below, I stuffed the item in one of my pockets without examining it. "*What is it?*"

"*My phylactery,*" Adriel said.

For a moment, I was dumbstruck. "*Your what? What were you thinking, bringing that here?*"

"*It is necessary,*" Adriel said serenely. "*Before I can take Draven's place, the phylactery will have to be broken to release my spirit.*"

I shook my head. "*But still... the risk. Couldn't you wait until we've won to do this?*"

"*No. Farren and I have talked it over, and we both agree. We can't wait until we defeat the harbinger to restore the guardian. We have to tackle both objectives simultaneously. The risk of failure is too great otherwise.*"

"*But... but...*" My thoughts raced, recalling what Adriel had told me of the void tree and the guardian. The sapling had wrapped itself around Draven and he couldn't be awoken unless... "*You want me to kill the void tree while you two fight the harbinger,*" I said, realizing what they intended.

"*If you can, yes,*" Farren said. "*But you don't need to kill the sapling, only survive its touch long enough to awaken Draven. Then Adriel can take his place.*" He paused. "*That way, even if we lose the fight against the harbinger, we still win. The guardian will be restored to full strength and he—she, I mean—can begin restoring the barriers around the dungeons.*"

I said nothing, recognizing the truth of his words.

"*It is a lot to ask,*" Adriel added, "*but of the three of us, only you stand a chance of withstanding the tree's psionic touch long enough to awaken the guardian.*"

I thought for a bit. "*If the guardian is awake, will he help us defeat the harbinger?*"

Neither sibling answered.

"*Adriel? Farren?*" I prompted.

Farren sighed. "*We don't know. The guardians are constructs and bound by the commands of the Game and their creators. The spirits who animate them are not free to do as they please. That way lies anarchy.*"

"*Farren is unfortunately right,*" Adriel added. "*It all depends on how much leeway the Primes granted the guardians to defend their sectors. Draven may be able to help, or he may be prevented from acting against any denizen of the dungeon. And there is no way to tell beforehand which it will be.*"

"*But what we do know,*" Farren said, "*is that the guardian can close the barrier. Once he does that, the void tree will be starved of nether and wither away. It may take months or years, but it will happen. The sapling is still too young to survive on its own without help from its elders.*"

"*So, will you do it?*" Adriel asked softly.

"*Of course,*" I replied. There was never any doubt of my willingness, only the how. "*But reaching the tree might be a problem. Even if you could draw the harbinger away from the tree—which is what I assume you intend—the moment the spores spot me, he will return.*"

"*Leave the spores and the harbinger to us,*" Farren said casually.

"*You have a plan for dealing with them?*" I asked.

"*We do,*" Adriel said.

"*Tell me,*" I said, even as I began working out how to perform my own role.

"*First,*" Farren began, "*we will...*"

CHAPTER 374: TWIN OBJECTIVES

As we entered the central fog bank, the lichs and I began our final preparations.

You have cast heightened reflexes, load controller, fade, and trigger-cast quick mend.

Farren has cast reaper's sanctuary, granting you the buff: <u>death immune</u> (+100% death magic resistance). Duration: 5 minutes.

Farren has cast reaper's shield on you, granting you the buff: <u>death's favored</u> (+75% death magic resistance). Duration: 1 hour.

Farren has cast lich's aid, increasing the effectiveness of all your skills and abilities by 25%. Duration: 1 hour.

Farren cast two separate death magic buffs on me, and while they did not stack with each other, the second would replace the first when it ran out. Together, they would ensure I was well-protected against death spells, and given the harbinger's penchant for such, I gladly welcomed them.

Adriel has cast undead's champion on you (+100% damage inflicted). Duration: 20 minutes.

Adriel has cast warrior's boon on you (+20 to all physical attributes). Duration: 20 minutes.

Adriel's own buffs were no less powerful than her siblings' but were more offensively inclined and would double my effectiveness in battle.

"*We're here,*" Adriel said.

We were inside the thick nether cloud obscuring the dungeon's center and had been in it for nearly the last minute, but by 'here,' Adriel did not mean the fog bank; she meant the void tree itself. We hovered directly over it, high enough that the stygians below could not sense us.

Glancing down over the dracolich's side, I tried to see what distinguished this spot from any other but beheld only opaque mist. "*You're sure?*"

"*I am,*" she replied. "*I do not need to see to sense the guardian's presence. Draven is directly beneath. Are you ready?*"

"*One moment,*" I said. There were two final preparations I needed to make. The first was establishing our position. Removing the pioneer's compass from my coat pocket, I clenched my fist around the artifact and focused on the safe zone.

You have attuned a pioneer's compass to the safe zone of sector 73,102.

Just like a beacon, the safe zone's location appeared in my mind's eye. We were due south of it. The compass could not tell me how far away it was, but I didn't need to know that. All I needed was a heading—a point to navigate by.

Stowing the compass in my pocket again, I turned my focus inwards. The last thing I needed to do was perform a casting of my own.

You have cast fortified mind, reserving half of your psi for your mental shields. Psi remaining for use: 50%.

As the spell fell into place, I felt my subconscious split in two, one half forming an unassailable wall around my mind, while the other part continued to feed me energy.

Now I was equipped to both find the sapling and survive its touch—or so I hoped. *"Ready,"* I pronounced with satisfaction.

Immediately, Adriel dropped into a dive, and we fell as silently as a stone.

Wind rushed by, brought into being by the ferocious speed of our descent, and tore at my clothes, face, and hair. Squeezing my eyes shut, I kept watch for the ground with my mindsight. Behind me, I heard Farren whispering to himself, but couldn't tell if the wild ride had him terrified or excited.

It was probably both.

The seconds ticked away, and with each, my anticipation and dread grew. This was it. My last battle in the dungeon. One final roll of the dice to save the sector and an untold number of lives.

My mental sight blossomed into life.

Hundreds—no, thousands—of mindglows had just breached the edge of my awareness. *"Ground!"* I yelled. *"A hundred yards away and closing fast."*

The dracolich had been waiting for my word, and in the next instant, she pulled out sharply from her dive to skim along the ground.

I took careful note of the safe zone's beacon in my mind. By its reckoning, Adriel was heading east.

Behind me, Farren fell silent. He could hear as well as I, the enraged hissing, chittering, and roars of the stygians below as the nest sensed the threat descending from above. *"How many?"* he asked tersely.

"Thousands," I replied laconically.

"The harbinger?" Adriel asked.

"Behind us and already in motion," I replied. I had sensed the stygian Power the moment the nest had come into range, a mindglow larger than any of the others nearby.

"Then we're off to a good start," Farren said in a tone that told me he was smiling again. *"Do it now, Adriel."*

The dracolich banked left sharply, causing her lower wing to almost brush the ground. I jumped off. So did Farren.

Protected by his shield, the lich weathered the short drop to the ground without suffering anything other than a few cuts and bruises while I broke my own fall using windborne.

"Good luck," Adriel called, wings flapping hard as she fought for altitude. The dracolich would cut a wide circle through the fog and return when we were ready.

I bounced back to my feet and scanned the area swiftly with mindsight. We'd been lucky in our choice of landing spots, and the immediate vicinity was free of stygians.

But the creatures were already converging from far and wide as an unknowable number of spores reported our position. Setting my stance, I drew a couple of stone flasks from my bomber's belt.

For now, I only had one job. Protecting Farren.

Glancing behind me, I saw the lich was already muttering the words of a spell under his breath. Leaving him to it, I whipped back my arm and flung the flasks in my hand at the closest clump of stygians.

You have ignited 1 acid bomb and 1 firebomb!

Acid splashed and fire ignited, then the pair mixed in a volatile combination that set the mist flashing orange and tossing asunder the closest creatures.

You have killed 5 stygian crawlers and 3 stygian serpents.

I drew another pair of bombs and threw it as quickly to my right. Repeating the maneuver twice more, I thinned the number of stygians approaching from the rear and the left.

You have killed 25 stygians.

Trying to hold back the nest was a losing proposition, of course. There were too many stygians converging on us, but all I sought to do was buy Farren time.

Farren has cast purifying dome. Duration: 12 minutes.

An electric ring rippled outwards from the lich. It passed harmlessly over me but burned away the mists wherever it touched it.

You have entered a purifying field. All environmental ill-effects have been nullified.

The circle kept expanding until Farren and I stood in a dome of crystal-clear and sweet-smelling air that was about twenty yards in diameter. "Much better," I said, throwing a grin at the lich behind me but, already in the midst of another spell, he failed to hear me.

Shrugging, I drew my swords. Farren's spell had laid bare the dozens of approaching stygians—a mix of hydras, serpents, and crawlers. There was no sign of the harbinger yet. He was certainly taking his time, perhaps to ascertain there was no trap lurking, but I did not doubt he would eventually arrive.

Right, let's see how many I can kill before he gets here. Drawing psi, I leaped towards the closest stygian.

*   *   *

You have charmed 8 of 8 targets for 20 seconds.
You have induced 6 of 6 targets to sleep for 40 seconds.

I danced between the stygians, my blades in constant motion. My right flank was protected by a pair of charmed hydras, my left by four bespelled serpents.

I couldn't hide. I tried twice already but failed, confirmation enough of the presence of the spores. Yet, even without my stealth, I wreaked havoc among the nether creatures.

A hydra nipped at me from the front. Swaying out of the path of the darting head, I chopped down with the sword in my right hand.

Courtesy of the lichs' buffs—Adriel's especially—my weapons were empowered beyond the norm, and the gray stygian blade cleaved right through the hydra's neck.

You have crippled a hydra!

Strengthening my arms yet further, I went on the offensive.

You have cast whirlwind and piercing strike.

Lunging forward, I ripped open the hydra's second head with the blade in my left hand, then pivoting on my heel, chopped off two more in quick succession.

You have crippled a hydra!
You have crippled a hydra!
You have crippled a hydra!

Shrieking in pain, the hydra attempted to retreat. I didn't let up. Dashing forward, I launched a blistering assault, cutting and slashing at my foe from two different directions at once.

You have killed a hydra.

The hydra crashed lifelessly to the ground, but its demise only marked an opportunity for the rest of the waiting nether creatures. Surging forward, a dozen crawlers rushed over the corpse in an attempt to reach me.

They failed.

You have teleported into a stygian serpent's shadow.

I emerged from the aether on the other side of the lich around whom the skirmish was centered. Farren was still blind to the world and unbothered by the few stygians nipping at his shield. The spell he was casting, I knew, was a long and complex one.

The serpent struck me. Somersaulting forward, I leaped over the blow and plunged both my blades into its torso.

You have killed a stygian serpent with a fatal blow.

Freeing myself from the dead creature's coils, I rolled away from the snapping jaws of another stygian and surged back to my feet to bury my blades in the crawlers attempting to sneak up on me.

You have killed 2 stygian crawlers.

A giant shape that dwarfed even the hydras thumped down less than ten yards from the shielded lich, causing the other stygians to scatter. It was the harbinger. I have been monitoring his careful approach for a while now and was not caught by surprise.

Ignoring Farren, the harbinger fixed his malevolent gaze on me. "Wolfling, you've returned. How foolish of you."

"Not as foolish as you falling for my ploy at the archlich's compound," I retorted. Retracting my blades from the dead crawlers, I advanced on the harbinger.

"I'm ready," Farren interjected. *"Should I release the spell?"*

"Go," I replied tersely, not taking my eyes off the harbinger as I drew psi in anticipation. *"I'm ready."*

"On my way," Adriel replied from above.

"So, that was your doing? The archlich was *your* pawn?" the harbinger hissed, unaware of our mental asides. "I should've known!" Not waiting for my response, he threw himself into motion, moving so rapidly he was little more than a blur in my vision.

I flung myself out of the way, barely avoiding his snapping beak and searching claws.

You have evaded a stygian harbinger's attack.

I laughed as I rolled back to my feet. "You should have," I agreed, continuing the conversation as if there had been no interruption.

The stygian's eyes glinted. "Arrogant cur, I'll—"

Farren has cast oblivion.

The harbinger broke off, seeming to sense the spell almost at the same time I did. Forgetting me entirely, the stygian whipped around to pin Farren with a menacing glare.

It was far too late to stop the lich's casting, though.

The air flashed black, transforming from one second to the next in a darkness so thick I could almost taste it on my tongue. Closing my eyes, I waited.

The spell rolled over me—

You have entered an <u>oblivion field</u>.
You have passed a magical resistance check! You have failed to disintegrate!

—then the harbinger—

A harbinger is immune to death magic. A harbinger has failed to disintegrate.

—and then, the rest of the stygians.

A stygian crawler has died.
A stygian serpent has died.
A stygian crawler has died.
...

...
A level 4 stygian spore has died.
A level 6 stygian spore has died.

My lips twitched upwards in a smile at the death notifications. Farren was nothing if not consummate a death caster, and both he and Adriel had been certain the oblivion field would extend all the way to the void tree.

Of course, the spell's strength would decrease exponentially the further afield it went, and that would allow most of the stygians to escape unscathed.

Not so the spores.

As mere rank zero creatures, even the faintest touch of the oblivion spell would slay them.

"Fools!" the harbinger crowed. "Your death magic cannot touch me!"

I wanted to retort, but wisely refrained. Because, of course, it was not the harbinger but the spores that were the true targets of the spell. Our foe had not seemed to have caught onto that fact yet, though. Flaring his wings and rearing back his head, the harbinger prepared to strike—at me or Farren, I wasn't sure.

And in the end, it didn't matter.

Before the stygian could release the attack he readied, Adriel crashed down, her clawed feet digging deep into his back as she landed squarely atop him.

A stygian harbinger has been critically injured!

"*Go!*" Adriel ordered.

I went. Targeting a lone crawler in the fog, I shadow blinked away.

I had a guardian to awaken.

Chapter: 375: Foreplay

You are hidden.

I emerged from the aether with a smile on my face. Our gambit had worked. The spores were destroyed, and I had my stealth back.

Everything was going smoothly.

The crawler I'd teleported to had still not spotted me, and I backed away before that could change. Orienting myself using the beacon in my mind, I crept westward in the direction of the void tree. My target could not be far.

The range of Farren's oblivion spell was two hundred yards, and since all the spores had seemingly been destroyed, the tree had to be somewhere inside that range. But, after less than a dozen steps, I ground to a halt as the harbinger let out a strident cry. It was a clarion call for help.

And the entire nest responded.

An instant later, every stygian in mindsight range was moving towards the harbinger. And there were a lot of them. Farren's spell had killed a few hundred nether creatures. But that still left thousands standing, and right now, each and every one of them was rallying to the Power's cry.

It didn't matter that the spores were dead, and they'd lost their shared sight; the nether creatures were experts at maneuvering by sound and they had the harbinger's call to fix on.

Multiple hostile entities have failed to detect you!

I rose to my full height, still hidden. Moving forward was out of the question. I would have to wait for the swarm to pass by. Until then, I would have to do my best to evade detection.

Forcing myself into a loose-limbed stance at odds with my keyed-up state, I watched the closest clump of mindglows draw closer. Three seconds. Two. One. Then, they were upon me.

Dancing left, I avoided a slithering serpent.

Ducking low, I dodged the low hanging head of a hydra.

Turning my body sideways, I let two crawlers pass on either side.

Throwing myself flat, I escaped trampling by a hydra.

I emerged from each incident alive and hidden. One of the crawler's tentacles had brushed my arm as it passed by, and a hydra had actually clipped me on the shoulder. Despite these close calls, though, my stealth—bolstered by fade and the mist itself—had held true.

A minute later, with my heart still pounding and a sickly grin pasted on my face, I picked myself up. The swarm had passed, and miraculously, I lived to tell the tale.

The path ahead was clear with not a single mindglow in sight. Focusing my attention eastwards, I winced.

I could barely make out Adriel and Farren's mindglows, so swamped were they by stygians. It did not bode well for my allies, and although the lichs had

had the harbinger at a disadvantage earlier, they would not be able to keep him at bay for long now.

But the two were still fighting, and while they were, hope remained.

I swung back westward. I would have to fulfill my own part quickly.

* * *

Ten yards later, I located my quarry.

The void tree was characterized not by a bright mindglow, but by the distinct absence of one. It sat ninety yards ahead, an almost perfect circle of emptiness, in the middle of twenty weavers.

It could only be the sapling.

I glanced back. My allies were fifty yards behind. Adriel had cut it close, setting us down less than one hundred and fifty yards from the sapling, but right now, I had cause to be thankful for that. It made my own task easier.

Pausing, I took a second to plan my approach.

The first challenge was the terrain. It was unlikely to offer much help. What I've seen of it thus far had all been flat rock, unrelieved by either crevices or outcroppings.

The second problem was the weavers. The creatures did not have their mind shields active, but that would change the moment they or the sapling sensed me, and while I could eventually break through their mental defenses with shatter, it would take time I didn't have.

Lastly, there was the void tree itself to consider. I didn't know what it was capable of, and the only way I'd find that out was in the doing. I could be certain, though, that if I was detected, it would call on the harbinger for help.

There was no question that my best chance of success lay in remaining undetected, but there were enough unknowns that I felt uncomfortable with the idea of advancing further without any contingencies.

Unfortunately, time was of the essence, and I couldn't afford to spend even a few minutes arranging the battlefield to my liking.

Full speed ahead then, I thought, creeping forward as swiftly as my stealth allowed.

* * *

I covered the next forty yards quickly, only drawing to a halt when I reached the fifty-yard line. The weavers were in teleport range, and I had another decision to make.

I could either cover the remaining distance in a single bound, the more dangerous option, or on foot, ready to retreat at a moment's notice.

"Adriel," I asked, reaching to her mindglow, "*how is it going?*"

"*Poorly,*" she replied bluntly. "*We will be overrun soon. Hurry.*"

I winced. The dracolich's response made my decision for me. "*I'm going in,*" I said, then shadow blinked.

You have teleported into a stygian weaver's shadow.
Multiple hostile entities have failed to detect you!

You have passed a mental resistance check!
A hostile entity's beguiling aura has failed to dominate you!
A hostile entity's beguiling aura has failed to dominate you!
A hostile entity's beguiling aura has failed to dominate you!
...
...

I stepped out of the aether, bombarded by a near endless litany of Game alerts. Momentarily overwhelmed, I froze in place while I waited for the messages to subside or for something to attack.

Neither happened.

It took me a split second longer to understand why. Despite the frightening proximity of the twenty weavers, I remained hidden. More alarming though, was the second alert. It was *still* scrolling through my mind.

A hostile entity's beguiling aura has failed to dominate you!
A hostile entity's beguiling aura has failed to dominate you!
...

The entity in question had to be the sapling, and if I was interpreting the Game message correctly, the creature had an aura about it that bespelled everything nearby.

How big the field was, I couldn't tell, and it didn't truly matter. I was already inside the void tree's sphere of influence. Nor could I leave. Besides, I was resisting its domination attempts.

For now.

That could change at any moment, though. All it would take was a single failed resistance attempt...

Let's get this done quickly. Slowly turning my head from left to right, I scanned my surroundings.

I was inside the perimeter of weavers. The creatures looked outwards and stood stock-still, unnaturally so, and were probably bespelled. A marble statue was in front of me, close enough that I could see part of it through the mist. Only its hooves and lower legs were visible, but from them I could tell it was enormous.

Draven.

A white tree, unlike any I'd seen before, and one that so closely resembled the guardian in color I had missed it, was wrapped around the statue, its branches creeping all over him in spider-like fashion.

The void sapling.

I examined it carefully. The sapling's central ash-white trunk was as spindly as the rest of its limbs and meandered down the guardian before burrowing into the ground.

The sapling had nothing so wholesome as leaves either. Its rail-thin branches were covered in ebon-black thorns that looked like condensed slivers of the void. Completing the hellish picture were the concentrated tendrils of nether slowly seeping out of the cracks and knots in the bark.

Right, so that's a void tree.

Letting my gaze drift downward, I scanned the base of the statue, looking for the indentation Adriel had told me would be there.

At first, I didn't see it, and my pulse began to race, but then my gaze alighted on a particularly dense patch of prickly thorns. The tree had gone to great lengths to conceal the spot in question.

That must be where the Emblem goes.

I only had to reach it—and brush aside the obscuring branches and thorns. All without alerting the tree.

Nothing to it, I thought sardonically.

Staying crouched and rotating my feet a few inches at a time, I turned around until I was facing the tree.

Multiple hostile entities have failed to detect you!

Step one complete. I rose into a half-crouch. Next, I had to cover the remaining distance to the guardian.

"*Michael!*"

I froze.

It was Adriel, and from the sounds of it, she was only a few feet behind me. Slowly, I glanced over my shoulder.

And found myself staring at a ghost.

"*You'd better hurry,*" the spirit said. "*I've died, and Farren will, too, soon.*"

CHAPTER 376: SHADOW GAMES

"Damn," I muttered, staring at spirit-Adriel in shock. She looked identical to her younger human form, and like Ghost, was fully formed. *"What about the harbinger?"* I asked, recovering.

"Close to death, but still alive," Adriel said, advancing closer to study the void tree. *"So, this is our foe."*

I glanced from her to the sapling. *"You're not afraid of it?"*

The spirit shrugged. *"It cannot hurt me in this form, nor even see me without the spores' aid."* She gestured at herself ruefully. *"But, like this, I'm equally powerless to harm it."* Her gaze flickered back to mine *"What's your plan?"*

"I meant to creep up to the base and place the Emblem, but now... I'm not sure. I may need to rush things."

She nodded. *"Don't let me keep you. Go ahead, I'll keep watch."* Her lips twisted. *"I can do that much at least."*

"Thanks," I replied absently, my mind already working on the problem.

Once Farren died, the harbinger and the rest of the nest would return. And if things were about to get noisy, staying stealthy didn't matter anymore—I paused, a thought occurring—or did it?

I was assuming that when the entire nest returned, I wouldn't be able to hide, but given the evidence of my approach, was that right?

"Adriel... If Farren dies, will he be alright?"

"Of course," she said casually. *"He did not bring his phylactery. His spirit will re-materialize in the court."*

"That's what I thought," I murmured. *"And the harbinger, just how badly did you say he was injured?"*

"Bad enough that, with a minute more, I believe we could have killed him." She studied me curiously. *"Why, what are you thinking?"*

"I'll tell you in a second, but first tell me about the battle with the harbinger—what worked and what didn't."

✳ ✳ ✳

I was about to change the plan.

Never a wise idea mid-execution, especially with the stakes so high. In my current position, I knew I could awaken the guardian. One quick darkness bolt at the obscuring thorns, then a speedy dash across five yards, and the Emblem would be in place.

But neither Farren nor Adriel had been certain how much help Draven would be able to offer against the stygians. It was conceivable he would be constrained from harming both the tree and the harbinger. And once I awoke the guardian, I lost the element of surprise—and perhaps my best chance of ambushing the harbinger.

Which led to option two, and the one I was presently considering: ambush the harbinger, kill him, then the void tree, and *only* thereafter restore Draven.

The original plan was the surest path to victory, even if that victory took months or years to be fully realized. Option two, on the other hand, would end in either complete and instant triumph or total and utter failure.

Both alternatives were not without danger either. With the original plan, if Draven did not—or could not—help, I would be revealed and stuck in the middle of the stygian nest with an angry harbinger and void tree. With option two, if I failed to awaken the guardian, everything we had done would've been for naught.

Still, I preferred the second plan.

If only because it left less to chance. Success and failure would depend on my own ability to execute and *not* on Draven's willingness or limitations. Then, too, I was always at my most dangerous when striking from the shadows.

And the risks were minimal. Yes, I could fail at slaying the harbinger. Yes, I could fall prey to the void sapling. But Ghost was safe in a soulbound cloak and would not be endangered. I, too, had an extra life to spare. Only Adriel would be at risk, but there were measures I could take to protect her phylactery.

"Farren just died," Adriel said suddenly. *"Whichever way you are going, now is the time to decide."*

The lich had listened attentively to my proposal and had not tried to sway me either way. I closed my eyes for a moment, contemplating both choices again.

"We go with option two," I said softly.

"Then get ready," Adriel said. *"Here comes the harbinger."*

✳ ✳ ✳

You have cast fade, blurring your form and making you 50% harder to see for 2 minutes.

While Adriel kept watch, I renewed fade, my shortest-lasting buff, then remained where I was, not daring to advance an inch further towards the tree and equally afraid to retreat closer to the circle of weavers at my back.

It was best to stay put.

With bare blades in hand, I observed the harbinger's approach through mindsight.

A hostile entity has failed to detect you! You are hidden.

The stygian Power was no more able to detect me than the weavers and void tree. Swooping down from up high, the harbinger descended near vertically. Mindsight put him almost directly above the guardian. Was he going to land in front or behind the statue? I wondered. Not that it mattered much.

Thirty feet from the ground and still outside my line of sight, the harbinger's mindglow stopped moving. I frowned. Was the stygian hovering mid-air? But I didn't hear the flap of wings.

"The wretch!" Adriel hissed suddenly. *"He has landed atop Draven!"*

I glanced at the spirit. Her lips were thinned, and she quivered with anger. Clearly, Adriel considered the harbinger's actions blasphemy.

"He's sitting on the statue?" I asked, startled. *"How is he managing that?"*

"Draven is a centaur," she said as if that explained everything.

And it did.

The harbinger had to have landed on the centaur's back, which from the stygian's point of view, was the only practical thing to do. Perched on the guardian, he would have an easier time landing and taking off, and as an added bonus, being thirty feet up meant he was protected from most landbound threats.

But not me.

Turning my mindsight outwards for a moment, I checked on the progress of the other stygians. The harbinger had not waited for the rest of the nest— and why would he? As a result, they still had some way to travel before they reached us.

Good. They would not be able to interfere while I dealt with the Power. There were still the weavers and the sapling to consider, but I couldn't do anything about them.

"How far up the guardian does the void tree reach?" I asked.

"The sapling is still young and doesn't extend beyond the centaur's legs."

I smiled. That reduced the chance of interference by the sapling, although what form that could take, I was at a loss to say. *"What about the harbinger, what is he doing?"*

"The wretch has curled up in a ball and closed his eyes," Adriel replied. *"He is either meditating or about to go to sleep."*

"Even better," I said with a grin.

Tightening my grip on my blades, I got ready to move. *"I guess it's time I introduced myself,"* I said for Adriel's benefit. *"Here goes."*

Then without further ado, I shadow blinked.

✳   ✳   ✳

You have teleported onto the back of a stygian harbinger.
You have cast whirlwind, piercing strike, and crippling blow.

I emerged from the aether with my blades held aloft and spelled energy rushing into my arms, redoubling their speed and power. Dropping down atop the harbinger, I spread my legs then snapped them shut to straddle his hyena-like neck.

Securely straddled, I brought my swords flashing down.

You have backstabbed a harbinger for 5x more damage! You have critically injured your target.

You have backstabbed a harbinger for 2.5x more damage! You have critically injured your target.

A hostile entity has detected you! You are no longer hidden.

It was not enough.

As devastating as my initial onslaught was, my foe survived. I had not expected otherwise, though. Even hovering on the brink of death, a Power like the harbinger would not be easy to kill. Withdrawing my blades, I unleashed a second flurry of blows.

You have injured your target.
You have injured your target.

The harbinger's eyes snapped open.

Absent of befuddlement or even surprise, they shone with burning rage. He was about to counter, I knew, and likely with an attack beyond my ability to evade.

I played my next card.

Reaching for the spell sitting idle all these long days in the ring on my right hand, I activated its casting. But not for an instant did I stop stabbing.

You have trigger-cast cold sphere.

A stygian harbinger has failed a magical resistance check! 1 of 1 targets have been chilled.

You have injured your target.
You have injured your target.

My gambit effectively froze the harbinger in place.

Any physical maneuvers he thought to perform now would take too long. He'd be dead before he completed them. The stygian knew it, as did I. That did not preclude him from launching spelled attacks, though.

A stygian harbinger has cast nether's cloying touch.

I made no attempt to dodge or evade.

The harbinger's response was one I had expected—sort of. While I had no way of predicting the exact spells my foe would employ, I knew his magic schools of choice—and was prepared for both.

Trusting in my defenses, I plunged my blades into the harbinger again, inflicting huge swaths of damage with each blow.

You have passed a magical resistance check. Your void armor has repelled your foe's attack!

You have injured your target.
You have injured your target.

Smiling grimly, I kept hacking at my foe's neck like a butcher at work. In. Out. Over and over.

On the ground below, I sensed the weavers and the void tree turn my way, but I didn't let up on my attacks. Before I focused on them, I had to slay the harbinger.

A stygian harbinger has cast leeching touch.

Your void armor has repelled your foe's attack!

I laughed, the sound an expression more of relief than joy. I couldn't help it. I didn't know if the harbinger had access to other spells, but the two he'd just employed were the wrong type—and I had resisted both. Thanks to my own training, Adriel's cloak, and the two lichs' buffs, my nether and death magic resistances were incredibly high.

The harbinger had guessed wrong twice. And now my task was almost done. Predatory instincts told me so. My foe teetered on death.

Ramming my blades down one final time, I lifted my head and howled in triumph.

You have killed a level 315 stygian harbinger!
You have reached level 199!
Your sneaking has reached rank 19, your shortswords rank 18, and your null death rank 4.

Congratulations, Michael! You have slain your first tier 7 creature and accomplished the feat: A Mighty Player! Requirements: be unsworn to any Power, possess an evolved Class, and reach player level 250. Or be unsworn to any Power, possess an evolved Class, and slay a foe above level 300. Your spirit signature has been etched with a new Mark!

You have acquired the Mark: Powerful Initiate, and have begun to tread the ways of Power yourself. The path to greatness is paved by death, and no player can rise to prominence in the Game without pitting himself against its strongest contenders. You have done so and emerged victorious. Note, as a Powerful Initiate, you have not yet ascended to the rank of Power but have merely set yourself on the path to reaching it.

As a result of your new Power Mark, you have gained the trait: Higher Evolution. This is a trait granted to all would-be Powers and allows you to evolve your Class beyond the limits imposed on ordinary players.

Your task: Cleanse the Corruption! has been updated.
You have slain a stygian harbinger, the primary protector and enforcer of the nether's ambitions in this sector. Your objective remains unchanged: rid Draven's Reach of the nether's corruption.

The glint in the harbinger's eyes died, his eyelids drooped, and his neck sagged. My nemesis' silent descent into death was almost anticlimactic, but I knew my own assault had only been the last in a series of blows dealt by my allies—and foes—both here in the fog and the archlich's courts.

In the end, none of that mattered, though.

The harbinger was dead. And I was not.

The battle was far from over, however. A glistening sliver of ebony, visible even through the thick mist and half-glimpsed around the corner of my eye, caught my attention.

Cutting short my victory celebrations, I jerked my gaze downwards. The sliver was a thorn from the sapling, and accompanying it were hundreds more.

All flying my way with deadly intent.

CHAPTER 377: MIND GAMES

The good news was that the thorns appeared to have been fired blindly. There was bad news too, though. As widely dispersed as the thorn barrage was, it would be impossible to avoid entirely.

So, instead of ducking, I huddled small, tucking my chin into my chest and shielding my head with my arms while I waited for the hammer to fall.

A stygian thorn has failed to injure you. Your mind shield has blocked the attack, absorbing the psi damage.
A stygian thorn has failed to injure you.
A stygian thorn has failed to injure you.
...
...

In all, two dozen thorns struck me—all of which were rebuffed by my mind shield. Amazed, but pleasantly surprised by the outcome, I raised my head.

More missiles were heading my way.

These, while thorns too, were of a different kind and were already too close to evade. With no other choice, I gritted my teeth and waited for the second storm to hit.

10 blight thorns have struck you.
Your void armor has repelled 7 blight thorns!
Your void armor has reduced the nether damage incurred from the remaining 3 projectiles by 100%.

Huh, I thought, impressed anew by the strength of my defenses. I had escaped two full volleys of nether and psi projectiles unscathed. But I was sure more attacks were on the way, and it was time to move.

My mindsight reported the immediate vicinity to be empty—falsely so, the weavers had shielded themselves—but I wasn't fooled. Slipping free of the harbinger's corpse, I jumped down from the guardian's back.

Halfway to the bottom, I materialized a ramp of air and coasted the remaining distance. I hit the ground running and raced towards the void sapling. It was time for my next kill.

A few short steps later, I was under its sickly branches. Another torrent of thorns descended from above, better aimed now that the tree could see me. Evading as many of the tiny slivers as I could, I lashed out at the ash-white trunk.

A level 201 void sapling is immune to necrotic damage! You have failed to injure your target.

Urgh, I spat as my blades clanged off the bark as if it were steel.

"Hurry, Michael," Adriel called from behind. *"The nest will be here soon."*

Nodding sharply, I rammed my stygian swords back into their sheathes and, reaching over my shoulder, grabbed ebonheart by the hilt. Another shower of thorns fell.

Dancing around them, I thrust the black blade point first into the tree's meaty trunk.

It, too, failed to penetrate.

A level 201 void sapling is immune to physical damage! You have failed to injure your target.

"Damn, damn, and damn," I cursed. What was it with this damnable tree?

Motion around the corner of my eye drew my attention—more blight thorns. The weavers had found me again. Dropping flat onto the ground, I let the incoming hail of projectiles sail over me.

You have evaded 6 blight thorns.

While I was presently resistant to the weavers' attacks, that would only hold true as long as my void armor remained active. Every attack my armor fended off drained it a bit further, and I couldn't afford to be needlessly struck.

Surging back to my feet, I materialized a psi dagger and flung it at the sapling.

Your target's mind shield has blocked your attack.

I'd more than half-expected the result but had flung the dagger anyway as a test. Now, I knew the tree was only shielded—and not immune to psi damage. That gave me two viable means of killing it. There was no quick way to implement either though, and I needed to regroup.

Turning tail, I fled.

Thorns raced after me—both stygian and blight ones—but before they could close, I shadow blinked out of reach.

You have teleported into a stygian crawler's shadow. You are hidden.

✳　✳　✳

An hour later, I was still in the mist.

Meditating psi and channeling mana, I listened to the frustrated cries of the stygians searching for me. Despite having numbers on their side, none of the creatures had come close to finding me.

Retreating from the void tree had been necessary if only to give the stygians a wider search area. Even with my ridiculously high stealth, I couldn't see myself going undetected once the nest's denizens crammed shoulder to shoulder around the tree.

And truly, time did not press down on me as severely as before. The harbinger, the biggest threat, had been eliminated—leaving me far more options.

Your psi and mana have been fully replenished.

Opening my eyes, I took stock of myself.

Most of the lichs' buffs had dissipated, but they were no longer necessary. None of my remaining foes were anywhere near as fearsome as the harbinger. It was time to return to the fray. Rising to my feet, I stalked through the mists.

"This is a strange way to fight," Adriel remarked.

I chuckled, relaxed and at ease despite the thousands of stygians between me and my target. *"I'm not one for a stand-up fight, not if I can avoid it."*

Adriel smiled crookedly. *"I can see that."* She, too, was in good spirits. Success lay close at hand. *"Are you going to whittle down the stygians' numbers before renewing your assault on the tree?"*

For a moment, I was tempted. Slaying a few thousand stygians would undoubtedly take me to level two hundred, making me an elite in truth, but that was not the mission and getting sidetracked was a good way to get killed again.

I shook my head. *"No need. Without the spores, the creatures can't find me, and I need to get rid of that sapling before it creates any more of those troublesome things."* And besides, I could always kill the stygians *after* I saw to the void tree.

Adriel tilted her head. *"I hadn't thought of that. You're right, but how do you intend on killing the sapling?"*

"There's two options," I said. *"Farren's spell or astral blades."*

"Hmm. Which of his spells do you have?"

"Darkness bolt."

The spirit grinned. *"Use that."*

I glanced at her questioningly. *"You're sure?"*

"Definitely. Few things in this world are immune to Force damage. I will be surprised if the tree can shrug off the bolts easily."

Nodding thoughtfully, I crept back toward the sapling.

✳   ✳   ✳

I did not approach the seed as closely as I had originally anticipated needing to. In fact, I halted my advance at the fifty-yard line and well outside of sight range.

I did not need to *see* the sapling; I only needed to know where it was. And from my current position that was glaringly obvious. The ring of emptiness ahead could only be the void tree. That it could neither move nor dodge only made matters worse for my foe.

"Ready?" I called to Adriel. The spirit had positioned herself twenty yards from the tree. She would act as my spotter, reporting the outcome of each of my attacks.

Just like Ghost used to do, I thought fondly.

Since our last conversation in the archlich's court, Ghost had fallen asleep in the cloak, and knowing how much she would hate missing out on the action, I had decided against rousing her. Better, I thought, for Ghost to awaken to the news that she could try out her new stygian form than to keep her waiting in breathless anticipation of the moment.

"*Ready,*" Adriel confirmed, unaware of my inner musings.

I drew mana. "*Alright, here goes,*" I said. Rising to my feet, I released the casting I had prepared.

Mana rushed out from my core, slipped down my right arm and out my pointing finger. Spearing through the mists, the black missile flashed towards my target.

You have cast darkness bolt. Multiple hostiles have failed to detect you.

Eyes fixed in the direction of my unseen target, I waited.

I'd chosen the launch site for my attack wisely, and even though the nearest stygians were already wandering closer to investigate the source of the bolt, I had time yet before I needed to retreat.

You have injured a level 201 void sapling.

"*A hit! A palpable hit!*" Adriel crowed.

I smiled, just as delighted by the outcome. Killing the tree could end up being easier than I expected. Weaving psi, I repositioned in anticipation for the next attack.

You have teleported 50 yards.

Emerging from the aether behind a stygian hydra, I slipped away unseen from the oblivious creature. "*I'm in position,*" I told Adriel. "*How did the first attack go?*"

"*You've hit the tree squarely, leaving it with a new scar running down its center. And from the looks of it, the sapling isn't too happy. Its branches are quivering, and its trunk is swaying. It's trembling, really.*" She laughed. "*All in all, I'd say, you've given our foe a good scare.*"

"*Perfect,*" I said. "*Time to hit it again, then.*" Stretching out my arm, I hurled another darkness bolt at my foe.

You have injured a level 201 void sapling.

I didn't need Adriel's report the second time around. The furious bellows and roars of the surrounding nest creatures made clear enough the stygians were unhappy and, just as importantly, uncertain about what to do.

Chuckling quietly to myself at my foes' impotence, I launched an entire volley of bolts at my target.

You have grazed a void sapling.
You have injured a void sapling.
You have injured a void sapling.
...
...

It proved too much for the void tree.

"*Wait!*" Adriel called. "*Something's happening.*"

About to reposition again, I paused. "*It's dying?*"

"No... It almost looks like it's uprooting—" Adriel broke off. "*Quick! Hit it again before it flees!*"

I didn't need to be told twice. Ignoring the nearby stygians rushing closer, I hurled another darkness bolt in the direction of my target.

You have injured a void sapling. Multiple hostiles have failed to detect you.

"*Again! Again!*"

I wasted no time in complying. Spinning mana, I flung forward another projectile.

A void sapling has evaded your attack.

"*It's airborne. Aim higher!*"

Airborne? Although I didn't question the veracity of Adriel's statement, I didn't ready mana again, I wove psi. If I was going to hit a moving target, I needed to get closer. Escaping the converging stygians, I shadow blinked.

You have teleported into a stygian hydra's shadow. Multiple hostiles have detected you! You are no longer hidden.

I emerged from the aether to find the hydra I'd used to relocate already turning to strike. I leapt over the first snapping jaws, ducked beneath the next darting head, then sidestepped the third.

Unfortunately, more attacks were already coming.

In a move that was either foolish or daring—or both—I had teleported to the center of the nest, right beside Draven's legs, in fact. That put the sapling dead ahead. Orienting myself in its direction, I dashed forward.

A weaver behind me raised its pincers, and another appeared on my left, both preparing to strike. Beyond them, even more stygians waited. Paying the threats no heed, I stayed focused on my target, drawing mana as I went.

Your void armor has repelled 2 blight thorns!

A couple of steps later, my quarry came in range.

Or, at least, the last vestiges of it did.

Jerking my gaze upwards, I spotted a tentacled mass of roots disappearing into the mist. Ignoring the absurdity of the sight, I took aim and cast.

A void sapling has evaded your attack.

Raising my arm, I fired blindly into the mists again at where I thought the sapling's trajectory would take it.

A void sapling has evaded your attack.

Swearing viciously, I dropped my hands, not bothering to fire again. The void tree had disappeared from sight, and even with Adriel's help, hitting it now was near-impossible.

A blight thorn has struck you.

Glancing over my shoulder, I saw that the rest of the stygians were closing in fast. If I was not careful, I would be trapped soon. I was out of options. A second retreat was called for. Sighing, I cut right and dashed back into the mist. Perhaps the sapling would return.

CHAPTER 378: END GAME

The void tree did not return.

At first, neither Adriel nor I wanted to believe it. The sapling couldn't just up and leave, could it? Eventually though, once the nest started to disperse, we accepted the truth. Our foe had fled back into the open void where it was beyond our ability to pursue.

It was possible, of course, that the void tree had chosen to relocate elsewhere in the sector, but neither Adriel nor I thought it likely. The sapling could not survive Draven's Reach alone and without its protector.

I sighed. I was sitting atop the guardian once more. Adriel hovered beside me, and together we watched the stygian nest unravel. Without the sapling's presence—or was that its guidance?—any cohesion the nether creatures had was gone.

Half the tree's former minions had already vanished from sight. Nor was it only the nether creatures that suffered in the sapling's absence. According to Adriel, even the central fog bank was shrinking, as were the mist tendrils leading to the other seeds.

The nether's occupation was over, rapidly reversing course with the void tree's retreat, and by every measure, we had cause to celebrate. The void tree was gone. The harbinger was dead. And the stygian nest they had left behind was in shambles.

So why are Adriel and I in such a dour mood?

It was the sapling's escape. It stuck in both our craws.

"We should have realized it would try to run," Adriel said finally.

I nodded morosely. *"Where do you think it's gone?"*

She glanced at me. *"You mean other than to the open void?"*

I nodded again.

"Probably back to the void father that birthed it. I'm no expert on stygian lore, but I know the trees have their own familial networks."

"But why flee?" I asked, returning to the central question still bothering me.

"Why should it have stayed?" Adriel shot back. *"The trees want to live as much as the rest of us do. But with the harbinger dead, and it unable to stop us on its own, there was nothing keeping it."* She shook her head, then added unhappily, *"I should have anticipated its flight."*

I said nothing, experiencing the same regret.

"You know, there might be another reason, too," Adriel added abruptly.

"What's that?"

"I said there may be another reason why the sapling chose to flee instead of fighting to the death."

Looking at her questioningly, I waited for her to go on.

"You said the harbinger knows you are a scion?" Adriel asked.

I nodded, not liking where she was going.

"That is information the void fathers would want. Even now, the sapling is probably reporting the rise of the new threat."

"What threat?"

A weary smile sneaked back onto Adriel's face. "*You, of course. You are a promise of the Primes' return—something the void fathers will want to stop. From what you've told me about life outside this sector, the nether seems to be handily winning the war in the ancients' absence.*"

I frowned. "*Who are the void fathers? You've mentioned them twice now.*"

Adriel shrugged. "*I can only tell you what I know, which is not much. If you want a more complete answer, you will have to seek out an expert. But as far as my understanding goes, the void fathers are the eldest amongst the trees. They are the driving force behind the nether. They are the enemy we fight.*"

I shook my head ruefully. "*I've been gathering quite the collection of enemies. Soon, I'm going to lose track of them all.*"

"*Then you must be doing something right,*" Adriel quipped, smiling more genuinely. I grinned back, and for a second, we forgot our troubles in a shared moment of humor.

Then the lines of Adriel's face grew grim again. "*But in all seriousness, Michael, you must be careful. Your enemies are legion, and your new Mark is only going to make matters worse.*"

I'd told Adriel about the feat I'd earned from slaying the harbinger. The news had seemed to trouble her, and she had begged off further discussion on the topic, but now, I sensed she was ready to talk. "*That sounds like a warning,*" I said lightly.

"*It is,*" she said, her expression no less grim. "*You earned the Mark too early.*"

I blinked. "*Too early. What does that mean?*"

"*Even in my time, hardly anyone ever followed the route you took to earn the Power Mark.*" Adriel shook her head. "*If I hadn't been away from the Game so long or distracted by events, I would've remembered that little bit of lore and would've stopped you from killing the harbinger.*"

"*You're not making any sense,*" I pointed out gently.

She sighed. "*Do you know what prevents the Powers from destroying any player that irritates them? And before you answer, by Power, I don't mean a creature over level three hundred like the harbinger, I mean an* actual *Power— new or old—a participant of the Game.*"

"*Uhm, I assume it's the Adjudicator himself who stops them,*" I said. "*Unless a player breaks a Pact, a Power can't touch him.*"

"*That's true, as far as it goes,*" Adriel allowed. "*But courtesy of your new Mark, you are not just a player anymore.*"

My eyes widened as the implications sunk in. "*You're saying any Power can attack me directly now? Without the Adjudicator intervening to stop them?*"

Adriel nodded solemnly.

"*But I'm not a Power yet! The Adjudicator's message was very clear about that.*"

"*It does not matter. You have the capacity to evolve your Class beyond master rank and you've slain a level three hundred creature. In the Game's eyes you can take care of yourself and no longer warrant protection.*"

"Right," I muttered, thinking this was another complication I didn't need. Rubbing the side of my face, I considered the rest of what else Adriel had said. *"So, I will be able to evolve my Class further?"*

"Theoretically, yes. But to do so, you must deepen your Wolf Mark."

I nodded, having known as much. *"What about the Power Mark? How do I advance it?"*

"Just in the manner the Game implied: by killing other Powers—or Powerful Initiates."

I groaned. *"Really?"*

A half-smile flickered across Adriel's face. *"Really."*

I shook my head in bemusement. *"This world seems to be rife with conflict— between the nether and the aether, between the Primes and the Powers, between Light, Dark, and Shadow. Even amongst the Houses and Factions. Does it ever end?"*

Adriel laughed. *"Welcome to the Forever Kingdom, Michael. It's not called that for nothing, you know."*

My brows furrowed.

Seeing my confusion, Adriel explained further, *"This world exists at the center of everything. It is a nexus. The nexus. Someone—don't ask me who, it was well before my time—once likened this world to a 'kingdom forever at war with itself.' The phrase stuck but was obviously too wordy for some. Hence, the name 'Forever Kingdom' was coined."*

"I would never have guessed that," I murmured.

Adriel shrugged. *"Few do."* Her gaze turned downward. *"But now that I've burdened you with one more pointless bit of trivia,"* she said with a smile to show that she was only half-serious, *"it's probably time we moved on."*

Glancing down myself, I saw that the last of the stygians roaming near the base of the statue had wandered off. *"Right, I guess it's time we did this."* I turned back to her for one last searching look. *"Are you still sure about this?"*

"I am," Adriel said, knowing what I meant.

Not about to question her resolve further, I dropped down to the ground and approached the front of the guardian. With the sapling gone, the small disk-shaped hole in the statue's base was clearly visible.

Removing the lich's phylactery and the Emblem of the Reach from my backpack, I held them in my hands for a moment, my gaze flitting from the items to Adriel and back again.

"Go on," she said gently.

I sighed. Knowing I had no real cause for further delay, I kneeled beside the indentation and reached out with the hand holding the Emblem.

"One moment, Michael," Adriel said, stopping me.

Pausing, I glanced at her, wondering if she was having second thoughts.

"Before... before you do that, I wanted to say thank you. You didn't need to help me on this quest or fight Loskin. What you did went—"

I brushed aside her words. *"I only did what was necessary."*

She smiled. *"Perhaps it was. But not many would have seen that, and even fewer would have risked as much as you have to see it through."* Then, surprising me, the spirit bowed from the waist. *"You will make a good Prime someday. Perhaps even a great one."*

"Uh, thank you." Rising to my feet, I returned her bow, albeit less gracefully.

Adriel laughed. "You will have to practice your courtly manners more, though. I imagine players will be flocking to your banner soon." Her amusement faded. "Be careful of who you trust. Be especially careful of Loken." She hesitated. "And any other Houses you may run across."

I tilted my head to the side. "Why?"

"The rivalry between the Houses is as ancient as, well, the Primes, and even facing utter defeat, some refused to form alliances." She held my gaze. "Not every House will be happy to see House Wolf rise again."

I inclined my head, taking her warning to heart. "Then you believe some of the other Houses still stand?"

"I don't know," Adriel said, her voice turning pensive. "But I refuse to believe the Primes' destruction was as complete as the Powers make out. If we of House Death managed to escape, perhaps others did too. Use Farren. He knows the Game as well as I do and can serve as your teacher. He knows the location of many of the Houses too. Seek out their scions and draw them to your cause if you can."

I nodded. It was all good advice.

"One last thing. Tell Ghost I will miss her." She smiled. "Perhaps she and I will meet on the other side someday."

"I will," I said, then waited to see if she had anything more to add. When she didn't, I kneeled beside the statue again.

My time in Draven's Reach was coming to an end. I was not entirely done, though. They were still the New Haveners to tend to. While Elron and his people didn't need my help any longer, I had big plans for them and would have to revisit the city.

There were also the possessed to consider. How they would fit in with my plans, I wasn't sure yet, but I couldn't let them roam free in the Game either. Somehow, I would have to bind them to my cause as well.

Lastly, there was the dungeon. Draven's Reach was a powerful resource, one which I had to secure for the exclusive use of me and my allies.

And those were only the things I had to do in *this* sector.

I sighed. My list of tasks that needed doing never seemed to grow any shorter. *Best get to them, then,* I thought.

Reaching down, I inserted the Emblem in the waiting socket.

Analyzing offering...

...

...

Analysis completed.
The offering has been deemed sufficient. Tithe accepted. Item lost.

Awakening guardian...

✳ ✳ ✳

THE END.

Here ends Book 5 of the Grand Game.
Michael's adventures will continue in **A Scion's Duty**.
Get it here!

I hope you enjoyed the story! If you did, please leave a <u>review</u> and let other readers know what you think.
<u>Click here to leave a review</u>.
Happy reading!
Tom Elliot.

MICHAEL AT THE END OF BOOK 5

Player Profile: Michael
Level: 199. Rank: 19. Current Health: 100%.
Stamina: 100%. Mana: 100%. Psi: 100%.
Species: Human. Lives Remaining: 2.
True Marks: Worthy Adversary, Powerful Initiate.
True Marks (hidden): Pack Alpha.
False Marks (fabricated): Lesser Shadow, Lesser Light, Lesser Dark.

Active Buffs
Damage reduction: Life: 5%. Death: 20%. Air: 45%. Earth: 45%. Fire: 45%. Water: 45%. Shadow: 15%. Light: 15%. Dark: 15%. Nether: 100%. Physical: 46%*.

Additional resistance (excluding inherent resistance provided attributes): Life: 2.5%. Death: 10%. Air: 22.5%. Earth: 22.5%. Fire: 42.5%*. Water: 22.5%. Shadow: 7.5%. Light: 7.5%. Dark: 7.5%. Nether: 70%*. Physical: 0%.

Other Boosts provided by Items*
Damage: +30% damage (ebonheart), +40% damage (faithful).
Abilities: perceive tier 6 spelled wards (sorcerer's helm), move soundlessly (wayfarer's boots), hands immune to hazardous substances (wayfarer's gloves), spellhold: empty (mage's surprise), psi-feed (psi bracelet).
Immunities: tier 2 entanglement immunity (unbound ring), tier 2 mind spells immunity (stillness ring).
Skills: +4 ranks stealth (ranger's armor).

Attributes
Available: 4 points.
Strength: 21 (13)*. Constitution: 27 (19)*. Dexterity: 84 (60)*. Perception: 40 (36)*. Mind: 119 (107)*. Magic: 48 (28)*. Faith: 0.

Classes
Available: 0 points.
Primary-Secondary-Tertiary tri-blend: voidstalker (fabricated). voidstealer X (hidden).

Traits
void heritage (hidden)**:** +2 Dexterity, +2 Strength, +4 Mind, +4 Perception, +6 Magic.
beast tongue: can speak to beastkin.
Marked: can see spirit signatures.
wolfwalker (hidden)**:** improved senses in all conditions.
anointed scion (hidden): bound to House Wolf.
inscrutable mind: +8 Mind.

secret blood (hidden): conceals bloodline.
mental focus IV**: increases effectiveness of Mind skills by 40%.
budding explorer: all key points in newly discovered sectors logged.
arctic wolf (hidden)**: +5 Constitution, +2 Mind, +3 Strength.
spell illiterate: cannot cast mana-based spells.
potion resistance II: potency of potions reduced by 2 ranks.
spirit talker: can speak to spirits.
higher evolution: can evolve Class beyond master ranked.

* denotes boosts affected by items.
** denotes Class traits.

Skills

Available skill slots: 0.
light armor (current: 157. max: 190. Constitution, basic).

dodging (current: 168. max: 600. Dexterity, basic).
sneaking (current: 193. max: 600. Dexterity, basic).
shortswords (current: 181. max: 600. Dexterity, basic).
two weapon fighting (current: 157. max: 600. Dexterity, advanced).
thieving (current: 118. max: 600. Dexterity, basic).

chi (current: 164. max: 1070. Mind, advanced).
meditation (current: 200. max: 1070. Mind, basic).
telekinesis (current: 169. max: 1070. Mind, advanced).
telepathy (current: 200. max: 1070. Mind, advanced).

insight (current: 200. max: 360. Perception, basic).
deception (current: 155. max: 360. Perception, master).

channeling (current: 189. max: 280. Magic, basic).
elemental absorption (current: 90. max: 280. Magic, master).
null force (current: 31. max: 280. Magic, master).
null life (current: 11. max: 280. Magic, master).
null death (current: 40. max: 280. Magic, master).
nether absorption (current: 200. max: 280. Magic, master).

Abilities

Constitution ability slots used: 10 / 19.
load controller (10 Constitution, expert, light armor).

Dexterity ability slots used: 56 / 60.
crippling blow (Dexterity, basic, shortswords).
minor piercing strike (5 Dexterity, advanced, shortswords).
improved backstab (10 Dexterity, expert, sneaking).
improved trap disarm (5 Dexterity, advanced, thieving).
superior lockpicking (5 Dexterity, advanced, thieving).
superior set trap (10 Dexterity, expert, thieving).

whirlwind (5 Dexterity, advanced, two weapon fighting).
greater fade (15 Dexterity, master, sneaking).

<u>Mind ability slots used:</u> 66 / 107.
superior mass charm (10 Mind, expert, telepathy).
stunning slap (Mind, basic, chi).
windborne (10 Mind, expert, telekinesis).
heightened reflexes (10 Mind, expert, chi).
twin astral blades (5 Mind, advanced, telepathy).
long shadow blink (10 Mind, expert, telekinesis).
quick mend (10 Mind, expert, chi).
fortified mind (10 Mind, expert, meditation).

<u>Perception ability slots used:</u> 36 / 36.
superior analyze (10 Perception, expert, insight).
improved trap detect (5 Perception, advanced, thieving).
conceal small weapon (Perception, basic, deception).
superior facial disguise (10 Perception, expert, deception).
superior ventro (5 Perception, advanced, deception).
lesser imitate (5 Perception, advanced, deception).

<u>Other abilities:</u>
greater slaysight (hidden) (Class, master, telepathy): shatter, sleep, terrify, blind.
superior void thief (hidden) (Class, expert, any void skill and telepathy): steal, siphon, negate.

Known Key Points
Dungeon Sector 14,913 (candidate's dungeon) exit portal and safe zone.
Kingdom Sector 12,560 (wolves' valley) nether portal and safe zone.
Kingdom Sector 1 (Nexus) safe zone.
Dungeon Sector 101 (scorching dunes) exit portal and safe zone.
Dungeon Sectors 102, 103, and 104 (haunted catacombs) exit portals and safe zones.
Dungeon Sector 105, 106, 107, 108, and 109 (guardian tower) exit portals.
Kingdom Sector 18,240 nether portal 1 (guardian tower), and nether portal 2 (Draven's reach).
Dungeon Sector 73,102 (Draven's Reach) one-way entrance portal and safe zone.

Aetherstone Bracelet Stored Points
sector 24,401 safe zone.
sector 12,560 (wolves' valley) safe zone.
sector 18,240 nether portal 1 (guardian tower).

Equipped
<u>Weapons</u>
ebonheart (+30% damage).

---

faithful (+40% damage).

Armor & Clothes
sorcerer's coif (perceive tier 6 wards).
ranger's kit (+40% damage reduction, +4 ranks stealth).
bomber's belt (4 x acid bombs, 5 x smoke bombs, 4 x ice bombs, and 4 x fire bombs).
belt of the chameleon (5 x rank 4 nether protection crystals, 11 x rank 4 disease protection crystals, 9 scent concealment crystals, 5 x mental concealment crystals, 4 x rank 6 disease protection crystals, 2 x rank 5 poison protection crystals, 1 x rank 4 strength enhancement crystals, and 2 x rank 4 magic enhancement crystals).
wayfarer's boots (legendary item, +8 Dexterity, move soundlessly).
wayfarer's gloves (legendary item, +8 Dexterity, hands immune to hazardous substances).
cloak of the Reach (legendary soulbound item, +10 Magic, +20% fire magic resistance, +20% nether magic resistance).

Rings & Accessories
goliath's ring (+8 Strength).
acrobat's ring (+8 Dexterity).
sharpshooter's band (+4 Perception).
hale stone (+8 Constitution).
savant's ring (+4 Mind).
troll's talisman bracelet (+6% damage reduction).
gift of the unbound ring (immunity to tier 1 and 2 entanglement spells).
band of stillness ring (immunity to tier 1 and 2 Mind spells).
aetherstone bracelet (3 / 5 stored locations, 2 stones charged).
simple potion bracelet (3 / 3 full heal potions).
veteran's trapper's wristband (128 / 200 trap-making crystals).
mage's surprise (+10 Magic, spellhold: empty).
psi bracelet (legendary item, +8 Mind, psi-feed).

Other
backpack, **small bag of holding** (50 slots), **large bag of holding** (200 slots), hunter's alchemy stone.
pioneer's compass (soulbound, attuned to safe zone).

Backpack Contents
Money: 73 golds, 5 silvers, and 3 coppers.
10 x field rations.
2 x flasks of water.
2 x iron daggers.
1 x bedroll.
goblin writ of safe passage.
bounty letter authorization.
1 x coil of rope.
tavern bill of ownership.

Tartan token.
Vivane token.
Kesh Emporium access card.
cat claws.
spectacles of ward seeing (detect tier 4 wards).
BHG ID (junior member, 1 / 10 active jobs).
simple map of Nexus.
1 x rank 6 cure disease potions.
dungeon notes.
commune rod.
greater trap detect ability tome.
enchanted leather armor set (+20% damage reduction, -35% Dexterity and Magic).
6 x acid bombs, 14 x smoke bombs, 10 x ice bombs, and 6 x fire bombs.
slotted-potion belt (2 x rank 4 cure poison).
adept's ring (+6 Magic).
mirror shield (reflect tier 4 spells).
quaker (+50% damage, paralyzing touch).
phoenix's feather shaft (soulbound).
small bag of hiding (tier 6 concealment ward).
a simple shovel.
1 x blue mages robes, 1 x black mages robes.
stygian shortsword, +3.
stygian shortsword.

Miscellaneous Loot

4 x legendary items.

Alchemy Stone Contents

(0 / 500 ingredients stored).

Bank Contents

Money: 1,655 gold, 0 silvers, and 0 coppers.
2 x full healing potions.
2 x full mana potions.

Tavern Money: 9,850 gold, 0 silvers, and 0 coppers.

Open Tasks

Find the Last Wolf Envoy (hidden) (find Ceruvax).
Heist in the Dark (steal chalice from the Power, Paya).
Silent Brethren (find out what has happened to the guardians).
A Perverted Trial (stop the Triumvirate abuse of the Combat Trial).
Brokering Peace (establish peace in sector 12,560 within 4 months).
Brotherhood Obligations (report to the brotherhood after 4 months).
Cleanse the Corruption (rid Draven's Reach of its nether infestation).

BOOKS BY THE AUTHOR

BY TOM ELLIOT

The Grand Game (series page)
Book 1: The Grand Game: ebook | audiobook
Book 2: Way of the Wolf: ebook | audiobook
Book 3: World Nexus: ebook | audiobook
Book 4: House Wolf: ebook | audiobook
Book 5: Wolf in the Void: ebook | audiobook
Book 6: A Scion's Duty: ebook | audiobook
Book 7: Ancient Debts: ebook | audiobook
Book 8: The Lost Reclaimed: ebook (coming soon)

The Grand Game Box Set (series page)
Book 1-3: Birth of a Player: ebook
Book 4-6: Rise of an Elite: ebook
Book 7-9: The Making of a Power: ebook (coming soon)

The Grand Game, Elana (series page)
Book 1: Empyrean's Rise: ebook
Book 2: Empyrean's Flight: ebook

Annals of the Runeguard (series page)
Book 1: Proving Grounds: ebook

BY ROHAN M. VIDER

The Dragon Mage Saga (series page)
Book 1: Overworld: ebook | audiobook
Book 2: Dungeons: ebook | audiobook
Book 3: Sponsors: ebook (coming soon)

The Gods' Game (series page)
Crota, the Gods' Game Volume I
The Labyrinth, the Gods' Game Volume II
Sovereign Rising, the Gods' Game Volume III
Sovereign, the Gods' Game, Volume IV
Sovereign's Choice, the Gods' Game Volume V

Tales from the Gods' Game
Dungeon Dive (Tales from the Gods' Game, Book 1)

AFTERWORD

Thank you for reading the Grand Game!

If you enjoyed the book, please consider leaving a review on Amazon [click here]. I'm already working on Michael's next adventure.

If you have any questions, comments, or want to support my writing, please feel free to contact me through my site, TomLitRPG.com or Discord.

Alternatively, if you wish to learn more about the world of the Forever Kingdom, understand the system of the Grand Game better, or are just looking for the latest news on the Grand Game, please visit my site at TomLitRPG.com or signup up here for my: Newsletter.

Regards,
Tom
Support my writing on **PATREON**
Amazon Author page | Goodreads | Facebook | Reddit | Discord |

Definitions

Accord: old agreement between new Powers ceding control of Nexus to the Triumvirate.

Adjudicator: controller and arbitrator of the Grand Game.

alchemy stone: a device used to store alchemical components.

ancient: old Power.

anointed scion: a scion who has bound himself to a bloodline.

ascendant undead: term the Adjudicator used to describe Stayne, meaning unknown.

blended Class: a combined Class.

blood awakening: the process of recalling blood memories.

blood infusion: the absorption of the essences from former scions.

blood memories: gifts from your forebears containing the power of the ancients themselves.

bi-blend: a combination of two melded Classes.

bloodline: reference to the ancient from which the player is a descendant.

civilian player: a player without a class or combat abilities. Civilians do not have a player level.

class-unique skill: a skill that is unique to a Class and can only be acquired through a Class stone.

closed sector: a landmass that does not physically border another, making the area inaccessible except by portal.

composite spell: a multi-stage spell made up of two or more individual spells.

controlled sector: a sector owned by a faction. Ownership of a sector gives the faction's players increased privileges in the region.

Class: a defined path or vocation that gives a player access to specific skills.

Class evolution: the advancement of a Class, generally to a better-ranked one, due to particular traits, skills, or Marks acquired by the player.

Dark: one of the three Forces.

Darksworn: a player pledged to the Dark who values the self over the collective.

deathwish: An ability that is triggered in the instant between a creature being dealt fatal damage and the spirit fleeing the body.

Elite: a tier five player, i.e. someone above level two hundred.

ebonblade: soulbound weapon found in the Twilight Dungeon.

envoy: a trusted representative of a Power authorized to speak on their behalf.

Endless Dungeon: A section of the Nethersphere where dungeon mechanics are active.

evolution: the advancement of a player's core characteristics.

follower: a player that has pledged themselves in a binding vow to a Force or Power.

Force: Light, Dark, Shadow. The building blocks of the cosmos and energy in its rawest form.

Forever Kingdom: the world of the Nethersphere and Kingdom.

forsworn: a sworn who has betrayed their Power.

Game: refers to the Grand Game.

gatekeepers: holders of ancient lore, guardians of the ancients' trials.

House: House of the Ancient.

House of the Ancient: a grouping of followers pledged to one Prime.

Kingdoms: the collective name given to sectors located in the aether.

lycan: werewolf.

ley line: magic threads connecting nether sectors.

Light: one of the three Forces.

Lightsworn: a player that champions the cause of the many, even to his own detriment.

marshmen: mysterious dwellers in the saltmarsh district.

meld: the process of combining multiple Classes into one.

mindglow: the visible signature of a mind as seen with mindsight.

neutral sector: a sector unowned and unclaimed by any faction or Force.

Nethersphere: collective name given to the sectors in the nether.

nethersight: ability that allows stygian to see through free-floating nether.

new Power: one of the Powers that usurped the ancients.

oath breaker: one who has broken a Pact.

Pact: a binding enacted between a Power and player, overseen by the Adjudicator.

Power: an evolved player.

power word: a blood memory ability.

Prime: head of ancient bloodline. An ancient.

Prime Conclave: a gathering of Primes referred to by Kolath.

Primehood: the act of becoming a Prime.

rift: unstable portal from the nether. Ley line created by stygian seed.

scav: short for scavenger. A player who loots kills not his own.

scion: one bearing the blood of an ancient.

scion abilities: the abilities Michael had earned during the Wolf trials: astral blade, chi heal, mind shield, shadow blink.

seeking spell: spell that distinguishes friend from foe.

stolen spell: a spell acquired from another and cast using their skills and attributes.

soulbound: an item that remains with the player after death.

sworn: as in sworn servant. A sworn is a follower of a Power who has sufficiently deepened their binding Mark.

the real: reference to the physical realm.

trap-making crystal: crystal in trapper's wristband. Can be manifested as different trap components.

trials of the ancients: tests created by the Primes for their successors.

tri-blend: a combination of three melded Classes.

trigger-cast: a spell held in readiness and invoked under specific conditions.

upgrade gem: a game item used to advance an ability a single tier.

voids: informal term used to reference players who possess a void Class.

void Classes: a rare subset of Classes that specialize in damage reduction.

void's chosen: term by which the stygians address the stygian seeds.

void fathers: void trees.

windslide: ramp of air formed by windborne spell.

were-trait: a trait carried by all were-players, fueling their ability to shapeshift.

weres: short for werewolves and other were-players.

wolf trials: ancient trials created by Wolf Prime.

wolfkind: used interchangeably with wolfkin.

Key Characters & Factions

Factions

Albion Bank: major non-aligned bank in the Forever Kingdom.
Awakened Dead: A Dark faction.
Axis of Evil: An alliance of Dark factions.
blackguards: Policing force in the Dark quarter.
dawn brigade: Policing force in the Light quarter.
gray watch: Policing force in the Shadow quarter.
Mantises: A Dark faction of assassins.
Marauders: small Shadow faction.
Shadow Coalition: A power bloc of Shadow, made up of like-minded Shadow Powers.
Tartan: the faction of Tartar, the god-emperor.
Tartan legion: the military forces of Tartar.
Triumvirate: A unique faction composed of Light, Dark, and Shadow that control Nexus.
Unity Council: the governing body of Light, made up of all Light-affiliated Powers.

Guardians

Kolath: mysterious construct in the Guardian Tower.

Guilds and Non-Factions

Bounty Hunters Guild (BHG): headquartered in the plague quarter, mercenaries.
Information Brokers: A gnomish organization in the plague quarter.
Kesh Emporium: merchant company owned by Kesh.
Stygian Brotherhood: headquartered in the plague quarter, experts in all-things-nether.

House Wolf

Atiras: Dead Prime Wolf.
Ceruvax: Last envoy.

Non-Players

Adriel: the exile.
Arden: gnome information broker.
Algar: human captain, New Haven.
Avery: New Haven magister.
Castor: possessed mage.
Cilia: first amongst the dark elves of New Haven.

Cyren: gnome senior information broker.
Elron: dark elf marshal, New Haven.
Farren: lich.
Gamil: New Haven shopkeeper.
Lorn: orc chief in New Haven.
Loskin: archlich.
Regus: court's security chief.
Sunfury: a phoenix.
Sienna: human lord in New Haven.
Storhammer: dwarven thane in New Haven.

Players

Anriq: werewolf criminal.
Barac: crusader, male centaur.
Beorin: senior BHG member, dwarf.
Bornholm: Michael's companion from Erebus' dungeon, dwarf.
Cara: alias given to Kesh's agent in plague quarter by Michael.
Dathe: unknown werewolf player.
Devlin: Viviane's guard, unknown aquatic species.
Ent: guard outside emporium, armsmaster, giant.
Eyes: The BHG HQ doorkeeper, species unknown.
Jasiah: duelist, human male.
Genmark: ward architect, gnome male.
Gintalush: mantis assassin, insectoid.
Hannah: BHG client liaison officer, human female.
Kartara: huntmistress at Stygian Brotherhood Chapterhouse.
Kesh: master merchant, owner of the emporium, human woman.
Lake: guard outside emporium, berserker, giant.
Michael: protagonist.
Misha: Marauder tracker, aka the Hound.
Moonshadow: aeromancer, male elf.
Morin: Michael's companion from Erebus' dungeon, the painted woman.
Orlon: Triumvirate knight-captain in the plague quarter, human.
Pitor: rank 15 warrior, Kalin sworn, human, Marauder sub-boss.
Richter: constable in Triumvirate citadel, human civilian.
Saya: apprentice alchemist, tavernkeeper in wolves' valley, gnome.
Shael: red minstrel, half-elf.
Simone: sharpshooter, half-elf female.
Stayne: Erebus' henchman.
Stonebeard: Triumvirate captain, dwarf.
Talon: the captain, Tartar's envoy.
Tantor: Michael's companion from Erebus' dungeon, high elf male.
Teg: Michael's escort in the citadel, human.
Terence: rank 2 human fighter, swordsman.
Teresa: rank 2 human fighter, blade devotee.
Tevin: Marauder knight.
Toff: player outside haunted catacombs, ogre

Trion: Triumvirate holy knight, Herat sworn, human.
Trexton: herbalist in Triumvirate citadel, Simone's contact, dark elf.
Wengulax: mantis assassin, blade dancer, human.
Wilsh: Blackguard captain, human.
Yzark: Marauder boss.

POWERS

Arinna: Light Power.
Artem: Shadow Power. Goddess of nature.
Erebus: Dark Power, leader of the Awakened Dead faction.
Herat: Light Power, member of the Triumvirate.
Ishita: Spider goddess, Dark Power, member of the Awakened Dead.
Loken: Shadow Power.
Kalin: Minor Shadow Power, faction leader of the Marauders.
Menaq: Dark Power, leader of the Mantis faction.
Muriel: Light Power contesting Wolf Valley.
Mydas: Shadow Power, member of the Triumvirate.
Paya: Dark Power, junior member of the Awakened Dead ruling council.
Rampel: Dark Power, member of the Triumvirate.
Tartar: Dark Power, also known as the God-Emperor.
Viviane: Power owning the Albion Bank.

WOLFKIN

Aira: dire wolf dame.
Barak: dire wolf elder.
Cantur: half-mad wolf.
Duggar: dire wolf alpha.
Oursk: dire wolf sire.
Leta: dire wolf elder.
Monac: dire wolf elder and former alpha.
Moonstalker: Oursk's pup.
Shadetooth: Oursk's pup.
Snow: arctic wolf pack alpha.
Star: Snow's mate.
Stormdark: Oursk's pup.
Sulan: dire wolf healer.
Suva: dire wolf elder.

Locations

bounty hunters guild headquarters: in the plague quarter.
court of the dead: archlich's stronghold.
Dark quarter: eastern side of Nexus.
global auction: auction in the safe zone.
guardian tower: public dungeon.
haunted catacombs: public dungeon.
information brokers office: in the plague quarter.
Kesh Emporium: merchant house in the safe zone.
Light quarter: western side of Nexus.
market square: square housing global auction.
New Haven: city in Draven's Reach.
plague quarter: southern side of Nexus.
saltmarsh district: area in the southeast of plague quarter.
scorching dune: public dungeon.
Shadow Keep: central castle in the Shadow quarter.
Shadow quarter: northern side of Nexus.
Sleepy Inn: Michael's tavern, aka Wyvern's Roost.
Southern Outpost: tavern in plague quarter.
Wanderer's Delight: hotel in the safe zone.